Praise for *Claude & Camille*

"Stephanie Cowell is nothing short of masterful in writing about Claude Monet's life and love. . . . *Claude & Camille* is both a historical novel and a romance, but Cowell's graceful, moving treatment of Claude and Camille's turbulent love defies categorization. It's an enthralling story, beautifully told. . . . Cowell's glimpse into Monet's life and art is convincing and intimate . . . vividly portrays not just the couple and their life together, but their time and place, their world. She writes in language that is simple, elegant, and extraordinarily evocative."
　　　—*Boston Globe*

"Historic verisimilitude cuddles with bodice-ripping fancy in this diverting fictional representation of the Impressionist maverick Claude Monet and his first wife."
　　　—*New York Times*

"Cowell presents a vivid portrait of Monet's remarkable career. She writes with intelligence and reverence for her subject matter, providing a rich exploration of the points at which life and art converged for one of history's greatest painters."
　　　—*BookPage*

"You'll never look at Monet's water lilies the same way after reading Cowell's luminous biography of the artist and his muse."
　　　—*Romantic Times* (Four stars)

"Fleshing out the artist's biographical outline with fresh imagery, well-paced dramatic scenes, and carefully calculated dialogue, Cowell mines the tempestuous relationship of Monet and his romantic and artistic inspiration with a nimble and discerning command as she indelibly evokes the lush demimonde of 19th-century Paris."
　　　—*Booklist*

"Rich and satisfying . . . Cowell seems poised on the cusp of very great things."

—*January* magazine

"A convincing narrative about how masterpieces are created, and a detailed portrait of a complex couple."

—*Publishers Weekly*

"There's more than one love triangle involved in this highly recommended tale. Don't miss *Claude & Camille*."

—*BookLoons*

"*Claude & Camille* will make you rethink what you thought about art, life, and love. With colorful period detail and deft emotional insight, Cowell re-creates the life of Monet and his world that adds an entirely fresh dimension to the paintings."

—*Big Think*

"*Claude & Camille* is by far one of the most beautiful books I have ever read! . . . An utterly engrossing read—the kind that makes you tune out everything and has you looking forward to every free minute that you can get back to it. Poignant and touching."

—*Passages to the Past*

"Like stepping into an artist's studio and finding oneself among the great Impressionists."

—*Tea at Trianon*

"Cowell has brought Monet to life and in doing so created a masterpiece of her own."

—*Muse in the Fog*

"Cowell has painted her own canvas, giving readers a unique look into Monet's life. . . . As I read the last words of this magnificent story, I was brokenhearted it had come to an end. Cowell's story will forever be etched in my mind when I think of Monet."

—*Chocolate & Croissants*

"I loved the book from the moment I read the first word. . . . Stephanie Cowell is one of those authors who has the ability to write in such a way that you feel like you're in the places you're reading about and almost feel shock when you move the book from your face and realize you're still in your own living room."

—*Book Drunkard*

"Reading *Claude & Camille* is like inhabiting an Impressionist painting filled with luscious, tactile imagery. But in this novel of passion and heartbreak, Stephanie Cowell never forgets the emotional price exacted by such vivid, trembling beauty."

—Lauren Belfer, author of *City of Light*

"An engaging, lyrical, and spirited work of fiction about the great love of Monet's life. Cowell creates a vivid world here of art, friendship, and ardent love within the Impressionist circle."

—Harriet Scott Chessman, author of *Lydia Cassatt Reading the Morning Paper*

"*Claude & Camille* is a wonderfully absorbing and romantic novel, the story of Claude Monet's passion for his painting and his equally passionate love for a woman who is as elusive as the water lilies that he strove to capture on canvas. This elegant novel was hard to put down, and once I did, I rushed to view Monet's paintings with a deeper understanding. Stephanie Cowell is a wonderful writer."

—Sandra Gulland, author of *The Josephine B. Trilogy* and *Mistress of the Sun*

"Stephanie Cowell's new novel of art and love is focused on Claude Monet's great passions: painting, friendship, and Camille Doncieux. With her uncanny ability to inhabit the hearts of historical characters, Cowell creates a wholly fascinating milieu as vividly as a filmmaker. She has a special gift for rendering the scene—knowing which moments excite the reader, illuminate the characters, and create memorability. I was touched by the novel's tenderness and compassion, and moved to immerse myself in my books of Impressionist paintings."
—Sandra Scofield, author of *Opal on Dry Ground* and
Occasions of Sin

"A novel as luminous as a Monet landscape. Cowell shows the reader the world through the great artist's eyes and paints a dazzling portrait of a passionate young man struggling to become the towering Impressionist we revere."
—Ellen Feldman, author of *Scottsboro*, short-listed for the
Orange Prize

"With elegant prose that blends color, light, and shadow to perfection, much as Monet did in his canvases, Stephanie Cowell offers us a gorgeously rendered tale of love, genius, and haunting loss set against the dramatic backdrop of a world on the verge of inescapable change."
—C. W. Gortner, author of *The Last Queen*

"Stephanie Cowell's Monet and his Camille are achingly real, and the miserable garrets of Paris where they struggle to survive are so sensitively portrayed, you can almost smell the paint. Cowell sweeps the reader up into a story as dazzling and turbulent as the art whose creation she depicts."
—Laurel Corona, author of *The Four Seasons*

"*Claude & Camille* offers a fascinating look at nineteenth-century Paris, the bohemian lives of the Impressionists, and their struggle to create a new way of seeing the world. From Parisian ateliers to Giverny's lush gardens, Stephanie Cowell paints an unforgettable portrait of Claude Monet and the two passions that framed his life: his beautiful, tragic wife, Camille, and his pursuit of art."

—Christi Phillips, author of *The Devlin Diary*

"So often, while reading *Claude & Camille,* I felt I had stepped into Monet's world and then through it into his paintings. Cowell movingly explores themes of friendship, love, betrayal; hardship, endurance, dedication; and the challenges innovators in the arts confront."

—Mitchell J. Kaplan, author of *By Fire, By Water*

ALSO BY STEPHANIE COWELL

Marrying Mozart

Nicholas Cooke

The Players: A Novel of the Young Shakespeare

The Physician of London

Claude & Camille

A NOVEL *of* MONET

Stephanie Cowell

BROADWAY PAPERBACKS

New York

BROADWAY

Copyright © 2010, 2011 by Stephanie Cowell

All rights reserved.
Published in the United States by Broadway Paperbacks, an imprint of the Crown Publishing Group, a division of Random House, Inc., New York.
www.crownpublishing.com

BROADWAY PAPERBACKS and its logo, a letter B bisected on the diagonal, are trademarks of Random House, Inc.

Originally published in hardcover in slightly different form in the United States by Crown Publishers, an imprint of the Crown Publishing Group, a division of Random House, Inc., New York, in 2010.

Library of Congress Cataloging-in-Publication Data
Cowell, Stephanie.
Claude & Camille : a novel of Monet / Stephanie Cowell.—1st ed.
          p.   cm.
1. Monet, Claude, 1840–1926—Fiction.   2. Monet, Camille, 1847–1879—Fiction.
3. Painters—France—Fiction.   4. Painters' spouses—France—Biography.
5. Impressionist artists—France—Fiction.   6. Giverny (France)—Fiction.
          I. Title.   II. Title: Claude and Camille.
          PS3553.O898C63 2010
     813'.54—dc22   2009023383

ISBN 978-0-307-46322-7
eISBN 978-0-307-46323-4

Printed in the United States of America

Book design by Lauren Dong
Cover design by Laura Duffy
Cover photography: top image copyright © Veer; bottom image
copyright © Harald Sund/Getty Images

10 9 8 7 6 5 4 3

First Paperback Edition

As always, to my husband, Russell,
and to my sons, James and Jesse

Prelude

DULL LATE-AFTERNOON LIGHT GLITTERED ON THE hanging copper pots in the kitchen where the old painter sat with his wine, smoking a cigarette, a letter angrily crumpled on the table in front of him. Through the open window he could hear the sound of a few flies buzzing near one of the flower beds, and the voices of the gardener and his son, who were talking softly as they pushed their wheelbarrow over the paths of the vast garden.

He had meant to paint his water lily pond again, but after the letter had come he could do nothing. Even now, he felt the bitter words rising from the ink. "Why do you write me after all these years, Monet? I still hold you responsible for the death of my sister, Camille. There can be no communication between us."

Outside, the day was ending, smelling of sweet grass and roses. He swallowed the last of his wine and stood suddenly, smoothing the letter and thrusting it in his pocket. "You foolish woman," he said under his breath. "You never understood."

Head lowered, he made his way up the stairs to the top floor, under the sloping attic roof, and down the hall to the locked door. He had worked in this small studio briefly when he first moved here years before and could not remember the last time he had gone inside.

Dust lay on the half-used tubes of paint on the table; palette knives and brushes of every size rested in jars. Rolled canvas and wood for stretchers leaned against a wall. Past the table stood a second door, which opened to a smaller room with another easel and an old blue-velvet-upholstered armchair. He lowered himself onto the chair, hands on his knees, and looked about him.

The room was filled with pictures of Camille.

There was one of her embroidering in the garden with a child at her feet, and another of her reading on the grass with her back against a tree, the sun coming through the leaves onto her pale dress. She was as elusive as light. You tried to grasp it and it moved; you tried to wrap your arms around it and found it gone.

It had been many years since he had found her in the bookshop. He saw himself then, handsome enough, with a dark beard, dark eyes flickering, swaggering a bit—a young man who did not doubt himself for long and yet who under it all was a little shy. The exact words they spoke to each other that day were lost to him; when he tried to remember, they faded. He recalled clearly, though, the breathless tone of her voice, the bones of her lovely neck, and her long fingers, and that she stammered slightly.

There she stood in his first portrait of her, when she was just nineteen, wearing the green promenade dress with the long train behind her, looking over her shoulder, beautiful, disdainful, as she had appeared nearly half a century before. He rose and lightly touched the canvas. Sometimes he dreamt he held her; that he would turn in bed and she would be there. But she was gone, and he was old. Nearly seventy. Only cool paint met his fingers. *"Ma très chère . . ."*

Darkness started to fall, dimming the paintings. He felt the letter in his pocket. "I loved you so," he said. "I never would have had it turn out as it did. You were with all of us when we began; you gave us courage. These gardens at Giverny are for you, but I'm old and you're forever young and will never see them. I'll write your sister again at her shop in Paris. She must understand; she must know how it was."

Outside, twilight was falling on the gardens, and the water lilies would be closing for the night. He wiped his eyes and sat for a time to calm himself. Looking around once more, he left the studio and slowly descended the stairs.

Part One

I have so much fire in me and so many plans. I always want the impossible. Take clear water with grass waving at the bottom. It's wonderful to look at, but to try to paint it is enough to make one insane.

—CLAUDE MONET

IN THE TOWN OF LE HAVRE THE HARBOR WATER CHANGED color every hour; sometimes it was bright blue-green, sometimes exhausted gray, and other times a mysterious inky black. Boats creaked against their anchors, from great English ships with towering masts to little shabby fishing boats, wind-worn and piled with soggy nets. The wind always carried the smell of salt and fresh, slippery fish, which spilled out daily on the wet rough wharf boards. The ropes were every shade of brown.

Seventeen-year-old Claude Monet strolled down the main street in his dark suit and starched lace cuffs, his thick dark hair tucked beneath his jaunty hat and an artist's portfolio under his arm.

Pushing open the creaking door of the art-supply shop, he called out, "*Bonjour,* monsieur!"

Old Gravier limped from the shadows illuminated by a few oil lamps. "There you are!" he exclaimed. "Did you bring more of your work to sell?"

Claude dropped the portfolio on the counter and lifted his new caricatures, drawn with huge heads and minuscule twigs of bodies in the popular Parisian style.

The old man chuckled, showing his broken, tobacco-stained front teeth. "You clever boy!" he lisped. "Yes, people will pay well for these. Commissions come in every day for you. Can you go to this address first thing in the morning? The gentleman who lives there is eager to have his caricature made. He's the father of your friend Marc from your lycée, which hasn't yet let out for today, I believe."

"Hasn't it?" Claude replied airily, taking the address and ignoring the subtle inquiry. He turned away to glance out the window and down the street to where ships bobbed in the water, their masts moving back and forth. Someone was coming past the shop and in through the door. Who is it? he thought, a little uneasily. Ah, no one much! Only Eugène Boudin, one of several local painters who haunted the area with an easel weighing down his shoulder, always wearing the same clothes and shapeless brown hat. He was perhaps forty; friends said you could set a firecracker off near him when he was painting and he'd never hear it.

As Boudin walked across the floor, nodding pleasantly to them, the closing door created a sudden small wind, which lifted a few sheets of drawing paper from Claude's portfolio. The young man dropped hastily to his knees to retrieve them.

"*Bonjour,* Monet," Boudin said. "Allow me to help." He also stooped to retrieve a paper that had blown against the counter and glanced at it. Stroking his beard, he studied a chalk sketch of boats. "But what have we here?" he asked, surprised. "Is this *yours?*"

"It's mine. *Merci!*" Claude replied stiffly, holding out his hand.

"But it's very good indeed. I didn't know you drew seriously."

"Oh, I don't draw seriously," Claude replied as he put his drawing away. "I just do it for my amusement between my real work."

"Your real work?"

"Yes. I intend to be the most famous caricaturist in France."

Boudin began to sift through a large wood box of oil paint tubes that Gravier had brought him. He weighed a few in his hand, his face thoughtful. Looking up at Claude again, he asked, "So that satisfies you, eh? But come! You've never tried oils or landscapes?"

Claude sensed both artist and shopkeeper waiting for his answer. He shrugged. "*Landscapes*, monsieur, such as you do? Standing outside in all weather to paint? That doesn't interest me."

Boudin shook his head. "Look here, then," he said. "Try it once and you might change your mind. I'm going to paint at dawn tomorrow, and I invite you to come with me. I'll bring an extra easel and supplies. Meet me in front of this shop at five in the morning."

"It is unreasonable to go anywhere at that hour, monsieur."

"It is totally unreasonable." Boudin touched his chosen paint tubes with love and carefully laid money on the counter to pay for them. "Accept it as a challenge if you like."

"Why of course, monsieur," Claude replied calmly. "Five in the morning, as you say. I don't suppose it's as hard as all that."

HE WALKED AWAY more quickly from the shop, glancing toward the wharf, where his father's business stood. Not for the world would he go that way. Things were bad between them.

It had not always been so. When Claude was younger, he had adored his father and loved to run down to the nautical-supply shop, delighting in the cut-glass inkwell, the pens, the samples of brittle ropes hanging from nails, the tin boxes of hard bread. He would go after school, climbing on his father's lap, being sent at last to the confectioner's to bring back cakes with hazelnut cream to eat on the desk between the accounting books. Then came the harsh quarrels of the last few years, his sarcasm and poor marks in school, the bitter confrontations. There was also his exemplary older brother, Léon, who was turning out (as his father said) the way a man should.

So much had changed since those early days. Then, his father and mother had slept lovingly in one room; for two or three years now they had separated into their own bedchambers. He knew the cause. Claude hunched his shoulders as he climbed the hill to their house in the Ingouville neighborhood above the harbor, breathing harder for his anger and clutching his portfolio as if to defend himself. His mother was delicate, sweet, and too kind for this world. She should never have been the wife of a tradesman but of some great man who would have appreciated her love of the arts and her gift of empathy; she was tenderly warm, welcoming all, from their friends to the beggar at the back door.

As he approached his large house up the path and walked through his mother's rose garden, he made his decisions on how best to manage the evening before him. Guests would be coming tonight for the monthly musicale; if he did not descend until they arrived and escaped upstairs again before they left, he could avoid the irksome problem of speaking with either his father or his newly married brother.

His shapely young cousin would be coming as well; that would likely make the evening bearable.

Claude mounted the stairs to his room two at a time and closed the door behind him. This room was his alone since his brother had moved away; with its narrow bed, washstand, and well-worn copies of novels, poetry, and plays on the shelf and in piles on the floor, it served as his refuge. He had also tacked some of his caricatures on the wall near magazine pages of women dressed in the latest Parisian haute couture of wide crinolines and embellished silk evening dresses.

Glancing at his small desk, he saw his schoolbooks waiting for him and, with sudden disgust, thrust them under the bed. Why had old Gravier asked him that stupid question? He put it from his mind as not worth thinking of at this moment and lay down to read a favorite novel.

Hours later, when darkness was falling and the clock below struck its melancholy eight times for the hour, he heard the voices of their guests for the musicale, dressed in his evening suit and shirt with lace cuffs, and sauntered downstairs to the parlor. Gaslight shone on the embroidered chair seats, the silk wallpaper, and the good French piano. He noted also the plentiful supply of wine.

Adolphe Monet stood near an oval portrait of his own mother on the wall, feet slightly turned out while his eyes darted about as if looking for someone to whom to explain his work. There was something irritatingly humble in his need to let all know that he did well by his family. With him stood Claude's older brother, Léon, already slightly round-shouldered, with his pale, dull new wife.

Claude frowned. I must keep to the other side of the room, he thought, and slip away if he comes near me.

He drank a full glass of wine to fortify himself.

A dozen or more guests had arrived, including his fifteen-year-old cousin, Marguerite, in a long dress of sandy pink, her flaxen hair in curls, her wide mouth smiling at him. She was always daring him with her blue eyes. He sat by her on the sofa, trying to capture her fingers with his. "The price of ship rigging . . ." his father was saying.

Rigging to hang oneself, Claude thought, his hand now entwined with the girl's smaller, moist one.

Claude's mother arranged her skirts to sit at the piano. She began to sing, her older, widowed sister, Claude's aunt Lecadre, standing near to add a soft contralto harmony. Madame Monet called, "Sing with me, Oscar," and Claude released his cousin's hand with a last squeeze and leapt up, bowing extravagantly to the general applause of the room. He pulled a chair next to the piano. Amid all the guests he felt his father watching him as he sang. *À la claire fontaine, m'en allant promener . . . Il y a longtemps que je t'aime.* By the clear fountain I walked; I've loved you for a long time.

He had had too much wine already. His youthful baritone faltered. A few other people had come in, and behind them the Latin master from his lycée. Who had invited him? Claude rose and walked to the side table, where he poured brandy; then he returned to the sofa and sank down onto it to join the girl again, frowning. The room was suddenly stuffy, and he unfastened his top shirt button.

She giggled. "You're drunk."

"I need air. Come with me." He rose, pulling her through the room and outside the house to the now darkened rose garden. He urged her around to the shed and kissed her mouth, his other hand feeling for her little breasts under the whalebones of her corset. More singing came through the window, and laughter.

"Oh don't, Oscar! *Non, s'il te plaît!*" She giggled as he pushed her against the wall of the shed.

His father had appeared on the house steps, holding a lantern, which he shined here and there in the flowers until the light moved to the shed wall. "There you are!" Adolphe Monet whispered angrily. "What the hell are you doing? I've just been informed that you've been in school only a few times this past month and that you're likely to fail the year. And you, young lady!"

He seized Claude's arm, and the girl fled.

Enraged, Claude shook his father off. "I'll do what I like!" he cried. "Just as long as I'm not like you! I know about your mistress and what it's done to my mother!" Their voices rose above the music.

Avoiding his father's blow, he ran back up the steps, past the guests, and to his room. There he spilled open the box of money he kept on his desk, and the coins rolled and clanked to the floor. He would be wealthy and take his mother away and they would live together and be happy. He felt the girl's lips on his and the smell of the flowers and was angry and full of longing, and then he threw up harshly from the brandy.

HE AWOKE TO sweet early darkness, that time when you should embrace the pillow and sleep hours more. Through the first birdsong he heard the sound of persistent tapping. He buried his head again, though the housekeeper, Hannah, was calling his name from outside the door, saying, "You asked me to wake you, Master Claude! You're to go out with that painter fellow. Your father's still asleep."

Claude recalled last night's confrontation in the garden. The last thing he wanted to do today was paint a stupid landscape. He threw on some old clothes and made his way down the hill, swinging his lantern.

The light showed the closed shop and the dark figure in front of it: Boudin, and beside him a wheelbarrow with two easels. I'll tell him I'm not interested and go back to bed, he thought.

Boudin's face came into view as Claude approached. "Slept late?" the painter asked. "A landscapist is up before dawn. Is everything all right?"

Oh, what the devil! thought Claude, and he answered, "Yes, why shouldn't it be? I had a little too much wine last night, that's all. Come on!"

How strange to walk through the town so early with only a few signs of people waking. The fishermen were just putting their boats piled with nets out to sea in the harbor beyond. Smoke rose from a few chimneys. As they walked on with the heavy wheelbarrow, even these houses fell away, and they found themselves on a dirt path with the first gray light of dawn rising over the fields. A grove of apple trees emerged before them, their blossoms scattered on the ground like ghosts.

Boudin began setting up the easels.

Claude looked around. "Here?" he asked incredulously. "We're painting here? There's nothing but trees, and beyond that fields and more trees."

The painter stopped his work and threw up his hands, his face no longer placid. He exclaimed, "Is that all you see before you, Monet? Perhaps I was mistaken to allow you to come with me today. Perhaps you haven't much of a gift after all. It begins badly! A painter does not drink late before rising early, not to mention that you kept me waiting for some time."

Claude flushed as he accepted the palette and brushes. He stared from the dim apple trees to the empty canvas on the easel before him. What was this odd man in his muddy shoes fussing about? Landscapes! It was only a matter of putting the right color paint in the right place. Then he could win the challenge and go home to bed. By that time, his father would have left for work.

The rising day was emerging behind the trees, and the dark tips of the leaves began to glimmer. "It keeps moving!" Claude exclaimed after half an hour, pushing back his hair with the crook of his arm. "You didn't tell me about this. How am I supposed to do this if the air keeps moving and changing and the light changes?"

The sun rose high above, warming him and the earth. His legs and right arm ached, his head pounded, and his eyes hurt from looking. A few hours later when he stepped back to study what he had done, he saw merely clumsy strokes of paint. The green was wrong. It had been right before and now it was wrong. If only the colors would stay the same; if only the air would stay the same!

"*Pas mal*—not bad at all for a start," Boudin commented, standing behind Claude to look at his canvas. "Your line's good because you draw well, but painting is . . . ah, painting! If you keep going, you will improve. Eventually you may reveal a little of your heart."

"That's not what a man does, is it?" Claude replied bluntly. "My father says that. I think he's right in that at least."

They stopped only once, for some bread and cheese and wine that the older painter had packed. By early afternoon, they both were tired. Claude shook Boudin's hand and limped back home, where he fell into bed and slept until morning.

When he opened his eyes he saw the painting on his bureau. The oddest thing was that as he gazed at it still half asleep, it seemed to gaze back at him. He rose somewhat shyly and approached it. Why, there's nothing there! he thought. It's all dead. Yet now a few branches of a tree seemed alive. There was a stiff cotton cloud and he thought, Perhaps I could make that a little better, as if it lived. Perhaps I could.

He looked down at his hands, intrigued.

Later that day Claude walked down to Gravier's shop.

He moved down the aisles full of fat metal tubes of English paints, their thick colors dabbed on a wood board to identify them. Near the back were canvases stretched on plain wood frames, as well as rolls of unstretched canvas, leaning like rugs against a wall. Another aisle held thick pads of paper, smaller sketchbooks, jars of pencils, crumbling pastels in a wood box, brushes that ranged from the most slender sable for ink drawings to ones as wide as his hand. There were boxes of watercolor pigment, each little square separate from its fellows; palette knives of several sizes in a jar; palettes of every shape.

What could I do with these supplies? he thought. What could I do? I may be terrible at it, but I have to try. He felt this with every muscle of his slender chest.

A few days later he discovered Eugène Boudin on the wharf with his easel, painting the boats. "Monsieur," Claude said politely, "I'd like to study with you if you'll have me."

The painter did not turn from his work, though he blinked a few times. He said finally, "I'm delighted, Monet. And the caricatures?"

"Maybe later."

That spring Claude went everywhere with the older artist. The two of them painted in Honfleur across the estuary, and they painted the estuary itself. It was oils for Claude, and the occasional red chalk or pastels. Wherever he looked he saw shadow, shape, and color, things receding and rushing toward him again, and each day he thought, Today I'll manage it; today I'll seize it all. Yet each day he felt he was beginning again. What he saw today made yesterday's work rubbish.

In the evening, during the peaceful hour before his father came home from work, Claude sat in the parlor with his mother as she embroidered. "I'm going to Paris one day to study," he told her. "Would you come away from him for a while to stay with me? We'd go to the opera and the ballet." By the lamplight, he looked at her more closely. Her face was in profile to him, and he could see that her neck was thinner under her high lace collar and her hands more fragile.

"What, aren't you eating?" he demanded.

"I am, but I know I'm losing weight."

The clock ticked; outside, the wind blew the trees and he breathed deeply to push away the sudden fear. He lowered his voice stubbornly and said, "You'll come to Paris with me."

FROM THAT DAY he did not cease to worry about her. Every morning when he left the house early to paint, he looked back at the window of her room, but the closed shutters told him nothing. She'll be in the parlor when I return this evening, he told himself, and I'll show her what I've done.

He forced himself to concentrate on his painting, but the moment he ceased, his thoughts returned home. Then he stared at the half-finished canvas on his easel and cried, "The harder I work, the more I want from it. How long will it take me to be good?"

"It takes all your life, Claude."

"There isn't enough time. I'm worried about my mother. There's the doctor coming in and out this whole month and no one tells me anything. And today I'm so uneasy I can't do any more. I've got to go home and see how she is."

As he hurried in the door, Aunt Lecadre was coming down the stairs, and when he climbed to meet her, her wrinkled face and pale mouth made her look as if all joy had seeped from her. "No one tells me things!" he whispered, looking up the darkness of the stairs to the landing.

"Claude, dearest, we hoped it wasn't so."

He rushed up past her. Wherever he looked, the hall turned into lines and colors and the shadows blended. In the bedroom, he pushed past the doctor and threw himself on the bed, burying his face in his mother's loose hair.

Two weeks later Claude listened to the earth fall on her coffin like measured blows. He broke from his family around the open grave and ran up the hill until he could not run anymore. Under a group of trees he felt that dreadful rising breath in his throat that warned him that his grief could not be kept down. Holding on to a tree, he wept so harshly he felt his chest would break apart.

The house in Ingouville fell silent but for Claude playing songs softly on the piano in the small hours of the night until his father called down, "Stop!"

A few days after the funeral he went into his mother's bedroom and put his face in her dresses, which hung in the wardrobe. He took out the gloves from her glove box and laid them on the bed. I never painted her, he thought bitterly. She saw only the very beginning of what I could do. I was going to paint the garden for her as a birthday present, and now it's too late. I was right that there wasn't enough time.

From behind his father's closed bedroom door he heard no sound.

FOR THE NEXT few years he did little but paint. Sometimes he took food and stayed away for days, sleeping in little houses or inns. He and Boudin walked and painted together.

As they put their brushes away one late afternoon, Boudin said, "Listen, my young friend. You're twenty now, and I can't teach you much more. Go to Paris to study. Speak to your father."

"He won't approve," Claude said. "Since I left school, he's been urging me to join him in the shop. But I'll ask again." He wiped the sand from his feet, put on his socks and shoes, and walked back to the wharf and his father's shop of nautical supplies.

Adolphe Monet looked up sharply from behind his desk under the hanging lanterns and ropes. "There you are, boy!" he cried. "This very morning one of the fishermen informed me you were sleeping with his daughter and wants to know when you'll marry her. I haven't laid eyes on you in a week, I told him."

He tore off his spectacles, which fell on his papers. "Damn it, Claude!" he shouted, slapping the desk hard with both hands. "You're gone when I get up and asleep when I come home. You're throwing your life away and leaving me here to work alone, though I'm growing old and you know it! And you don't earn so much as a franc from this new obsession. Landscapes!"

"I want to go to Paris to study art."

Aunt Lecadre hurried toward them through the crates, looking anxiously from one to the other. Claude snatched up her rough hand and kissed it. "Talk to him, Tante! You must!" he begged. "I can't put it off any longer. I've got to go to Paris. If I fail, I'll come home again. I promise."

The tall old woman touched his cheek. "*Alors,* Adolphe!" she said. "Let him go for a time and see what he makes of it. You know how mad I was about painting as a girl. I have artist friends in Paris. They could find him lodging."

"I won't give him any money!"

Claude said hotly, "I don't need your money; I have a lot of my own left from my caricatures."

Adolphe Monet felt for his spectacles amid the papers. "Then go," he said wearily. "Perhaps things will blow over with your girl here by then. I tell you, though, my son: you'll be back."

1861–1862

When I've painted a woman's bottom so that I want to touch it, then the painting is finished.

—AUGUSTE RENOIR

IT WAS THE IMMENSITY OF IT HE COULD NOT HAVE IMAGined: Paris, where the emperor and his wife rode through the streets in their carriage, where mansions and palaces rubbed walls with hovels. Thousands of cafés, their windows painted with wine advertisements; thousands of alleys, whose brick houses were pasted with posters. Filth ran in the streets in one neighborhood while those in others were washed daily; in stately green parks, sunlight danced through the trees onto the women's fine dresses and onto the feathers and silk flowers on their hats. Clean, bright children skipped about with hoops. He had never seen so many people in his life.

About him whole neighborhoods were being torn down, and magnificent boulevards with elegant terraced houses were being erected, the work of the emperor's deputy, Haussmann, who had vowed to make this cramped medieval city the most beautiful in Europe. Claude had read about it in the news journals for years.

He would not go straight to the room that his aunt had arranged for him to have in Pigalle; no, he would go first to the annual state Salon of French artists in the Palais de l'Industrie on the Right Bank. He got lost twice, and his arms were aching from carrying his suitcase and easel when he finally found it and, for a small fee, walked inside and climbed the broad stairs to the exhibition hall.

Claude moved carefully from room to room, gazing at the hundreds of canvases hung from floor to ceiling. Sculptures of dying heroes and quivering virgins loomed above him; it was not the sort of art he liked at all, for he found it artificial and suffocating. But here and there, amid huge, old-fashioned paintings of allegories of the gods, he found the bright, humble paintings of the artists of whom Boudin had spoken—Corot, Daubigny, Delacroix, Millet—with their dreamy forests, fields of hay, and a house by a canal at twilight that seemed to glow with an unearthly radiance. All were painted not within studio walls but outside, *en plein air,* in wet, cold, or glorious sun. He felt he did not stand there looking at them but instead that he stepped inside, where the light gathered about him. This is art, he thought, almost touching the canvases. This is the new, true way; this is the path I will follow.

The next morning he joined a small school to learn.

A model posed naked on a stand. Dust lay on everything, clinging to the windowsills and the lamps. The other thirty students seated on benches at the stained tables hardly bothered to look at him. Claude took his pad and charcoal and began, sometimes working quickly, sometimes erasing with a bit of rolled bread.

Many hours later when he left, he was so tired he could hardly climb the seven flights to his room in Pigalle. By his oil lamp, he saw that his lace cuffs were gray with charcoal. He washed them in the cold water of the basin and draped them over the back of a chair. All about him, every angle and every color was more vivid than before. Even the chair with the drying cuffs and the worn wicker bottom cried out to him. He lay down and covered his eyes with his arm.

He walked to the studio every day, passing the new horse-drawn omnibuses that made their way through the rubble of wrecked neighborhoods and across the bridge to the Left Bank. At night he went home alone, too overwhelmed to speak with anyone.

Boudin had told him last summer, "The only thing I see you lack, Claude, is humility. When you learn that, you will do your best." Claude winced, thinking of it as he walked through the darkening streets. I'm humble enough, he thought wistfully. It should come easier.

HE WAS YOUNG, and he had not left sensuality behind; it followed him here, it hung about the studio. Amid the chalk and dust at the long tables of the art school, he looked from the model's rich breasts to the few demurely clothed female art students who diligently sketched her. Seated quite close to him on his bench was a plump, blond student from the Netherlands called Damek; he could feel the warmth of her leg against his trousers.

When he looked up from his sketchbook one warm afternoon, a male model stood where the lovely female had lately displayed her beauty; he was not, however, naked, but wore large white underdrawers. At that moment Damek pressed so near to Claude that he felt the edge of her breasts. "Because women study here too, the government says it's not decent to let us see what's between a man's legs," she said. Her voice dropped discreetly lower as she felt for her charcoal. "I wouldn't mind seeing what's between yours, Monet. Shall we? I don't live far away."

The chalky air stood still for him. "I only sleep with duchesses and maids; a duchess's maid would be ideal," he blurted as coolly as he could.

She closed her sketchbook sharply. "Oh, very well, then!" she whispered. "Keep what's there to yourself."

He leapt up as she took her things and hurried from the class. He caught her on the stairs, taking her in his arms and kissing her long and hard. "Actually," he gasped, "what I have is best shared, and I assure you, it's more than worth a look."

In her boardinghouse room, they latched the door. He was in her then, thrusting hard, gasping. After, Damek lay naked beneath him wonderfully contented, her finger running slowly down his bare back.

He took her again. The strange sensation came to him then: he was with her in the height of their shared sexuality—laughing, grasping, pulling together—and then they fell apart and the intensity was but a memory. It was the same with his painting. There was his passion, and then his energy was spent; he tried to hold it in and it was gone, leaving an odd sadness for his loss of power.

"This certainly does not mean," he said practically as he buttoned his shirt at last, "that we're falling in love. I'm so glad you agree."

They were lovers through the hot summer when the class emptied and the city sweltered, and they remained lovers as autumn came on and then the winds of winter. He bought coal for his own fireplace as seldom as possible to save money, and he sometimes sat with his back against it, wrapped in blankets, reading. He bought sausages so cheap they tasted of fat and wood. One franc purchased a jug of bitter wine. Almost all his money went to canvases and paints. The room had a few rats, but they were friendly. He wrote home that he was doing brilliantly.

He was making friends.

"There's a café in the Batignolles district on the Right Bank where a bunch of us go," a cheerful, thin student told him after class. They stood in the street and shook charcoal-smudged hands. The dark-skinned young man wore his usual workman's blue smock and always looked as if he needed a good meal. "Pierre-Auguste Renoir," he said, introducing himself. "I used to paint china but gave it up for canvases. My saintly widowed mother and many sisters are pinning all their hopes on my success! *Allons-y!* Come on!"

The windows of the Café Guerbois in Batignolles were dirty, the letters half worn away from the advertisement for wine painted directly on the glass. Claude recognized a few students seated around a long, cracked marble table. Their coats hung on hooks on the wall above them.

One man with a long, black rabbinical beard spoke with the cadence of the West Indies. "Jacob-Abraham-Camille Pissarro," he said, introducing himself. "*Plaisir!* You don't want to sit next to my friend Cézanne from Provence because he hasn't changed his clothes in two months. Perhaps it's a custom there in the south."

"You *merde;* this shirt is new," growled the dark painter.

Édouard Manet extended his pale hand to shake Claude's. Manet was the only one of them who had already gained some public recognition. He painted scandalously provocative nudes. Claude had seen him walking brusquely down the street in his top hat, swinging his walking stick as if clearing the street before him.

As the waiter took their order, Claude felt for his money. He was burning through it at a great rate with art supplies and presents for Damek, but he did not worry. Well, here I am, he thought. My path is clear before me. I'll keep working until I'm good enough to be accepted by the annual Salon and I begin to earn a living. Nothing can stand in my way.

He ordered sausages, cheese, and wine for all and began to tell them about the sky in Normandy. Of his family he said nothing: the one he loved was in the ground and he could never speak of her.

The artists met several times a week. They always carried paint boxes or sketchbooks and sometimes tied canvases; they came from painting the cold winter river, trying for a portrait commission, or persuading some framer to let them have credit and display their work in his window. Except for Pissarro they were all under thirty.

Around the café table, they talked all at once, shouting one another down and then listening quietly, nodding their heads before breaking into argument again. They spoke of perspective and shadow, brushwork, priming, layers of paint, leaves dancing in the wind, the fresh colors of a woman's bare arm, darkening skies over the water, mist on the roofs of village houses, and fields of new wheat. They discussed the shape of Parisian rooftops and the many colors of snow that lay over them this winter.

A new student from the school walked into the café one rainy day, bending to accommodate his height as he came through the door. He had a wide, crooked, endearing smile and such a wispy beard and mustache that it looked as if he had just been blown in from a storm. "Jean-Frédéric Bazille, from Montpellier," he said in his light bass voice when they all shook hands. "I'm a medical student, but my only love is painting. I shall murder all my patients through incompetence!"

He blinked as he shook Claude's hand, suddenly serious and a little shy. "I saw your work in class, Monet. You're good!"

CLAUDE STROLLED HOME on a late spring evening and was halfway up the stairs when a hoarse voice called him down. The concierge did not take the cigarette out of her mouth but waved a thick letter in the air. Claude took it, mounting the stairs more slowly now. It had been forwarded by his family and bore the stamp of the department of the army at Le Havre. Inside his crowded room, he read the letter.

For a few hours he walked back and forth in the dark until the seamstress below shouted up for him to stop. When he finally fell into bed he did not sleep but stared at the cracked ceiling in the dim glow of the streetlamp far below.

Claude caught the morning train back to Le Havre in a crowded third-class compartment with a family who ate garlic sausage and drank thick wine. Arriving in midafternoon, he trudged up the hill to his family house. He felt he had been away for years.

He washed in the basin in his old room and paced again to calm himself. At eight he would go down. He studied himself in the bedroom mirror, arranging his face, trying to find an expression between indifference and self-assurance. That had been his face at seventeen, and he did not know where it had gone. He passed his hand over his mouth, but it was no use. Damn it, then, he thought, descending the stairs two steps at a time at the sound of the dinner bell.

Gaslight illuminated the photograph of his mother on the wall. The long polished table with its ten chairs now seated only his father on one side and his aunt in her white, frilled matron's cap on the other. He kissed them and sat down before his soup.

"So you received the letter we forwarded," his aunt said.

"I did, dear aunt, and I came at once."

She shook her head, her soupspoon poised in the air. "Oh, Claude, such bad luck that your name was called in the army lottery! So many other boys here escaped it. We understand your training is to be in our French colony in Algiers. The seven years will pass quickly, we hope."

"But surely you don't expect me to go!" he exclaimed, appalled. "It will only cost you a thousand francs to buy me out. I don't doubt you'll do so. I'm on my way to great success!"

He waited in the silence, only the gas lamp sputtering.

His aunt and father were looking at each other.

"Yes," said his aunt reflectively at last, fingering the edge of the embroidered tablecloth. "We have been discussing your prospects, dear Oscar. Paris is full of thousands of artists, I'm told. And you haven't sold anything yet. We know also that you've met a Danish girl there; one of my old friends heard from your teacher. You oughtn't be thinking of *les filles*. No, it won't do. A thousand francs is a huge sum."

"However," his father said, clearing his throat, "if you stay here and work with me, we'll buy you out. You can paint on Sundays. Many men do."

Claude put down his napkin and stood up abruptly, startling Hannah, who was waiting with the dish of chicken. "Then I will go into the army," he said coldly. "I will never waste my life in a dark shop selling nautical supplies."

1862–1864

*My family thought they would catch me when I was con-
scripted, because then I would sow my wild oats, come
home, and settle down to a business career.*

—CLAUDE MONET

ATER THE NEXT DAY IN HIS ROOM, CLAUDE PACKED THE
uniform he had been given of his exotic Zoaves regiment:
red billowing trousers, tight black jacket, fez, high boots, and a great
curved sword. At least he looked handsome in it. As he sat wistfully
on his bed selecting the books he would take, he raised his eyes to the
old magazine pages of elegant women still tacked to his walls. Then
he opened his sketchbook.

He had missed his train to Le Havre by two minutes and, sitting
on his box near the ticket windows in the great Gare Saint-Lazare to
wait for the next one, he had sketched the tobacco and news-journal
kiosk. When he looked up to catch the shadows of the stacked news
journals, three women stood there, one older and the other two likely
her daughters, both still in their adolescence. The younger yet taller
girl was weeping beneath her blue hat veil. "But I won't just do what
you want me to," she sobbed, bunching her glove in her hand. "All
the social things you plan are so wretchedly tedious. I want to go to
the theater; you promised me!" Her mother and sister tried to pull
her away, but she shook her head and they hurried off without her.
She stood alone then, pulling up her veil and drying her eyes with her
handkerchief. Why she's scarcely fifteen, if that, he thought, moved.

Now she gazed about, her lovely, long desperate face wistful as if she hoped someone would rescue her. He turned the page and surreptitiously sketched her.

As he was about to approach her, his train was called.

Still sitting on his bed, he closed his sketchbook sadly, all his fond sketches of Paris within it. He straightened and tried on his hat. He thought, I am an army man now.

WITH A FEW hundred new soldiers who had volunteered or whose names had been chosen in the lottery, Claude sailed away across the ocean. Toward sunset some days later he and his fellows crowded on deck for their first sight of the glistening white city of Algiers rising up before them from the bay of the Mediterranean Sea.

They disembarked with their bags to the market amid French soldiers and men in colorful Arabic robes and merchants and horses and dust and walked to their barracks, set in the former receiving room of a crumbling Arabic mansion. Claude fell asleep that first night in a bed protected by netting amid the snores of others and woke thinking he was back in his room in Paris with the cries of the market outside.

For months he threw himself into his new life. He excelled at rifle practice; he won most practice duels, marched stoutly and gracefully, executed complicated drills with his fellows. Sometimes in his mind he saw himself as a great military man saving his country.

Yet the colors would not leave him alone.

He felt the subtle shades of sand and crumbled walls, of trees, of brown feet in sandals, of veiled women, of music played by men on instruments whose chords quivered in the air as the musicians squatted in the dust: brilliant reds and thick, deep browns, gold embroidery, and a hot, burning, sleepy sun. He climbed the steep hills to the Casbah, from which the Sultan had ruled before France conquered the country, and wandered among the old mosques and minarets.

He unpacked his sketchbook; he had to capture the city.

After a time he visited the Casbah regularly, returning with chalk drawings in his book. He managed to buy some paints and some old canvases. When he worked, he drank freely from the wells because it was so hot, and one day, hurrying back late as always, he fainted and rolled down the street.

Someone picked him up and half carried him to his bed.

He vomited; his bowels turned to hot, sick liquid, and he crawled to the chamber pot. The barracks in the ornate mansion with the stained blue tiles faded, and he thought he was scrambling over huge rocks to get to the sea.

"Typhoid," a voice echoed above him. "Did you drink unboiled water? We'll telegraph your family in Le Havre and you'll leave on the next ship. You may die before you reach there."

"But where are my sketchbook and canvases?" he managed.

On his berth on ship, the mosquito netting blew back and forth, catching the sickly, dull, hot air. The sea rocked beneath him and death felt near. It descended upon him like the weight of stuffy still darkness, filling his mouth, filling his lungs, forbidding breath. This was it, then. He was only twenty-three and he would be carried off to where death takes a man, though he had no idea where that could be. Tears ran down his unshaven face, stinging it; he managed to turn his head. But I don't want to die, he thought. This can't be the end for me when my life has hardly started.

Then he was back in Le Havre in his boyhood room.

Lying in bed, he gazed miserably at his magazine pictures of beautiful women, which looked down at him from the wall, as did his old drawings and caricatures. A week later, he managed to stand for a moment. Ten days later he made his way down the steps and outside as far as the gate.

His father visited him a few times a day, his weary face full of concern, and his aunt brought him trays of food and read him amusing stories from the local newspapers. Léon, his older, married brother, arrived weekly, looking the proper businessman in his dark suit and with short hair, having just opened his own engraving shop. "How's the soldier?" he said with a slight smile. "Made commander yet?"

Claude's aunt mounted with the supper tray one evening, her face a little somber. "We've inquiries from the army, Oscar," she said. "Someone came to the door a few hours ago, a corporal of some sort in uniform. As soon as you're well enough, they want you back."

He was strong enough to walk as far as the wharf, leaning on a stick, staring out at the vast, churning water. He longed to be in that Paris café with his friends, the long marble-topped table cluttered with glasses of cheap wine and everything smelling of cigars and old coats and paint. He slid out a pad and charcoal from his bag and sketched their profiles from memory. Back in his room, he wrote a letter to Auguste Renoir, whose address he found on the flyleaf of a book.

> *You may as well know I have made a mess of everything. I got myself sick in Algiers and they had to send me home for a time. I miss you all so much I can't stand it. What are you doing in Paris? How are Cézanne, Sisley, our medical student, and your homely self? Are you are cheerful and determined to put beauty into the world? Though why you should be cheerful with your poverty, I don't know!*
>
> *Why don't I come and surprise you all? I can't. I haven't any money. I have to go back to the army again just as soon as I'm well. The life I planned won't happen and I've been stupid enough these last days to want it again rather desperately. Yes, I want to create art more than anything else, and it was that that got me sick in the first place. It aches and aches in me and won't go away. I figure I have about a month or so more before they put me on a ship for Algiers again. Here it's a tomb! Even my old artist friend Boudin is traveling and there's no one I can talk to about these things at all. I wish one of you would visit me. I am almost perfectly well and have to pretend that I'm not.*

Claude tacked his sketch of the artists on his wall where he could look at it from his bed. He drew his room in Paris from memory. And one late afternoon he looked up and saw the medical student Frédéric Bazille bending his head to step through the door as he did in Paris to enter the café.

Claude jumped up and shouted, "You walked out of my drawing! I was two days away from expiring from loneliness!"

"Ah, that would be a pity, Monet! Is there a bed here for me?" He looked around the room. "You know, I could see from the train window that your Normandy has the most amazing light."

THEY HAD BARELY dragged the folding cot from the attic when the dinner bell rang below. "Ah *connard*—the ass!" Claude muttered, looking around for his dinner coat. "Come down and meet my father. My aunt's away tonight. We'll have a meal of recriminations. Recriminations in the soup, the chicken, the salad, the cheese."

Frédéric changed his shirt and slipped in gold monogrammed cuff links. "The only reason these aren't pawned yet is my grandfather just gave them to me," he said with his lopsided grin. "Come on, Monet. I'm going to charm the hell out of your father. I'm sent on a mission here."

They descended the stairs, hands behinds their backs like lawyers. Frédéric Bazille did not walk shyly as he did into the art class but strode past the china hutch to shake Claude's father's hand, saying, "I am your son's friend Frédéric Bazille from Montpellier. I am hoping you will extend your hospitality to me for a few days in your beautiful province."

Adolphe Monet studied the tall visitor with some bewilderment. "From Montpellier, monsieur?" he asked. "I have just read an article in the news journal that spoke of the scientist Bazille of Montpellier. Are you his son?"

"I am, monsieur."

"And he has sent you to Paris to study *art*, monsieur?"

"I study art only in my leisure hours, monsieur. I am a medical student; my family intends me to be a physician."

The three of them took their seats and shook out their napkins. Adolphe Monet poured the wine, and when the soup had been served, he said with a sigh, "Your father's fortunate in you, Bazille, if I may say so. Medicine's an honorable profession. My younger son wants to do nothing in life but paint clouds. Seven years in the army will make him a little more realistic. I also expect your serious studies will be a good influence on him."

"Do you want me to study medicine also, Father?" Claude asked. "After my years as a soldier are done?"

"You know what I mean, Oscar."

"Yes, I suppose I must. What I want is not important." Claude stared angrily at his wineglass until it wavered for him and he felt Frédéric kick him under the table.

"I don't think you understand, monsieur," Frédéric said, his spoon poised neatly above his soup bowl. "Claude influences me. He's the best of all of us. You must buy his freedom from the army. You must continue to support him. The world will later thank you. He's a genius."

Adolphe Monet stared at him. "The world will thank me!" he exclaimed, throwing down his napkin. "You looked like a sensible fellow. A genius! He's a dreamer! He'll serve his seven years and make his own way in the world as I did. Landscapes and girls! Oscar, you'll drive me to an early grave."

THREE HOURS LATER both young men had thrown off coats, ties, and vests and sat on their beds in Claude's room in their shirts and trousers, a wine bottle on the table in front of them. They were drunk, and two empty wine bottles had already rolled under the bed. The clock downstairs struck eleven, and outside, the harbor city slept.

Claude said, "So your family's old? Respected?"

"Both. I come from generations of men of great achievement, city fathers, benefactors of good public causes such as hospitals and the poor."

"That was kind what you said! I'm not better than the rest of you."

"You are. You have an uncompromising vision. I want to paint, but my style's not free like yours. I wish I were like you."

"Don't wish to be like me. If my friends think I'm any good, they're almost the only ones."

"My mission was to get you back. I may have failed. I'll be skinned alive with a dirty palette knife."

Claude stared down at his glass and then out the dark window. "Wind's rising," he said moodily. "A storm's coming; I feel it. I always used to lie here when storms came after my mother died and wish the house would blow away to the harbor. Now you know how pleasant it is here. I bet you never have to compromise, Frédéric."

Frédéric frowned. "On the contrary; I do. Do you think I want to be a doctor? The professors in medical school hardly know my face except for the look of panic on it just before examinations. I only agreed to attend so I could come to Paris and study art. My family keeps me on a small allowance to rein me in, though they're wealthy."

The lantern flickered, and the wind blew. Frédéric sat quietly with his knees drawn up, his voice low and words stumbling from the wine. "I'll be . . . wealthy one day when I'm old or married. I'm engaged. I have a little time to live before I get shut up forever and become a Bazille."

AN HOUR OR so before dawn, a tree branch banged against the window, leaves rustling. Claude sat up. On the cot across from him, he made out the shadow of Frédéric Bazille still sleeping, long bare feet hanging over the edge.

The wind was pressing at the window, and somewhere a shutter swung and knocked. "Frédéric," he whispered, shaking his friend. "Frédéric, wake up! Storm's coming. Come on, get dressed. We'll watch it over the sea."

He threw Frédéric's trousers at him. In the dark, they banged into things and sent the water pitcher crashing. He hushed Frédéric and led him by the hand out of the house and across the garden to the stable, which housed old Mirabelle. The docile mare nuzzled him. Claude saddled her quickly and jumped up. "Come behind me," he whispered. "*Dépêchez-vous*, Bazille! Hurry!" He felt pulled by the wind.

Frédéric jumped behind him, throwing his arm around Claude's chest. He whispered, "This is crazy, you know."

"I don't care and neither do you! If they're going to shoot me in some war, I might as well go now in my own way. Besides, it will be all right. I haven't died yet."

Claude pressed forward, whispering in a seductive voice, "Mirabelle!" He thought she shifted a little, turning her old dignified brown face as if to say, "You're crazy, my young master! *Tu es fou!*" They turned down the road, he kicking her gently to go forward. The wind whipped them, smelling of salt, blowing away his hat. The mare trotted fast now, her face down, the road rough, bouncing the riders. Claude and his friend heard the sea and slid down, tying the mare's reins to a thick tree branch.

They ran across the road and climbed down the wet, slippery rocks, holding the lantern, balancing in the fierce wind, shouting and laughing. The wind was full of cold, salty seawater. Claude grabbed Frédéric's arm and shouted, "Look!"

Dawn emerged from the sea with a streak of dark gray light blended with blue. Clouds pushed up from the darkness of the deep, hardly able to separate themselves from the heaving water that staggered toward the shore.

Frédéric ran in the face of the wind and Claude ran after him until they came to the water's edge and the waves hit them. Their wool trousers clung to their legs. Now for a moment sky and sea were one.

A sudden wave knocked Frédéric off his feet. He fell to his side, clothes and beard drenched. Claude shoved him and they fell together with the tide dragging at them, shells and stones on their back, rolling over and shouting.

Cold salty water filled Claude's mouth; he spat.

Above him, lightning split the sky in two until it seemed clouds and sky would fall on them and rise again, pulling him and Frédéric into them and melding them with the dark sea.

HANNAH WAS ALREADY awake when they returned, shivering, to the house. They poured coffee in the kitchen, drawing their chairs as close to the fire as possible to dry themselves, laughing and eating bread and butter. The storm pelted the window. Under the noise of the thunder they heard footsteps and looked up to see Claude's father in his dressing gown.

Adolphe Monet poured his own coffee with hot milk, and sat down opposite them. He rubbed the side of his nose with his finger and said slowly, "I've come to a decision, Claude. When your aunt returned last night and you were both in your room, she and I talked about your future. She'll buy you out of the army and I'll support you for two years. I expect you to work and succeed as with any business and remember, no girls. *Pas de filles!* And Claude . . . if I ever need you, you will come?"

Claude stared at his friend and then at his father. For a moment he could not speak, and then he said humbly, "Anything . . . always . . . as you wish, Father."

Interlude

The old artist could not work well for some days after he received the cold letter from Camille's sister, Annette. He left a canvas on the Japanese bridge where he had been painting, and the rain came suddenly before the gardener could retrieve it.

He mounted the stairs to his room and pulled out an antique lacquered Japanese box with two drawers he had discovered several months before when cleaning out some things. He had given it to Camille as a birthday present a long time ago, and the finding of it had precipitated his communication to her sister. Now he decided to look at it more closely; he had not done so in more than thirty years. Sitting on his bed, he opened it.

The drawers were jumbled. The first contained some letters from him to her and a bit of what Camille called her diaries. They were not proper diaries in a leather-bound book, but a few small portfolios of odd notes and impressions. The second drawer held small keepsakes: a candle stub, some seashells, a fan, calling cards, opera tickets. In touching these things he felt he touched her.

He read some of the papers here and there, only lightly because his eyes were tired. Each one opened a world of memories for him. Unfolding one scrap, he found the address and hour of a theater audition.

Here was a poem, also incomplete, written, he suspected, nearly half a century before because it was on the bookshop stationery. *Quiet love, so quiet it is as if I am walking early in the morning, hearing the call of the blackbird. Which am I?* On the back of this was a list for blue feathers and ribbons for hat trimming. There was a paper with the address in his handwriting of his Paris studio to guide her there the first time.

Each item led to another, some of which he did not understand. Everything moved him deeply. Yet only Camille's sister would know the story behind some of these things.

No, he thought suddenly. *Que le diable l'emporte!* The devil can take her! She'll have nothing more from me. I've allowed this woman to distract me when I'm working. What can these paintings of water lilies, which are such a struggle for me, have to do with my long-lost love? What has my past to do with me now?

He closed the box and stuffed it away in his wardrobe.

He would not risk another letter to her.

Part Two

1864–1866

My family at last begin to take me seriously . . .
—CLAUDE MONET

THE STUDIO CLAUDE AND FRÉDÉRIC RENTED TOGETHER was on the rue de Furstenberg on the Left Bank of the Seine. They walked through the huge porte cochere across the cobbled courtyard to the back house. The concierge gave them the key, and Claude took one of the tin candleholders with a slanted stub of candle.

Above them the wood stairs to the studio ascended into darkness. They began to mount, the tiny light showing them just one step at a time. Some steps were cracked. On the top landing, the iron key scraped in the lock and they walked into the room. The wallpaper was peeling, and the stove's rusty pipe snaked up the wall. The floorboards were old, and the windowsills were stained from the dust of coal fires; when they opened the huge window, light poured in, and the roofs and chimneys of Paris stretched as far as they could see. There were two small bedrooms. Claude noticed that the ceiling sagged in his.

They carried up their bags and boxes. Frédéric knelt by one of his wicker trunks and withdrew a few small framed studio portraits of his family. Claude dropped beside him to pick up one of a lovely girl. "And who is this gorgeous creature?" he demanded. "Your sister? Introduce me! I promise I'll behave horribly."

"No, you *merde*! That's Lily, the girl I'm going to marry when I move back home to begin my medical career."

"The one you don't particularly *want* to marry?"

"I don't mind marrying her," Frédéric said carefully. As he unpacked the trunk, his long fingers moved more slowly, a habit Claude had observed when Frédéric was unsure of himself. "I spoke rather rashly when we were drunk at your house. Lily and I have known each other since we were children; she used to follow me around. She plays the violin and she's good and beautiful and besides, she adores me." He gave one of his lopsided grins.

Claude shoved him lightly. "So you're intending to move back home eventually? How does a slob like you merit such a girl? Is she nice to sleep with?"

"What? Sleep with her! She would never. I have to make my promises in church first and suffer until then."

"Poor bastard. Are you still a virgin?"

"Certainly not, but I've no one now."

"Well, I guess we'll both have to keep our trousers buttoned for a bit. Damek's found someone else. Don't go with whores, Bazille; you'll get syphilis, which can kill you. Maybe all the desire will go into the painting."

"I intend to live a long time," Frédéric replied and began to hang his clothes in the wardrobe. Since the days painting by the sea near Claude's house and the leisurely barge journey back to Paris by the Seine, they had talked of many things, laying down the first path of a friendship. Now they could be utterly irreverent about the present one moment and more somber about the future the next. As hard as they tried to look into it, it did not seem very real.

They were hanging their paintings on the studio wall when Auguste Renoir and Pissarro came in with their own work in roped bundles. Auguste walked from room to room. "Surely you'll need company here," he called. "You don't have enough pictures on the walls! I'll bring some of mine to cover up the broken plaster. You don't mind if I sleep under an easel now and then?"

"You don't mind if we step on you when we get up?"

Pissarro put down his paintings and rubbed the rope marks on his palms. He said modestly, "I could also use a place to stay when it's too late to go back to my mother's house in Louveciennes. Besides, things there aren't so cheerful since our maid Julie bore my child last month. Lucien keeps me up nights, but I've already made three drawings of him—best work I've done. Do you have any food? I can't remember if I ate today."

The four artists gathered around the small table with its green oil-cloth, all talking at once. "But why can't you remember?" Claude asked.

Auguste took a large bite of sausage and bread. "Because he's not sleeping and we've both changed jobs again. We left that job at the wharf. A falling crate almost took off his arm: no arm, bad for a painter. So just an hour ago he found work painting blinds. I'm painting a large picture on a café wall, did I tell you?" He leaned back in the chair, thumbs in his trouser waistband, grinning at them, his small teeth a bit darkened from tobacco. "Lucky me! It'll take a month and they feed me and give me a little money for my own canvases. There are ten thousand cafés in Paris, and by the time I've painted all their walls, somebody will know my presently obscure name."

The studio became the meeting place for all their friends. It was cluttered with books, shawls, props, chairs; everyone's work hung on the walls and leaned in piles against them. There were dirty glasses, a plate of drying bread and cheese rinds, greasy cheap sausage paper, and a few cracked saucers with cigar butts. The artists often stayed up very late talking over a keg of wine Frédéric's family sent from their vineyards in Languedoc. Sometimes when they ran out of money for food, they had dinner at the *hôtel particulier*, the town house, of Frédéric's bourgeois uncle and aunt, Commander and Madame Lejosne, who patronized the arts and whose rooms were full of musicians and actors. They took home leftovers and dined on cold pheasant, lamb, and cake for days after.

Toward the time the quarterly rent was due, Claude and Frédéric would sit across the rickety table from each other composing clever letters to their families, reading them aloud. Auguste Renoir, who slept on the floor more often than not, would pace the room extemporizing, suggesting florid phrases. Then they would run down to their mail slot as soon as they heard the postman's bell. They pawned their good clothes, their watches, and once, their clean sheets. Someone got a portrait commission in the end and redeemed things. Sometimes several people came over and they talked about art until two in the morning. Frédéric's friend Edmond would raucously play cheerful songs on the rented spinet piano.

CLAUDE WAS STANDING before his easel on a February day, fingernails embedded with paint, when Frédéric came slowly in with the post. "Of all bad fortune, I have to go home for a week to my family in Montpellier!" he groaned, dropping his long form into a chair. "I can't put it off any longer. Come with me as a shield?"

"Now? You know we have less than a month to finish paintings to submit to the annual State Salon! I can hardly sleep thinking of it."

"I thought you already chose your submissions. Anyway, we can paint there and maybe come up with something good."

Claude hesitated. "Well," he said carefully, "if we can paint, I don't mind spending half an hour with your young lady. Is the light good? I shall do my best not to be rude."

"That's more than I can hope for myself," Frédéric replied.

They threw their clothes in a couple of valises, packed their paint boxes and a few new stretched canvases, and caught the train. It was a journey of several hours to the old province of Languedoc.

Claude sensed the weight of the house when he entered it. Every chair and ancestral painting and the capacious library full of rare books seemed to say, "We are old France; we live as all men ought to live."

When he came to dinner, he recognized his friend's fiancée from her picture. There were many people at the table, but she sat between her parents as if protected by them. He took in her curled hair and ivory wool-silk dress, her small mouth. She looked curiously at Claude and gently at Frédéric.

After the meal they all moved to the music room, where coffee came on a silver tray and delicate cups were passed around. When they all had been served, Lily lifted a violin from its case and tuned it, and Frédéric took his place at the piano. "Mozart, violin sonata in B-flat major," he announced. The firm sounds of piano and violin began together at once, followed immediately by a poignant soaring line from the violin. The instruments answered each other.

Lily's curls trembled as she dipped and played; she was very skilled, but it was Frédéric who amazed Claude. After the last chord, Lily returned to sit between her parents on the sofa with the violin on her lap, but Frédéric did not rise. Suddenly he began to play again, and Madame Bazille's shoulders grew tense at the thick, driving music.

"It's Schumann," Frédéric exclaimed over his shoulder. "He went mad." He stood up and excused himself and bolted from the room, leaving the last unfinished chords of the phrase vibrating in the air over the coffee cups.

Everyone glanced at one another; Lily looked as if she was going to cry. She seemed to want to run after him. "What did we do?" Madame Bazille asked.

His father cleared his throat. "We let him go to Paris to study medicine, but between his passion for music, art, and amateur theater, I think he's doing badly in his studies. I suspect he won't pass this year again. Have you any influence on him, Monet?"

"Yes, his studies are likely weighing on my friend. I'm sorry, mademoiselle. If you'll excuse me, I'll go and find him and bring him back."

Where the hell had Frédéric gone? Claude looked in his friend's bedroom and saw hundreds of books and some of Frédéric's earlier paintings on the wall. He was walking down the hall again when a door above opened and Frédéric's voice whispered, "I'm here."

Claude took the steep back stairs to the attic, which was lit only by one oil lamp. The large space was full of broken furniture, old toys, a dressmaker's dummy, and many trunks. Frédéric was kneeling beside one, his shape long and thin in the shadow.

Gripping Frédéric's shoulder, Claude said, "*Courage, mon brave!* The girl's stunning and obviously mad about you."

"*Merde!* Claude! My father's already been lecturing me. It's what they say, the way they say it. It's all subtle. They mean well, and I love them, but sometimes I feel none of them knows me at all. I was born a Bazille. I know what my great ancestors did. I know what I'm supposed to do and to feel, but I don't always. Your father wants something of you; mine wants something of me, but what am I? So I hide here as I did when a boy."

Frédéric opened the trunk. "I wanted to show you this stuff anyway," he said. "We could take some away to paint if we wanted to. These are my great-grandfather's uniforms from the Napoleonic wars in Russia sixty years ago. He came back with the flag, but his foot and one arm were amputated for frostbite."

Claude knelt to feel the stiff, tarnished gold braid, which crumbled a little in his fingers. He took up the rapier.

"That's still sharp," Frédéric said. "Never mind; I remember now you were in the army."

Claude folded up the uniform and laid it in the trunk, closing the lid. "Come on," he said. "I'm supposed to bring you downstairs. Your mother's crying a little and your fiancée looks very sad. She'll be up here looking for you any moment, I suspect. Tomorrow we'll go out to paint. We must submit to the Salon when we get back. Frédéric, quit medical school. You want to. Listen to me. You have one life. Be what you are. You're gifted, damn it. We'd manage somehow. We have to live just for our work."

Frédéric shook his head. "I won't submit this year." They rose and went downstairs to the sound of chatter and the smell of coffee.

IN LATE MARCH, a month after his return from the Bazille home in Languedoc, Claude wrapped two of his paintings in canvas and set off. He could see the crowd at the door of the enormous Palais de l'Industrie between the Seine and the Champs-Élysées. Hundreds of artists were already lined up, squeezing in one at a time to submit their work and receive a numbered receipt. Men carting sculptures in wagons, some women carrying paintings almost larger than themselves, all pushing like people on a bread line. Two men began to shout, and one shoved the other. "I was standing here first, monsieur."

"You are a pig, monsieur."

Almost every artist he knew in Paris was there: the old hopeful ones, the successful painters, who barely glanced in his direction, the students from the art school, which had closed. They would have left anyway. The teacher had predicted no future for any of them if they insisted on painting in such a loose style.

Paul Cézanne called to him, "Pissarro's submitted already and gone to work. Where's Auguste?"

"Either already submitted or settling some problem with his mother and sisters." They spoke briefly, and then fell into silence, inching forward slowly. When Claude looked back sometime later, a few hundred men had taken their place behind him. He put up his coat collar against the March wind.

A while later he passed through the enormous triumphal arch of the entrance. Within the arch high above, huge sculpted angels blew their stone trumpets and a heroic statue personifying France sat crowned with a halo of stars. Each artist fell silent at the grandeur.

A withered man sitting behind a table accepted his paintings, logging them into the large book with a slow, scratchy pen. "M-o-n-e-t," he spelled, writing as carefully as an aged schoolboy. Then the two paintings were lifted onto a cart by a muscular workman and Claude walked away, hands in his pockets.

It was like leaving his soul to see his paintings stacked with so many others and wheeled away to echoing rooms. The judges will stare at them for a few minutes, he thought, and then pass on to other work. He could see the committee in their dark coats and hats. Everyone knew how it was in there when they chose among twenty thousand works of art: a minute's glance, an off-the-cuff decision. Giving a shake of the head for a negative vote, then passing on to the next. A mark noted on a scrap of paper to be counted later. Was the work original but not too original? How was the perspective? Was the subject properly executed? Just the sort of things *they* wanted, in other words, something with a style of fifty years before. Nothing vivid and moving and real, nothing like he and his friends were trying to create.

He paused, finger against his lips. Still, perhaps not; perhaps it would be different. Perhaps when looking at his they would stroke their beards and mutter among themselves, "A work of genius!"

Two weeks later the concierge yelled up that a letter had come for him, her voice echoing up the long flights. Claude rushed down, almost falling.

He walked back up the stairs, into the studio and into Frédéric's bedroom, where his friend was studying at the desk; Claude leaned against a wall, covering his face with his hands. "*Putain*—the whore!" he cried bitterly. "Both declined! They're good too."

Frédéric leapt up. "The bastards. They don't see. They can't see! Listen to me, Claude. Just go on painting. I'll pay the rent myself if I have to. I'll lie to them at home."

"You already lie to them at home. Suppose I'm not worth it? Suppose I'm fooling everyone?"

~ 2 ~

EVERYTHING HE PAINTED that spring displeased him, and the last thing he wanted to see was the barely disguised empathy of his friends. "You're not fooling everyone!" Frédéric had shouted after him as he bolted down the stairs and ran he did not know where.

He took a wealthy woman he had met at the theater as his lover for several weeks and painted nothing until he was thoroughly disgusted with himself; by late autumn, he had decided to return to Le Havre to work. As he walked to his train in the Gare Saint-Lazare, he remembered the tall girl in the veiled hat he had seen three years before—recently he had been looking through old sketchbooks and found her picture, which he had tacked on the wall of his studio bedroom. He wondered what had happened to her. Was her life as unsettled as his was? He imagined meeting her and saying, "I am the famous artist Monet," but of course he could not say that. He bit the edge of his thumb and looked out the window.

For many days after he arrived home he slept a lot and read. Then on a damp November morning he went off alone to the riverhead at low tide and began to create a new painting. A storm was coming; a horse and cart made its way through the low tide, and a few other weary horses lifted their hooves from the wet sand while the clouds almost fell into the sea. He took the painting back to his bedroom and worked on it there and then continued in the Paris studio when he returned. In March he submitted it to the Salon with a smaller painting of a road in Chailly.

Again the concierge yelled up to him one morning as he was shaving. There were three letters in their slot, including one from Frédéric's wealthy aunt and uncle, presumably inviting them to dinner again. He stood in the hallway to open the one addressed to him, using the ragged letter opener that hung from a string on a nail. He read it several times. Half an hour later he was still sitting on the stairs, flushed and breathless.

Claude went with his friends on the opening day of the spring Salon to see his work hung. They looked for the paintings for half an hour until they discovered both twenty feet above them, just under the ceiling, where little could be seen of them at all.

A party of men and women pushed past them on the way out of the room, knocking into them. "It's not a failure," Auguste cried above the noise. "Come back here, Monet! At least you got in. That's more than the rest of us can say. Success takes a long time."

"I haven't got a long time," Claude cried as he strode out under the great arched entrance. "I've got six more damn months of money from home and then I'll have to find a doorway to sleep in."

Auguste threw his arm around Claude's back as they walked. "Look, Claude!" he said. "Start planning for a submission next year. Never mind painting seascapes and shores for now, even though they're the best around. Paint beautiful women and paint a big canvas. If you do it well enough, the world will notice you. Find some models. You'll do it. We'll help."

FOR HOURS HE wandered alone. When he was troubled, he always sought refuge in the streets and by the river. Sometimes he saw everything; other times he saw nothing. Dusk was falling when he entered the bookshop on the rue Dante near the Sorbonne; the window lamp had been lit and an elderly cat was sleeping on a French encyclopedia. The hand-painted hanging sign read Libraire Doncieux.

A young woman was seated behind the desk. She was so absorbed in writing a letter that she did not hear him come in. Her thick, brownish-red hair, which was secured demurely in a topknot on her head with combs and a heavy black velvet bow, glistened in the light of the desk lamp. She wore a little gold cross against the high lace collar of her dress, and she bit her lip as she wrote.

"*Bonjour,* mademoiselle," he said.

She raised her face. It was the veiled girl he had seen in the train station on his way to join the army nearly four years before.

Claude was so startled that his heart began to beat a little faster.

She was looking at him oddly now. "*Bonjour,* monsieur," she said in a clear, sweet voice. "May I help you?"

"I merely came to look."

"Very well. *D'accord.*"

"Do you carry any secondhand books?"

"Some, in the box against that wall."

A few customers came in as he browsed the shelves, glancing back at her secretly several times. She was so much lovelier than he remembered her because she was real. There was a sort of warmth from her as from the earth on a summer day. He felt it drift across the shop and cause the titles of the books to blur before him.

The customers departed, and he heard the rapid scratch of her pen again until it stopped. The silence was potent. She called, "*Je suis desolée,* monsieur! I'm sorry, but we're closing in a few minutes."

He pulled an old book from a box and walked toward her with it. She looked at the title and smiled. "*Birds of Central France,*" she said. "That will be two francs, monsieur."

Now the day was ending outside and the bookshop grew darker. Behind her was a staircase leading to the upper shelves and then above to he did not know where. He had the odd sensation that she would go up those steps, her skirts trailing, and disappear as she had before.

He said, "What's up there?"

"Books people seldom buy, and above that, my uncle's rooms. He's rather the black sheep in my family to own a shop like this, but I like it."

"I've shopped here before. I've not seen you here until now."

"My uncle's not well, poor thing! I've come to help for a few days. My parents don't let me do too much because I'm just eighteen, but this time they said I might in compensation for . . ." She pressed her lips together and shook her head.

"You were writing passionately to someone and I interrupted you."

"I have passionate words to say."

"Ah, do you?" Claude could see from the quality of her dark wool dress and the real gold cross about her neck that she was not one of the harried Parisian shopgirls struggling to buy a pretty pair of shoes but some daughter of the petite or even haute bourgeoisie whose father had plenty of income. She likely spent most of her days drawing a little or playing the piano or deciding what she would wear. He knew that if she really looked at him, she might see a somewhat shabby young man who had just endured a moment of tremendous disappointment and who, under his slight bluster, was deeply sad.

He walked home by gaslight and then through the studio into his room, where he stared again at the sketch on his wall, which he had made of her when he had first seen her. Marvelous—but what could it mean for him? He locked his door and lay down on the bed with his copy of *Birds of Central France* lying open on his chest.

His mind was not still, though. Ideas for paintings moved in the dark room before him. He jumped up and flipped through his sketchbooks to find a rough sketch for a huge painting of picnickers under a tree. He had made it the year before and forgotten all about it, but now it came to life for him. The room changed: trees grew, people ate and drank on a picnic cloth, and everything was dappled by sunlight. And the girl in his drawing was in the middle of it.

HE WAS SWEATY and sensually excited; he tried to sleep and ended up making further sketches. His hopelessness of the day before was swept away. He was up by dawn, though he had hardly slept at all. He endured the hours until the shop opened. Suppose she was not there? For it was her face and figure and no other that he saw in the great painting he would make.

She was at the bookshop desk again, writing another letter, but when he came close she quickly turned it facedown. What was in it? It did not matter. He had nothing to do with her personal matters; he did not even know her. "*Bonjour*, mademoiselle," he said in a more charming way than he had the previous day. "I did not mention this yesterday. *Je suis peintre*—I'm a painter."

Her large brown eyes studied him, her hand over the turned letter. "Are you, monsieur?" she asked.

"I'm planning a huge picture of picnickers on the grass to be painted outside, *en plein air,* in the forest of Fontainebleau, a short train ride from Paris. I need a young woman to model. You're very lovely. It would take a few weeks. I plan it for June. I would of course pay for your time and your lodging. Would you model for me?"

"But I am not a model, monsieur," she replied demurely. "And I don't know what my parents would say if I went from the city alone." From her now downcast eyes, he could imagine exactly what they would say.

He flapped his hat against his trouser leg, keeping the other hand securely in his pocket. "I assure you I'll ask nothing that could be considered immodest or offensive. You would be fully clothed; I would ask you to bring your loveliest dresses. As for my references, others can speak well of me. My family has a prosperous business in Le Havre. My best friend, also from a fine family, is coming to model. Look, here's my address. Will you send word to me if you decide you can come?"

He walked home and through the studio, where his friends were painting, and threw himself on the bed. He wondered why she had been allowed to work in the bookshop, in compensation for what, and to whom she had been writing. She would not come, of course, and she was the one he wanted. He was uncomfortably aware of something about her that had haunted him since he had first seen her with the family.

But at twilight, when he was hurrying out to buy sausages before the shops closed, he noticed a sheet of blue stationery in the mail slot. "Dear Monsieur Monet," it said in neat handwriting. "I could come for one week only if I can bring my sister as chaperone. We regard it as an adventure and hope it will be of help to you and further the

cause of art. Sincerely, Camille-Léonie Doncieux." The other side of
the paper had a few words crossed out. He thought they said, "My
dear love," but it did not matter, for they were not for him.

FONTAINEBLEAU WAS AN ancient royal forest that artists had discovered more than a generation before. Claude wandered about until he
found the place he wanted to paint, then set up his easel and a small
canvas to begin to capture the leafy beech trees in the foreground and
the background that he would need for his picture of picnickers.
Later in the studio he would repaint everything on a very large canvas that no one in next spring's Salon could possibly ignore.

He had taken places in a rustic inn that catered to artists: two tiny
rooms in the attic for himself and Frédéric, and one lovelier and
larger room for the girls to share. Everything was ready when
Frédéric arrived a few days later. He had brought his paints and
easel, hoping to have time to work himself.

That night they smoked their pipes outside the inn in the warm
air, waiting for the Doncieux sisters to arrive by coach from the local
train. The young women did not come on the first coach or the second. Already it was ten o'clock at night.

"They're not coming!" Claude said. "It's all over for me."

"They're coming. There's one more coach."

"I bet you a pack of tobacco they don't."

"I bet you your future prize in the Exhibition they do."

Claude leapt up from the stone bench to pace the dirt road. A faint
lamp glow was coming closer, illuminating the trunks of oaks. The
horse stopped, the door opened, and two tall girls wearing bonnets
and struggling with large wicker trunks cautiously put their feet on
the step to descend. Both men ran forward to help and nearly toppled
the luggage.

"We nearly couldn't get away," the girls cried, their words tumbling over each other. "And we're so dreadfully tired! Did you get
the hatbox?" He had a feeling they had been arguing on the way, and

indeed when he and Frédéric carried the bags upstairs and closed the door, he heard the muffled intense voices.

HE ROSE VERY early and descended the stairs with his paint box. The sisters' door was firmly closed, and no sound came from within. "Are the young women who came last night still here?" he asked the innkeeper's wife as she came toward him carrying clean linen, and she replied, "*Bien sûr!* But of course! One of them has already walked in the garden; she's below with her coffee. It will be a fine day, monsieur."

Camille-Léonie Doncieux was standing by the window, two hands holding her coffee bowl; she held the curtain back just a little with her shoulder and was gazing out at the flowers. She turned to him with a smile and said cheerfully, if a little shyly, "Good morning, monsieur!"

"Good morning, mademoiselle."

She put her coffee bowl on the table and gave him her bare hand.

She was young indeed and very lovely; hers was a strong, almost classical Grecian face with full eyebrows, beautiful eyes, and a strong nose. Neither was she too slender, he noted appreciatively: a full bosom pressed against the bodice of her blue and white striped dress. He had had the impression before she turned that she had been waiting for someone; under her outer restraint he sensed a certain anticipation that something she would like was hurrying toward her.

He felt a strong frisson of attraction and immediately frowned at himself. She must be only a model to me or I won't do well, he thought.

He heard skirts on the stairs as her sister, Annette, descended, still looking half asleep. Frédéric came down shortly after and drank his coffee hastily. The four of them left a clutter of bread crumbs and empty coffee bowls on the table as they walked out to work on the painting.

Claude spread a picnic rug with dishes and food on the ground beneath the beech tree and set up his easel and the canvas. He called sternly, "Now, Mademoiselle Camille, if you please, over there. Sit on the rug. Yes. Now pick up that plate and hold it out a little. Very good. We'll work this way for a while and then I'll have you change places. I'll paint you as different women. And you, Mademoiselle Annette, sit there if you will." The women took their places, laughing a little, arranging their full dresses over their crinolines, which were fuller in the back in the new style, tidying their hair. Frédéric stretched his long body on the grass, propping himself up on both elbows.

Paris was full of professional models who knew how to hold a pose; would these girls be still? Yes, it appeared they would be still, though they did talk softly back and forth about the theater, which they both adored.

Sun touched the bright colors on Claude's palette as he painted the first stroke, then the second. He always began in apprehension. If it worked, there would be a time when the painting took him, when it reached out and he became it, when he smelled of oil and mineral spirits, when he and the air became one.

His hours passed radiantly; with every stroke, he enclosed himself more in the canvas. By the afternoon's end, he noted that his models had begun to sag this way or that, into the ground or leaning against the air. Claude sighed; he felt his own weariness with intense reluctance, but there it was. He could wring no more of himself from the day or his models. His arm ached and the light was going, going. He wanted to rush forward under the trees and snatch it in his arms.

THE SISTERS LOOKED somewhat alike and were almost the same height. Both were beautiful. He saw that when he painted and again as they sat down in the inn kitchen for dinner that night. Annette sat quite straight, showing off her long, lovely neck above her high dress collar as if she might be presented to the nobility at any moment if someone from the ancien regime before the Revolution should sweep into this farmhouse kitchen past the blackened stove. Camille was more open; she broke into conversation and then pulled herself back with a shy smile. She picked up her fork and forgot to eat the bit of lamb. She wore her brownish-red hair in a thick bun at the back of her neck, with several shorter strands falling against her cheeks as if they resented being constrained.

They were well-bred young ladies suddenly stolen off for an adventure together. Their parents likely did not know they were here. Claude looked toward the dark window. If they should be followed!

He was still so much in his painting he had no idea how he would make conversation with them. He looked at his friend and at the girls at the table, rearranging them in his mind on the canvas as he had seen them that afternoon.

Frédéric poured the wine gallantly. "So, mesdemoiselles!" he said in his charming bass voice. "Have you both always lived in Paris?"

Annette shook her head. "No, monsieur; we're from Lyon, where we studied at the convent school. We came four years ago. Our father's a silk merchant and continues his work here."

"Yes, everyone comes to Paris for art, for music, for theater! Do you go often to the Louvre?"

Camille leaned forward, both hands on the table. "We go to the Louvre all the time, and to the theater," she replied, stammering slightly. "I love the theater so! Almost as much as books. I am always coming home with books, aren't I, Annette? I have read a lot of Balzac, much to my mother's disapproval, but I prefer the novels of George Sand. They're more tender. And Victor Hugo makes me cry."

"Do you read poetry too?"

"Oh, yes."

They all ate hungrily. Annette glanced now and then at her engagement ring as if appraising it; Claude had heard she was to be married in the autumn.

When dessert was served, Frédéric exclaimed, "How can it be you've never modeled before?" He sat back boyishly, his thumbs in his suspenders, smiling happily, surveying the girls. "You're both beautiful and sweet. Tenderhearted, I would say."

Annette shook her head, pushing her wineglass away a few inches and then surreptitiously drawing it back. Her voice was now just the slightest bit unsteady. "Camille's the one who's tenderhearted! Why, if she likes someone, she gives everything."

The younger sister flushed. "Really, it's not so. But how odd we've been to the Louvre many times and not seen each other. Paris is so big. You see someone interesting and then they are gone, gone. I've seen faces and remembered them always. I wonder sometimes what I'll do with my life. I have so many plans."

"What plans?" Frédéric asked seriously.

"Oh, well, *plans*!" she said, flushing.

Claude was now so tired he could hardly follow the conversation. In addition, Camille kept changing for him: he recalled her in the train station and then the book shop and now here she was across the table from him in an inn kitchen in Fontainebleau, her eyes a little unfocused for the wine. He struggled for words and managed to ask Annette, "But if you are to be married so soon, mademoiselle, why did you come here?"

Annette raised her hand to tuck in any loose strands from her hair. *We regard it as an adventure,* the note of acceptance had said. "To chaperone my younger sister, of course! *Bien sûr!* She came home the day you asked her, monsieur, saying we must go, we must go, and I couldn't let her go alone." Ah, he thought. Camille wanted to come and so she did, and left behind her passionate letters. But to whom were they written?

Annette drank delicately and dropped her voice. "Camille is also expected to become engaged by summer's end; actually my betrothed and hers know each other well."

Camille's face became serious. "Yes," she replied. "Monsieur is a dear man, very kind. I didn't expect my sister and I to find husbands so close together, but she's engaged and will marry first."

LATER IN HIS narrow room he heard them below wishing each other goodnight and then Frédéric's footsteps as he mounted to his own attic room. Claude put out his lamp and lay in the dark, his mind still seeing the heavy green trees of the painting, the little white flowers, the people moving languidly as if time had stopped and they would be there forever with Annette's arms raised to unpin her hat and Camille in a white dress, leaning forward, offering a plate.

The opening of the inn door below woke him. He felt for his watch and read the hour by the moonlight: nearly one. He could hear Frédéric snoring through the wall. Claude rose in his nightshirt to look out the window.

Camille was standing alone on the path in the white light of the moon.

What was she doing down there by herself? He thought to call out and run down to her, but what then? He must maintain some distance between them, and though he so much wanted to go to her, he only bit his lip as she turned away and walked toward the woods, her pale dress disappearing around the bend. Now he regretted his decision. Should he run after her? He doubted anyone would come to disturb her, but still he was not certain she should be out alone.

I'll go after her in ten minutes if she's not returned, he thought. He slipped back into bed, his eyes on the hands of his pocket watch. The wind blew the tree branches a little, and out of exhaustion, he slept. When he woke he still held his watch, which read half-past nine in the morning. Light usually woke him, but today rain was beating relentlessly against the window. *Merde!* They would have to work in the kitchen without any real light at all.

Frédéric was painting a still life of vegetables at his own easel when Claude came down for coffee. Shortly after, he heard a door open above and the two sisters descended, still adjusting the pins in their hair. Annette looked as if she had a headache. "Rain," she observed.

"It may clear," said Frédéric, looking from the window to the sideboard, which held the plate of potatoes and onions.

All of them drank their coffee and ate their bread with few words, half watching Frédéric paint an onion. Camille rested her hand on the table and Claude, who sat next to her, noticed how closely her fingernails were bitten. She looked toward the wet window. "I couldn't sleep last night," she said dreamily. "So I went out. It was a little like being at my *grandmère*'s in the country the way the wind shook the trees. I was looking at the moon."

"I wish you hadn't!" replied her sister irritably. "You shouldn't go walking alone; Mother wouldn't approve."

"She wouldn't approve of anything about our being here," Camille said. Her sudden joyful laughter rang brightly against the hanging pots and saucepans.

Claude began to make a neat pile of the bread crumbs near her plate. He said in a low voice, "Mademoiselle, you know I saw you one time before I came into your uncle's bookshop. You were in a train station with your mother and sister. You wore a blue hat with a veil. It was four years ago. I sketched your picture and that's how I remembered."

Her face was quite close to his; he could see the few freckles on her nose and how the loose strands of hair danced against her cheek. He could smell the powder she used on her body. Her eyes were hazel. "Oh, did you?" she murmured. "How odd! Sometimes wonderful things can happen and we don't know anything about them, perhaps never."

THE SUN CAME out shortly; they had sun for three more days and rain for two more. Then Claude hurt his leg and spent one rainy day sullenly in bed with his leg elevated and Frédéric painting him. The girls left on the sixth day, wishing them well.

After the coach rolled away, he limped to the kitchen with Frédéric to drink the rest of their coffee and watch the rain through the tree branches. He thought over the week. In spite of difficulties, he had accomplished a lot with his painting. Dinners, however, had been more discreet. Perhaps the older sister had reprimanded the younger.

The only sound was that of the innkeeper polishing the stove.

"Lovely, weren't they?" Claude remarked. "Flirtatious and at the same time not to be touched in any way. What a pity!"

"It's always that way with girls of their class. I told you. They don't unfasten their collar buttons before marriage."

Claude rubbed his leg. He said, "I'll write them in Paris when I need them to model again, though I almost wish I didn't have to: the older one's chatter of china and silver patterns for her marriage puts me to sleep. What a thought that when a girl looks at us, she is thinking of what silver we can't afford! I suspect the younger one really prefers other things but won't quite say it." Claude rearranged the bread crumbs between the table cracks as he had done some days before. There was only a swallow of his coffee left in his bowl.

He felt Frédéric's silence and asked, "What about you, *cher ami*? Something's been on your mind since yesterday. I saw you got a letter."

Frédéric pushed away the bowl and unfastened his top shirt button; he leaned back his head and swallowed. "It's all *merde*. Word came from the medical school: I failed my examination again worse than ever before. Damn it, Claude! I don't want to be a doctor; I never did. All I want to do is paint. I need to go home and tell them."

Claude exclaimed, "We've all been waiting for you to come to this decision! You'll manage them. Do you want me to go with you?"

Frédéric stood up. "No, go back to Paris and finish the painting. We can't live with you until you do. Never mind me. I'm just a dead man." By now the coach was long gone and the rain fell steadily against the kitchen window.

1866-1867

We were all one group when we started out. We stood shoulder to shoulder and we encouraged each other.

—AUGUSTE RENOIR

CLAUDE RETURNED TO PARIS ALONE ON A WARM SUMMER day a week later. He had bought and stretched the enormous canvas on which he would repaint the smaller portrait of the picnickers. Hands in his pockets, he prowled before it. He worried he would run out of paint. He found a half-used tube of dark brown near the oil cruet in the cupboard. He took it as his own, though he could not remember which one of his friends had bought it. Under his brush, it grew into earth and trees.

He painted the picnickers, some strolling, some sitting. He painted flowers and shadow and movement. In the center, Camille Doncieux perpetually held out her empty plate.

At night, when the last summer light had faded away, he lit his pipe and for the first time that day was lonely. Where the hell was everyone this late summer? The clock ticked, noises of carts and quarrels from the street below moved through the open window, and a mouse scurried across the floor.

The burly artist Courbet, who had come to Fontainebleau to model for the painting, knocked on the door one day unannounced and came in. "Hot as hell in Paris this summer!" he said. "Here's a letter from Bazille; the postman had just come below and I brought it up. So he's home with his family?"

Claude took the letter. "Thanks. Yes, he's gone home to tell them he wants to paint full-time."

"Ah! *Abandon all hope, ye who enter here,* as Dante says. The same quote might apply to you and this painting you're making. Manet's painting of picnickers with the women naked caught more attention. Pity not to show a woman's best qualities."

"Well that's Manet, and this is me!" replied Claude irritably. "I like the flow of dresses."

Claude opened the envelope as soon as his visitor had left. I should not have let Frédéric go alone, he thought.

> *Claude! Well, it is over, and I am relieved enough to be able to hold a pen. I broke the news of my repeated failure to pass my examinations to my family and then—you will be proud of me—I told them I want to throw over medicine to the benefit of all healthy beings and paint full-time. My mother wept gallons. The maids came with buckets to clean up. My father puffed his pipe and failed to look stern and called me* cher ami *as he always does when he is not sure whether to take her side or mine. Still, all is well.*
>
> *So,* cher ami, *I have done some painting here; not very much. Now that I've won my freedom, I'm a bit afraid to try. I wish you'd come here! I have a cousin I'd like you to meet, a very pretty girl. And how are you getting on with the Doncieux sisters modeling for you in the studio as they said they'd do if asked? Send them my greetings. By the way, my Lily sends regards and says she looks forward to knowing you further. Not that she would understand you one bit: you are an incomprehensible wretch.*
>
> *F. Bazille*

Claude studied the letter again. It was like Frédéric to lighten the difficult.

That night under the shadow of the huge canvas, he sat at a

corner of the table cluttered with paint tubes and bits of old bread, and wrote a heartfelt response to his friend.

Frédéric, I'm happy for you and miss you a lot! I'm sorry I was so absorbed when we were away. I get so crazed I can only think of myself. I don't even remember if I ate today. Courbet stopped by, the ass. If he wanted to unnerve me, he couldn't have done better. Auguste isn't here, though some of his clothes are, as always. He's still somewhere for the summer. As for Cézanne, who knows what river he's fallen into or if he's begging his way through Provence. Pissarro wrote; he's trying to earn some money. I think of you and wish you the best and am so glad things have worked out for you. I presume your words "all is well" mean that your family will continue your allowance and we will not have to sleep like beggars by a church door. You are really talented, you know. Now you have to get down to it and create a body of work, as do I!

I am going to try to do some chalk portraits for quick cash, and as soon as I get some, I'll pay the next quarter's rent. The butcher's wife says perhaps, if I make her pretty. (She is not; you know her.) Come back and we'll do a dozen things this autumn. We could hire models and split the cost.

I can't send your greetings to the Mesdemoiselles Doncieux because they have disappeared. I went to the bookshop but the younger one was gone and her bastard uncle would not give me her address. I am in a fine situation to go on without them, outside of the fact that Mademoiselle Camille keeps coming to my mind.

CM

All that summer he worked on his canvas, painting, retouching, scraping, remembering. He worked on the dresses, the leaves, the couple strolling; he pushed away every other thing. Friends returning to the city in the autumn stopped by to admire it; they told others about his great painting. Frédéric came back triumphant from his visit to his family; within an hour he had stacked his medical books to sell, thrown on his old suit, and set a new canvas on his easel. Sitting at it, he began a still life of dead herons. He sat blissfully for so many hours that he was quite stiff when he rose.

He threw his arm around Claude's shoulder as he surveyed the large painting of the picnickers. "It's perfect," he said. "I'll never do anything half so rich!"

More friends visited, all giving advice. "It's the best thing you've done!" "It's wonderful but for . . ." Then Courbet came around with talk of some new commissions he had obtained and persuaded Claude to let him retouch some spots he said were clumsy.

The portrait of the eighteen-year-old Camille looked out at them all, well bred and polite, spots of sun on her white dress.

Colder winds blew from down the hills across the river, and the leaves on the trees, which he could see from the studio window, turned yellow; after a heavy autumnal rain, they fell in sodden heaps to the cobbled street. Claude painted into midwinter.

One dark morning, he stumbled out to his painting as soon as he came from bed, as always. The studio floorboards were cold to his bare feet and he wiggled his toes to lift them. He rubbed his eyes and raised them to his great canvas, then drew in his breath.

What he had seen so clearly on a summer's day in the forest was not on the canvas before him. People were clumsily placed; the brushstrokes were all wrong. It had been repainted many times and he had never found the balance of human form and light. It was not a masterpiece at all. How could he not have seen it before? How could he have made such a mess of it?

With a shout he ripped the top of the canvas from the stretchers. The supporting boards shuttered. The frame cracked and fell amid the heavy canvas. Frédéric ran from his bedroom in his nightshirt crying, "You idiot! *Tu es fou!*" but it was too late.

Later Claude sadly rolled the painting up, and yet even then he could not escape its presence. He could still feel the strollers walking under the trees; he felt them escape and float around the room.

FOR DAYS HE walked moodily about or lay on the sofa trying to read, ignoring the brushstrokes of Auguste and Frédéric at their easels. As the short winter light was fading one late afternoon, Frédéric glanced over at Claude and called, "You haven't left that sofa all day! Paint something else. Come on, Monet. I know it was eight months' work and a fortune but you're deader than the herons I'm painting, and they're starting to stink."

Auguste walked over to Claude, hands on his hips. "Get up, you sloth," he said firmly. "I have an idea to make money since there's nothing left to pawn. Let's walk over to the Café des Ambassadeurs near the Champs-Élysées. We can solicit drawing quick chalk portraits for twenty francs each. We both need money. You owe everyone for what's rolled up in the corner. You paid those girls and they probably spent it on new gloves. Frédéric can stay here with his stinking birds."

"My stinking birds will win me a place in the Salon!"

"Oh, the hell with the Salon!" Claude cried savagely. He sat up. "*Merde!* I'm such bad company I could hire myself out as a professional mourner. I wish I could do caricatures, but I can't stand the idea. Now you're going to drag me someplace. Good-bye, birds." He buttoned his coat reluctantly and, with Auguste's arm in his, descended to the windy evening street with its torn blowing bits of news journal and smell of coal fires.

The Café des Ambassadeurs was the largest of the fashionable new *café-concerts* in Paris. Claude and Auguste squeezed in the door past a few drunken men smoking cigars and left their coats in the cloakroom before entering the enormous central room, which was ablaze with gaslight. Hundreds of people seated at tables talked at once, and a soprano tried to make herself heard over the orchestra;

waitresses shouting orders pushed by him. Many more revelers sat at tables in the balcony, leaning on the rail and calling down to friends.

"Come on!" Auguste cried, taking his sketchbook from his bag. "You take the left side of the room and I'll take the right. Go from table to table and ask if they want a fifteen-minute portrait."

Claude pushed past a waitress and approached several people at a round table who were drinking champagne from fluted glasses. "I beg your pardon, mesdames and messieurs," he asked, "but would you like a quick souvenir of this enchanting evening?"

He caught sight of his reflection in a wall mirror: untrimmed dark hair almost to his shoulders, angry eyes. It's my sternness, he thought, retreating after a fourth table of friends had refused him, backing into waitresses carrying trays of foaming beer in glasses. Tonight, when I must be charming, I can't. And there was Auguste across the large room, head bobbing convivially, already having begun a portrait of a young couple.

Claude elbowed himself through the crowd to the bar and threw down a coin for a glass of wine. No, he thought, swirling the wine, I've got myself into a very deep hole and there's no way out of it. The Salon entries are in two months and all my friends will do well. Frédéric had begun that painting of a gorgeous model in a green dress playing his spinet and will redeem himself in the eyes of his family. But as for me . . .

He looked about the room, raising his eyes to the balcony.

Camille-Léonie Doncieux was sitting at a table there, her arm on the rail, gazing down at the crowd. She wore a pink dress cut low and seemed to slightly shimmer in the flickering gaslight.

Swallowing the last of his wine quickly, he elbowed his way past people to mount the stairs to the balcony, exclaiming breathlessly, "Mademoiselle Doncieux!"

She turned quickly. "Oh, Annette, do look who's here!" she cried as the two men at her table and her sister turned to gaze at him.

He bowed to them. Annette, who had drunk wine so freely in the inn kitchen, had now turned into a matron. Though she was some-what alluring in her low-cut pale blue evening dress, which showed off her long neck, she seemed, if possible, even more aloof than she had before. He also could find little interesting in either of the two men at the table, each near forty, obviously prosperous, and one of them married to her.

Annette took up her fan delicately. "Henri," she said to the man at her side, "here's the very artist who painted us last summer during our little adventure! Monsieur, we hope you and your friend have been well."

"Quite well! And both of you?"

"Henri, I believe I saw monsieur come in before and solicit por-traits below. Charming!" Annette added.

Camille had not ceased to smile shyly at him and now gently tapped the back of an empty chair at her side. He sat, tucking his sketchbook under the table, aware of a faint sweatiness under his shirt. He had worn it for five days; since he had destroyed his paint-ing, he had hardly bothered to care about his clothes, nor had he shaved above his beard.

He asked, "Mademoiselle, where have you been all these months? Your uncle wouldn't give me your address, so I supposed your fam-ily had found out about your modeling."

She whispered, "Yes, we confessed and were scolded and I couldn't write you because I lost the address."

"Please forgive my shabbiness. I didn't expect . . ."

"I can see our escorts are wondering who you truly are! My sis-ter's husband likely thinks you and your friend are gypsies."

"No, not gypsies," he protested, "but struggling artists." His eyes were a little dazed by the shimmering fabric of her dress and her soft bare right arm, a flimsy mauve shawl touching it. His old fascination for her was returning; he felt it slowly moving through his body. "So one of these fine gentlemen has married your sister and, if I recall the conversation at the inn, perhaps the other will shortly be your fiancé."

She whispered conspiratorially, "Oh, yes, it's expected, but one never knows. Monsieur Lucien Besique has indicated as much to my father concerning me. But Monsieur Monet, I often wondered what happened to you. I imagine your painting was a great success."

"No," Claude replied, shaking his head. "I gave up on it. It didn't do justice to you." He leaned closer to her, his arm on the table between her wineglass and the thick white napkin on which she had undoubtedly wiped her lips. He murmured, "If you had been there, the painting wouldn't have failed."

"Then I wish with all my heart I'd been there!"

He touched the edge of the napkin and drew it stealthily toward him as if he would pocket it. He leaned so far forward that his lips were only a few inches from her ear with the little pearl earring. "I could do better," he said softly, "if you would give me a chance. You remember the studio my friend and I have on the Left Bank near Saint-Germain? He rented a sumptuous green dress to paint and hasn't returned it. He wouldn't mind if I kept it for a bit. It's for a tall young woman and would suit you; you would look beautiful in it. I could make an unforgettable picture of you in that dress." The vision had formed in a moment and left him almost breathless. The whole large and noisy café dissolved to nothing but the green train of the dress draped across the studio floor.

Claude lowered his eyes and asked, "Can I prevail upon your kindness to endure the weary task of modeling for me just once more?"

The chanteuse had ended her song, and the piano and horn took up a dance melody while below the dance floor filled quickly. A chair scraped and Monsieur Besique's pale leather glove descended to the pink frills of Camille's shoulder. "If monsieur does not mind," the gentleman said scathingly, "I would borrow mademoiselle to dance."

"Monsieur," replied Claude, standing proudly.

He retrieved his sketchbook and followed them down the stairs. Leaning against the bar with his second glass of wine, he watched

Camille Doncieux move among the other dancers in her pink dress. Could this lovely girl be almost engaged to this forty-year-old dullard? Did she want to be? Could this man be the recipient of those passionate letters she was writing when he found her in her uncle's bookshop? And here he was in his old shirt and wrinkled coat, not even able to ask her to dance.

He'd had enough then.

He pushed past the others to the men's cloakroom to claim his coat and was buttoning it when Camille Doncieux came to the door.

"But where are you going?" she whispered. "I wanted to say that I *will* come to your studio to model. I'll tell my mother I'm visiting a friend. Is tomorrow at nine good? Give me the address again."

He took a book from his pocket and scribbled his address on the endpaper, tearing out the page. She folded it neatly and undid the strings of her silk purse, dropping it inside. The strings drew together and she was gone amid the crowd.

SHE WON'T COME, he thought. But she did.

He was looking out the window when she emerged through the porte cochere of the courtyard, lifting her skirt above the muck. He opened the door. He could hear her low-heeled shoes tapping on the wood stairs as she mounted with a candle until he could see her, slightly breathless, the silk flowers in her hat bobbing. She climbed the last steps and at once smiled at the caricature on his door of two men, the first scowling, and the other very tall, reading, "Monet and Bazille."

"Oh, it's clever!" Camille said. "It's not like the forest painting, though."

She stepped in, looking about at the paints and books crowded on the dresser top and the dozens of pictures hung on the walls. He watched her as he took her coat. She was not quite the shy girl he had engaged to paint over the summer. Girls at that age changed quickly as they understood their beauty. They glided into the world in their

lovely dresses and hats as if it had been waiting for them and then disappeared with rings on their fingers behind the door of matrimony
and grew severely into matrons as her sister had begun to do.

Camille Doncieux was not there yet. She was now gazing with
particular fascination at nudes by Auguste and Frédéric. Claude
studied the floor.

She exclaimed, "What an enchanted place! I've never been in an
artist's studio before. There are so many paintings!" She glanced at
the closed bedroom doors and hesitated, asking, "But where's your
friend?"

He took her arm, fearing she would turn and leave. "Frédéric
went home very early this morning; he got a telegram that his grandfather had had a stroke. It's quite all proper to be here with me. In my
bedroom there you'll find the gown. I think it will fit you perfectly.
Close the door." He added meticulously, "Your privacy will be
undisturbed."

Shortly after, she emerged in the green and black taffeta promenade dress with its train and the fur-trimmed jacket and hat.

He studied her, arms folded across his chest, walking this way and
that, moving his hand to touch the edge of her shoulder, arranging
the hat, and helping her mount a little platform that had been standing against a wall. He placed the train of the dress behind her. "Turn
this way," he ordered. "No, more, more. I want to see your back so I
can get the sweep of the fabric, but I'd like you turning as if someone
has just called you. Look back but keep your eyes lowered. You're
haughty; you're a little annoyed at being called."

"Like this?"

The sweet face turned disdainful and the girl became a woman of
the privileged haute bourgeoisie who expects everything will be
given to her. "That's it!" he cried. He began with a quick charcoal
outline and then dipped his brush into the paint.

Time passed and she did not move. Outside, carts clopped along,
and somewhere someone practiced the violin. "Break and stretch,"
he said, unwillingly. "Your neck will cramp badly after a time.

Unfortunately I will need you to again look over your shoulder. I want you to look as if the world's too dull to notice. You're a woman of riches; you have everything." He bit his lip under his mustache; he had almost added, *ma chère,* and he wondered if she guessed it as she once again assumed her sullen look.

The distant sun of late February retreated. He breathed in cold air and the smell of turpentine and paint and the warm scent of her. He felt as if he rose above his body, looking down at both painter and model, a young woman dressed for the opera but in reality standing in an artist's studio with smudgy walls.

She turned, hand on her back. "It's too much," she said. "My back aches."

"Yes, it must!" he replied, putting down his brush. "Are you hungry? I have some beans. I buy them by the sackful; they're cheap. Sometimes we live off them for weeks. You better keep that jacket on. I'm sorry it's cold. I meant to buy more coal." He glanced at the stove, which gave off only the remnants of heat as if it had betrayed him.

The beans were yesterday's, mushy and dressed only with a flicker of oil and no herbs, but she ate them hungrily. Now and then, she raised her eyes to look at him. He smelled her faint scent: she wore a floral perfume. Again, as in the Ambassadeurs, he felt her presence through his body, and to put distance between them he jumped up to examine his painting. She rose as he did and began to study all the paintings on the wall more closely. "Well, what do you think of them?" he asked.

Her voice was more quiet and serious than he had ever heard it. "They're so real, so beautiful! I feel the wind. They're not like the paintings we have. I'm not sure people want real things. My mother wants life to be just as she arranges it; she wants to arrange mine too, so that I'll live undisturbed by anything unpleasant—not cold, or want, or heartbreak. She'd like me never to encounter anything that might hurt me or make me live differently than the way I've been brought up. Sheltered, you might say, as most girls are." She looked down.

He stayed across the room. "Ah, does she want that for you?" he replied. "If we can't risk, we can't have anything real, can we?"

The striking church clock made her start.

"Oh, I must go," she said. "I had no idea it was so late! I'm very sorry, but I need to meet someone! I must take off this dress at once." She unpinned the hat, put it down, and then disappeared into his bedroom.

He bit his lip, standing outside. "But the painting!" he called. "I'm afraid I've just begun. Please tell me you'll come back tomorrow."

The voice moved within his room. "Yes, I'll come," she called, and in a few moments she emerged in her dark day dress again, looking about for her own hat with the flowers. As she pinned it on she gazed toward the easel and he implored, "Before you go, look what we've made today."

She slowly took in the sketched face and the bold strokes of the dress. She stood so close that the buttons of her nearly closed coat almost touched him. He only needed to encircle her waist with his arm and pull her in, but then what? He closed his eyes, imagining her lips against his. When he looked again, she was already at the door, her cheeks flushed. And then she was gone.

HE MISSED HER; there was a silence in the studio that he seldom had minded before, but that evening he counted the hours until she would come again.

She returned exactly as promised, but if she had ever come close to kissing him, she obviously did not want to recall it. Oddly, she seemed a little removed from him this day and a little sad, as if struggling inside herself. Sometimes she did not look at him directly. Perhaps her sister knew Camille was modeling again and had spoken sharply to her. Then he reconsidered and thought that no one in the world knew they were here alone together.

If I ask her too many questions I will alarm her, he thought, and then she will go and my painting will remain forever unfinished.

He said, "I believe you told me your father came to Paris for his work?"

"Yes; he's the representative of an old silk manufacturing firm."

"May I ask where your sister lives now?"

"She has beautiful rooms on the Parc Monceau. What woman could want more?"

"Indeed, what more?" he replied. She said nothing of the man who had been her escort at the *café-concerts* and he could not bear to ask. But at times she did talk freely of books. She had read a huge amount and could quote a lot of poetry by heart.

"Did you ever draw a little?" he asked. "Most young women do."

"I tried watercolors, but I have no gift for it."

After the last session he thanked her and tried to believe she let her gloved hand remain a longer time than necessary in his. There was no movement toward a kiss, though he felt the impulse between them. He heard her footsteps descending his stairs, and she was gone. She never had been and never would be his *chère*.

"IT'S NOT LIKE anything you've done," his friends remarked as one after another they came to see the portrait of a woman in a green dress. "There's such longing in it, and she's such a mystery! I wouldn't be surprised if you had a chance to get it taken by the Salon." Claude nodded. He would have liked Frédéric's opinion, but his studio mate still had not returned from Montpellier. Frédéric wrote that he would miss the Salon submission and hated to be apart from his unfinished still life. He would return with more birds. He wished Claude all good fortune and sent two hundred francs, an impulsive gift from his family, for rent or other needs.

On the last day of general submissions, Claude brought the painting over to the Palais de l'Industrie in a wheelbarrow; Pissarro walked with him, talking of playing with his three-year-old son. They stood on line once more, and when they passed through the enormous triumphal arch of the door under the statue of France crowned with stars and reached the acceptance desk, both Claude's and Pissarro's paintings were taken away.

Claude locked himself in his room for the next few days and reread favorite books. He heard the chatter of his friends from the studio but could not bear to go out to them.

Auguste finally struck open the door. He fidgeted when anxious, swinging his arms, dancing a little on his narrow feet. "I can't stand to wait another day to find out if any of us got in. Let's try to waylay someone from the judging committee at the Palais and grovel at his feet to tell us something."

Hands behind their backs, the two artists walked solemnly under the lovely new spring trees to the Palais on the Right Bank and climbed the steps. The choosing of work among the thousands of submissions was in progress. They ambled as indifferently as they could past a stack of paintings marked for acceptance, hardly daring to glance. One was of ravished naked virgins against a ruined temple. "Pissarro would throw up," Auguste muttered. His loose shoe sole flapped slightly on the floor. "When will people ever see that good art is living and real, intimate, not grand? That real beauty is in ordinary life? Not in a palace built to the great grandeur of France and her immortal emperor, I'm afraid."

They went from room to room.

Finally someone referred them to the next room, where the committee was even now selecting whose work would be accepted. Auguste held up the straight pin that had belonged to his tailor father and that he always carried in his pocket for good luck. His eyes met Claude's and they went forward, as directed, past a crated statue of an angel. The great painter Daubigny noticed them and came forward smiling with his hands extended, saying, "Ah, Monet and Renoir! Good news for both of you . . ."

CLAUDE SAT BY his window, gazing down at the blossoming spring trees. When he went out in the streets it seemed every other artist he knew and men he didn't think he had ever seen before had heard about the annual Salon's acceptance of his painting; they stopped him as he left the *charcuterie* with his sausages or shook his hand when he entered the local fragrant *boulangerie* to buy his fresh bread.

Pissarro had had a painting taken as well. Frédéric wrote effusively from Montpellier.

> *I am so happy for both of you! I sensed it; I knew it. So the great Daubigny and Corot both fought for your acceptance! Their work with its softer, more realistic style paves the way for yours. Maybe your father will extend your stipend for a bit longer. As for me, I'm painting here a lot and can't wait to see all your sorry faces again. My grandfather's a little better. Lily is well.*
>
> *FB*

Only one person in his world knew nothing about his fortune. She was the most important of all, and he did not have her address.

The cat was sleeping in the bookshop window on the rue Dante when he opened the door to the soft tinkle of the bell. A few students were browsing the shelves. Camille Doncieux was not there.

In her place sat a thin young woman with spectacles, the sort he thought went to meetings on women's emancipation and poverty in the colonial world.

He walked up to the desk. "*Bonjour,* mademoiselle," he said softly. "May I ask if you are acquainted with Mademoiselle Doncieux? If so, would you be so very kind as to give her a short letter from me?"

"*Mais, oui,*" the girl replied, smiling. She gave him paper and pen and he wrote quickly while standing, leaning on the desk. "Mademoiselle Doncieux, your portrait is in the Salon, which opens in a few days. My heart is full of gratitude to you. Let me take you to see it. Send word when you can come. Yours sincerely, Claude Monet."

The girl slipped the note inside a book. "Baudelaire's poems," she whispered confidentially. "Where I always leave her letters. But she's not in as much these days." Letters? he thought. What letters? Who else writes her here? That man who took her to the *café-concerts?*

Three days passed with no reply. He prowled up and down the rue Dante, always seeing the girl at the desk, who smiled through the window at him and shook her head. I shall never see Camille Doncieux again, he thought.

Then she wrote: on fragile paper this time, scented with perfume, left modestly in the corner of their mail slot. She would wait for him in front of the Palais de l'Industrie for the festive opening day of the Salon at four the next afternoon; she was thrilled—she underlined the word twice.

AH, THE CROWDS in front of this immense structure built for the great Exposition twelve years before! He walked among them wearing a new dark suit and a mauve vest. He had visited here a few days before for the vernissage, when all the nervous painters had a last chance to dab at or varnish their work before it was viewed by the public. Now everyone in Paris was here, eager to be the first to see the new work.

Camille was standing by a streetlamp, wearing the blue and white striped dress in which she had modeled for him in Fontainebleau. A hat with white silk flowers was perched above her hair. Under it, her face seemed very young. "I came alone, you see!" she said. "I wanted to see it just with you."

"News about the painting is already in the papers. The one this morning called you the Parisian Queen."

She looked almost alarmed. "No, that can't be," she murmured, shaking her head and looking both anxious and delighted. "No, they can't say that of me."

He gave her his arm in his most courtly way and led her under the great archway to the crowded, echoing central hall. "Close your eyes! I want you to be surprised!" he whispered as they mounted the palatial stairway, brushing past the flowing dresses of visitors, of older women with lorgnettes and brusque men, most talking loudly and clutching programs.

At first they could not even get into the room he sought for the crowd of noisy schoolgirls pushing out. When an opening came, he guided her in.

The painting hung prominently on the far wall in its heavy frame. There she was, her head turned disdainfully, the gorgeous train of the green gown rippling out behind her. "Now," he whispered, "open your eyes."

She looked. "Oh, it's me!" she whispered.

"Yes, it is you indeed," he said close to her ear. "I'm so very grateful to you! I want to take you for an early supper to celebrate and to thank you."

She gazed at the picture as if trying to understand it, clutching her purse, and finally she turned to him as if she had just heard his words. She stammered a little. "But I couldn't now!" she exclaimed. "Please forgive me. My mother expects me in an hour; we're to go to a friend's for supper."

"Mademoiselle, allow me! This day is a celebration of many years of effort, and the only person to truly share it with is you."

She hesitated, looking down at the polished parquet floor. A small smile passed her lips. "Well, then," she said. "I will come with you. For shortly after this, I don't know . . . my whole life will be different. There will be fewer adventures. Isn't that what proper life is?"

"I don't know," he replied passionately. "I'm certain I wouldn't want it. Let's go to the park, the Bois de Boulogne. We'll walk and talk and rent a boat. There's a little Swiss restaurant on a tiny island in the middle of the lake. And I'll have you back by the time it's dark." All the time he was urging her from the room through the other Salon visitors, some of whom turned to stare at them.

He breathed more steadily once they were seated in the omnibus, bumping along the rough streets. She was not going to rise, ring the bell, and descend suddenly. She would stay by his side. All the thrilling energy of the Salon still poured through him. He wanted to seize her against him so that her hairpins fell down and her hair tumbled free. Did she like him? Did she see him? Was he so far from her class? Not by birth, but by circumstance—this little convent virgin who had come from one cell door and would soon enter another.

He thought, I've succeeded because of her kindness. I must take this day as it is and be glad for it and ask no more.

They entered the park via a huge avenue of trees and wandered arm in arm until they came to the edge of the lake. He said gallantly, "Here's where we rent a boat."

A little water on the boat's bottom darkened her hem. He saw the edge of her lavender shoe and wondered if her mother was now impatiently looking out a window somewhere, waiting for her daughter to come. He wondered if Camille noticed how strong he was and how easily he rowed.

In the Swiss restaurant, they were seated at a little table and discussed the menu board. A pot of melted cheese came with bread and salad, and he found he was starving. He poured her wine and they both drank. The terrace band played.

"Will you explain Baudelaire's poems to me?" she asked suddenly. "I heard you talk about them with your friend at the inn. I must confess a lot of them confuse me. For instance, *'Je te donne ces vers afin que si mon nom.'* The part at the end where the poet cries to the accursed ghost."

She wants to discuss poetry? But why not, he thought, when I feel I want to say so much to her and not one word will come? "Ah, yes," he said, folding his hands on the table. "It has many meanings. I mean, it's the way you interpret it. To tell you the truth, I'm not sure what it means. He writes most of his work on opium, friends tell me. A strange dark poet for a young woman!"

"I don't understand him either, but still his words frighten and thrill me. They're filled with experiences, even if dark ones. And because I don't understand doesn't mean I don't want to. Even if I may have few experiences in my life, at least I can read about them."

"Mademoiselle, surely you don't want experiences like that!"

"No, if I could choose my experiences I wouldn't choose those. It's just that to be free to choose seems so wonderful."

Camille's eyes were very bright, her hand was half open on the table, and her lips were parted. He drew in his breath. "I wish I knew more about you!" he said. "Please tell me something. I looked at you so long when I was painting you and sometimes I thought, What's she like? Now I want even more to know."

She sat back, breathing a little deeper, carefully arranging the fork and the now empty wineglass before her. "Myself?" she said in a low voice. "There's so little to know! My sister and I are the only children. She's four years older. I loved the convent school. I love to learn things. Sometimes I wanted to be good the way girls are, to be approved of, to be loved—and sometimes I didn't."

She lowered her eyes, again moving the glass as if the exact distance of it from the plate was important. "My mother takes me into society, where we all talk politely of things that don't matter. It bores me. Mostly I love working in the bookshop. My uncle who owns it has been somewhat estranged from our family since he and my father were young; he was the first to move to Paris and turn his back on bourgeois life. He's led a secret life, we suspect; no, we don't suspect. We know."

She looked at her empty wineglass and he refilled it. She said firmly, "If I had my way, I'd be an actress and go on the stage, but the idea of it scandalizes my mother! Nothing but amateur theatricals for me, and only in the parlors of our good friends, of our own class, *comme il faut!*"

Camille stumbled a bit over her words now with eagerness and she leaned a little forward, her full breasts pressing against the blue and white striped dress. "I've many plans for the future. I began a novel this past year but haven't shown it to anyone. My family hopes all these yearnings will settle when I marry." She looked down at the floral tablecloth, blinking gently as if trying to read her future in the pattern of violets.

"Do you *want* to be married?"

"I'd like to have my own home. My sister and mother say I'm not practical, and it's true. I wish I had a great passion as you have, something to dedicate my life to." She wound her fingers together, stammering a little. "I don't want life to simply pass me by without my having any of it! I'd like to suffer for some great cause, to give all of myself!"

Claude crumbled a bit of bread. "Well, as to suffering, I'd prefer not to suffer for any reason. I find one needn't look for it; it comes for you!"

"Then you think I'm silly?"

"Oh no, not at all," he replied as the waiter swept away the bread and brought little plum cakes. "You're wise. I think your imagination is very great indeed and you couldn't be satisfied with a dull life."

"No, truly! I never could. And yet I've been raised to . . ."

The side of his laced shoe touched hers under her full skirt beneath the table. He thought to withdraw it but instead let it remain. She looked harder now at the cake and the wineglass and he suspected that she also debated moving her own little lavender shoe and yet did not. What did this mean? He was too confused and thrilled to know.

He reached in his pocket for his briar pipe and began the careful process of lighting it, narrowing his eyes. He said, "Mademoiselle Camille, I must confess I've thought about you. I sensed a hidden passion in you when I rediscovered you in the bookshop. That's why I wanted you for my model."

"Did you really think of me for nearly four years after seeing me once?"

"Yes. Your spirit and your beauty."

"Am I beautiful? I'd like to be; I have moments. It's truly more important to be educated and wise." She leaned forward, almost touching his hand, which lay a few inches from hers on the table between the coffee cups. She straightened then, her palm patting her hair, a gesture of women that he always felt meant that they were deliberating their next words. Her foot under the table moved away from his.

"Well, it's late." She sighed. "My poor mother! What excuses will I make now? She thinks I'm forgetful, which I'm not. I don't forget things ever, ever."

"Don't you?" he asked sadly. The joy of the day was leaving him, and he felt tired.

Dusk was falling as they rowed back in silence. In the park again, he walked on by her side without a word, his hat low on his forehead. Every way he looked the paths turned under the heavy, hanging trees, and small clumps of flowers seemed to cup and hold the last of the day. Now a lamplighter had climbed his ladder to ignite a flame, which shone down on the empty bandstand.

She took his arm. "May I tell you something?" she said softly. "I think I can tell you things! I've always felt in my sister's shadow; she always tells me what to do. Everyone at home thinks I'm not fit to make my own decisions about my life, but I'm perfectly fit. They worry about me; they say I'm moody. Women have such a short time to bloom, you know. Your portrait of me is the way I am inside: mysterious. You saw me inside. Do you think I'm silly?"

"No," he said.

She spoke on, almost to herself. "They want to keep me in a little box, but it's really so unnecessary. I don't miss Lyon at all except for my widowed *grandmère*. I love it here. You're from Normandy, right? From Le Havre? Do you miss it?"

"I do, so much! I miss the boats and the smell of the sea; I miss the country, and yet if I want to make a name for myself I must do it in Paris. I'd like to return to the country one day when I make my fortune. I'd like to live outside Paris in one of the little villages. I want desperately to have a garden."

Claude felt the day slipping from him. It had been such a lovely adventure, but it would be put away and forgotten until a moment years later when he was old and something would remind him: the smell of the air, a lamplighter, the darkening trees above on a long walk. She would drift away, and the Salon would continue for a time and then be taken down and he would hear of the marriage of this lovely girl who wanted and would have beautiful things.

He said abruptly, "It's late. I'll take you home."

The horses wearily pulled the omnibus through the city until Claude descended with her near the bridge, walking toward the seventeenth-century houses of the Île Saint-Louis. It's almost done now, he thought. A minute more and she'll disappear down the street into one of those formidable dwellings and be gone.

He took her arm and, as they leaned on the bridge railing over the Seine, suddenly demanded, "Camille, how much do you really like your old fiancé?"

"He's not old. He's very nice. He's kind, a true gentleman."

"Is he? Well . . ."

Claude drew her toward him and kissed her mouth. To his amazement she did not pull away but pulled him against her, her arms about him, returning his kiss. I am dreaming this, he thought. I am dreaming it.

She whispered against his lips, "I don't want to go home to my family. I want to go home with you."

He felt the shock of her words and his sudden, intensely rising desire. He thought, Is she willing? Can she be truly willing? He slipped his fingers through an opening in her dress buttons and felt the silk and whalebone of her corset. He undid another button and a corset hook. Now she will push me over the bridge rail into the river, he thought, but she did not. As his fingers moved down to her hardened nipple, she kissed him more deeply, pressing against him. At any moment all we are wearing will fall away, he thought, and be carried down the river to the sea: her cloth buttons, my vest . . .

He said, "Are you sure, dear?"

"I'm sure, I'm sure," she whispered.

He took her hand and they ran across the bridge. Several times he turned to her and they kissed again. They hailed a carriage and clasped each other tightly on the leather cushions that smelled of cigars and other lovers. *Mon Dieu*, he thought, don't let this moment melt away!

In his building on the rue de Furstenberg he almost pulled her up the stairs, fumbling with his studio key in the lock. Who the hell is here? he thought. I'll kill them! To his joy no one was there, though the nude pictures looked down thoughtfully from the walls, observing them. She'll go soon, she'll go, he thought. She'll come to her senses or I to mine. This is a good girl, a convent-bred girl, and I am a wretch of desire and know only that.

Oh, such desire.

He pulled her into his bedroom and felt for her dress hooks as she coaxed eagerly at his buttons, pulling down his shirt so that it tangled in one arm, leaving his chest bare. A few pins fell from her hair, which tumbled down her naked back. Such hair! Way down to her round bottom, dangling against the bare flesh. When he pushed her to the bed, he had to knock away the open novel he had left there.

"Camille, Camille," he repeated.

Thought left him. His breath came faster and she flung her head back and forth, reaching up for him as he entered her. She was warm, warm. He pushed harder, stopping her gasps with his mouth so that her feeling should remain within her and grow warmer there. He cupped her full breast in his hand and thrust faster still. I'm dreaming this, he thought, before all thought left him. Still he held her and felt her own mounting joy. She rose up against him, melding with him, shuddered and cried out, and fell away again.

He held her, kissing her shoulder, and then felt something warm and wet on his cheek. "What, are you crying?" he asked. "Did I hurt you?"

"No, never."

"Why then, *ma très chère fille?*"

"Nothing, just the loveliness of it, the amazing loveliness! Oh, I thought . . . Claude."

"What?"

"*Rien*—nothing worth speaking of!"

She flung her arm across his stomach. In a moment she was asleep, and he also slept, unable to help himself, keeping her warm body in his arms. He dreamt they were rowing, not over the tiny lake of the park as they had that day, but on the vast sea. He rowed steadily while she kept her hand on his knee; before them was nothing but more churning waters as far as they looked.

He awoke suddenly at the sound of loud cracking and pulled her over to his side of the bed, sheltering her body with his own just seconds before something crashed to the floor. "*Merde!*" he shouted, leaping up naked. "*Merde*, the ceiling! I knew it! Are you all right? Let me light the lamp."

"What?" she asked. "Has the ceiling fallen? How could the ceiling fall?"

"Water leaks from the roof. Look."

Holding his shoulder, she gazed down at the large pieces of ceiling and rotten wood on the floor. Plaster dust hung in the air, making her cough. Looking up she saw the beams that separated the floors and a new hole several feet wide. She stood, just before he shouted, "Watch out, you'll cut your foot!"

"I think I stepped on something."

He swept the broken plaster from the sheets, urged her back on the bed, and held up the lamp. "*Merde*, there's a splinter in your heel. I used to get them all the time climbing around the shore. There was broken wood from old boats. *Quel bordel!* I make love to you and then my damned room falls on top of you."

"Stop! It hurts!"

"Just one moment and I'll have it. I'd never hurt you, you lovely girl! There! Come here, come close! Are you sure you're all right?"

"I will be once it stops hurting."

"Let me kiss it."

He kissed the bottom of her foot and playfully licked it and she took hold of his hair and cried, "Now it tickles. Your tongue tickles." Still he continued until he realized she was laughing. She shook her head and her long hair whipped around and her shoulder shook. She laughed so hard she gasped. He was shouting with laughter then, saying, "And this is what you did not expect . . ."

"Really, it's quite marvelous! Such a thing has never happened to me before, truly, truly, Claude!" She pushed him away and then dropped back on the pillows, holding out her arms to him.

HE WOKE EARLY to gaze down at her as she slept. Swept into a corner were the ceiling pieces; he had found the broom in the studio last night after they carefully removed and shook out the sheets and then slept, exhausted, curled together once more.

Outside the window, he heard a few neighbors crossing the courtyard below on their way to work.

Watching her, breathing softly so as not to disturb her, his mind returned to the events of last evening. He could have expected none of it, least of all that in spite of his concerns, this lovely girl was not a virgin when he took her in his arms. All girls of her class were delivered untouched to their weddings. It was none of his business, but he did wonder.

Claude rose quietly, sweeping any further pieces away. A plaster flake was caught in her glimmering hair, and when he touched it Camille opened her eyes and smiled at him.

He sat down on the bed. "I thought I dreamt you. All the time I painted you I felt such tenderness inside me for you, and there you were on the model's platform, so far away, with the easel between us."

"I thought of you sometimes too," she replied. "I didn't know you saw me as more than a painting."

"When we were away at the inn, I saw you from the window."

She lowered her eyes; her eyelashes were like silk and her cheek faintly red where it had pressed against the pillow in sleep. "Did you?"

"So you walked about on the path alone at night?"

"Yes. You've no idea how often I've been alone in my life, Claude. Sometimes I think always."

She moved away now; she felt for the sheet to cover her. He tried to tug it down but she shook her head. The languid look turned to a frown. Her voice changed and she looked past him toward the bureau, saying, "Let me up. I must go now. What will my family think? I never came home; I stayed away all night. I stayed all night with you!"

He pulled her against him. "What? You're going?"

"Of course I'm going!" she said, looking at him sorrowfully. "I'll have to lie to them. How could I have come with you last night? I'm getting married in two months." She rose from the bed and looked desperately for her stockings. Her dress was draped over the chair where she had thrown it last night.

He cried, "Then it's settled? Your life's settled?"

"I won't forget this night, Claude. I promise. Never. I'm crying now, you see. Don't look at me like that. You have the most beautiful, haunted eyes. In my heart, years from now, this night will be safe there."

He shouted, "But you mustn't . . ."

She was sobbing as she dressed and kissed him again many times. She tore herself away from him and he heard her little heeled shoes quickly descending the stairs to the courtyard as she fled away.

The room was so quiet after she was gone.

He stumbled through his day. I must forget her, he thought that evening. It is all too complicated. He stood at the edge of his door, imagining her tangled in his sheets as he watched her sleeping.

Then with a cry he pounced on something that had fallen beneath the bed. In leaving quickly, Camille had forgotten her little bag. He spread the contents on the covers. Powder, lip rouge, a little mirror, a handkerchief, the studio address, a few chocolate sweets, which were partially unwrapped and had smudged the calling cards. He arranged these things, trying to make some sense of them. One of the calling cards was her mother's and bore her address; a small shopping list for hose and a parasol was scribbled on the back. Powder and chocolate smeared his fingers and nearly obscured the house number.

HE WOULD HAVE liked to have gone at dawn, for as soon as he made up his mind to do something, he wanted to have it done. However, he felt it best to be mannerly. Milkmen came before sunrise, not gentlemen. Dressed carefully in his new suit and the shirt with the lace cuffs he had worn the day before, he did not present himself at the third-floor apartment in the house on the Île Saint-Louis until the church clock struck the hour of ten.

A maid peered around the door and, perhaps impressed by his cool manner, admitted him while she went to call madame. Claude looked about the salon with its chairs and divans carved with lyres and urns reflecting the classical style of the deposed monarchy. All were upholstered in fine pale silk, reminding him of the family business. There was not a single painting of any merit on the wall, only mediocre work from the last century, which the family likely had brought from Lyon. It was all very formal, as if royalty was expected. All in all he could not imagine the bright girl who had cried out in his arms walking impetuously through these rooms.

Madame Doncieux approached him in her dark dress. He assessed her quickly: her thick hair was neatly piled on her head, her lace collar starched. She looked as if she had never eagerly pulled the shirt off a man in her life. Still, something of her nose and mouth confirmed that she was her younger daughter's mother.

"Monsieur," Madame Doncieux said. "My maid told me you wished to see me. I do not believe we know each other."

He inclined his head; he was not sure if he should kiss her hand. "I have not yet had the pleasure of meeting you, madame," he replied. "I am the man who painted the picture of your daughter that hangs in the current Salon."

Her back stiffened as her eyes swept from his newly washed hair to his polished shoes. "So you're the *artist*," she said. "My daughter finally confessed that she had modeled twice for you. It was indiscreet on her part, to say the least, and unwise. What can it say of her good name? A girl who received holy pictures while at school for her piety!" Madame Doncieux blew the last words out as if she wished to blow him away. "I am amazed you come here."

If Camille was convent bred, it was one with wide windows, he thought wryly. Well, if he had expected any welcome, he had been wrong. Even his fine clothes did not excuse his questionable profession.

Claude glanced at the door that madame had closed behind her and that likely led to the bedrooms. Perhaps Camille was in there, listening. He wanted to rush through that door to find her, but madame would cry for help. And then—*Merde!*—suppose Camille herself did not want him there, that she had taken pleasure in him for one night the way he had a few times with women, and now returned to her own world? He imagined her room with a wardrobe full of dresses, floral curtains, a dressing table with a large oval mirror, and books. What kind? Baudelaire? She had said she read the novels of Balzac but preferred George Sand. Did she have theater programs autographed by actors? When you saw someone's room, you knew her. He would have liked to see it even if he could not see her.

He held out the bag. "But I have stopped by for a very ordinary reason, madame—to return this to her."

"This was the bag my daughter had with her two days ago. How did you come by it?"

"She went to see her picture at the Palais. I happened to be there, as I might be. When she left, I found it beneath the chair where she'd been sitting. She was hurrying off to meet you to pay a call on friends."

"What? We were to make no call that day!" Madame Doncieux shook her head as she accepted the bag. "She left here two days ago to go straight to her sister's and has been there since. I hope your picture is a good likeness; she told me you're very drawn to painting trees and air."

His artist's pride intervened. "True, madame, but I believe I drew her well."

She smiled a little. "Now, I know nothing about you, monsieur," she said, "but that you take good girls from their family homes without permission. Let this be an end of communication between you both. If you attempt to see my daughter again, my husband will be forced to have words with you. I trust this warning is all you need as I see that, in spite of your profession, you are a gentleman."

AS CLAUDE WALKED away from the Île Saint-Louis, he said to himself: But Camille will write to me. Yes, for I miss her with a strange ache that was not there before, and she must feel the same. She cried when she left me. He could still feel her kisses on his mouth. What did it matter if she told him she was to meet her mother when it was her sister who expected her? She had only said it to avoid spending the day with him, knowing perhaps in advance that it might end in such intimate passion on his narrow bed.

Days passed, though, and there was no word; the situation was made worse by the presence of other women in the studio. Auguste brought a plump, dark-haired beauty called Lise home and slept with her on his cot near the easels, both breathing gently under the blankets. Once someone stayed behind Frédéric's closed door all night.

Perhaps it is true, then, Claude thought, as I suspected when I stood amid her mother's silky classical chairs: she had her fun with me and now has hurried off to her proper marriage. One day our paths will cross on one of the great boulevards or perhaps at the annual Salon. I will be famous then and she will arrive on the arm of her husband and lower her eyes when she sees me. She will flush and murmur and I will keep my hands behind my back and nod coldly and say, "Madame."

Claude imagined her years from now approaching him across a parlor as her mother had done, saying, "My maid told me you wished to see me. I do not believe we know each other." She would be near fifty then as her mother was now, all her heedless charm gone, turned into the proper matron, upholding the values of the empire and French petite bourgeoisie, not ever remembering she had thrown off her clothes to the last petticoat for him.

To escape her memory he began a painting in a park, yet every woman walking down the path reminded him of her. He could do nothing well. That's it, then! he thought, putting down his brushes. He would have no peace until he found her again.

With his folded easel over his shoulder, Claude marched toward the Sorbonne, turning down the small rue Dante. The cat slumbered in the bookshop window on the second volume of the French encyclopedia and the fat uncle was arranging books on a shelf and puffing on a cigar whose acrid smoke circled above him.

"If you're the artist," he growled, "my niece and her parents have gone away to Lyon for a week. You know the girl's mother wishes you to stay away from her. Do you understand me, monsieur?"

How had Camille described this renegade uncle? His values were as restrictive as those of the rest of her family. Gone away then; torn away. Claude crossed to the Île Saint-Louis but the shutters were closed outside their rooms. Looking up at them, he felt his sadness harden to anger.

As he and Auguste walked toward the colorist shop near the

École des Beaux-Arts off the rue Bonaparte the next morning, Claude confided the whole story. "So she came like the night and fled with the dawn!" Auguste said compassionately as they opened the door. "Isn't that what the girls do in the great ballets: dance away to the dawn, fluttering their arms to some virtuous end? She's not coming back; it's been three weeks. She's thinking of her wedding trousseau. Isn't that what girls think about? A ring, then clothes and furniture."

"How could she?"

"Family pressure. She'll have a bit to conceal on her wedding night, I imagine. She'll probably close her eyes and dream it's you, you devil. Come on, you'll get over it. And anyway, you got a few more raves in the news journals for your picture. You can have anyone you want. Upper-class women!" Auguste shuddered and raised his eyes to the frames hanging from the ceiling. "Spare me! You know Frédéric would agree if he weren't still home visiting his sick relative."

Claude took up the parcel of paints from the shopkeeper. "Very well, then," he said coolly. "Monsieur, I will pay you next week for this."

HE FORGOT HER: he relegated her in his mind to the future, where she had faded, all her youthful beauty gone. He could not quite remember the sound of her voice. Then, just as he no longer thought of her several times an hour, the Salon ended and he brought his painting back to the studio and hung it up, hitting his thumb in the process.

After, he walked out to the street again.

The problem with having loved, however briefly, he thought reflectively, is that you can't ever get back to yourself just as you were before. It changes you. He looked in the mirror and saw the same man but angrier, shoulders hunched, defensive. He sank into a terrace chair at a small café on the rue Jacob and ordered wine, and taking out a small pad of paper, began to make a list. He had had a success, and his family had sent him extra money. What should he do next?

I will go home for the summer, he said to himself resolutely. That's first on the list. I will go home and paint the sea again because it calls to me. Hannah's meals are excellent, and there's plenty of wine. And in the autumn, I may come back here and I may not.

He looked up from his wine.

Camille Doncieux was standing at the edge of the café chairs.

SHE WAS HOLDING the same purse, looking lovelier than ever in a polka-dotted white dress, a folded parasol in her gloved hands. It is someone else, not her, Claude thought. He stood up, scraping back the chair on the cobbles as she hurried past the other tables to him.

She said, "I was going to your house to leave a letter for you."

Ah, one of her passionate letters! he thought dryly.

He resolved to be formal and polite. He took her gloved hand and let his lips brush hers. She flushed and looked about. She must conceal me, he thought resentfully. The hidden boudoir, very much like a play. "What a surprise to see you," he said. "Do sit down."

She took the chair opposite him at the small table. "How have you been, Claude?" she asked, never taking her eyes from him.

"Oh, very well! I'm busy, very busy. Had you appeared a few days from now I wouldn't have been here. Sorry you left. I do understand. A woman's wedding is a great thing. I was, perhaps, your indiscretion." He did not want to speak angrily, so he controlled his voice. He could feel a touching humility from her across the table. Pigeons pecked at crumbs between their feet. He raised his face and saw tears in her eyes.

"You've every right to be angry," she said. "But where would you go?"

"Many places. I have to get back to my work. I've had a great success. I thank you very much for it. I truly mean that. Look, I've been making a list!" He turned it over. It was not much of a list, with only one item so far. How can I be at such loose ends? he thought.

Camille felt the edge of the table nervously. "I have to tell you this," she said. "When I was away at my *grandmère*'s little house in the Rhône-Alpes, I thought of how the ceiling fell. I left my purse. I know you returned it. I know my mother was cold; she knows nothing. I have to explain. Please excuse me if I do it clumsily because I've never done anything like this before. I decided to forget you, but I can't. I was all prepared to live the life of my mother and my sister if you hadn't walked into my uncle's bookshop that day. Something in me turned and went the other way and won't turn back around."

She raised her eyes for a moment, then looked down again. "I cried for you. I stifled my tears in my pillow. I wrote letters to you but didn't send them. And I knew last night suddenly because it all burst out. I had to be with you again. No, Monsieur Monet, you are far more than my 'indiscretion,' as you called it. I almost wish you weren't more because you were so haughty when I came across to you just now."

"I . . ." He was stunned.

"I heard the Salon closed. Did my picture sell?"

"Not yet; it will."

"I should have said your picture," she added. Tears fell down her cheeks. He wanted to stand up and crush her against him, but he said cautiously, "My haughtiness is an old habit. I'm sorry. I was a little hurt. So here you are."

Camille raised her face hopefully, her eyes still full of tears and her nose a little red. He did not have a handkerchief, but she pulled one from her purse, stained somewhat with powder and chocolate.

Claude looked down at a pigeon and asked cautiously, "But what does it mean that you've come for me after you disappeared? You're engaged."

"I don't know if I want to be. Lucien Besique is good man, a kind man, and would give me whatever I wanted but I want only to be with you. He would never understand me; he would indulge me. He would say, 'Oh, those are her little ways!' I would have cards engraved like my mother and pay calls."

She had anxiously pulled off her glove, and he could see her fingernails were bitten more closely than he recalled. She raised her chin and said tremulously, "Now you can send me away if you wish and I won't come back. I've humbled myself. I want to be with you. I had a friend who died so suddenly, young, and she never had the chance to be with the man she was drawn to, but I took that chance. I went into your arms; I couldn't help myself. I can't now. You may send me away, but I won't go on my own. I want to be with you for a little time, some days, a week. I can at least have that!"

He thought, She has yearned for me as I have for her. He exclaimed, "Yes, I want that too. The hell with everything else!" The heat of desire and relief so flooded him that his voice carried. The elderly waiter turned around and looked benignly at him as if to say, Young love.

"But where can we go?" he cried. He thought of the studio as it was now, without a cleaning woman for weeks and full of unwashed dishes and someone's socks drying over the edge of a chair. Sometimes there was just he and Frédéric and other times two or three more artists sleeping all over the floor. He couldn't take her there; besides, he couldn't see his friends' faces after he had sworn to them he had forgotten her utterly.

He took out his pad and pencil again. "I know. I have a friend who stayed in this lovely rural area just outside the city, Sèvres, in a farmhouse. We'll go there, just us. We'll hide. Come. What will your family say?"

She smiled slightly, so touching with the tears still wet on her face. "They won't know where I've gone. I'll send a note that I'm safe. Yes, let's go away together where no one can find us."

~ ⚬ ~

NOTHING HAD EVER happened so fast in his life. An hour later he and Camille caught the train together to Sèvres, where they walked to the farmhouse. Dusk was falling and smoke rising from the chimney over the tiled roof with the fields and hills and stone walls beyond. He signed the registrar Monsieur and Madame Claude Monet before they climbed the creaking stairs past the pregnant farm cat to their room, bolting the door behind them.

They lit no candle but immediately began to undress each other in the dark, not hastily this time, but contemplating every lace and button. He felt the air on his bare back and legs. She stood waiting as he unfastened the eight hooks of her corset. He slipped off her chemise. In the dim light her slender body with its large breasts was the most beautiful thing he had ever seen, and they were alone, alone. No one would bother them. Outside, they heard the goats coming down the road and the voice of the boy shepherd. A gate opened. Below, a pot was placed on a trivet; the smell of soup rose. The still, sweet night lay against the window listening to them.

He wanted to go slowly so that it would never end. He kissed her breasts and belly and thighs. She murmured and moved against him. As he entered her, he willed the very air to stand still. He felt he would remember always her softness, the bedposts, the cotton bed hangings, and the smell of cooking soup. When it was done he held her until he was ready to begin again.

An hour later hunger drove them downstairs, where the farmwife smiled at them and served them tenderly. His leg pressed against Camille's under the table and they soon drew each other up the creaking stairs once more. The world became her body pushing against his, gasping in delight. The touch of her hand on his stomach made him cry out with longing.

On the third morning, as they still lay in bed, he said, "You were walking in the garden yesterday in the sun and I saw you as a painting of four women, all you. Will you model for me?"

"But we left so quickly I didn't have time to try to run home and secretly take any other dresses but the one I'm wearing, and you didn't bring your paints."

"I can paint other dresses in later, and I'll write Frédéric. He wrote me a week ago that he'd be back by now." He sat down at the desk by the window, glancing back at her in bed. Already she was slowly and languidly turning into the painting for him, and on top of his letter he roughly sketched how he would place her on the canvas.

F., cher ami! *I'm so sorry I never even left you a note—you and our friends must have thought I drowned in the Seine. I went away quite suddenly with the enchanting Camille, the younger sister whom you met last summer in Fontainebleau (the older sister is fast become a terror of respectability) and whom I painted in your rented green promenade dress. Anyway, I did not bring my paints, so can you buy the enclosed list of colors and also a large canvas and stretchers and some new brushes and put them on the train? I'll pay you back. I know I owe you a fortune already but it will be repaid in good time! I am on my way to remarkable success. Don't tell a soul where we are, as her family doesn't know. We are entirely happy together and she is in all ways* lovely. *Envy me!*

CM

THE STRETCHED CANVAS was so large he needed two boys to help him dig a ditch lined with oilcloth so that he could lower it a little when he needed to paint the top. He ran about gathering a huge bunch of flowers and placed them in Camille's arms. He painted her that day and on the many that followed. She stood in a loose garment smelling another bouquet; she passed behind the tree, retreating. The four of her moved and blended into one. He would change the one dress into several in the final painting. That dress was now dingy at the hem.

"Can I see it, Claude?" she called.

"Later. Don't move your mouth or I'll kiss it."

"Then I'll talk away so you'll kiss me!" She raised the flowers so that only her large eyes could be seen, following him as he worked. He smiled, slightly sweaty under his shirt. The sun was exquisite.

At night when they undressed he sometimes remembered that he was not the first man to make love to her. Who was your first lover? he wanted to ask. Surely not that old man, your fiancé? And were there others before him? To whom did you write letters from the bookshop, and who wrote them to you? As she lay on the sheets before him, naked but for her last petticoat and arms open to him, he bit his lip. His inquiry would come out strident and jealous. He would say nothing now but keep the question inside of him.

The painting was done; he had captured the last small white flower.

"Well," he said a few nights later with a sigh when they returned to their room, "we must go home tomorrow. My money's gone. How sad to leave this place. You belong in a garden." He stood at the window, looking out at the dark night, and they fell asleep later without touching. In the morning he took his now dry canvas from the stretchers and laid large sheets of paper on top of the painted surface, rolling it loosely so that the paper was outside and tying it with rope. My love is inside there now, he thought sadly; my love is rolled away in darkness.

Slowly they walked away from the farmhouse and the garden to the station to catch the train back to Paris.

Her sister, Annette, was waiting for them at the Gare Saint-Lazare.

THAT TALL YOUNG matron in her ornately decorated hat who looked so like Camille came rapidly toward them through the crowds under the huge glass domes of the station, calling over the shouting porters and screaming newsboys.

Claude whispered, "*Merde!* What's she doing here?"

Camille gave him a quick, tragic look and stammered, "It's my fault. I wrote her the day before yesterday that we were coming back this morning around eleven because I just knew how she'd worry. But . . . I *told* her to tell no one."

Annette was within a few feet of them now, clutching her pink parasol so tightly that he felt she would hit him with it. "Are you out of your mind, Minou?" she exclaimed above the noise of the crowds. "To go off a whole month with no word? We finally traced you to this man's studio and his peculiar friends. One of them told us you were with him. You're fortunate we didn't know exactly where until last night when your letter came!"

Claude opened his mouth to speak. "Madame," he began, but Annette Lebois' words rose over his. The sisters were now not a foot apart.

Annette's slightly freckled face was pale with outrage. "What about your engagement, Minou? My husband wanted to go to the police but Father dissuaded him to avoid scandal. We have kept it from your fiancé; we told him you were away outside Lyon with our poor *grandmère* and likely too distraught to write. And how will he marry you after you have simply run off with some painter? Yes, monsieur, that is what you are indeed. Minou, you swore you'd never do this again!"

Camille stamped her foot. "This time has nothing to do with that!" she cried passionately. "You said you'd never mention it again; you broke your promise! I went away with Claude because that's what I wanted to do."

A porter with a trolley piled with luggage was trying to make his way around them, bumping against the standing rolled canvas, but neither sister paid him any attention. "Yes, you always do what you want!" Annette replied. "You always have! Are you planning on staying with this man? What proper home can he give you? What sort of income does monsieur have? Where does he live? In a studio with half a dozen other painters! And what sort of a man is he to take you away and cause you to lose your good name?"

Annette began to pull her sister's arm. "You must come now and talk to Maman and Papa! And your dress is dirty! How could you be seen in public with such a dirty dress!"

Camille was crying now, tearing at her gloves and stamping her feet. "Leave me alone! I'll go to them without you. I know what I'm doing. Go away, go away!"

"Madame," Claude said, raising his voice. Several people had now stopped to stare at them. "I beg you, madame . . ."

Annette Lebois turned away from him; she was also crying now. "Your good name is lost unless we can conceal everything."

CLAUDE COULD FIND no seats for them on the crowded omnibus. He kept one arm around Camille, while the other balanced the rolled painting, which was taller than he was by a few feet. A bit of the protective paper had ripped and showed a riot of painted white flowers. People climbed over them to descend. The stopping and starting of the horses in the heavy traffic threw them against each other and once nearly knocked him into an elderly man's lap. He tried to find his handkerchief as the tears still ran down her face.

As the omnibus crept over the crowded bridge to the Left Bank, he whispered, "Did you really run off with someone before me?"

"I did, and it was a stupid thing," she replied sadly. "I was sixteen, an innocent girl, and he lied to me."

"Will you tell me about it sometime?"

"One day when I get the courage."

"You can always tell me the truth."

Her warm eyes looked at him as gratefully as they had many times before, but now it was more poignant because she had been weeping. She pressed his hand and whispered, "Oh, thank you! I know that and I will!"

More passengers squeezed on board and glanced angrily at the huge, rolled painting. He stared at the dirty floorboards and black shoes of the woman sitting in front of them. "Well, we're back in Paris. Does this mean good-bye, Minou? If that's the pet name your sister calls you, I'll use it too. Do you intend to keep your engagement and marry that man?"

She stared at him, her long Grecian face indignant. "What? What do you think of me? Don't you understand? I'm in love with you; I'm so much in love with you!"

They descended at their stop on the rue Jacob, where he took her face in his hands and kissed her. "I love you too," he said. "I don't want you to go away."

She stepped back. "I'm going now to settle things with my mother and father," she said quietly. And then she was gone, hurrying down the street.

HE BALANCED THE heavy canvas on his shoulder like an itinerant peddler to mount the stairs to the studio. His good friend the painter Sisley ran down to help him as he approached the top, but Claude shook his head. When he maneuvered his way into the room, he saw Frédéric standing by a new painting of a nude girl; he wore his old painting suit as if he had never left. "Claude!" he exclaimed. "You didn't write. I see you got everything I sent you."

Claude stared at Frédéric's face and managed to catch his breath. "And I thought you all were my friends!" he shouted. "Which one of you or the other idiots told Camille's family she was with me? Was it you, Bazille, when I wrote you for my paints and easels? You have a blissful time at home with your Lily and now you want to ruin things for me."

"What? Let me help you with that!"

Claude shook his head, but together they brought the canvas to rest on the floor. "You're wrong," Frédéric said bluntly. "It wasn't any of us on purpose. Pissarro saw your letter lying about and forgot he was supposed to be quiet about it. He was carrying his portfolio and his son the other day when someone stopped him in the street and asked him if he knew you. He said you were away with your pretty model and gave them the studio address because they said they wanted to commission a painting. He didn't think; he's so honest. Now he says he'd rather return to the West Indies than face you. Yesterday her family walked in our door, which we hadn't locked. Auguste's Lise was modeling naked on the stand. What a mess."

Claude grunted. "Sorry," he said. He walked back and forth, gently touching the bristles of the brushes in the jars, turning over a tube of paint to study the color label as if he had never seen it before, fingers drumming on the dresser and the table. "I mean it, I'm sorry. Come on, help me unroll this and put it on the stretchers again. Thanks for sending the paint."

They unrolled the canvas on the floor and placed bricks carefully on the edges to keep it from curling. Claude stood between his friends, who were studying it. "What do you think?" he asked.

"It's the best thing you've done," Frédéric said after a time. "It's far better than the portrait of her in the green dress. I don't think anyone's done anything like that, the movement of the women, the sun. So you went away with her, you lucky bastard. Of course I'd never betray your secret. So she's 'in all ways lovely,' eh? But I've met her irate parents now and gotten an even clearer idea of her situation."

Claude grunted. "So what idea do you have?" he asked.

Frédéric knelt to admire the painting. "It's just girls like this. Good, upper-class girls. They're raised like precious flowers to take their place in society, to live the lives of their mothers in paying calls, hiring carriages, eating dinner off fine china. You don't know what trouble she'll be in for climbing into your bed these weeks."

Claude placed his hand on his friend's shoulder and thought of Camille now with her family telling them the news. "It's not for weeks, Bazille," he said seriously, "it's for always. We love each other. We want a life together. As for the things she'll miss, I'll make them up and more. I'm on the edge of doing very well. We all are. I'll take care of her. I'll find someplace to live. It would be too crowded here." He nodded, suddenly filled with calm: he envisioned the world he would have with her eventually, the elegant city rooms and the house in the country with a garden.

"So you're leaving here?" Sisley asked, looking up from the painting.

Claude looked around the studio at all the hanging paintings. "I bet I'll be missed," he said.

Frédéric shook his head, making a wry face. "I won't miss your snoring," he exclaimed. "Auguste is looking for a room and he can have yours. Besides, nothing much will change. You'll be here every day to paint."

"Yes, every damn day! Can you clean up the dirty socks if she comes too? What can you do? Friends fall in love and move on. Speaking of love, how's your Lily these four months you've been home?"

Frédéric stood up. "She was sad when I left. She asked me when I'd come back to live. I said three years. So I have a little time to learn to be the artist I'd like to be with all of you before I become I don't know what. I have a little more time."

Interlude

The old artist put aside thoughts of Camille's unforgiving sister. Something so large and extraordinary was happening in his painting; it was the most extraordinary work he had ever done. For four years steadily he had been painting the lily pond and little else; he felt that at the age of sixty-eight, the greatest challenge of his work was yet before him. He could not quite conceive when he would exhibit this work, which was so very personal.

And yet sometimes at the end of the day he also thought of the lacquered Japanese box and all its mysteries. One night after supper he put his pride aside and went to his room to write her once more.

My dear madame,

I must tell you what a great hurt it was to me that after all these years you still hold me responsible for your sister's death. I was also very angry and resolved never to try to contact you again as you wished, but that is impossible for me, so I am writing once more in hope of beginning a communication between us.

I realize you did not even know I had moved to Giverny. It's a small hamlet forty miles from Paris in farm country. You may remember I loved to garden, and over the years I have made a large and beautiful one. In varying seasons it is full of poppies, marigolds, sunflowers. I also have a lower garden with a pond and many paintings of this, which today I have understood I may not have the courage to exhibit next spring, though many people are urging me to do so. To show my heart, as my old mentor once told me to. Today I do not have that courage, but still I must write this letter.

I did not even know you were in Paris until a friend mentioned that you had returned there a while ago and owned a successful millinery shop on the Champs-Élysées. It has been nearly thirty years since our last meeting. I am older than my years, paunchy and white-bearded, my just rewards from tramping long hours out in inclement weather to paint. My vision has also begun to trouble me.

I cannot say how many memories opened to me when I first wrote you. All I have now of your sister are my many paintings and the contents of a box. It seemed impossible that all that is left of her can be crammed into two drawers. There are things I do not understand, and I believe you can explain them to me. Of all those who knew her well and loved her, we alone remain, but for my friend Auguste, who is now far from me and not well.

Can we meet somewhere after all these years? Would you do me that kindness? For suddenly I must search for your sister

again. Perhaps it is my age—one knows one is not immortal and
it is time to think back on all we loved.

Yours sincerely, C. Monet

He enclosed a sprig of lavender before posting it.

Part Three

1867

❦

Don't work bit by bit, but paint everything at once by placing tones everywhere.

—CAMILLE PISSARRO

THE ROOM HE AND CAMILLE MOVED TO A FEW DAYS LATER was long and dark with only one small window. It was located in a workmen's neighborhood of Pigalle above a laundry. She brought her beautiful dresses and her fluffy white dog, Victoire, who was getting on in years and peed wearily in corners. "Come, Victoire! *Viens, vite!*" she called and the hysterical little creature leapt after her, tongue out. The smell of hot water and heating irons rose up from dawn to dusk with the chatter of the laundry girls.

Claude received another check from his aunt. He wrote a gracious letter thanking her but decided not to tell her yet that he was living with Camille. To pay for immediate expenses, he drew portraits in red chalk of neighbors, and Camille contributed money she had accumulated from family gifts over the years, which she kept in a little black-beaded purse.

They were both astonished to have found each other. You are not a dream, they whispered to each other in the middle of the night. Still at times he woke and thought he was in the studio again, and he listened for his friends' low voices in the other room.

They had been living together only a few weeks when her father showed up at the door. Monsieur Doncieux was a weary-looking and not large man of perhaps sixty years. He knocked very politely and Camille rose from mopping up after Victoire, crying, "Papa!"

"So this is where you . . ."

Claude put out his hand, but Monsieur Doncieux ignored it. Claude felt a rising anger but decided to say nothing for Camille's sake. Hastily he cleared laundry and books from their chairs, saying, "Will you sit, monsieur?" They all sat, and Claude took Camille's fingers, which were suddenly cold.

Monsieur looked about the room at the canvases and his daughter's many dresses hung from hooks as they had no wardrobe. He glanced at the murals of the bucolic countryside on the cracking plaster walls that Claude and Auguste had painted together one night until four in the morning.

Her father began clumsily. "Minou, your mother's desperate. We can only hope you'll return soon. At least you've not married yet. You may have thought we preferred it, but we feel that step would be more irrevocable." He added sadly, "I only hope you have enough to eat."

She reached out her other hand for her dog to come and said uncomfortably, "Claude is a very good cook!"

"Your mother and I want you to know that we will receive you back home anytime and that though we have sent back the ring as you asked us, your fiancé says that he will excuse you this for your youth, and that he still loves you."

"But I don't love him," Camille replied intensely. "And I love Claude and I love his work. I'm proud to stand beside him as he paints. You must not insult Claude. I won't have it."

Claude cleared his throat. "I shall take good care of her, monsieur," he said. "And I shall do well." He listened to more of the arguing back and forth, his body aching from withheld anger. When her father rose to leave, he did not offer his hand again, but when he and Camille were alone the blood rushed to his face and he hurled the pile of laundry to the floor, shouting, *"Merde! Merde!"* The terrified dog crept whimpering under the bed.

"Oh, Claude!" she said, her long face tragic. "He barely kissed me good-bye! I've hurt him and that poor dull man they wanted me to marry. I never wanted to hurt anyone, and yet I have, but I can't live their lives. I can't. And yet . . ." She covered her face with both hands.

He took her in his arms. For hours he seemed to hear her father's footsteps descending the stairs.

THEY THOUGHT THAT evening that they could not soon forget the visit, but within a few days they again plunged happily into their busy lives.

At first his friends mostly left them alone, but after a time they visited regularly. They came up the stairs bearing food and wine, and soon she was throwing her arms about them, kissing them, welcoming them. They treated her like something precious. If there had been any shyness between her and them, it had left. Only Paul Cézanne did she find odd.

Sometimes Claude took her with him over the bridge to the Right Bank and the café in the Batignolles district. She wore her blue and white striped dress and a little cloth hat with a feather. The artists all sat together at the same marble table in the back. She ordered cake and Auguste finished it; she drank from their glasses, putting her pretty lips to the rim. In her exquisite dresses she sat among them like the lady she was.

Other times he wished he had had finer friends to introduce her to: not the shabby, genial Pissarro, who looked like a farmer with his old boots and untrimmed beard, nor even Auguste. But she loved them. She learned to cook two dishes and invited them to dinner with their women: Pissarro's outspoken Julie, who had been his mother's maid and who gazed about her, saw what had to be done, and quietly accomplished it; and impulsive, idealistic, and volatile Lise, whom Auguste was falling more in love with every day. She was the eighteen-year-old daughter of a philosophy teacher who did not mind that his beautiful daughter had taken a thin, intense painter as her lover. Her mother had run off years before.

One bright, clear winter afternoon they all met in the studio to celebrate a portrait commission Auguste had just completed of a little girl. Several painters had work stored here or hung on the walls, and others had brought new paintings. They were discussing to whom they might market them and what they should submit to the Salon, now several months away in the spring.

Camille knelt to gaze at the new work; she studied the canvases of fields in flower, country paths, and Auguste's portrait of the child, which he was to deliver the next day.

"It's difficult, mademoiselle," Pissarro said from his chair across the room. "We sell something and then nothing. Most people say what we do is a sketch and against all the rules of classical art. I can count on one hand those who really believe in us."

"This is yours, monsieur, I think! Where did you paint it?"

"Louveciennes, where I live. It's the village road."

Still on her knees with her skirts flowing about her, Camille let the edge of her hand hover over the painting and then looked at all of the painters. She asked, "Don't you all understand what you are doing, all of you? You can smell the earth and the moisture in the air; it's all here. And oh, Monsieur Renoir, your pictures of young women! They're so fresh and happy. Someday people will pay a fortune for all of your work, but only if you allow nothing to come between you; you must remain together. Do you remember the three Musketeers, who lived *un pour tous, tous pour un*—one for all, all for one?"

Auguste gave her his hand to help her rise. "Yes, that is the way, of course! How generous and kind you are, mademoiselle!" he said. "What can we do for you? Claude tells me you love theater. Would you like some tickets? Lise adores theater. I can get some free for the Théâtre de l'Odéon through an actress I know."

She turned brightly to Claude. "I would love to go!" she said. "I love it more than anything."

"I know you do!"

"It's not exactly the expensive box seats," Auguste added, reflecting, but she declared, "Will we be high up? I always wondered what it was like!"

A small group of them made their way into the theater the next evening, exclaiming over the ornate lobby with statuary and glistening chandeliers, then mounting to the highest gallery, where they squeezed into their seats. Frédéric had nowhere to put his long legs. Camille said, "I feel like a bird looking down on everyone, that this is a secret place."

Auguste bought nuts to eat and trod on their feet during the interval trying to climb back to his seat. "Pig!" Lise cried, kissing him. They had a playful, sharp relationship.

The friends went again that week to *Le malade imaginaire* by Molière; the great actress Sarah Bernhardt played Angélique. Camille and Lise wept over the translation of Shakespeare's *Le roi Lear* and of the tribulations of the king's faithful daughter Cordelia. They were fascinated by *Passant*, in which Bernhardt appeared as a boy Florentine singer, her shapely legs in close-fitting leggings.

"Women should wear leggings," Auguste whispered. "Down with skirts. I mean that in every sense of the word."

After the play, they all walked to a cheap restaurant, where they were served bread and some meat that claimed to be pork. The rooms were full of poor writers and poets; the actors who had smaller parts came in as well and talked loudly about what roles they hoped to have. The gaslight was so scant that they could hardly see what they ate.

"I think it's tree bark," Lise said, poking with her fork.

Auguste shook his head. "No, likely a corpse, and not too fresh."

Camille put down her spoon. "I'll just have the bread," she said and Claude cried out imperiously, raising his hand, "*Garçon!* Bring your best cheese for madame!"

They climbed back to the room above the laundry, where they lit lamps and Camille found a copy of a Molière comedy, which she persuaded others to read with her. "I want to study acting," she cried breathlessly to Claude when everyone had left. "Lise and I discussed it when we were walking together. We'll share lessons. My family never let me. Would you be proud of me?"

"I'm proud of you in all you do," he said. "I know this is what you want." He saw a paper under the table and retrieved Auguste's sketch of the two young women bending their heads together over one play script. He kept it carefully among his things.

Camille and Lise began to study elocution and dramatic movement privately with an elderly retired actor. They went twice a week at five francs a lesson, and Claude sometimes came back from doing his chalk portraits or painting around the city to find the furniture pushed back and Camille and Lise reciting scenes with each other, one of the two dishes Camille could cook simmering on the stove.

One evening he found Camille crying out the last words of the tragic Phèdre, expiring in her dressing gown at the foot of the table set for dinner. Lise sat cross-legged on the floor prompting her and reading all the other roles. He leaned on the door, arms folded, portfolio at his feet, smiling at them. "Monsieur! Monsieur!" they called to him, laughing and giggling. They utterly charmed him. How happy I am, he thought.

SNOW FELL OVER the city one night in November until the steps and horse posts and signs were covered; it surrounded the chimneys on the roofs and piled outside windows slowly, sealing them inside. They fell asleep wrapped in blankets before the fire.

Claude woke to scratching noises, and in the shadows he saw Victoire worrying a paper that had been slipped under the door. He rubbed his eyes and crawled over to rescue it, knocking down a small pile of playbooks on the floor that rested on the large purple theatrical cape Camille had acquired somewhere to wear while practicing tragic queens. He leaned near the last of the firelight to open the paper. A flush of heat shot through him. *"Merde!"* he muttered.

Camille stirred from sleep. "What is it?" she asked in the more resonant voice of her training.

He rose, pushed aside the lethargic Victoire, who was settling in to sleep in their one armchair, and dropped heavily into it. He would have given anything not to tell her, but he could think of no way around it. "It's about the damn rent," he said. "We have to pay it all or be out by the morning."

"But I never heard of such a thing." She came across the room barefoot, wrapped in her blanket, and looked gravely down at him. "People don't do things like that. It's not civilized. Don't we have the money to pay them? Oh, Claude! Is it because I bought that hat? It is my fault, isn't it?"

"But that hat belonged to you," he said. "It was wrong that any other woman should have it. Hats! I'll buy you twenty of them, just wait!"

"I'll hurry over in the morning and ask my father for a loan." She had visited her family a few times since her father had come to them.

Claude cried, "Never! And it may be too late by then." He jumped up, pulling the carpetbag from under the bed. "I'm sending you to your sister's now," he said over his shoulder. "Get dressed quickly. Get your hairbrushes and your good dresses. Now, dear, now. I'll come later." He threw a few of her dresses into wicker trunks and bundled her into her coat. She picked up Victoire.

"I want to stay!" she said steadily.

He shook his head. "I'll leave as quickly as I can. I know these people."

"What do you know?" she asked him fixedly.

He fell silent, thinking of friends tossed from their houses, two painters he had met. One was thrown out without his clothes. One had been beaten. He remembered a story told in art school of the sound of old copper pots hitting the courtyard as some sculptor's wife threw them from the window to save them. "Come on!" he cried more harshly than he wished.

She looked a little frightened at his tone and distractedly picked up the playbooks and the cape. He came forward swiftly and kissed her. "It's all right," he whispered.

Outside, the snow fell on her coat and hat and on his suit jacket. At last a carriage appeared, the driver huddled on the top seat. Claude settled her in with the paintings and boxes. "Ask your sister to pay for the cab," he whispered. "I'll be there shortly. I need to take some things to the studio."

He stood for a moment watching the carriage turn the corner and then hurried inside again up the steps. There was such stillness about everything; the whole house was sleeping. He heard snoring from behind one door.

In his room, he stood looking at all his things, the murals on the wall, his clothes and dozens of paintings. *Women in the Garden* was already stored at the studio. He could not take everything at once; he had to choose what was most important and take it there tonight. He felt in the pocket of his overcoat, which hung by the door; he had a few francs for a wagon or carriage if he could find one.

Somewhere a clock struck one.

He wrapped several of his best paintings in oilcloth and packed a large valise. He would empty it at Frédéric's, borrow money for another cab or two, and come back for more of his things. He could get back by half past two in the morning if he could find some transport now and the vehicle did not get stuck in a snowdrift.

As he shoved his mother's picture into the valise, he heard the opening of the door far below, the sleepy murmur of the concierge, and then footsteps ascending. They mounted until they stopped on his landing. Someone knocked hard on his door. "Monsieur!" someone shouted. "Open up, monsieur. We know you're in there!"

He sprang for the bolt, but someone had fitted a key to the lock. Claude threw his weight against the door to hold it closed. Someone pushed, and the door burst open, sending him sprawling back. Three strangers stood in his room, men in wet coats who looked as if they could get no better work to do.

One growled, "Was monsieur thinking of slipping out with

something? Nothing belongs to monsieur anymore. Monsieur can redeem his things when the rent's paid."

Claude seized the tied canvases and pushed past them to the dark stairs, where he slipped. He got to his feet, cursing the sharp pain in his ankle, and half hopped down the remaining steps with the canvases. When he got to the bottom he realized no one had followed. I should have beaten them, he thought, his heart pounding. For a moment he was so appalled he had not that he could not move.

They might follow, he thought grimly. He had best go on.

The concierge had closed her door.

The snow was worse than before, swirling all around, obscuring the doors of the dirty brick buildings and the alleys. It was a while before the rage left him enough that he could think at all and remember that his hat and overcoat were upstairs, the few francs he had in the coat pocket.

He put up his collar and limped to the alley. An overhanging roof sheltered a cart, and he squeezed toward it to get out of the snow and stumbled against a bulky form under a blanket. It moved and cursed him.

Claude felt his way, trying to protect his paintings under his jacket, and took shelter in a church doorway to feel his ankle. A bad twist, likely not a sprain, and nothing broken. Still, it hurt like hell. I need to figure out what I can do, he thought. I can't walk very much, but I'll go as far as I can toward the Right Bank and try to make it across the river to the studio. It will take me a few hours to reach Frédéric's in the snow. Suppose he and Auguste are not there and they have taken away the concierge's key?

Claude limped on, staying as close to the buildings as he could, sheltering his paintings. Now and then a carriage passed him and drove on. What was worth noticing about a man limping somewhere at night without a coat?

He was heading toward the river when a solitary cart moving down the avenue slowed its old horse and the driver called out, "All right there, young fellow? Had too much to drink?"

Claude sheltered his eyes to look at the cloaked shape and the horse's snowy back. "Not drunk, monsieur," he called, his voice sounding lonely in the snow. "I'm trying to reach the rue de Fursten-berg, across the river."

"I'll go as far as the Seine and turn west then. Come on."

He parted from the man at the river and painfully made his way down under the bridge, where he saw the light of a crude fire and a number of men gathered around it. They moved to make a place for him, and he sat down on the stone. After a time, he broke the stretch-ers from his paintings and fed the wood to the flame. It was easier to carry the canvases rolled under his coat anyway.

He reached the rue de Furstenberg as dawn was breaking. The concierge came grumbling, awakened from her warm bed. "What a night!" she said crossly. "You'll catch your death, young man! Imag-ine leaving this lovely neighborhood for Pigalle! Take the key. No one's there, I think."

There were the familiar steep stairs, and the same chamber pot someone always left out. In the studio, Claude crossed the darkness to his former bedroom, which Auguste Renoir now rented. He stripped off his suit and crawled under the covers.

He woke to the fragrant smell of coffee and pulled himself from bed.

The studio was filled with white light, which reflected from the snowy roofs. Pissarro and Auguste were at the table drinking black coffee and breaking off pieces of fresh bread.

Auguste reached over and slid out a chair. "I heard you snoring!" he said. "Lucky I didn't come in drunk and fall on top of you. I spent the night with Lise, and Pissarro just arrived. Here's a cup for you! Where's Camille? What happened? You look like *merde*."

Claude wrapped his hands around the warm cup. "She's at her sis-ter's; we were thrown out. The rent, you know."

Pissarro shook his head. "Why didn't you tell us there was a problem?"

"It happened very fast. It was . . . *putain!*"

"Why are you limping?"

"Damn foot; it's better now. A bruise, I think. Where's our good Doctor Bazille?"

"Some relatives are in town and he's taking them to a concert. Pissarro and I had better go over to your room and see what can be done."

IT WAS AFTERNOON before Claude gathered the courage to fetch Camille. The omnibus moved slowly through the snowy streets, and he turned from the window, wincing. He did not want to remember how he had walked last night.

The omnibus left him near the Parc Monceau. He walked past the black and gold iron gates and crossed the slushy street, marked with horse droppings and carriage wheels. The apartment building rose with its mansard roofs high above him. He passed through the wide oak doors; the young, sharp-nosed concierge studied him doubtfully but motioned him up the polished wood stairs. He looked back at her critical face and the marks of his wet shoes.

Camille's sister cautiously opened the door.

He glimpsed the parlor, the mauve-velvet-upholstered furniture, the silver coffeepot and porcelain cups set before a fire just before she closed the door behind her. She was not going to ask him in.

"What are these goings-on, monsieur!" she whispered. "Minou arrived half frozen past midnight. How could you take a girl from a good home to endure such an experience! My mother's inside. We think it best, monsieur, if my sister never sees you again. Please send back her dresses if indeed you still have them."

He said, "It was a misunderstanding; it was an oversight."

"In fact, she doesn't want to see you."

"That's a lie!" he shouted as he glanced down to see the concierge mounting the stairs toward him with a heavy stick in her hand. At that moment the apartment door opened and Camille ran out. She wore only her dress and held her corset, hose, and barking dog under

one arm. She seemed like something wild and tangled. "I was looking from the window!" she cried. "I saw you crossing the street! I
couldn't sleep for worry! Did they come? Did they hurt you? I
would kill them if they hurt you!" She threw her arms around him so
hard he almost lost his balance. He could feel the wild beating of her
heart.

NIGHT HAD FALLEN when they reached the studio. Their many
boxes and wet bags and canvases and paintings were heaped in the
hall and against the studio walls. Pissarro and Auguste and Sisley had
rescued some things from the landlord of the Pigalle room, who
promised to deliver the rest tomorrow when the remainder of the
money was raised. *"Les putains!"* Pissarro said angrily. "The
whores. Landlords should be exiled. Rent should be free." He kicked
the wall.

Frédéric said, "I'm so sorry, Claude. Are you both all right? She's
not!" Camille was sneezing and feverish. Lise took her into the other
room to help her out of her wet clothes and into a dressing gown and
then tucked her onto the sofa and covered her with blankets.

They pushed the table to the sofa and Claude coaxed her to eat a
little chicken. They opened a new small keg of wine sent by
Frédéric's family. The room was made warm by the puffing stove.

Auguste said between mouthfuls, "You both take the bedroom
again. I'll sleep on the cot until you find another place."

Frédéric was too angry to sit down; he walked back and forth between the easels. "We've got to prevent this from happening again,"
he said. "It kills me when I think how gifted you all are. Claude
couldn't even sell *The Green Dress* after all the praise it got. And we
never know if the Salon will deign to take us, and then if they do,
most people can't find our work amid all the other work."

He sat down then, drumming his long fingers on the table. "We
need to arrange our own independent exhibition: the lot of us, Manet

too, and Degas and Cézanne. We have to show the public what we can do with our new style."

"But how do we know it'll succeed or if anyone will come?" Pissarro asked. "Manet had an independent exhibition and lost his shirt."

"But he was alone and we're all together."

Camille leaned back, holding the pillow against her. She croaked, "Ah, you see, there's your answer! I told you! As I said before: one for all, all for one. Whatever I can do to help, I will!"

Claude lifted her and carried her into his old bedroom, which was now half filled with her rescued clothes, and tucked her in bed. "Now you must rest," he said softly. "If my friends talk too loudly, I'll throw them out the window."

"Our friends," she corrected him.

"Are you sure you don't want to stay with your sister until I do better?"

"Never. You'd forget me and I'd grow ugly missing you. I intend to be brave. We must all be brave together."

"You're so beautiful! You must rest now. Shall I sing you a song? One my mother used to sing with me?"

"Yes, do! That will make me sleep. I didn't sleep at all last night worrying about you, my love."

"Well, then," he said. Stroking her hair, he began to sing softly. *"À la claire fontaine, m'en allant promener . . . Il y a longtemps que je t'aime."*

From the other room he heard the voices of his friends taking animatedly about when they could have their exhibition and how they could afford it. She was asleep, her face in profile. He ran his finger down her nose to her chapped lips. As he sat watching her soft breath, he remembered something her mother had whispered as Camille had kissed her rapidly and hurried down the steps ahead of him that late afternoon. "Monet, take care of her. She's delicate. There are things you don't yet understand about our Minou."

1 8 6 7 – 1 8 6 8

If God had not created women's breasts, I don't know if I would have been a painter.

—AUGUSTE RENOIR

CLAUDE TOOK CAMILLE TO LIVE IN A ROOM OWNED BY AN ancient lady in a wheelchair until the woman insisted that the smell of paint made her ill. They left in haste and for one week lived on a damp, cold houseboat in the Seine. He liked to watch Camille looking over the river at sunset. He was twenty-seven and she just twenty.

He had made a tentative rapprochement with her family during a stiff Sunday dinner in their rooms on the Île Saint-Louis. He had sat back in what Auguste called his lordly way, lace cuffs showing, and exclaimed, "I am heir to a prosperous Le Havre business."

"But do you intend to take it over from your father?" Madame asked as they sat down to dine later and the maid served them.

"Not exactly, no."

"Le Havre is after all too provincial for Minou."

"It is, of course! But I don't have to think of that. I'm on the cusp of doing very well here, madame! My prospects are great. Just this month, several new patrons have expressed interest in commissioning my work."

For some moments Claude felt he had convinced Camille's parents of his future. Later, thinking over her father's mumbled assent and her mother's cold look, he realized they had temporarily given up in weariness and were merely biding their time until their errant daughter would come back to them with some of her good name intact and marry the sort of man who would not take her to live on a houseboat. Madame Doncieux said nothing of the odd remark she had made when he had fetched Camille from her sister's apartment. It likely meant nothing.

I must make a life for her, he thought. I will soon.

Then Claude heard of a spacious room in what had been the ballroom of a sixteenth-century *grand hôtel* in the poorer section of the Marais district, now given largely over to immigrants, artists, and the Paris Jewish population. Though crumbling, the mansion still had its wide and grand marble staircase. They moved in at once. The windows stuck. Cherubs still decorated the ceiling, but they had been blackened by years of coal smoke from the capacious, cracking marble fireplace.

Lise fell in love with it. "It's full of ghosts!" she said. "It's so theatrical! Oh, *chérie,* we shall give tragedies here! I feel the ghost of some poor royalist who was guillotined in the Revolution!" She came by daily, walking impetuously in the door to take Camille away to their elocution and movement lessons. The theater books piled up among her poetry and novels; his and her books mingled again. The tattered purple cloak hung from a hook in the wall amid her beautiful dresses.

SHE ROSE LATE that January morning, stumbling about the room in her robe, wearing a pair of his warm socks, and gazing at the frost that clung to the windows. He had already brewed coffee and heated milk. Once more they had stayed up too late visiting with Pissarro and his Julie, who now lived upstairs with their little son. While Claude and his friend lingered at the table, Camille had disappeared with Julie to the sleeping alcove, where their whispers and giggles floated from behind the curtain.

Claude poured her coffee as she sank down at the table. He said, "I'm off to paint the boulevard des Capucines from a high window, and you have your lesson and something else with Lise. I forget. Well, what are you thinking? Did you dream of guillotined counts? Lise's imagination is sometimes too much for me."

Camille clasped her coffee cup with both hands and shook her head.

"You'll never guess," she said.

"I can't. Tell me."

"I'm pregnant."

"You're . . . ? How many days since . . . ?"

"Nearly two months, and my breasts ache so much."

"Two months! You said nothing."

"I wanted to be sure."

"But we use the sheath."

She bit her lip playfully and gave him that coy look, head to one side, hair tumbling down. "We haven't *always* used the sheath, Claude! Perhaps once or twice we didn't."

This is me, he thought. This is me, sitting opposite her at our table drinking our coffee as we do every morning. This is our room and our life. The boulevard is waiting. He squeezed her hand and kissed it. "I don't see how it could be!" he said lightly. "Your bleeding's irregular sometimes."

"But it's got to be true! Julie read it in the tea leaves, Claude!" She searched his face, crossing her arms slowly over her dressing gown. She said thoughtfully, "Then you don't think I'm . . ."

"Oh, likely not at this time, *ma très chère fille,*" he replied.

STANDING AT THE window above the snowy boulevard later that morning, he thought at first, I can't. Then the painting took him and swept him along, but when he paused a few hours later, his heart began to pound.

As the day ended, he left the unfinished painting in the empty room high above the boulevard and walked reflectively home. Camille was standing by the stove wearing an apron, stirring a pot.

"I've made pot-au-feu," she said cheerfully over her shoulder. "I bought the sausages. Our teacher is very pleased with us; he thinks we may be ready to audition soon! Oh, Claude! He thinks there may be places in the Comédie-Française or at the Odéon. I won't tell my family until it happens. How did your work go?" She raised her face for him to kiss her.

"Well," he answered. "I can sell this one with no trouble. My old framer Isaac Clément will exhibit it." She was humming brightly and wore a secret smile that seemed to radiate from her entire body under the apron. She hovered over the pot and ground in a little pepper, dipping her hand in the water basin.

We will not discuss it, he thought. There's nothing to discuss.

Then he thought, We have to discuss it.

He waited until they sat down at the table, a jug of wine between them. "Well, I suppose your time came as always?" he asked cheerfully, and she pressed her lips together as if she could not begin to keep the smile inside and shook her head.

He hesitated, speared a piece of sausage, and ate silently for a time. "I suppose you want a baby."

She reached out to touch his hand. "It's all so wondrously strange! A few months ago I did think when we were in bed together, 'He could give me a child,' and that made me feel warm all over. Aren't you happy? Wouldn't you like if our love turned into a child?"

"I hadn't planned on it yet," he muttered, looking down at his half-empty plate. His appetite had gone. "And the stage? You've been working so hard."

"My audition would merely be deferred a little," she said. "I didn't tell you, did I, that my sister's with child? Claude." She looked at him hesitantly, her lips slightly parted. "You don't sound happy."

"Yes, of course I'm happy! Only I don't want you to get your hopes up and then find it isn't so."

He took a deep breath, wanting only to escape into his painting of the snowy boulevard, to flee into its brushstrokes and disappear. It will come to nothing, he told himself firmly. She has whims and they pass, and this is likely just something she wants for now. Her sister is having it and she wants it.

How had he not noticed? he asked himself the next morning as he hurried down the stairs with his paint box. She loved children, stopping often when they walked in the Jardin du Luxembourg at the octagonal pond, the Grand Bassin, where children rented small boats and ran around in their pinafores while mothers and nursemaids watched them fondly. They sometimes took Julie's son, Lucien. Once he had come home to find Camille minding a neighbor's two little boys, sitting on the floor with them, cutting out shapes from scrap paper. With some chagrin she had told him she had missed her elocution lesson and that Lise was angry with her.

Each night that week he hardly dared ask her if her time had come as usual, and by Friday he only gazed beseechingly at her when he came in, hanging up his hat. He poured water in the basin and washed his hands, rubbing at the paint under his nails.

"Well then, it's true," he cried, turning to her as she set down the casserole for dinner. He threw himself into a chair. "I'm not as successful yet as your sister's husband; one day I'll be even more successful. But now, how can we manage? How can I take care of you and a baby? Yes, you would have to defer your audition. Don't you care about that? You can't go on stage looking like a Renaissance Madonna! I'd borrow again, but I haven't even paid my friends back for the last time, and they're struggling as well."

His voice rose. "That woman who bought my work hasn't introduced me to other patrons yet, but she might take this new work herself. And when *Women in the Garden* is accepted by the Salon this spring, things will change for me, but that's months away. Until then—*merde!* What on earth are we going to do?"

"But none of these things matter!" she insisted calmly. "All will be fine. I know it; I sense it. It's in the tea leaves. We'll manage somehow. We always do."

"What do you mean 'somehow'? Do tell me, Camille!"

"Don't you have faith in your gifts and in mine? I *will* go on the stage; I won't always look like a Renaissance Madonna. It's only seven more months."

"I don't know what to do! I don't know what the hell to do!"

Camille jerked her hand away and snatched at her coat, and before he could get to his feet, she had flung open the door. He heard her footsteps before he was able to take the dinner from the fire and run after her. Now what? he thought. Where in Paris has she gone? Likely to her sister's. Oh, not that; not that!

He hurried through the old palatial courtyard, now filled with peddler's carts and a tent with some straw on the ground and a wretched horse pawing it. Claude ran into the street. There were fewer gas lamps in this part of the city. He hurried past a café with its dim light showing through the frosty window and saw her in front of the closed dairy shop, her face against the window, her shoulders shaking under her coat.

He approached her tentatively, but she did not turn away from the dark window with its tin milk containers. "Why did you follow me?" she sobbed. "You don't want the baby! I don't need you. I could go home to my family. Then I would never see you again. I would never want to see you. They've been right about you all along!"

A horse and carriage trotted by, splashing them. Claude stood erect; though only a few moments of silence passed, he felt them to be hours. "Why do you say I don't want our child?" he said at last. "Even if we face some difficulties, it will work out." Still, under his breath he murmured, "What am I saying? What have I said?" He stood smiling slightly until he felt he had disappeared and only a bit of air remained where he stood, hardly visible under the gas lamp on the filthy snow. At least her sobs had subsided. He would have done anything to stop them.

She turned from the window, wiping her cheeks with her hands, the faintest look of joy in her eyes again. "But how will we manage?" she asked. "I could try to find modeling work until I'm ready to audition. Shall I do that, Claude?"

"I don't want you modeling for anyone but me and our close friends! And you'll start to show soon, won't you? Have you told your sister? Maybe your family will help us. I'll go home and speak to my father. It's just for a time until I can earn money more regularly. I'm trembling. I don't think I could hold a paintbrush if I tried, Minou!"

DURING THE TRAIN ride home through the countryside to Normandy, Claude thought of what words to say, biting his fingernails. As he descended at Le Havre and walked toward his father's shop by the water, he could not remember how long it had been since he'd written. And yet the letters from his aunt to him were affectionate, and his father's postscripts were warm. They had been thrilled at the great success of *The Woman in the Green Dress*, and Claude's father had written that perhaps he had been wrong to stand against his gifted son. The checks, never large, had mercifully continued, and for some time his aunt and his father had begged him to visit.

Large snowflakes drifted down here and there amid the masts and the water. He walked under the shop sign and opened the door.

Nothing had changed here; he peered into the shadows at the ropes, at the shelves of boxes, and then at the desk with its old paid bills speared on the iron spike of the paper holder. And there was his father, sitting back reading a newspaper through his spectacles. The lenses were not clean, and his old sweater was missing buttons.

Hearing the shop bell, he looked up. "Claude!" he exclaimed happily. "What a surprise! Your aunt will be delighted."

Claude thought, Growing older is mellowing the old man. He kissed his father's bristly cheeks and sank into the chair beside the desk beneath the hanging samples of rope. "How are you, Papa?" he asked.

Adolphe patted his rounder belly. "A little older and stouter, but the same, the same. Your brother's well. Your aunt keeps all clippings of your Salon success. Poor woman: she's living with me now all the time. Has rheumatism, walks with pain, stays home mostly. If business remains good I can help you a little each month for another year."

He folded his wide hands over his sweater vest and took off his glasses. "And you, my son? How is the rising young artist getting on?"

Claude set both hands on his knees. "*Pas mal*—not badly! Since last spring's success, I've had a great deal of interest in my painting. I was quite prepared to support myself without your kind monthly checks." He studied the inkwell on the desk and his voice dropped. "Unfortunately, another small problem has arisen that makes me need to ask you for a little more each month."

He hesitated. "I'm going to be a father." He looked harder at the desk, now touching the steel tips of the pens. "We didn't mean for it to happen," he said. "She's my model, comes from a very good family; her father's in silk exports. She's the woman in the green dress. We fell in love; you know how that is. I need a loan until I can see us through. It's a temporary thing."

Adolphe Monet rose. He paced the wide, creaking floorboards under the hanging ships' lanterns, hands clasped behind him, his heavy gray mustache concealing the expression of his mouth.

He has not mellowed so much, Claude thought.

His father said, "Ah, this isn't good. I was glad to see you, and now what are you telling me? You make hardly any money, Claude; you're all hope. Now you want a loan to help support some woman and child?"

Claude cried, "She's not just 'some woman.' She's a good girl, a beautiful girl! You don't know her."

"You can't do this, Oscar. Send the girl home to her family. Where was her self-respect? If she chose to behave herself so loosely, she must bear the consequence."

Claude jumped up, clenching his fists. "How can you say that?

Send her home? Never, never! I love her, Father. And what about your mistress? You have a love child, though you keep it hidden. You broke my mother's heart."

"Claude," said his father wearily, his voice echoing to the dusty hanging ropes. "Life is more complicated than you believe. What do you really know about me and your mother? You were a boy and judged things as a boy does. People's hearts are more complicated."

Adolphe Monet leaned on some wood boxes. "So you love her, eh? I think you do. Will her family help her?"

"I don't know."

"This is bad. I need to talk things over with your aunt. Come to the house toward dinnertime. I'll close early. I can't think anymore."

Customers came into the shop and Claude nodded and left. Wrapping his scarf tighter, he walked quickly through the wind. Then through the wet window of a fishermen's café, he made out his old schoolmate Marc reading a news journal. They had walked miles together, skipped school, once stolen a rowboat for an hour and took it so far out to sea that they almost were lost. His friend had grown fatter. He opened the door and walked in through the sawdust and the smell of fish soup, exclaiming, "Marc!"

"Monet!" Marc exclaimed, shaking Claude's hand vigorously. "What are you doing here in the dead of winter? I'm working at the family bank. Did you hear I'm engaged? Berthold's daughter, the younger one."

"I wish you all happiness, Marc. As for me . . ." Claude fell into a chair, patting his cold beard and blowing on his hands. He ordered soup, his face stern, and as he ate it, he told Marc a little of the story.

Marc slapped his hands on his knees. "You always had all the luck with girls, Monet! Your father will relent, of course. He's always relented with you. He brags about you all over town. It was just a shock to him, that's all: the son becoming a father. By the way, my older brother's in banking in Paris now. If you ever want work . . ."

"That sort? No, thanks!"

"Good luck, Monet."

"Yes, good luck to you too," Claude replied.

Darkness was falling as he walked up the hill to his old house. From outside he could hear the voices of his father and his aunt, and the sound of her cane as she walked back and forth. Poor woman! She had bought him his first colors and canvases. He mounted the stairs and sank into a hall chair, biting his lip. His right hand stretched inside his pocket, the thread pulled.

Finally a door opened and his father came through the shadows. Claude stood. "Well, Father?" he asked, almost wistfully.

"Claude, your situation's impossible. Send the girl home to her family and we'll continue to help you as long as we can. Admit you have made a mistake. Don't go forward with this thing that you cannot do."

THE WATER SLOSHED against the pilings, the gentle night wind nudged the sails, and the blue-black water lifted and released the boats by the wharf as an afterthought. The boards smelled of old fish and seaweed and all was deserted but for a watchman, whose pipe bowl glowed. A church bell rang two in the morning. Claude sat on a pile of nets, as he had for some hours, muttering under his breath, "What shall I do? What on earth shall I do?"

Finally he returned to his father's dark house and fell into bed fully dressed, feeling the presence of some of his old caricatures, which he had tacked on the walls years before. Maybe he could still sell them; he had to raise money.

Early in the morning he sat at his boyhood desk to write Camille. Six drafts he tore up and crumpled on the floor. "Sweetest love of my life," he wrote once more. *"Ma très chère fille!"*

My father won't help us. This is unexpected and terrible but we must make the best of it. I agree you should put off your theater audition until you feel more ready. Now you must go to your parents if you haven't done so already and see if they will do something. If they will not, go to the art schools and post that you are available to model but only clothed, dearest, or I couldn't bear it. A lot of artists know that painting of you and will be glad to have you as a model. My friends can't pay, but they may know others who can. You said you weren't averse to the idea. We must bring in some money. Don't go to Manet or Degas, because I would not trust them with any beautiful girl, let alone mine.

Now I hope you will hear me with patience and fortitude, darling Minou. I think I had best remain here for a few weeks. I want to paint some more seascapes and harbor views, which will surely sell in Paris, as I've sold a few there before. I intend to paint the lighthouse; you should see how marvelous it is. I also can slowly work on my father's good heart. Enclosed is all the money I have for now. Please take good care of yourself, and I send a thousand kisses on every part of your lovely body. By the way, have you finished reading Zola's Thérèse Raquin? *You were nearly done and you're such a fast reader.*

Claude

She will write back soon and tell me I have made the right decision, he thought as he mailed the letter and took his easel to the wharf. From there, over the tumbling water, he had a good view of the stone jetty reaching out into the sea with the rising white lighthouse. Lamps dotted the jetty, and warmly wrapped women walked carefully, sprayed by the sea. The water rose to the sky, the sky eased to the water.

Acquaintances stopped by to watch him, young sailors and captains, holding on to their hats. After a while he breathed more easily, slowly becoming the painting that had its own reason and was an entire world that held him. The people he painted quickly as outlines: it was sea and air that beckoned and left him breathless. He thought of nothing but that: the whole rest of his world disappeared. He vaguely felt the comforting daily presence of his father in his shop of nautical supplies and that there had been a truce. There would be enough time to make everything right.

Claude was so swept away by his work that it was not until late afternoon when cleaning his brushes that he remembered why he had come to Le Havre. She will agree with me, he thought.

Three days passed and neither she nor anyone else wrote him.

He wrote a second letter and sent it with the picture of the lighthouse that was propped on his bureau and again went out to paint, once more blissful until he saw a man and his pregnant wife walk by and sharply remembered. By the time he had been home five days, his concentration had left him. Coming back to his father's house on the hill late that day, he thought, surely a letter would be waiting.

More days passed and still there was no reply. Now the anxiety of it was mingled with the water and jetty each day, and his brush staggered a little. Surely the postman today had brought something from her, he thought. However indignant it might be, just to see his name in her hand would soothe him. He returned to the house early and wrote yet again, underlining much.

> *Why haven't you written? We are in an impossible situation. What has your family said? What of the modeling? I am painting here, trying to do something deep and dramatic enough to catch the attention of some Paris art dealer or gallery so that we can live a better life together. Don't you know I love you?*

He went on for several pages and posted the letter at the post office in the center of the town, also mailing intense letters to his friends.

Then he went out to paint the estuary but could not even see it. Staring at the waters, he saw only his room in the Marais. He imagined Camille sitting on the bed's edge crying, unable to be comforted. She rose to pack, hurling her things in a trunk. Their room was left empty, the windows open. She had moved back to her

parents'. Claude threw all his paints into the box and hurried back
to his father's house, his long dark hair blowing against his unshaven face.

His aunt was making an apple tart in the kitchen, moving slowly,
holding on to the stove, her cane resting against the table. She poured
him a glass of wine and pulled a letter from her apron pocket for him.

Frédéric had written. He tore it open at once.

> *Claude,* mon ami, *you know I was away, and as soon as I
> came back and got your note I hurried over to your room, where I
> found the poor girl sick, confined to bed, throwing up a lot, weep-
> ing. Her sister was there yesterday and told me I must not dare
> mention your name! Her family has sent food but says they will
> do nothing more unless she forgets you and goes away to have the
> child in secret and gives it up for adoption when it is born. Need-
> less to say, this made her quite hysterical.*
>
> *The poor girl, Claude! She's so distraught none of us knows
> what to do. She believes you have deserted her forever in spite of
> your loving letters, and talked of ending the pregnancy. Do you
> remember that pretty blond model who did that and bled to
> death? I don't believe Camille would do such a thing. If no one
> else has written to you, it's because they don't know whether to
> take her side or yours.*
>
> *Well, my friend, you have got yourself into a damn mess, but
> what can be done? Come back and we'll all stand beside you in
> this as we can.*
>
> *Yours in all affection, F. Bazille*

Claude did not see the kitchen then, but only his Minou lying on
the sheets of some abortionist, pale in death. He saw her limp hand
dangling off the bed's edge.

When he looked up he noticed his aunt gazing down at him tenderly, a few stands of her gray hair escaping from her white cap. "I
must go home," he said, standing slowly.

"Yes, we knew you would."

"You needn't help me anymore. I'll do this on my own."

"I also knew you'd say that, Oscar," said his aunt, kissing him.

The next morning Claude packed his things, took his new paint-ings, and caught the first train to Paris, sitting in a third-class car, hand clenched on his knee. The winter sky outside was dull, and the sound of the gulls was soon lost under the wheels of the train. He whispered, Frédéric's right. We'll manage. I have nothing to give her now, but I will one day. I love her. I love her.

1 8 6 8

I would have bought paint but your mother needed the money.
—CAMILLE PISSARRO IN A LETTER TO HIS SON LUCIEN

CAMILLE DID NOT WELCOME HIM; SHE PUSHED HIM SO hard when she opened the door of their room that he almost lost his balance. All his clothes were heaped in a pile by the door, a few of the lace cuffs of which he was so proud half hidden under his new trousers. "There you are!" she cried, her mother's contemptuous look about her mouth, her pale face flushed with anger. "If you'd returned one moment later, they would have been given to the rag-man!"

"The ragman!" he cried, putting down his easel. He stood between her and his best suit. "You didn't answer my letters. I was painting. I really was coming back almost at once."

"I don't believe you!" she shouted.

"I needed only a little more time." He felt both righteous and humble, but when he glanced up again he saw the terror in her eyes. She fought tears; he could see how angry she was at herself for weeping. "You make me pregnant and then leave me," she gasped. "You can go back to . . . that place and paint again. That place where your philistine father won't help us."

"Your family won't help either."

They stood glaring at each other and she plucked a crumpled handkerchief from his pile of clothes and wiped her eyes. "I didn't want to throw them out," she said. "I wouldn't have in the end, but I have no one really but you now. No one. You understand that. I want to see where you were born and stand at your side when you paint. You are . . . all the baby and I have in the world."

Slowly they gathered his clothes, folded them, and humbly returned them to the wardrobe and drawers. He found the shirt she had bought him last Christmas. They laughed a little about his passion for his lace cuffs. They stood close, almost knocking into each other, apologizing with another small laugh, putting the room in order. He watered the potted plant, which had withered in his absence. The clutter of dresses and paintings and books seemed to close in around him to protect both of them. By nightfall he felt he had never been away.

"How is your dear aunt?" she asked as she shook out her hair to brush it before bed. "Oh well, well," he replied. Now the sound of the sea had utterly left him, and all the world extended no further than her once again gentle looks and the corners of this room.

SLOWLY THAT SPRING their lives began to change.

Camille's body swelled every day, and as it did she moved farther away from her family. Before her pregnancy she would sometimes meet with friends from her former life, drinking coffee or shopping with them. She drew away from this also. In late spring, when she was visibly with child, she and Claude encountered two young women she knew at the theater. The women looked oddly at Camille's figure and at her finger, which was bare of any wedding ring. When they had entered their box and she and Claude began the steep climb to the high gallery where they were sitting, she whispered, "Did you see how they looked at you, Claude? In their narrow hearts, they envied me!" Yet there was a slight breathiness in her voice that showed their expressions had hurt her in spite of her light defiance.

She did not go for coffee with them again, but spent many hours with Julie and Lise sewing baby clothes. She embroidered exquisitely. She went a few times to see her sister's fragile newborn baby girl but did not ask Annette or her parents to visit her. She knew very well what they thought of where she lived, amid bricklayers and craftsmen and seamstresses.

CAMILLE'S WATER BROKE on an early hot August morning when she was walking across the floor while flies buzzed about the room. Claude sent a boy from the café with messages and the midwife arrived shortly. "This is no place for you, monsieur!" she told him. "Go for a walk. Take the dog. Come back in a few hours."

"Hours?" he murmured.

He took Victoire on the leash, but did not go far; he sat down on the stairs, wincing each time he heard Camille scream. He left, walked about the neighborhood, and hurried back. "It is progressing," the midwife told him when he opened his door a little.

I will never touch her again, never, he thought. He went out once more with Victoire until he began to count how shadows moved on the stones of buildings as the day wore on. He sat down at a café table and ordered wine and left without drinking it. He ran back.

He heard her cry out and then another, higher-pitched cry.

He raced up the stairs.

Camille lay in bed, one fair plump arm outside the cover, her face dark and tired. By her, wrapped tightly in a soft cloth, was a wizened face with a bit of black sticky hair. The basin of water the midwife had left on the table was tinged as if scarlet paint had been mixed with it. He knelt and covered Camille's hand with kisses. As he rocked his newborn son, he thought: Thus we begin, so small and unblemished, and how complicated we become!

He woke at two, reaching for her, but she was a dark shape pacing the room holding this small, strange new thing. "Oh, look at him, Claude!" she whispered, lighting the lamp and sitting down beside him with the tiny baby. "Have you ever seen anything so beautiful?

It was worth any pain; it was worth everything. I care only about him and you!"

"Yes, he's beautiful," he whispered with awe.

But for weeks after, the baby cried half the night. Just as Claude got to sleep, he would be startled by the piercing shrieks. "It's crying," he muttered, exhausted.

Camille rose and walked the child, but the little one would not cease to cry. "Well, what is the matter with it? What does it want?" he glowered from his pillow. "Can't you do something?"

"They cry. Haven't you heard them in the house?"

"It doesn't mean ours has to."

"And his name is Jean!" she said fiercely and protectively.

"Merde!" he muttered. He stumbled into his clothes and went out, but he could hear the howling as if it persecuted him. The child seemed to cry down to him, You don't love me. He made his way back and took up the light, little thing. "How can anyone so small cry so loudly?" he whispered. "Did you feed him?"

"Of course I fed him," she replied.

"How long are they like that?"

"They change, Julie says."

Not only life changed in those months, but his room as well. His paintings were pushed to the corner as the room filled with so many things. There were baby garments from her sister; from Julie came hand-knit baby caps, from Auguste's mother pots of food and advice, from Lise constant visits and cooking, from Sisley's sweetheart a carriage to walk the baby, which Claude carried up and down the stairs. His aunt sent a generous check, not telling his father. Camille's parents sent a cradle draped with printed cotton. Once, passing it when his son was not there, he kicked it slyly. It rocked; the fabric danced. He resented that they had to accept help from anyone.

Once more the play scripts and props were piled on the dining table, and Lise came regularly to practice. She had presented two monologues before the directors at the Odéon last spring and been engaged as an ingenue. Together at the table with coffee bowls amid the scripts, she and Camille wrote to the Comédie-Française on Camille's behalf. They were also looking for an ingenue. Ten weeks after Jean had been born, a letter came saying that they would hear her Thursday morning.

Claude walked with her to the venerable theater and inside past the huge painted sets on their rollers. He and Camille stood in the wings between a tangle of rope on the floor and an intricately painted set of ancient Rome. "Wait outside," she begged him. "I'm too nervous." Then she kissed him and walked on toward the stage with a few other actors who were also being heard that day.

He was pacing back and forth in the alley behind the theater near trash boxes and an old cart when she came from the door, calling his name. She walked swiftly toward him, her face very bright. "Oh, Claude!" she said. "They liked me. I'm engaged to begin rehearsals after Christmas. Now you need only support us until I can help!" He nodded. He knew from Auguste how little young actresses were paid but decided to say nothing. Not for the world would be disturb her happiness, and besides, he did not need her to earn a living. He would do it.

LATE NOVEMBER, AS dingy as the skirts of a prostitute. Crowded omnibuses moved through the streets, the drivers huddled on their high seats outside above the horses, reins in their gloved hands. In such wet, muddy weather he would rather have stayed home painting by the window, but their money was low. The few paintings Claude had sold during the pregnancy had carried them through, and he had paid some old bills with the gift from his aunt.

Wearing his best suit and with his portfolio in hand, he walked over the Seine to the rue Saint-Germain and through the courtyard of a *hôtel particulier* where he had sold his work before. He was always fascinated by the apartments of the middle and upper classes, so beautiful with their tall doors, their molding, their wainscoting. So will our Paris rooms look soon, he thought as the maid took his coat and hat.

Madame Mathieu and another woman were embroidering together behind a silver chocolate pot. "Why Monsieur Monet!" she cried. "Will you have a cup of chocolate and a cake? Do you recall, Susanne, that lovely painting of the church in our bedroom that we bought from monsieur last year?"

The chocolate was creamy and sweet. Claude dabbed at his upper lip and mustache with his handkerchief. "I have some more paintings to show you, this time of Paris parks in summer," he said charmingly. "You said you would like more."

"How kind of you to remember!" the woman exclaimed.

He placed the canvases on the long sofa opposite them. The dull light from the window did nothing for the paintings and he thought to ask his hostess to open the curtains more. Still, both women stood and looked carefully at them, and then at him. Had he been too light in his tone? He suddenly felt they would have had more than the paintings from him if he had been willing. In such a house a few years before, the husband had been away and Claude had gone upstairs. The nipples of the woman had been dark against the white scalloped sheets; he could not remember her name.

Ridiculous to recall! He brought his thoughts back to the room.

"Oh, I do want at least one, perhaps a whole set," Madame Mathieu exclaimed. "Unfortunately, I can't purchase them now. Can you come again in the spring? That won't be inconvenient?"

He knocked on a few more doors that morning, doors of men who had bought his work in the past, but their servants declared that monsieur was not home and Claude should call again. He stopped at a café for coffee, looking through the window at the people walking by, now and then writing his options on a bit of news-journal column torn away, crossing off the names of the patrons and writing "spring" next to one. With some reluctance he left for the damp street again.

He turned to the shop of the frame maker Isaac Clément on the rue Bonaparte.

The shop was small, paintings for sale in racks wherever he looked and examples of every sort of frame hung from the ceiling. A sleepy gray cat rubbed against his trousers and he knelt to scratch it behind the ears. Clément had framed all of Claude's work over the past few years.

"So, Monet," Clément said, without looking up from painting a frame with a small brush dipped in gold paint. "What brings you here?"

"I was hoping you'd buy a few of my paintings."

Claude placed his six small canvases of the city parks and gardens on the racks in front of the others. Clément stroked his gray mustache, silent for a few moments. "You paint like a bird sings," he said. "You know how a bird sings, Monet? Even if no other bird can hear him, he hopes to be heard, or he doesn't care. But these look half finished. You don't want to work more on them?"

"They are finished," Claude said stiffly.

"That's not what people say of your work, or that of your friends! They say they're sketches. They don't want to hang sketches on their walls."

Claude repacked his paintings and left, walking down the boulevard Saint-Germain toward the church. He had not sold a painting in some time. If Camille had to send to her family for help, he felt he could not bear it.

A cart rode by, splashing him.

Dusk was falling as he arranged the paintings against the church wall, their bright green trees and the soft pale dresses of the women strolling beneath them giving a faint glow to the dull street. Many people passed; some looked, and some did not bother. Just as he was about to pack everything away, an older English couple stopped and bought two. When they left he had to lean against the church wall for a time before he was able to pack away his things and go home.

~ ⚬ ~

BUT FOR THE birth of the child, which seemed to bring them all together, the painters had not met as much since the previous spring, when their work had once again been refused for the state Salon, even Claude's magical painting *Four Women in the Garden*. That had stunned him, and he had been slow to tell Camille about it.

Now they had called a meeting at the studio on the rue de Furstenberg. Claude came up the stairs late, pausing to listen to their voices. Seven or eight of his friends were sitting on chairs or on the floor, all wearing their coats. The room was almost as damp as the street; likely wood was in short supply. Frédéric was between checks from home and had been reprimanded for the money he was spending on this foolish pursuit of art.

Claude rubbed his hands by the glow of the small stove fire. "Sorry I'm late," he said over his shoulder. "The baby cried half the night again. Is this your fault, Frédéric? You're godfather."

Pissarro shook his head. "They stop within the first ten years," he said, his kind face now morose. "Or so I hear. Julie's pregnant again. I love them, but how . . . You get used to one and then there's another."

Auguste indicated the one empty chair. "Don't feel bad you're late," he said. "You missed a gloomy talk. What's happening to us? We haven't been to the café in months. Claude, here's the bad news. We have to admit it. None of us has the money to front for a private exhibition this winter."

Claude nodded grimly. "I thought so."

"We'll do it next year for certain. Things will look up by then. Maybe you'll be famous." He made a wry face. "Meanwhile we've been sitting here trying to figure out how we'll even pay our rent this winter. I may have a portrait commission. Pissarro's painting blinds now. What will you do?"

Claude sat down, touching the coffeepot on the table; it was cold. He rubbed the back of his neck. "I don't know. I can't get a good art dealer to look at my work. They say they can't sell it. I sell something and then I'm scrounging again. I have enough for a short while thanks to a street sale, but Paris has lost its charm for me. I'd like to just escape to Le Havre for the winter and paint."

He pulled a letter from his pocket. "My old mentor Boudin is traveling this winter with his wife and has offered me the use of his second cottage on the sea. He wrote that there's a maritime exhibition in Le Havre; he feels I could walk off with a prize and then sell those seascapes for a lot. I could borrow them back for our exhibition next year. But I can't ask Camille to come because her rehearsals start soon."

Still, when he left his friends, he was so much back by the sea in his mind that he hardly noticed the old newspapers blowing down the street. Snowflakes landed on the journals in front of the kiosk and he turned toward home, thinking only of the sea. He was running as he reached his house and took the stairs two steps at a time.

Camille was sewing by the lamp, singing softly, one foot rocking the cradle in which his son slept blissfully. Since Jean's birth she had kept the room beautifully; pillows were brightly covered in scraps, the floor was swept, food was neatly put away. He gazed at her, thinking, She is truly a portrait of mother and child.

He pulled up a chair near her, kissed her, took away her sewing, and held her hands. "Here's the situation," he blurted and told her his thoughts. "I feel it's the best opportunity for my work, but we said we'd stay together, and you have your rehearsals. I couldn't ask you for such a sacrifice. And we'd need to give back the key here. I couldn't afford both."

She took a few more stitches in the soft linen baby dress. "I would have come anyway; you know that," she said. "I don't want you to miss any chances and I know how hard you work for us. But there's no sacrifice. I wrote a letter to the manager at the Comédie-Française this morning. I've decided not to accept the engagement."

"But why, Minou?" he cried. He looked around the house quickly. He had been working so hard he had not noticed that the scripts and crown of papier-mâché were nowhere in sight. "Why, after all your hard work?"

"I simply can't do that to my family. My audition was very successful but my mother begged me not do to it; it would so hurt my father. He's been patient with our living together and I can at least not disgrace our family name on a theater poster. And anyway, now I can go with you."

Claude bent to kiss her hair. "You can meet my father!" he exclaimed. "I know he's coming around. My aunt is longing to meet you."

"Oh, I'd like to meet your family! I've longed to see where you lived! From your paintings, it's so real to me!"

He stroked her hair tenderly, winding a loose strand around his finger. "That was hard for you to decide about the theater," he said. "You're so gifted! My poor love!"

"Yes, it was. Very hard. I'll envy Lise."

"You can decide differently in the future."

"Perhaps I will. I shouldn't let them influence me so much."

He can only see things from one point of view, but have there ever been geniuses who could see things any other way?

—Henri Bang on Claude Monet

Boudin's small stone fisherman's cottage sat back a short distance from the seacoast; it lay a few miles north of Le Havre and not far from the huge natural stone arch within the sea called Étretat, which Claude had always wanted to paint. The cottage consisted of a few rooms and a low attic, which still smelled of the old apples that had been stored there. It was not Boudin's main house in Honfleur, where the artist lived with his wife, but a place where he retreated to paint; several unfinished paintings were stacked against the china cabinet and many hung on the wall. Every drawer and door stuck and groaned when opened, and you could not get away from the sound of the sea; you felt you were in it.

Claude had sometimes cooked fish here with Boudin.

It was a plain, masculine place that long before had belonged to a retired fisherman; it was not a place, he thought, for Paris dresses. It was far away from the huge new department stores, the opera, and the boulevards. Would Camille like it?

But she exclaimed, "It's enchanting." He saw in her bright eyes the girl who wanted adventures. She stayed by the window, arms clasped over her breasts, mouth opened breathlessly as she watched the waves crash and retreat again. Victoire climbed on a chair at her side, quite hysterical at the sight of the fierce white swooping gulls.

Boudin had arranged for the wife of a local fisherman, a plump woman over fifty with worn, thick hands, to help them. She had a fish soup waiting. "I brought a cradle from the attic and wiped it down well," she said. "It's not been used these fifty years. Give me the little one. There's fresh linens there and on your bed, madame."

They ate the fish soup and the woman rocked the child. "Take madame out, monsieur," the woman urged fondly. "Your babe's asleep already and madame is longing to walk down to the sea. If you look very hard, madame, you imagine England there across the water."

They left the cottage hand in hand. The dry high grass blew in the wind, and gulls shrieked above.

Light wind tugged at the scarf Camille had used to cover her hair as they approached a pile of black rocks that led out into the sea. Claude climbed up on one and held out his hand. "Come out with me and walk a little!" he called. "It's slippery; hold on to me."

Holding hands, they slowly made their way from one rock to another out into the sea, the water lapping about them. "Oh, what an adventure being here!" she cried. "I was so envious when you were here without me! It will be lovely just to be alone with you, without our friends and my family."

They stood kissing on the rocks with the sea spraying playfully on the bottoms of his trousers and her hem. Yes, just us, he thought, dazed. And the way she pushes against me! It mystified and thrilled him how she would change from the demure girl to such a sexual woman. She moved her hand down to his crotch and cupped him.

He drew in his breath sharply; all he was seemed to be rushing down to where her hand enclosed him. He whispered, "Can you see all the mussels on the rock? They are somewhat like barnacles, which even cling to the flesh of the great whales out in the sea when they dive so deep! And—I know this for sure—there are creatures who can only be pacified by munching on a beautiful young woman. They eat her up very slowly." He dropped his voice. "Beginning at her toes, then her pretty legs and thighs."

"Unless she eats them first, you see. Can we go back and send the woman home very quickly?"

"There's a more secret place," he whispered as best he could.

They climbed down to the wet sand, where he pulled her steadily toward a rough little windowless shack and opened the door. Within it was almost dark but for the light coming through a few loose boards. It smelled of old nets, seaweed, and wood. She felt for him; they laughed, stumbling. He threw some tarps onto the floor, and she dropped down before him, pulling him on top of her.

They turned over and over, tussling with each other, her hem wet against him, her leg over him. She pulled hard, and one of his trouser buttons popped. He felt the cold on his bare back where his shirt pulled up—intense, biting cold. And she bit as well, his ears and shoulder, not gently but hard. They rolled and laughed and a box fell. She smelled like salt.

"I'm stronger, madame!" he said. Outside, he heard the sounds of the sea and the wind, as if it were trying to get inside. Now he held her down, looking into her bright shining eyes. How beautiful she was! "I'll have my way with you, and then I'm at your mercy. This is a lesson in maritime life. Now, concerning those creatures that come from the sea to devour women, I'll show you how they begin at the toes and slowly mount to the thighs with fast little tongues . . ."

There was never anything warmer than her body as he tasted it. He led her to near explosion and then pulled away again. She slapped his shoulder in protest. After a time, when he could bear no more, he moved into her and whispered in her ear, "Now I will go very slowly, as the sea moves; very slowly, until you can't bear it."

She reached for her passion, pulling him down.

"Now you know my secret! I am the sea." He felt then that he would die of loving her. He lay back and she bent above him, her hair loose, falling over his belly. He felt he could not and then he did.

They could hardly stand for the cold and their feelings, and they stumbled back to the cottage holding on to each other, hearing the great pull of the ocean behind them.

"Goodnight, madame and monsieur," said the woman. "Baby's asleep and bread is rising for the morning."

HE RODE THE public coach the few miles to Le Havre the next day and submitted his four best seascapes to the annual maritime exhibition that Boudin had spoken of in his letter.

In the next few weeks he painted the sea passionately and took long walks with Camille, yet under it all he was always aware of his work in the old town hall where it was hanging and wondered what would happen with it. In a way he wished to hide himself in the cottage with his small family and the dog, only painting, away from people's opinions. They had enough money left for a month more and he had canvases to last that long; a sale would come. There were few other cottages about, and they were alone with each other and the baby. They read to each other; they were always together.

A few times a week, they wrapped Jean warmly, took Victoire on a leash, and walked the road bounded by high wild grass to the small shop where they bought provisions and received letters. Friends wrote, but the one letter he waited for did not come. At last, in mid-December, the old proprietress handed them a small package from Le Havre wrapped in brown paper.

They put the package in their basket with the cream and the to-bacco, and headed home quickly. He hardly dared unwrap it. She took it from him and prayed over it before they opened it. In a small box lay a silver medal engraved with a ship.

"I've won second prize!" he shouted. He picked her up and swung her around the room.

"I knew you could!" They sat on the floor by the fire with Jean on her lap and the dog sniffing them, examining the medal. He draped his arm around her, wanting her close.

He said, "Now people will read about it and hurry to buy the paintings. I'll have commissions. I'll paint and paint. We'll go to Le Havre and see friends. *Now* I can face my father! I'll come back to Paris triumphant with more commissions in my pocket! And we'll move to better rooms and invite your family to dinner. It's all happening, Minou. This, the exhibition with all of us in the autumn!"

They ran out the next morning to catch the first coach to town, where he burst into his brother's shop. On the table was a newspaper opened to the page announcing the winning paintings. He introduced Camille and shook his brother's hand. He asked, "Does our father know about my prize? The shop was closed when I went by."

"He's gone away for a few months with auntie. It's for her health; he's taken her to the south. So, Oscar, do you expect to make a sale soon?"

"*A* sale!" he exclaimed. "I'll make many sales."

His brother dropped his voice and looked over at Camille in her gray wool dress as she held her child in one arm and with the other hand browsed through engravings of old Le Havre in a rack. "You have found yourself a real lady, Oscar," he said. "I wish you the best of everything."

THROUGH ALL THIS he painted: outside when the sun was warm and the wind not too fierce, inside through the window when it was too cold. One day as he painted he noticed her carefully placing a small candle in another window. "For the *Fête des lumières,*" she told him, pinning back the curtain. "If the *Sainte Vierge* with her child comes down our road, she knows she will be welcome."

"Well, ask her in for coffee if you see her."

"Silly!" Camille said, setting out the bowls for dinner. "Don't you know Christmas is coming? You're a perfect heathen! Can we go to your brother's Christmas Day? And to Mass Christmas Eve? You will come!" Passing him, she pulled his thick hair affectionately and began to sing. "Painting, you're always painting!" she teased.

He put down his brushes and kissed her hand. "I have something for you for Christmas," he whispered in her ear. "You must wait until after Mass! Yes, I will go, heathen that I am, and all to please you."

On Christmas Eve, they set out on the road away from the sea, carrying Jean. The night was full of stars. Inside the small stone church dedicated to the protection of sailors, he looked around curiously at the crèche and the candles in front of it. The consecration bell rang hard in the cold air. He watched her kneeling and thought about her rare bursts of spiritual fervor. Now he felt ashamed that he had something so insignificant to give her.

Still, when they came home again he fetched it, at her insistence. It was under his socks in the drawer, wrapped in fragile paper. She unwrapped it carefully. It was a ring of dried grass he had made one day. "Minou," he asked, "it's not the real one yet, but will you marry me and be mine always?" She nodded and kissed him. "There will be a real one someday," he assured her again.

"Dance with me!"

"I'm not so good at it!"

"Oh, please do!" she said. Outside, he heard the sea pull in and out. With the fragile ring on her finger, they danced, dipping through the room and into the bedroom and back again. He sang a few songs in his light baritone voice. In the middle of one of the songs they heard a knock on the door. They looked at each other and heard the knock again.

"You go! I hear Jean from the bedroom!"

"Coming!" he cried gaily, crossing the room.

He flung open the door.

The old woman from the shop stood there. "*Joyeux Noël,* monsieur," she said politely. "My son was driving me home from church in his cart and I heard the singing. I've not seen you lately. I hoped that perhaps you had the amount you owe me on your bill."

"Ah, the bill!" he said softly. "Give me until next week, madame! I'm expecting money soon. *Je vous souhaite aussi un joyeux Noël!*"

"Just a well-wisher for the season," he explained when Camille returned. As they ate the late *réveillon* dinner of Christmas Eve, he looked at the guttering candle in the window and felt for certain that the old woman was not the saintly person expected this holy night.

THAT WAS THE first night he did not sleep well but tossed and tossed, listening to the sound of the sea. She slept deeply and peacefully, as if nothing could ever disturb her. He rose and, lighting the lamp, looked at the paintings he had made here. He felt the great pull of his other maritime paintings hanging alone in the town hall with yet no offers for them. He felt them sad and abandoned. And yet as he knelt there by his new work in the cottage, hearing the sound of the sea, its only murmur to him was "Paint me." It called to him like a lover. How could he paint, though? He had no more empty canvases. He stayed awake until dawn, waiting for the sun to rise, and then fell into a deep sleep.

"I can't go to my brother's today," he told her when he opened his eyes to her leaning above him. "I couldn't sleep." And yet he felt her sadness as she moved away, this girl who with her warmth and her charm so glittered in the company of others. Still, he could not bear to have his brother ask cheerfully, "Sold anything yet, Oscar?"

The day after Christmas he took the coach into town. He turned his back on the town hall with his paintings inside, and walked grimly to the art-supply shop of old Gravier. It hardly seemed to have changed since he had last been there. Gravier moved more slowly and squinted at him. "My dear Monet," he said, smiling. "It's been a while."

"Can you extend me credit for a few canvases and a little paint?"

The old man sighed. "There's a rumor you owe money all around this town since your last visit, that even your Paris creditors know you're here. You owe me as well. Not good, old friend. If you had stayed with caricatures, you would be a wealthy man. I will give you three canvases and some paint."

Claude walked back to save the coach fare, his face in the wind, past the grocery shop, where he stopped for his letters alone, murmuring to the old woman that he would pay her soon; they had food left in the house and they would manage for a time. He walked past the shack where he had made love with Camille. Surely a sale will come tomorrow, he thought.

At least Frédéric had written. A few minutes from the cottage he stopped to read the letter.

> *Claude, I changed studios to one on the narrow rue Visconti. They wanted more rent on the other. All of our same pictures are hung on the walls and your big easel's in good light. Auguste is sleeping here sometimes. Yes, we're all around. Paul's in the city and Manet keeps painting that red-haired model. Sisley's father died, so he's as poor as any of us now. I hope you and Camille and my godson are well.*
>
> *The date of my marriage has been set for two years from this autumn. To be honest with you, this is what kept me from writing, admitting this. I'm not ready to marry, to take on my father's life, and yet life goes on even if we're not ready for it. It pulls us along. Sometimes I wish we were twenty-four again, all of us crowded in the studio.*
>
> *Meanwhile I expect you are doing wonderfully there and have sold several pictures as you hoped. I saw in the papers here that you won a medal, as I knew you would.*
>
> *F. Bazille*

I can't write him for help, Claude thought as he put the letter in his pocket. I just can't.

❦

HE HAD ONE more canvas and hesitated to use it, and so he ceased to paint. He slept badly, was up every night looking out at the steady sea as if it might tell him something. He was so ashamed he could not tell Camille, though she sensed it. He was amazed at how tied together they were; when his moods fell, hers followed. She burned what she cooked when she did cook. They tracked in sand and it was not swept and the dishes were not washed. They could no longer afford the fisherman's wife to help and missed her cheerful presence. He dreaded that his old teacher would return and find his cottage in such a state.

Outside the window the sea was docile and the dirt road largely empty but for the daily milk cart. Each day they spoke less until they ceased to speak much at all, but he could sense their feelings rising so much that they had to struggle through them to walk across the floor.

She spoke first one gray, windy January morning when he had buried himself in a book. "Oh, Claude, what is happening to us here? We see no one, we go nowhere, and all's silent between us." She jumped up and held out her hand. "At least walk with me! We can talk a little. You're not sleeping. It's bad, isn't it?"

With her forced joy she sounded like her sister. "Everything's fine," he muttered.

"It's not and I know it."

"We owe a little money, and when I sell the maritime pictures, I'll cheer up. There! I can't tell you how disappointed I'll feel if no one buys them."

She sat down on a footstool beside him, took his book away, and draped her arms over his knees. She looked away, then at the fire. "Our problems begin when we don't tell each other things," she began earnestly. She blinked a little and hesitated and then shook her head.

"I'll tell you something you've wanted to know for a time, I think," she said, stammering a little. He could see she had been biting her nails again, down to the quick. "About what happened when I was sixteen. I ran away with a young actor called David. It was my first experience. I found out he was married. I wrote him for a time after he went to Canada. I was writing him when we first met."

He looked wearily at the waves and the gulls from the window. "Were you writing him when we first knew each other? When you were engaged? And did the letters to him continue? I am not in the mood to hear this today, Minou, when I can't manage so much."

She rose suddenly and looked down at him, appalled. "Why did you answer me like that when I told you my secret? It took courage to tell it. We left our friends and my family for this place. Lise writes me of what a marvelous season it is in the theater, and I'm missing her performances. I gave up my own theater engagement to come with you."

"You gave it up for your father."

"That's not the truth; I gave it up for you."

"Oh, indeed! Was that before you knew I was going away? "

She crossed the room to the shelf that held their remaining sup- plies—some beans, some coffee, a few sausages—and stood before them as if protecting them. Her long face was flushed with unhappi- ness. "If you wanted simply to be silent and shut yourself away from everyone and from me, why did you bring me here? I haven't seen a soul for days and I can't bear it, I can't. You're up half the night. I miss my sister. I miss my friends, and you're a ghost. Yes, you're a ghost."

He jumped up, gathered together his coat, easel, paint box, and the last empty canvas, and left the cottage.

Outside, he turned away from the sea toward the farms inland. He walked down the road resolutely, his scarf blowing, slowing a little. The field in front of him was covered with snow, as was the dark wood, rough-hewn fence. He set up his easel, fixing the canvas to it. A few lines in charcoal marked his boundaries. The snow was so many shades of white.

Now that he painted he could breathe a little. It didn't matter that it was cold. Damn the cold.

The fence was no longer empty. A single black magpie huddled there, contemplating the field. Claude painted it swiftly. It might have taken a few minutes or more. The bird turned its head and stared dark-eyed, then leapt into the air; it took flight and was gone. Yet now as he finished, painting a bit more slowly, a calm returned to him he had not felt in weeks. He had told the canvas what he could not tell her. He could manage her now. He was sorry he had been so abrupt with her and that he had stayed away several hours. His watch, which he only now looked at, told him the truth.

He walked toward home slowly, and as he came closer he heard the wailing of his son.

The door to the cottage was open, the fire was out, and Jean was shrieking until his little face was red. He was cold, and his diaper was soaking wet. Claude lifted him, covering his tiny body with a blanket, and rocked him while the boy tried to nurse from Claude's coat between screams. Victoire had made a puddle in a corner.

Camille was nowhere to be found.

He discovered the last of the clean diapers that the laundress had left and changed the baby. The child still screamed, puffing out his little chest. Claude bundled him in blankets and ran out, shouting Camille's name. The sky was bitter gray and the wild grass bent, defeated before the wind.

Now darkness was coming. He sheltered the baby in his arms.

He had gone a short distance when he saw the shed where they had made love a few months before. An elderly cat looked at him, terrified. It ran around the side of the worn gray boards. Instinct made him run down across the sand. Inside it was quiet, yet he knew.

He opened the door.

The shed was dark and smelled of rotting wood and salty nets. An oilcloth was spread over the floor, and Camille was sitting on it, absolutely silent. She looked as if she had been there all day. He called her name but she did not answer. He knelt, shaking her shoulder, calling again and again.

She turned and looked at him indifferently.

He grasped her against him. "What is it?" he cried. "What is it? How long have you been gone? The cottage was cold and the baby was . . . the baby was. . . . You can't just go. You have to take care of the baby."

"I want to go home," she said.

She began to cry. He tried to give her the baby but she pushed him away. "I don't want you," she sobbed. "I don't want either of you. We're almost out of food. They won't give me credit at the store. I want my old life back, my pretty room, my dances, theater, people, laughter."

His head was pounding. "You have to feed the baby."

"A letter came when you were out. They've confiscated your paintings from the exhibition for debt. You're a dreamer, just a dreamer. Now I'm here and I miss everyone. I feel so empty. We're alone and you don't talk to me!"

He heard her words with a terrible shock, sitting down on the cold floor, rocking the baby as best he could, his ears pierced by the child's hungry shrieking. I have to keep the child warm. Who can feed the child if not her? he thought. She just sat there, her back turned to both of them; the child shrieked, and Claude's paintings were gone. Where had they taken them? How could he pay his debt? And what was the matter with her? Even if she had found the letter, how could she leave the child and let the fire go out? How could she refuse to feed their son?

"Yes, yes," he stammered. "It's all true. I'm careless with money, and maybe I have too much faith in myself. But Jean's helpless and innocent. I beg you, feed him. We can discuss everything later."

She took the child, and as Jean suckled, her face softened. "I left the door open?" she asked. "I don't remember. How long was I gone? I feel so odd."

"I'll comfort you," he answered, touching his son's head. "I love you."

Slowly they walked back to the cottage with the child. He made a fire and a thin barley soup. He read the letter about the paintings and shook his head. He could not eat. He sat across the table from her, reaching out to touch her hand. He said, "What will I do?"

She was utterly calm again now. "Claude," she said. "I was wrong to get so upset and run out. We'll raise the money to get your paintings back, and meanwhile, you have the new ones you've made. We must return to Paris. I miss my sister and our friends. We need our friends. We must stick together. We're too alone here. You're not just a dreamer. I believe in you."

He could hardly trust his voice. "We've no money for the train."

"We can sell our books and I'll pawn my wool dresses."

"Your dresses? *Putain!* Minou, your dresses?"

He sought her in bed that night, parting her legs and moving into her. She clung to him. "You're not empty at all," he said. "I shall fill you with all that I am."

"I shall give you all that I am."

"Only love me. I am the sea."

1869

What can be said about a man who is interested in nothing but his painting?

—CLAUDE MONET

THE JOURNEY HOME HAD BEEN DIFFICULT: MANY HOURS in the third-class train car with its hard seats and no heat, carrying their lighter trunks, his paintings by his side and all three of them shivering with colds and blowing their noses into damp handkerchiefs. In Paris he sent Camille and Jean to stay with her sister while he slept at the studio. He was feverish, and Frédéric gave him his bedroom so he could rest.

In the middle of the night, he heard Frédéric walking about, and rose in his nightshirt. The studio was dark but for the table lamp, and the easels stood in shadow with the paintings above them. "Couldn't sleep?" Claude yawned. "This feels like old times. You were always pacing at night. What smells so good?"

"Julie brought some beef broth before and I heated it a little, thinking it would put me back to sleep. Sit down and we'll have some." Claude pulled out his old chair. He looked down at the chipped soup bowl placed before him. For a few minutes there was nothing but the sound of their pewter spoons against the bowls.

Then Claude let his spoon hover as he slowly began to tell his friend what had happened, making light of it when he could. He could see Frédéric's long hand press down on the table. *"Ah putain!"*

Frédéric said. "Maybe I could have done something. You didn't let me know."

"I wanted to manage things for myself, I felt until the end I could. Only sometimes I wish my life was as easy as yours, *mon ami*."

"My life isn't easy," Frédéric replied thoughtfully in his low voice, gazing at the flickering lamp between them. "You should know that. Look at me. I'm not in love and I'm marrying. I can't love Lily the way you love Camille. It's all compromises to get what I want, which is to stay here with all of you and paint." He looked from the lamp to Claude with a sudden smile and exclaimed, "Anyway, I've some good news, worth my waking you!"

"Tell me anything good."

"I couldn't sleep so I read my new letters from home. Don't fall off your chair. My family's agreed to sponsor our exhibition next autumn."

Claude stared at him. "Really? You're not dreaming?"

"No, it's in my father's authoritative, manly script. *Cher ami,* etc." Frédéric leaned back in his chair, hands behind his head.

"Really? Truly?" Claude flung back his head and began to laugh. "How can such a marvelous thing—you slob of a genius! How can you say it so calmly? How could you wait to tell me? Do the others know?"

"I just found out."

"But that makes up for everything!"

Frédéric stammered a little, frowning shyly as he sometimes did when he gave a gift from the money raised by a pawned watch or pulled the cloth off a basketful of food sent by his wealthy relatives. "I hate it that you have to struggle so. It won't be long, it can't be long. I've more good news. The letter said something else. You want to know what? I have permission from home and funds to be your patron. Yes, your old friend who hauled you out of your fate as an army man can serve you a good term. You know that painting of Camille as four women, *Women in the Garden*? I'd like to buy it and pay for it in installments."

"You should have shaken me awake for that! I can't believe you'll . . ."

Frédéric laid one long hand on the table near his soup bowl and said firmly, "You were snoring too contentedly. It's nothing. Claude. It's a small thing. I'm not due thanks for what's been given me. I need all of you. I need to make sure we're all safe together."

"But you're going home when you marry."

His friend hesitated and then pushed his bowl away. "Not completely, only half the year. Lily has agreed to live in Paris half the time. Did you think I'd let myself just end all I value? We negotiated and I was firm. I'll buy a house in Paris and the top floor will be a studio. You'll all have the key. Do you think marriage will change me?"

Claude murmured, "So it's true? It's all true? *Incroyable!*—incredible. I was so unhappy and now suddenly it's changed. Yes, I'll come paint in the studio, but you'll have to understand something." His voice rose joyfully. "With the help of the exhibition, my real success will come *sooner*. I'll buy a house of my own and you're invited to come and paint *there* with your lovely, delightfully agreeable wife at your side."

He drank some broth and hesitated. "Bazille," he said more solemnly.

"Monet."

"I love Camille so much, but sometimes I can't talk to her honestly about things. Her things, mine. If I'm going to go forward at all, I have to have peace between us, so I keep silent. And she does too, I think. It was like that between my mother and father. Something builds up inside and we want to cry out and fight, but it's awful when we do. And there are things I'm ashamed of . . . I'm afraid it won't last between us with all our difficulties. She has her secrets, and I have mine."

"What's yours?"

"Shame that I don't do better."

"You will! This autumn! All of us. And women are secretive; they're all like that. Maddening." Bazille grinned and stretched; the lamp threw his shadow larger on the wall and the ceiling, and it seemed to hover above both of them as if it had a life of its own.

TWO DAYS LATER, Claude found a thatched cottage in Montmartre to rent.

With Jean, who was now six months old, he and Camille took the omnibus as far as it went up the hill and then climbed a snowy dirt path. Montmartre was not part of Paris: it stood alone, dotted with small farms.

He watched her face uneasily as they entered the sagging cottage. If she felt a moment's disappointment after living some days in her sister's exquisite rooms, she quickly hid it. "It's not too awful, is it?" he asked hopefully, noting how the odd snowflake drifted lazily through a broken windowpane. "It's just for a little while until I get on my feet again."

"Oh no, it has such character, and besides, we're near friends!" she replied gaily. She put Jean down on the sagging bed and took off the fur hat her sister had given her. "I can make it beautiful," she said. "We'll be happy here with you painting and I writing."

"Writing?" he asked.

She shook her head mischievously. "Yes, of course," she said. "I hope all our other things come tomorrow! I can hardly remember who we left them all with when we went away. Where are the sheets? My sister is sending our plates. Why yes, of course, I have my own plans."

"What?" he said, gazing at her elegant face so flushed with the cold and wind.

"Never mind," she said.

The humble cottage with its sagging floor and walls took on its own charm. A hired donkey cart brought up their books, which had been stored with friends, and he hung his pictures, all of them crooked. The bed ropes creaked and mice chased each other under the scant furniture at night. In the day she sang snatches of Offenbach breathlessly in her slightly hoarse contralto, her voice dropping out and coming back again as if she had forgotten some words in each phrase. He went out to paint, but never farther than Camille could walk to him with some bread, cheese, and hot coffee at midday.

"You don't want to change your mind about the stage?" he asked her one late winter evening. The setting sun shone on the wide, rotting floorboards in a glorious way, and Jean tried to capture it with his small hands.

She wiped her hands on her apron. "No," she said. "I told you, *mon cher*! Do you remember that I started a novel in the bookshop? I'm going to complete it. I want to make it brilliant, the very best. Jean is chewing on something, Claude! Can you take him in your lap?"

Later that evening he lay back in bed, hands under his head, and the baby asleep on his chest as she walked about the room, one hand behind her back, the other holding her few pages as she read him the opening chapter. It was about a girl who wanted to become an opera singer but who is trapped by her family's expectations.

When she had done, he exclaimed, "The characters are so real!" and she sat on the bed's edge and kissed him. "I have found my true gift, I think," she said a little wistfully. And that month and the next she sat at the table and wrote.

When spring came, they wanted nothing more than to be outside and took long walks together, carrying Jean. Will the spring astonish me every year forever? Claude thought. The first buds on trees, the first dusting of green. All around them orchards, vineyards, and small pastures unfolded.

He sold a few paintings and settled with his creditors, redeeming his maritime paintings, which were shipped to Paris by train and which now would take pride of place in the planned exhibition with his friends in the fall. He redeemed her dresses. He was relieved to receive a letter from his father saying that he and Claude's aunt had returned and that she was better. Aunt Lecadre enclosed amusing articles from the local paper.

More than twenty friends climbed the hill on the day of Camille's twenty-second birthday and made a picnic under a huge old tree between vineyards and a wild field. Jean crawled about pulling up fistfuls of grass, following six-year-old Lucien Pissarro, who now and then sat down in the grass with him. The Pissarro family was back living in Louveciennes with Pissarro's mother.

Frédéric walked up the path in old green plaid trousers, bearing wine and cake, followed by his friend Edmond, who had a guitar slung across his back. Auguste brought Lise, who wore a straw hat with flowers; he now lived in Montmartre as well. Sisley came with his new wife and a few musician friends. They did not expect Camille's parents, who were to take her for lunch the following day, or her sister, whose little girl was again sick.

Lucien and the older children tried to catch butterflies and picked wildflowers. The sun shone on the leaves and the ground and the bright dresses of the women. A great number of cheeses and sausages and breads was laid on plates on the picnic rugs. Camille opened a few small presents. Edmond tuned his guitar and sang some songs by Schubert to his own accompaniment.

But the subject of their first private exhibition that autumn drew the painters apart to one picnic rug, where they talked and smoked pipes. Claude sat with his back against the tree trunk and Frédéric stretched out on his side. "I found rooms for it yesterday," Frédéric said excitedly. "I have to paint like a madman until then. I can start on the draft announcements to the news journals and magazines this summer. We need to invite all the gallery owners and art dealers, perhaps even Durand-Ruel, the most important art dealer in Paris now."

"He never wanted to see my work before," Claude said ruefully. "He sent word by his assistant that he couldn't sell it, it was too modern."

"He'll change his mind," Frédéric answered gravely. "They'll all change their minds. What do we call ourselves?"

They looked at one another. "The Society of Poor Broke Bastards?" suggested Sisley.

"Shut up! How about The Society of Anonymous Artists—*La Société anonyme coopérative d'artistes*?"

Claude glanced at the women, who were sitting close together with the children. How lovely they looked with their summer straw hats, the ribbons stuck with flowers. Camille lay on her stomach, her white dress floating about her. "I'm writing," she was telling them. "Something magical will happen. I'm going to be like George Sand, who took a man's name to publish. I find her smoking cigars and wearing trousers most alluring. But she's old now, way over sixty. Terrible to be old. I can't imagine it. I'm always going to be young and happy!" She burst out laughing and sat up, reaching for Jean, who was examining a fistful of grass.

Pissarro fell asleep on a picnic cloth on his back with his hat covering his face, snoring slightly. The air was still sweet and the earth was warm, though the sun sank low in the sky over the vineyards. They packed the dishes and walked dreamily down the hill. Claude held his jacket slung over his shoulder; his sleeves were rolled up.

They said good-bye at the turn and he watched his friends walking back to Paris, Frédéric with his hands in his pockets, Pissarro's son riding on his shoulders and the others in front of them.

Interlude

Now that winter had come, the water lilies were long gone, but he continued to work on his paintings of them from memory in his studio. More requests had come for him to settle on a date to show them, and more than ever he deferred his promise. In his last major exhibition he had shown the Japanese bridge and the trees and pond surrounding it, and endured criticism for his shallow subject matter. Why paint only a bridge, a pond below, a willow tree? the critics had asked.

What would they say now to an exhibition of nothing but lilies, water, and reflections? How great would be their contempt! And why did one ever give us the need to be understood? When was anyone ever indifferent to the opinions of others or the feeling that one should be better at work and with those one loved?

When his work did not please him and he thought of all the things that irritated him in his life, he sometimes remembered that Camille's sister had not responded to his second letter, sent months before. Then it would not leave his mind. Finally he put down his brush and took up a pen, sitting at the table in the midst of his pictures.

My dear madame,

I am hurt and angered by your silence, and though I may be foolish to interrupt my work to write you again, I must do so. I still hope we may have some communication about some of your sister's things that I have found. In particular, when I looked in the box again, I realized some papers were missing, a handful of love letters she wrote before I knew her and which she never sent. They may have been destroyed by her or perhaps are still in your possession. I would like to have them. It is odd for me to be jealous so many years after her death, but, as I said, discovering the Japanese box has awakened many old feelings.

Yours, C. Monet

He hesitated as he put the letter out to be mailed by his chauffeur. He had not told Annette the whole truth in his previous letter, for he had known very well that she had returned to Paris not recently but many years before.

Part Four

1869

I'm chasing the merest sliver of color. It's my own fault, I want to grasp the intangible. It's terrible how the light runs out, taking color with it.

—Claude Monet

As the opening of the first exhibition of The Society of Anonymous Artists approached that autumn, the artists themselves were so excited they could talk of nothing else. Claude and Auguste met at a new framing shop near the École des Beaux-Arts to decide how to frame their work. Each painter could contribute six or eight paintings, and Claude had decided on two of his redeemed seascapes from Le Havre, which were already framed. The others needed framing, including some he had made the past summer while staying with Camille and Jean in a small village near a little bathing spot on the Seine called La Grenouillère. Auguste, whose parents lived nearby, had painted with him.

The two artists stood together under the hanging forest of frames hung on ropes from the ceiling: they were of every sort of wood and weight, painted or gilded, or carved with flowers. Each seemed to whisper, "Within me might live the work of a great artist."

Auguste asked, "Do you remember how we met in art class? You spoke to no one."

"I didn't feel very confident."

They reached up to take down samples of one frame or another. They touched them gently and set them swinging like chimes, clinking into one another and moving away again. They knelt and tried the samples around the paintings.

After several hours they chose, deliberating between beauty and cost, compromising.

"Monsieur," Auguste told the framer. "You will accept a small deposit from us, the rest payable in three months?"

"*Bien sûr,*" replied the man. "Come back in a week and all will be ready for you."

ON THAT BRIGHT autumn day they went whistling up the street to their old café in the Batignolles district, leaping up like boys to touch branches of trees, knocking into a baby carriage and raising their hats, saying, "*Pardon,* madame!" Claude looked around the streets of Paris, at the churches, the shops, the chairs on terraces of cafés that would offer outdoor seating for a short time more. Glasses glittered on the tables, and the trees hung gravely in their late September fullness.

The painters were waiting at their table with its cracked marble top, their hats hung on hooks above them. They shook hands and sat down and ordered. "Well, we've chosen our frames," Auguste said, beginning to eat someone else's bread.

"What did you choose?"

"Second-best for me, best for Claude. The dandy!"

"I'm not worried. I'll sell the ones we did over the summer for six hundred francs each. You'll do the same. Have you seen the two rooms where we'll exhibit? They're right on the Champs-Élysées. I saw the first few posters for the show this morning, and the first newspaper announcement. But where are Sisley and Frédéric? We did say two o'clock." They peered through the dirty window at the street and the tables and chairs outside.

They had been there an hour or more when they spotted Sisley walking gravely past the inside tables toward them. He bit his lip, looked at them all, and took off his hat. Slowly he took a chair. "The exhibition is postponed," he said. "I've just come from the studio. Frédéric was running out when I arrived. All he said was that his family's gone back on their word about sponsoring our exhibition now. Something happened; he was terribly upset and said he was returning to Montpellier at once to talk with them."

Claude jumped up. "They've gone back on their word? Why didn't he come to tell us? How he must feel! I'm going to find him."

"It's too late. His train's gone by now."

THE PAINTERS STAYED in the café talking for a time after they heard the news. "Well," Pissarro said, "we are more of an anonymous society than I suspected. In all honesty, we are completely anonymous. In fact, we don't exist. The newspaper announced what will not be."

Everyone began talking at once, but Claude took a deep breath and sank back on the worn velvet banquette. Now he understood that no one would see the exquisite paintings made in La Grenouillère that summer. All they had planned for this autumn was suddenly gone: the exhibition, the crowds, the celebrations, the contract with an art dealer, the sales. Most bewilderingly, he had no idea why. And what on earth had happened between Frédéric and his family now? He had no way of knowing.

"The cost of framing," Auguste said sadly, eating the last crumbs of the bread.

Claude stood up. "I'd better tell Camille," he said and set out walking back to the river. The very streets he had passed before seemed different, as if all the shape and color were gone. He saw no light or shadow anywhere as he crossed the bridge to the Left Bank and the Quartier Latin.

On their return to Paris after the summer, he and Camille had moved into a medieval building near her uncle's bookshop. Claude slowly mounted the stairs, but no one was home. He remembered then that she had gone with little Jean to her parents'.

He walked about the two narrow rooms, looking at all their

things, mostly still stacked against the walls in boxes. Camille's little statue of the Virgin lay on its side on the bureau. He righted the lady, remembering the burning candle in the cottage and the shopkeeper demanding money it had brought. Would there be more such visitors? He cleared the second volume of *Les Misérables* from a chair and sat down with his head in his hands.

He could not bear to be with his friends or to be alone. Perhaps he would go and have a glass of wine to calm himself. He remembered that Camille sometimes hid her money in the portfolio with her novel in progress. He found it under the bed and opened it. Several francs were there, but only a few pages of the novel that she had been writing all spring and summer. He wondered what she had done with the rest of it. He would go fetch her. Still dazed, he set out toward the river.

With all his heart he did not want to enter her parents' beautiful rooms on the Île Saint-Louis today; indeed, he had been there for dinner only a few times since the birth of his son. Now he walked heavily into the salon with its chairs and divans upholstered in pale rose silk. The Doncieuxs' only concession to his relationship with their daughter was a painting he had given them of a sumptuous gathering of flowers in a vase.

Madame and monsieur were sitting on the sofa before the silver coffee service and the delicate cups. "Monet," Monsieur Doncieux said, rising and shaking Claude's hand heartily. "Just the man we were speaking of! You had a good summer, I hear?" His words did not add "living over a shoemaker's shop," but his eyes added them.

He said, "Sit down and join us, Monet. So tell us: Is all ready to proceed with your venturous exhibition?"

"Nearly," Claude murmured, sitting. Was it this they spoke of?

"We'll come, of course."

"Yes, of course."

Madame and monsieur looked at each other and monsieur sat down again, patting his mustache. He said, "So you both are perfectly happy and all your troubles will be over soon. Yes, we were speaking of you and our daughter. Minou's gone out just now with the boy to buy him an ice and see a friend." He nodded more seriously, like a doctor over a patient who is not well.

That half hour was one of the longest Claude could remember. The Doncieuxs rambled on and on, contradicting each other, while he looked at the blowing window curtains and thought about painting them. He did not believe a word they said. It was just another incomprehensible thing in this incomprehensible day. To go away and paint would be easier, but where could he go? He must post a letter to Frédéric today. And where was his love? How could he get out of this room?

The china clock struck three in its tedious way as if counting off another hour of life with some relief, and Claude jumped up, upsetting his coffee on the rug. As madame rushed to mop it with her tiny handkerchief and cried for the maid, he heard Victoire's bark on the steps and his son's voice. They tell ridiculous stories, Claude muttered angrily under his breath. He wanted to slam his fist into the glass cabinet of curiosities and gazed from the apartment door to the trembling maid who had brought a cloth and bowl of water. "Let me help you," he said, kneeling. The tall doors opened and Camille came in.

She was there, so pretty in her straw summer hat with flowing, pale blue ribbons, carrying Jean, whose face was smeared with white ice cream. Victoire scampered about in his usual excess, careening from his mistress to the bowl of coffee-tinted water, splashing it further. Claude gazed hungrily at Camille, who was the one reasonable, lovely thing in this room. "Claude!" she exclaimed happily. "Why, what are you doing here?"

"Change of plans, must go back now," he muttered. He thrust his hands into his pockets and then remembered and held his right hand out for monsieur to shake. "So sorry to leave you," he said rapidly. "Wanted back at the gallery." He could not wait to leave this room; if he never came back it would be too soon.

As he and Camille walked down the rue Saint-Louis-en-l'Île, he hoisted his son to his shoulders. Taking her hand, he felt the tales he had heard dissolve in his head though he was too weary to consider why they had been told. Would they never leave the poor girl alone?

She said tenderly, "You look terrible. What is it?"

His voice broke a little as he told her about the cancellation of the exhibition.

Camille at once ceased to walk. "I can't bear that you've had another disappointment, all of you!" she exclaimed. "It's not right! And poor Frédéric! What could have happened? Didn't he send you word? All your plans! But it will happen somehow; you'll find out more when he returns. We'll just manage until then."

He looked at the women's hats for sale in a shop window and said in a hollow voice, "I'm not sure how. Your father offered me a job working with him. As a sales representative."

"Is that what they talked to you about? No wonder you looked like you wanted to bolt when I came in, to have that upon the other loss. Let them find out about the exhibition in their own time. Claude, you can't work in silks! I have a better idea! Let me work for my uncle in the bookshop every day and have him send his assistant away; his heart's bad and he needs more help. He can pay proper wages and we'll manage until you can earn something."

"What, you can't work!"

"I can."

"Poor man! He's the best of your family. And your novel?"

"It's nearly finished! I don't mind waiting."

Their voices had dropped very low over Jean's murmuring as he played with Claude's hat. As they slowly walked on, Claude said, "Well, work a little if it amuses you, but I assure you we don't need the money. I'll see us through. You'll have a house and garden soon, I promise."

WITHIN A FEW days, the Doncieux family and everyone else he knew had learned about the canceled exhibition and his head began to clear a little. Only then did he remember what he owed the framer, but by that day he was able to cancel only some of his order. His letter to Frédéric received only a few words of reply on folded stationery, "Don't worry, back soon. So sorry." Several days later, he heard Frédéric had returned, and he ran over to the studio, climbing the stairs two steps at a time.

His friend was in his old painting suit, standing by his easel, but Claude could see that something of consequence had happened to him in Montpellier.

Frédéric barely looked up. "There you are," he said.

It was an abrupt greeting. Claude nodded and replied as casually as he could, "What on earth happened?"

"Nothing much. The main thing is they wanted to make sure I marry first because they're afraid I won't go through with it. They damn well know I don't particularly want to go through with it but I will. Lily will still move here. And we'll have our exhibition next fall, after I'm married." Frédéric raised his brush to paint the edge of a flower with maddening care. He's half here, Claude thought. Everything about him seemed to say, "Don't touch me."

He thought, my friend is hiding something.

He said, "You're painting that flower too tightly."

"I'm painting it the way I want to paint it."

"*D'accord.* Very well, then do so."

Frédéric hardly spoke that day as they painted side by side. Only when Claude put on his hat to go did he reach in his pocket to give Claude some money toward the purchase of the painting. Their eyes met for one moment and Frédéric looked away. Given so coldly, the money felt dirty in Claude's pocket. It's nothing I did, he thought as he went home. It's something with him and he'll tell me eventually.

But weeks passed and Frédéric remained withdrawn.

THOUGH CAMILLE BEGAN working for her uncle, leaving Jean with the Sicilian woman next door, it took Claude some time to gather himself together to figure out what he would do next. In October he tried to place the paintings with an art gallery and met with the same lack of success he had had before.

It was only a year more until their independent exhibition would really happen; he could manage somehow until then. Everyone was trying to manage, and none of them was quite sure how. He felt Frédéric also had something to struggle with, though it had nothing to do with money. The tall artist withdrew, and the others slowly went their own ways.

Through the autumn, Claude walked about the neighborhood asking if people wanted a chalk portrait. He applied for work in several colorists' shops and with his old framer, but they did not need anyone. Another framer said he would display a painting of Claude's in the window. Over the next week Claude painted a church in winter, using up all his oils in the process, and though the work was displayed as promised, it did not sell. He had no more money, he owed everywhere, and the rent was coming due. There was no way Camille could pay it on her small salary.

November blew in, and Jean caught cold. Camille set off for the bookstore each day wearing Claude's much-mended little grass ring, though Claude could see how the work tired her. He hated that she worked. No woman in his family ever had. She should not have had to do it; she was a lady. He knew her uncle was irritable and that she found working for a living much less pleasant than minding the shop now and then on a whim as she had done when he first met her.

What shall I do? he thought. Where shall I turn?

As he was walking down the rue Jacob one windy day he peered through the window of a café under renovation and made out Auguste in his blue smock standing on a chair painting a wall. "Good to see you," Claude exclaimed. "I haven't seen anyone. No one goes out for wine anymore; no one comes to us. Frédéric hardly talks when I see him."

"I know. He's withdrawing from all of us. He stands and smiles but he's not quite there."

"And you go on making your beautiful world." Claude looked at the wall with the lovely rosy-cheeked girls dancing and the handsome men.

"It is my answer to sorrow."

Auguste carefully painted the lips on another girl. He said suddenly, "You need work, *c'est vrai?* Do you want to join me and take those other walls? They just said this morning they'd pay for another painter if I could recommend one." He wiped his forehead with the crook of his arm. "They want a lot of people in the murals, you know, pretty girls having a good time, dancing, laughing."

They worked for the next three days with the tables and chairs piled in the center of the room, and on the third afternoon the manager stopped by to see the progress. When he looked at Claude's wall, he frowned. "Monsieur, what are you doing? What is it?" he asked. "My customers will not buy more wine with only dabs to look at."

"I told you," Auguste said under his breath.

"*Il peut se faire foutre et sa mère aussi!* He can fuck himself and his mother too," Claude replied, not too softly.

He strode away through the Paris streets with his shoulders hunched and his face burning. I am meant to do one thing only, he thought angrily, and that is to make real paintings. The only thing was to paint the Paris streets again and try to sell them to his old patrons.

He poured cold coffee from that morning, and began to write to his patrons. Time passed quickly, his pen hesitating as he searched for the right words. He did not realize the late hour until he heard Camille on the steps. He glanced about. He had not taken their clothes to the laundress. He stumbled over his son's small wooden wagon as he hurried to the door. Camille was so tired these days he could not bear it. *Merde!* he said under his breath.

She stood in the door in her hat and coat, frowning a little. She said, "I thought you'd be at the café working."

"I lost that job. I thought I'd try selling work to galleries again.

I'd lower my prices, though they're already to the floor. I'm sorry about the laundry. I can't think of a single cheerful thing to say."

She stared at him, stunned. "You've lost the job? How can we pay the rent?"

"I'll try the galleries again," he said, looking at the dishes piled on the counter.

"But we must pay it by tomorrow. Will we lose this place too? I'm trying to keep our situation from my family. I didn't know you'd go more than two months without earning anything. If we're thrown out, everyone will know. The woman downstairs knows my uncle, and he'll tell my parents. Oh, Claude."

The breathless fury he had felt at his dismissal from the café job huddled in his throat. He scraped the floor with his shoe. " 'Oh, Claude!' you say," he repeated. "As if I didn't try."

"But it's not just a matter of trying!" she cried. He dared not look at her, but he could see her lovely face was splotched with emotion. "You do try. You try very hard."

She came close to him and put a tentative hand on his arm. "Claude," she said. "Listen to me. I can't bear it. We can't live this way anymore. When the private exhibition opens next autumn, everything will be fine. Until then . . . my father stopped by the bookshop. Remember how he offered you a job with his silk concern? He mentioned it again. It pays fairly well. I think you should take it for a time."

Claude stared at her. "I can't do that," he said, shaking his head. He began to pace the room.

She followed him. "Then we must borrow again from my father or your aunt. You'd work for him for only a little while, Claude, before your painting begins to sell more. My sister came by yesterday in a new pale gray wool dress and hat on her way to a concert and told me she wished I could come. My father said it breaks his heart to see my life go so badly."

"So your life goes badly, does it?" he managed. "I'm very sorry to hear that."

Victoire, who had been snoring in a corner, awoke and began to growl at his feet. He shouted, "Your wretched dog! You had to bring your wretched dog with us!"

"Did you want me to give up everything I valued for you?"

"Who asked you? You came for me!"

She snatched the dog in her arms. "I think it's time we faced the truth, Claude. You must find some regular employment. Perhaps for a bank . . ."

"A bank!" he cried. "I can't, I can't!"

"Why can't you?"

Suddenly he recalled all the strange things her parents had told him that afternoon when he had spilled the coffee; suddenly he believed them. His words flew out. "Why do you tell lies? Why didn't you tell me you ran to your *grandmère* instead of away with an actor? And came back to your family as innocent as you were born? Why didn't you tell me the truth about the audition, that you sent me outside and then decided not to take it? You told your sister and she told your mother. I wouldn't have minded the truth, but I don't know what's true with you. You don't trust me. I think about you all the time; I try so hard."

She backed away a little, stunned. He could not stop his words. "Whom did you write letters to when I first met you? This actor whom you told me you wrote to who I learned had died of consumption the year before, the actor you never ran away with? And who wrote you? Your fiancé, I suppose. And where's the novel you were writing? I don't care if you don't sell it—I'll support us—but where is it?"

She stammered, "My parents were wrong. I never tell lies."

"For God's sake, Camille!" He was shouting.

"I didn't write my fiancé. Sometimes students from the Sorbonne wrote me because they liked me; they thought I was pretty and fascinating. I kept most of the letters I wrote; I never sent them. I think they got left in our room when we had to leave that night in the snow. I liked to be fascinating. It wasn't good. I'm not clever. Now you know it." She was gasping now, but she was angry as well. She stepped forward. "If I've told any untruths, they didn't concern you. Have you told me everything, Claude? You know you haven't! And until you are successful you must swallow your pride and do some sort of ordinary work. Tell me you will!"

"A few months ago you wouldn't hear of it."

"Everyone says you must. Let's go live with my *grandmère*."

"Do you mean to make a farmer out of me? 'Here is my poor Claude, who can't earn his way as other men can.' Shall I press walnuts and milk goats? Or will you? You live in a fantasy."

"I have absolutely had all of this life I can take!" she cried. "You've got to make things better for us. I trusted you!"

He walked back and forth, one hand in his trouser pocket, the other cutting the air, not looking at her. "The thing is . . . ," he said to his book on the table and the dimly burning light. He swallowed hard. "I think the time has come that we both face this, Minou. I want you and I love you, but I can't manage. We should never have begun, you and I!"

She cried, "What are you saying? That you don't want me? That you don't want our child?"

"I don't know . . . I don't know," he muttered, looking at the unmade bed with the dirty laundry piled on it. "Of course I love you; of course I do. I don't know anything. I seem to have no power to make my life as I'd want it, no matter how hard I try."

His voice grew more bitter. "You don't really believe I can have such a house and a garden. You expect me to go on when you don't believe in me! Before you came I had given up on women! You were so sweet, so loving, so beautiful, I couldn't help thinking of you all the time. I tried to avoid you, though. I knew you'd be disappointed in the end."

Camille rushed at him, turning him, but he did not want to meet her eyes. He was so angry he was afraid he would shove her away. "You tried to avoid me?" she cried. "You wanted me. So it's my fault that we began? There, take your ridiculous grass ring!" She held it out on her open palm, mended and fragile as it was.

"No, I won't take that," he said stubbornly, shaking his head. Now he did not know how to wipe away all the words that had suddenly poured out between them. How can you scrape words away as you do paint from a canvas? The air was thick with them.

She still held out her hand. "*Je vous déteste!*—I detest you! Take back your . . . this."

"No."

He heard her footsteps on the floorboards and the opening and closing of the stove door before he understood what had happened. Then he shouted, "Did you burn it? Did you burn your ring?"

She was sobbing through her anger. "It's not a ring, it's grass!" she cried. "It never was more than grass! Other women have real rings, real marriages."

"Yes," he said slowly, "it was only grass. And no, it's not your fault. We're both at fault. You shouldn't have gone home with me that night I took you to dinner. We shouldn't have had a child."

His voice rose. "Go away then, both of you! Leave me alone! Take our son and go live with your sister and her officious husband, the man who is so successful at everything, the man who can tell me what I ought to do, the man who is the way you'd like me to be! And then your mother and father, whom you fled from, will visit you! Why didn't you marry your rich fiancé? Minou, all the things you thought about me, all the bright, wonderful things, are wrong."

He gave her a last bitter look and without taking his coat, stormed out into the night.

ALONE HE SET out across Paris. He walked so fast the air parted before him as if afraid to hold him back. But where am I going? he thought bitterly. Away from her, away from them, away from my romantic foolishness, the idiot I've become. Taking on a family!

So we have ended it! he continued as he strode past cafés and theaters, their placards stained with rain. I mustn't be soft and let any longing lead me back. For without them I can go on as I was meant to do. I can make my bed in the corner of Frédéric's studio. He'll marry and have his town house and studio and I will live there humbly with nothing but my art. We'll find that caricature I made of us with our names that we hung on our first studio door and tack it up again. Below in his parlor with his wife he'll pretend to be happily married, whereas above I will have the pleasure of not pretending anything at all.

He walked for hours. Normally he felt such a part of this city, but now he felt all alone. How bitterly he regretted the words he had spoken! Well, it was her fault. There was a way he could end it completely.

He walked steadily toward the Right Bank and one of the houses that overlooked the river. He had gone there so often his feet knew the way. He would go there as he had the year before he met Camille, up the stairway and into the bedroom with its pale yellow satin drapes. His relationship with the woman who lived there had lasted a time. Winter mornings he would wake to the soft crackling of the fire and sit up barechested in bed for the breakfast tray with its pot of coffee, its warm milk, its buttery rolls. This wealthy widow who had bought a few of his paintings really wanted only one thing from him and, as he had confided in Auguste, that at least he did well.

She had given him presents: paints, canvases, silk nightshirts. And one day she had said lightly, tousling his hair, "Without me you'd have nothing. You're only a painter with a lot of extravagant dreams, but you are a beautiful one, Monet." He had not returned.

Claude stood by a lamppost looking up at the house. The lights were on in her bedroom, and as he watched through her curtains he saw the shape of a man. He watched even when the lights were dimmed, and he heard laughter. Then he thought, *ah connard!* What am I thinking? What did I almost do in my anger? Minou is the one with the right to be angry; I'm the one who has failed.

Hours later, he walked home through the empty streets, over the bridge. Sometimes he was aware of where he was going and sometimes he was aware only of where he had been. He wanted to scrub away what he had almost done and all the words he and Camille had spoken. He wanted to forget her parents' words, which had haunted him from autumn until now: "Minou makes up things sometimes and doesn't remember what she said and then says something else. She likely never auditioned. She had periods of deep despondency as a girl when she would fall silent or cry and not get out of bed. Often we didn't know why."

So she never ran away with anyone, he thought. As for her despondency, he also had been moody as a boy. Maybe she made up tales to protect herself from such a mother! Likely it was her old fiancé then who had been her first lover and to whom she had written letters. One day they would talk about it; one day it would all be clear. Meanwhile he loved and needed her.

She will not be there, he thought. Suppose she ran out like she did from the cottage and left the baby alone? Jean walks now! He could be eating my paints or pulling down the knives.

He raced up the stairs.

She was there, sleeping in bed with Jean sleeping next to her. He dropped his clothes and slid into the other side of the bed, pressing his naked body against hers, carefully draping his arm around her so that it also touched his son.

She was awake. "Oh, Claude, I missed you!" she whispered. "I'm so sorry we quarreled. I want only you, even as we are. Once or twice I've said things that aren't true. They aren't lies, but they aren't exactly true because when I look back, it seems that things that didn't happen ought to have, and those that did happen perhaps should never have. You see."

"I am trying to," he whispered. "So your audition . . ."

She was sobbing. "I tried to take it, but my voice died away. I was suddenly terribly shy. I don't know if I could ever be anything really magnificent. I did burn my book. It's not as good as Zola or George Sand."

"But it was good, *ma chère!*"

"That's not enough for me. Only paint! You will do well! I'm sorry I broke down. From now on all is well if only you love me."

"Yes, I do," he replied. "There's no one I could ever love like you. You are the sun on the grass and the light on the water." *Mon Dieu,* he thought as she fell asleep in his arms, let all memories of this night pass away and all ghosts that were before me.

1870

I never had a fighter's temperament and I would have given up many times over had not my good friend Monet, who had a fighter's temperament, backed me up.
—RENOIR TO A YOUNG PAINTER

THAT, HOWEVER, WAS the last time that winter he made love to her successfully. They had laughed when it happened the first time. Of all things he could do, that had never left him before.

Camille worked in the bookshop every day; it was but a few streets away from their room, so she ran back and forth, sometimes leaving Jean with a neighbor and sometimes taking him with her. She left him only occasionally with Claude because she felt Claude needed his time free to paint. He still hated that she went to work. He scraped down canvases in order to have new ones. He borrowed paint. He knew she had taken money from her family and dared not confront her. They were alone at Christmas with their child; all their friends had scattered and he would not go to her parents' Christmas Eve *réveillon* dinner. She had cried herself to sleep.

Claude's father wrote in January and Claude put the letter away unopened between books to read later and forgot about it. It was weeks later when he met someone in the street who told him that Claude's funny, tolerant old aunt had died of heart failure. Tears blurred his eyes. He began to write his father and did not. After a time, his brother, Léon, wrote him an angry letter, to which Claude also did not respond.

～

As the winter progressed, he became ill with one thing after another. For a time he had a thick cough and a fever, and Camille wrote to her *grandmère* asking for an herbal mix to brew as a tea. Sage tea, was the advice that was sent back. Do you still have any of the holy water? Sprinkle it on his pillow at night.

The letter was beautifully written by a priest, for the widow Faucher was illiterate.

The package held dried sage and rosemary in a piece of cloth. Camille bought black currant jelly, and stopped at the chemist with its rosewood cabinets to purchase a small brown bottle of sweet spirits of niter. In their room she mixed the jelly and the spirits with boiling water, sitting by him while he drank a whole cup and keeping the rest in a covered bowl. She bound a kerchief around her hair and walked about in her large apron. And there was darling Jean, his soft, sweet little boy, now a toddler exploring everything; more than once Claude found him trying to get the cap off a tube of oil paint or chewing thoughtfully on a brush.

Victoire snored at the bed's end.

He did not go to see his friends, and they seldom came to see him, for after the postponement of the exhibition to the autumn, they all seemed disgruntled with one another. Everyone was struggling. There was no time or money for meeting in cafés. Frédéric was unhappy but would not say why.

Claude lay awake most nights at Camille's side listening to the sound of the city; he was exhausted but could not sleep.

One bitterly cold day he found a letter in the mail slot from his father and shook it out to read as he mounted the steps, the tin milk container in his hand and bread under the other arm. "My dearest Claude, I think it best not to keep my bad news from you any longer. The doctors believe I have a cancer. I'm too weak to work in the shop anymore. I'm planning to sell it, which saddens me. I've not heard from you in over a year. What can you be doing? Write when you can."

He had to fumble to get the key in his lock for the tears that filled his eyes. How many times had he composed future triumphant letters in his mind to his father saying, I am doing so well and have a country house and a garden. Come live with us. Come stand beside me in my marriage; know your grandson.

He could not write home until his plans were realized.

Claude stood in the middle of their room, letter in his hand, and then sank down onto the tumbled, unmade bed. He lay on his back, covering his face with his arm. His father would not live long enough for the triumphant letters. All sorts of things were ending around him, and his position was just the same . . . beginning, trying, stumbling. Whatever troubles he had faced before, there had always been painting to run to, but no more.

He saw the color of snow, winter trees, or sunlight on a path no longer with passion but with indifference. He had stood by the window with his brush poised and could find no reason for it to touch the canvas. Where had his passion to paint gone? It had never left him before. He thought, This thing I loved so has become nothing for me but a canvas worth selling. The parks, the churches, the sea, the fields—all have stopped shimmering for me.

Lying in bed with his arm over his face, he murmured, Auguste, damn it, what would you do? You see, Frédéric, the situation's this. My fault, of course, but damn it! He gestured a little as if they were in the room, sitting at the table, nodding. They had all been over the familiar ground before. Why they all had to paint, why they must paint. No one discussed what it was like when they no longer wanted to do it, when the intimacy of it was gone and left you with nothing. Frédéric was getting ready for his marriage, withdrawing into his own proud petit bourgeois world. What did he know? Everything was so easy for him. He had even achieved a great success in last spring's Salon while everyone else was refused. They were strangers to each other now.

That was it, then. Claude strode across the room and knocked his small easel and new painting to the floor, sending the colors on the palette chipping and flaking over the floorboards, spilling the linseed oil. He seized every picture on the wall and slammed it to the floor; he hurled his sketchbooks after them. He would have burned them all but there was no coal for the fire. He could slash them with his artist's razor.

He stepped over the paintings, losing his balance, falling, the razor cutting into a canvas. He looked down at it. A man could end it all and with it end all the aching. What would death be like? Like the darkness of water at night, perhaps.

He drew the blade across his wrist. It hurt like hell. Someone had said you were supposed to put the wrist in hot water before cutting. It was not a deep cut, but the blood dripped onto the floor and canvases. This isn't me, he thought. His heart began to beat so fast he felt he would faint. He had to find a cloth to bind his wrist. Stupid, stupid, he thought. He pressed it hard and cried out with the pain. He found one of Camille's stockings and bound it. He stumbled to the bed.

He fainted, perhaps; he knew nothing else, and even in his dreams when he struggled to the surface there was a tremendous pain for everything. Someone was banging on the door. He had no idea what time it was, if night was falling or dawn was coming. He didn't know for a time what room he was in and how he had got here. He struggled for consciousness and fell away again. He looked with blurred eyes about the room and saw everything on the floor. Camille was at the door banging and shouting, and along with her voice he heard the voices of his friends.

He had bolted the door; her key would not open it.

"Go away!" he called, but they did not hear him.

He made his way across the room. His fingers could hardly grasp and move the bolt. He let them open the door and come into the room. He looked at their shoes and at the bottom of her skirt. "You see how it is," he managed. "You see things have not been well . . ."

Frédéric cried, "What have you done?"

"Go away!" Claude stumbled toward the bed, but Camille already had her arms around him. He half lay on the bed against her. "I'm sorry," he gasped. "I should have cleaned up. It was a mistake. Why don't you go away? Just go back to your lives . . . go paint a café or marry an heiress or something, whatever you do. Just . . . go away . . ." He would have cried with shame but he could only heave.

A light shone in his eyes, then moved away. Frédéric was kneeling before him, unwinding the bloody stocking. Renoir cried, "Jesus, you idiot, what did you do?"

"Frédéric, get off. Go back to your privileged life."

Frédéric cried, "You couldn't have sent for us? You locked yourself in and did this? Let me see that. It might infect; I have to wash it. You had some sense to cut the left wrist at least, not the right. Stay there, damn you."

"There are more stockings in the bureau," Camille gasped. Claude was aware of the beautiful softness of her and wanting to melt into it, and yet he wished he never had to look at her again. She held him fiercely in her terror.

Frédéric washed and rebound the wrist. "You didn't tell me," he said. "You didn't tell me."

"When do you talk to me anymore?"

"Shut up, you idiot! I always came when you needed me, but you don't need anyone anymore, do you?"

Frédéric wiped his face with the back of his hand. Auguste paced the room, swearing under his breath; he picked up a few canvases, and then kicked the wall. "It doesn't need to come to this!" he said. "It doesn't need to come to this for any of us if we stand together. We're together. Damn it, Monet! We're together! I have dark periods, you have dark periods. I'd stay up the night with you. Haven't you done it for us?"

Camille held him against her, clasping his right hand.

Auguste tried to make a joke. Finally when they had arranged the brushes twice in their cups, he looked at her under his eyebrows and said, "Will you both be all right? Should we leave you? We'll be here first thing in the morning. Claude, will you sleep?" He put a small blue bottle on the table. Now his voice was tender. "I used this for my aching arm. It helps with pain."

Claude nodded. "Yes," he said, "I'm all right. Camille, are you all right?"

He sensed she nodded, stricken, from behind him.

"We could sleep on the floor," Auguste offered. "Or in the hall. I've been so near homeless I don't mind halls. I'll just put my head on my paint satchel."

"No, you *merde*. That's your one good suit."

Frédéric stood blinking, the wash basin in his hands. "Claude, you must never . . . never . . ."

"I won't, I promise. Throw the water out the window."

His friends' footsteps sounded on the stairs and their murmured voices, and then they were gone. Claude lay facedown, right arm folded under his head, left arm with the bandaged wrist dangling to the floor. Camille ran across the room, climbing in beside him. "Claude," she sobbed. "How could you?"

His voice was muffled. "I'm sorry, Minou." She drew the blanket up and tucked it in over his shoulders.

His face still buried, he asked, "Do you remember my painting of the magpie on a snowy fence in a field? I am that magpie, you see. He's so alone. I face the canvas and there's nothing there, because I think it's all been vanity with me and I've never been good enough. And I can't paint."

He turned his head now to face her and touched her cheek with his right hand. "That scared me to say," he added hoarsely. "That was the hardest thing to say. Maybe I wouldn't have tried to do that stupid thing if I had been able to say that. I didn't want to kill myself, I just wanted to say . . . enough. Enough of so much here, my failures, your exhaustion, my shame. I kept pressing the wrist to stop bleeding. I was scared that I had tried. We can talk about it later. I haven't any more words now. I'm so sorry. I'm so tired. I feel I haven't slept in days."

"I'll hold you."

"Don't cry, beloved. It's all right. I never want to make you cry, Minou."

HE ROSE BEFORE dawn and looked at her for a long time as she slept, and then he looked at his sleeping son. Jean's chubby arms were spread out; his mouth was open and dewy. Theirs was the sort of warm, stuffy, sweet, scattered life some others might paint, shadows of hanging clothes, books leaning against one another on the shelf, Camille's garters in a small heap on the bureau.

Claude wrote her the most passionate letter of his life on a sheet left over from her unfinished novel. He would have cried, but he felt so drained he could not, and his wrist hurt so much.

He left the house in the dark, feeling his way down the stairs without a candle. Once in a cab he slept; he woke to the driver shouting at him that they had reached the train station. Dawn was rising over Paris as he saw the train roar toward him majestically, filling the air with noise and smoke. Hiding his bandaged wrist under his coat, he boarded the third-class car and slumped on the seat as the countryside rolled past him.

He went home to Le Havre.

IN A WAY he hoped to go home as if he were seventeen again and just returning from painting with Boudin: to find his mother singing at the piano and his aunt sewing in the corner. Many visitors would be expected, and his cousin might let him kiss her. He wanted it so much he almost thought it would happen.

It was not that way, of course. Only his father came anxiously from the shadows of the house as if he feared a thief. "Claude," he said. And Claude saw that his father was sick indeed, his formerly full face haggard, his trousers held up by suspenders.

Claude said abruptly, "I've come to help you. I'm done with painting. I'll take over the shop."

They stood a few feet apart, unwilling to come closer. "You're done with painting? What do you mean you're done with painting? What have you done there with your wrist? But what about the young woman and your son?"

Claude shook his head; he remembered his words in the letter and knew she had read them by now. He looked down the hall to the back garden door. Any moment his younger self would rush in the door, mud on his shoes. Then his father said, "Claude, *mon fils*—my son!" and he felt he could not bear it.

IT WAS AS if his father's ship chandlery on the wharf had waited for him—the nautical lanterns, drying rope, and paint. Sails rolled in the back. Claude sat down clumsily in the swivel chair behind the desk, pulling out old letters and bills.

The air was musty and cold because the shop had been locked for some weeks since the last assistant had gone away. Seeing the lantern in the window this dull day, a few men came in wanting small items but mostly to talk and warm their hands by the stove. The talk was of fishermen and boats and prices and someone they knew who had gone down with his boat the month before and had not been found.

He walked to the shop every morning through the winter wind. More old customers stopped by, having heard that Adolphe Monet's son had returned. At night he went home to eat what Hannah had cooked. Once or twice his brother came, bringing his wife and their twin girls, who reminded Claude so much of his son.

Two days after he had come he received her letter.

I cried and cried at your words. What do you mean you aren't coming back? You're my life and I'm yours. All our friends are very kind to me, but I want you. You wrote no one is to visit you. I don't know what to do. I know you'll be back. I know you will.

He missed her so; he went to sleep that night holding the pillow against him and pretending it was her. He kept her letter under the pillow.

Every day letters came from her and his friends, and sometimes he did not read them. He could feel the compassion and love and disappointment and hope seep from under the envelopes, and he could not bear it. He forbade them to visit. When he wrote to her he hardly remembered what he said. He said he was coming back; he said he would not come back.

If only I could paint again, he thought. I must try. At least I can try. Then I can think.

One morning three weeks after he had arrived, he left the house before breakfast, taking his easel and a canvas and some paints from a few years before that he had forgotten in a burlap bag at the bottom of the wardrobe. He walked until he came to the sea, and then he walked over the sand, choosing a place to set his easel. There was the white wild surging of the sea, sometimes darting so close to his shoes it washed over them. It half dared him and half regarded him coolly.

He raised his hand with the charcoal, but it did not meet the canvas.

He stared down at his tubes of colors and at his hand.

He waited for nearly an hour, but the world that had leaned into him like a lover and flowed out again through his brush did not approach him. He cried aloud, hurled the canvas into the high grass, and went home.

Mon cher Frédéric, This will be sad, so prepare yourself. Drink a little brandy, perhaps. How to begin? I owe you so much. Perhaps you saved my life. Can there be more than that?

What I regret most is not confiding more in you in the past several months, but then neither do you confide in me as you go forward in your marriage, which I feel can't make you happy! One day I came to the studio hoping to find you, but you weren't there. I saw your painting of the girl in the pink dress with the village far behind her and understood again what a fine painter you are.

The truth is, I believe our independent exhibition to be the fantasy of a group of tired, struggling artists who will one by one find this whole thing too difficult and give up. I write different things to Minou every day; she must think I've lost my mind. Don't come here, any of you. Don't fetch me again; don't rescue me! What for?

Right now I don't think I'm coming back. Please make sure Minou and my son don't lack for anything.

Claude

That was that, then. Outside, men in weatherproof coveralls shouted above the rain and ran for shelter, wet fish glistened, and the dark gray clouds paused and thickened and rained harder into the sea. He rose and cleared a place in the glass to look at the colors. Some man ran past the window, shouting something, his voice lost in the thunder and rain, and then he was gone.

The rain ended after several days. The thick gray clouds were silent, the air was cold and damp, the water lapped uneasily. Men walked in wet footsteps down the wharf. As Claude watched them through the window, he heard the shop door open, and his old friend Boudin came in.

Claude stood up from the creaking chair.

Boudin greeted him with a brief handshake and turned to examine some hanging nets. Men who lived in these parts were not quick to words: they did not hurl them out and knock them about for the pleasure of it, but took them carefully from their pockets and laid them on the table before them. Boudin said lightly, "So, my young friend! I'm back from wintering in warmer parts and was surprised to find you here. How's the painting going?"

"It's not. I can't," Claude said. He stayed by the desk. "It's stopped and with it I've stopped as well. I'm not there if it's not there." He reached down to feel the edge of an accounting book. "I'm sorry to tell you this above all men, believe me. I will never forget your kindness to me, arrogant boy that I was."

Boudin nodded. "To be honest, the painter Daubigny wrote and told me," he said. "One of your friends must have told him. It happens, you know, but never before for you, eh?"

Claude shook his head slowly; he folded his arms across his chest. He frowned and looked out the window. Boudin's voice carried to him over the damp wood of the shop.

"Happened to me three or four times . . . maybe a dozen. Threw down my hat, locked up the paints, tried to tell my wife, and found my throat closing."

Claude sat down in the chair again, stroking his beard. Boudin sat down as well, taking off his old brown hat and looking from the window now and then.

"It gets battered," he said after a time, scratching his thick gray curly hair. "The part of us that paints—if not by want of success, then by us always demanding more from it. Not enough to paint the same thing for us, but we always want to do better. And so we have to . . ." he raised his hands and shaped the damp air ". . . let it rest wherever it's hidden and after a while coax it a little. Coax it out. Life makes one humble, doesn't it? You have a great gift, Claude. It's what you are. I sensed it from the first time I saw your drawings and, yes, you were arrogant but you were young and unhappy. You have open seas now, my friend. I hear your father's ill, poor man."

The concluding words were few and yet they touched Claude so he could hardly respond to them. In a way he dreamt of them. As he slept, the harbor water seemed to lap at his bed until it reached the edges of his blanket and his dangling hand. Outside, the wind, which troubled the sails, knocked also on his window.

He woke in darkness one morning to the sound of a pebble against glass. Climbing from bed and going to the window, he made out Boudin below with a lantern. "Claude," the voice whispered, rising past the winter trees. "Come with me. I have a room overlooking the harbor I paint from early mornings. The sun will rise within an hour. Just to keep me company, if you will."

They turned down the road from the hill to the harbor, where they drank coffee at a fishermen's café before climbing the stairs of the old hotel.

He looked out the window in the room. There was the dark sea, and on the horizon, far away, the first hint of orange-gold light. He slouched in a chair and watched his mentor paint. "It's gone for me; it's gone," Claude said.

"Be still and wait. I'm here every morning in this hotel room for the next week."

For two more days Claude woke before dawn. On the third morning he threw on his clothes and made his way down to the harbor with his lantern. It was still perfectly dark. He went to the room and saw that Boudin was sleeping. Instead of one easel facing the window there were two.

From the depths of the blankets, the older artist stirred. "Monet," he said, *"I challenge you."*

Claude took up the palette, which was not his, and prepared it by the lantern light; he felt the weight of his teacher's brush.

Far across the water, low on the horizon stretched a thin line under the clouds of rosy orange gold, and the sun rose. As he worked, his brush became the sea and dark bits of boats and the spreading light. He raced the color; he snatched at it as it changed.

When he paused for breath he felt Boudin standing behind him. "Not bad for a start, Monet," he said.

HE KNEW CAMILLE'S uncle had suffered a heart attack and retired to the country and that she had decided to take over the bookshop and had moved into the rooms above it with Jean. Claude had written to her often, and then, for a time, seldom. He said he was coming back, and then he said he wasn't. She answered him that she would wait for him. He wrote her passionately. Then she was silent for three days and her letter, when it arrived, was cautious.

He read it several times in his boyhood room in his father's house, walking up and down. Had he really been away more than three months, the period of his terrible darkness and then the rapturous reunion with the world through his art? Having that again, his heart opened to everyone. Now he reread her last several letters and saw them for what they were. A sentence at a time, they had ceased to implore.

"Do you want me again?" he wrote wistfully from his desk, but he could not wait for an answer. He paced and chewed his nails, which always smelled of paint. No, he could not wait anymore; he must go to Paris and find the truth though he was sick to do it. His heart was heavy that evening as he told his father that he was returning. "I shall close the business," the old man said. "But it's right that you return to your woman and child. Bring them here to meet me soon."

Do I have a woman? Claude thought.

The four hours of the train ride seemed days, and then when he arrived he could hardly make his feet go quickly enough to the rue Dante.

The ancient cat was sleeping in the window on one of the volumes of the encyclopedia in the bookshop when he walked cautiously through the door with his paintings and bag on an early May day. A young man who had worked here before sat behind the desk. Claude glanced up the stairs and asked, "Madame has gone out? She expects me."

The young man replied, "She's gone out with the little one. Go up, monsieur, if you like, and wait for her."

Some of her things in her rooms were still in boxes, but others lay scattered about: her pink petticoat, her hair combs. He picked up one of her white chemises and held it to his nose. His paintings were stacked against the wall, and his son's wooden wagons and donkeys were heaped in a corner under the window. He lay down on the bed, her dressing gown in his arms, and slept until he felt his little son climbing on his chest, exclaiming, "Papa! Papa!"

He said, "You darling. Yes, it's me." Holding his wiggling son passionately against him, he turned his head to see Camille standing tall and gravely at the door in a little gray veiled hat, something so very removed about her. He knew then he had been away too long. He rose, forcing himself across the room. She stood as if waiting. He lightly kissed her mouth as an inquiry. He could feel her shudder slightly with emotion, but she did not move, only waited as if watching them both.

His voice was unsteady. "Have I lost you by what I've done?" he murmured, his forehead against hers. "In going to recapture who I am, have I lost what I love? In some weeks more would it have been too late, and you would have gone on without me?"

She put her hand on his. "I would have come back," she said. "I would have come after you, but I couldn't bear it if you sent me away."

Later, when night had fallen and the child was asleep, he came cautiously into the bed where she lay smiling, her hair loose on the pillow, arm behind her head. He kissed her tentatively then, thinking, but what if I am not able to make love to her as I mostly could not in the months before I left? Then he forgot and it returned naturally. The bed creaked and she clung to him.

They lay together as if listening to all the books below them. Shadows hovered on the ceiling from the streetlamp below.

"I've done so much clumsily," he whispered. "But I can take care of you now. Boudin introduced me to some possible patrons; they're commissioning me to paint several pictures of the resort of Trouville just across the estuary from Le Havre this summer for a good deal of money, but I'll go only if you go. I want you to meet my father . . . and I want to take you there as my wife. It will be our honeymoon."

He rose and felt in his trouser pockets, taking out a tiny box. By the streetlamp he opened it. "This was my mother's betrothal ring," he whispered, lifting out the gold band with its one small pearl. "It's not dried grass, it's real."

ALMOST EVERYONE HE knew came to the restaurant in the Batignolles district for the wedding reception. The private room glittered with brass fixtures, engraved glass, and polished wood. He often sought her hand, because the secular wedding ceremony had dazed him.

Her parents had come from Lyon. They brought Camille's *grandmère*, a tiny, intelligent woman, her back crooked and her smile wide and generous. She gave her granddaughter one of her own brooches and kissed Claude warmly. Annette came with her husband, who frowned at everyone. On Claude's side of the family, his brother arrived with his wife, a bit bewildered by Claude's boisterous friends but impressed enough by Frédéric, who carried himself gravely as best man. Claude's father sent money and his regrets; he was too ill to travel that day. Claude's old friend Marc from Le Havre walked about telling everyone of Claude's wild boyhood days, drinking a great deal.

Little Jean, who was running as fast as he could around the table, collided with Claude's legs. Claude picked him up and tossed him in the air, and the boy shrieked happily, ran away, and climbed on Frédéric's lap. Frédéric clasped him tightly and whispered in his ear.

Their good friend Edmond Maître played Offenbach for an hour or more until Camille rose and took her sister's hand. "Let's sing the aria from *La Périchole* together," she begged. "Let's sing together as we did as girls back in Lyon!" They stood together by the spinet, Camille in her dusty pink silk wedding dress with delicate silk roses in her hair. Claude sat back in his chair and watched her. He remembered the first day they had spent alone together and how she had gone home with him impulsively and thrown off all her clothes.

As the song died away to whistles of approval, Claude glanced down the room. Frédéric's napkin lay on the table, his glass of champagne half drunk, and his chair pushed back and empty. He was gone.

Claude rose at once, a bit unsteadily. He looked around the restaurant and finally pushed open the street door to the soft early-evening air. He was now in a state so strange for him, so emotional, so precarious, that his friend's leaving affected him deeply. His homecoming and the marriage had been so sudden that he had had no time to speak to Frédéric about what was happening to him. Once more Frédéric had managed everything, and though he did not seem a ghost anymore, he seemed a little dazed, especially this evening.

Claude sent word by a waiter that he would be back directly.

It was three streets to the new studio on the rue de la Condamine where Frédéric had now moved, and Claude walked them carefully, crossing once between the early-evening traffic and the omnibuses carrying clerks and shopgirls on their way home from work. He mounted the building steps, fumbled with the key in the lock, and pushed open the door to the large studio.

An unfinished painting rested on Frédéric's easel, and his coat was thrown over a chair. "Damn it, Bazille! Where are you?" Claude cried as he climbed the open wood steps to the sleeping loft, holding a little to the wall.

Frédéric was lying facedown in his bed. He raised himself on his elbow and blinked. "Sorry," he murmured. "I drank too much. What are you doing here? Isn't everyone still celebrating?"

"Why did you disappear?"

"I'm wretched, Claude. I got a letter from home this morning. Lily's changed her mind about living in Paris half the year. She wants me to live there full-time."

Claude pulled off his tie impatiently and opened a few of the buttons on his satin floral vest. "What did I tell you?" he exploded. "That's it, then. Damn it, Frédéric! Tell her to go to hell. Stay with us. Stay with us."

"I don't know what I'll do. The world's a little crazy now. Did you see the newspapers today? The Prussians want to put one of their princes on the Spanish throne, which means another country could align against us. What I do seems insignificant next to the decisions of our emperor, who says we will go to war to prevent them."

"*Merde!* I don't give *merde* for the emperor! What do we have to do with this anyway?"

"Nothing!" Frédéric said, rising. "You're too drunk to be walking the streets. Let's go downstairs and make some coffee, and then you should go back."

Hand on the wall, Frédéric descended the steps before Claude. "What answer will I give them at home? It keeps rolling around in my mind," he said over his shoulder. "Damn it, I have to start the stove to boil water." Below, he picked up the bag of coffee beans on the shelf. He said, "Maybe I'll come with you. I knew you'd worry when I left, but there's nothing to worry about."

"You're my best friend, so I worry." Claude felt for a chair and sat.

Frédéric hurled the coffee grinder, which clattered across the floor and came to rest, rocking, beneath the table. He shouted, "Stop thinking that! There are things I haven't told you. Do you remember when we went to Fontainebleau for you to make that painting?"

Claude said, bewildered, "Of course I remember. What's the matter?"

"I made love to Camille that night."

Claude shook his head and laughed. "You're drunk. Now I know it."

"I'm telling you the truth," Frédéric exclaimed. "It wasn't planned."

"You're not drunk."

"I'm drunk enough to tell you the truth."

Claude stared at him. "I think you'd better tell me then," he said.

Frédéric crossed the room, so close that his arm brushed against Claude's shoulder. "I had gone outside to smoke alone because I couldn't sleep, and she was there, crying. We started to talk and suddenly we were pouring out all sorts of things. We found a little deserted chapel and went inside. She didn't want her fiancé and I'd just had a bad letter from home. She told me she had already had lovers."

He picked up a tube of paint and turned it over, staring at the label. "It was the first time for me and then, damn it, it seemed she had lied and it was the first time for her. I knew what that meant in our class. I felt then I should marry her, tell them at home and marry her, but she wouldn't hear of it. She said we should never refer to it again. And she went home with her sister and I went home to my fiancée, but I thought of her. I have never stopped thinking of her, though I have been a perfect gentleman, except of course with you, my best friend. . . . I've held this secret. I'm sorry. I shouldn't have told you, but I was sick with jealousy tonight and sick of all my broken plans. She had made me promise never to tell you. She knew it would upset you."

The chair wobbled as Claude jumped up. He wrapped his arms around his chest and walked back and forth, kicking the coffee grinder. "It's true, it has upset me," he answered. "Then again, should I blame you? You didn't know back then, of course, that later she and I would fall in love. Only it makes me damn uncomfortable."

He stared at his friend, who remained by his easel with his half-completed painting of a fisherman. Frédéric had taken up a tube of paint and was turning it over and over in his hands; he kept his eyes lowered.

Claude cried, "So it's the truth. You made love to my wife. My wife—*ma femme* . . . but she wasn't my wife then. But when I went away those two times over the past few years, you and she were alone. I know you helped her, looked after her, took her to dinner, but *was* there more? Was there?" He forced himself to stay by the table.

"The first time, when she was pregnant, no. We were shy with each other. And she loved you so."

"Very good, but then? This last time? This past winter? Tell me!"

Frédéric reached out and put his hand on the top of the canvas on the easel. He cried, "Damn it, you said you weren't coming back. That's the last thing you said. I wanted to and she wouldn't; then once she wanted to, and I said no. The main reason was you. She loves you. And I love you. I do, damn it. If you came back I knew she'd return to you. If you came back."

His head shot up; a dark patch of his chest hair showed where he had opened his white shirt, and his neck seemed very thin. He cried, "But I couldn't stop thinking about her. I bought the picture of her in the garden for that reason. Four women in the garden. After we had made love that one time and I returned to Montpellier, I thought I'd break my engagement to Lily and find Camille. Then suddenly she was yours."

But all Claude could think of was the many months in which he could not make love and that perhaps she had confided this to his best friend, and that perhaps when he could not, his friend could very well. He fiddled with his vest buttons, flushed with shame, and shouted, "You wanted to take her from me, you . . . !"

"We thought you weren't returning. I could give her what she needed, which you have tried so hard to do. A calm, pleasant life."

"You . . ." Claude pushed Frédéric against the wall near the window, and the back of his hand struck his friend's face. He felt the cheekbone. The easel wobbled and Claude caught it. Frédéric put up his hand.

"Did you have to hit me?" Frédéric asked. "Damn you!" He pushed past Claude to the table and sat down.

Claude dropped down on the chair next to him. He muttered, "How could you? Nothing can ever be the same now between us." He let his hand hover over Frédéric's shoulder.

Frédéric jerked away. "Don't touch me!" he gasped.

Claude shouted, "You've hurt me! Bad enough you slept with my wife in Fontainebleau, but then she and I weren't lovers. Worse for you both to lie about it to me these past few years and, yes, to ask her to come to you. What about your marriage? You're ending that possibility and helping yourself to mine!"

"You have never understood anything!" Frédéric shouted, looking up.

Claude slammed one hand on the table. "I understand you tried to persuade Camille to come with you. That's all very well and good with all your family money. Of course, you were thrown together when I was away. When she was pregnant and I stayed with my family for a time, when I went back again because I couldn't paint anymore, I trusted you. I thought you were . . ."

"Utterly honorable?"

Claude flung back his head and cried out to the sleeping loft above, "I did, God help me. But you spent a great deal of time together. Or maybe there are more times with her you haven't told me about."

"One time. I told you the truth."

"How do I know? You could give her just what she needed, a lovely life. It's easy for you, damn it! Everything's always been easy for you. You've never had the courage to stand on your own two feet."

Frédéric reared up and shoved him so that Claude's chair almost fell over. "I have more courage than you know!" he shouted. "I have the courage to paint and yet not to walk away from my family. I love painting and I love people, but the truth about you is that all you really love is what you can create. You went away this past winter once more, to leave everyone waiting. 'Oh, it's all right!' you'd say. 'I'm a genius. Everyone will wait for me!' "

"You called me a genius, not me!"

They stood glaring at each other. Claude said bitterly, "So you thought to relieve me of the burden of Camille and my son by taking them over! I should never have let you pay our rent, or lend me money. One day I'll pay you back for everything. I swear it. I want no obligation to you. I came after you tonight because I was worried about you. You had some fantasy about your very provincial Lily living in a house in Paris with a bunch of grubby painters."

Claude wiped his mouth. Once more he was aware of the wedding party at the restaurant, that people by now must be wondering when he would return, and that Camille was laughing and dancing, quite unaware of any of this.

He said stiffly, "I think I'll go off with her and pretend you never told me this. That painting you made of all of us and our friends here last week: It's not true. It was a vision. You'll knuckle under and go home. Likely when I come back you'll have moved back to Montpellier. I wish you well. I do."

"You have never understood anything, least of all what you are to me."

"I understand you live in a dream of all of us. I have to go on, and I expect you will too. I will read about you in the news journals one day: the successful Dr. Bazille, kindly, aged, stooped, father of eight children, off to church each Sunday, city father, benefactor of this and that, because in the end that's really what you want most."

His words dried. He said, "*Putain!* I have to get back. Everyone will be wondering. Let's shake hands at least."

Frédéric extended his cold hand without emotion. "There."

"Why didn't you hit me back?"

"I wouldn't have stopped, Claude. For lots of reasons."

CLAUDE CAME BACK to the wedding dinner dazed, not realizing how long he had been gone. He fell into bed that night and dreamt nothing. The next day he was in a hurry to put their things in storage. Camille was busy too, arranging for a cousin to keep the bookshop open. They were to honeymoon in Trouville, where he would paint.

He left some of his paintings at the shop. Many were at Frédéric's;

he did not know what to do about that. The last few dozen, including the one he had made with Boudin of the rising sun, he brought to Pissarro's house in Louveciennes, walking from the train station up the road in the bright morning to the stone cottage.

"We'll put them in the empty stable, where I store mine," Pissarro said.

Light poured through the stable windows, and in each of the four standing stalls Claude saw hundreds of his friend's paintings, mounted or rolled on low wood stands, endless landscapes of the French countryside with its village roads and abbeys and markets and trees in spring. "It's my life's work," Pissarro said. "Put yours here. When you come back I'll bring them to you. Good luck you have your commissions this summer. We'll see each other in the fall. Is something on your mind? You look as if there is."

"Nothing to speak of."

There was, of course, and it was of such magnitude he had not been able to form the words; he felt oddly that if he said nothing it would go away. He had told Camille that Frédéric had felt sick from his news from home and she shook her head in disbelief and wanted to know if he was better. He watched her face closely, but it registered nothing but loving concern. Then what had happened? Had Frédéric told him the truth?

We will talk in the fall when we return, Claude thought.

He could not bear to recall that he had struck his best friend in the face.

Man is born free, but everywhere he is in chains.
—JEAN-JACQUES ROUSSEAU

E HAD SEEN THE RESORT AT TROUVILLE SEVERAL times but had never stayed there. Now he walked down the wide boardwalk with his little family and their dog, Victoire, the sea on one side and the hotels rising like castles on the other. His father was not in Le Havre; Adolphe Monet was away in Orléans visiting his brother. But Claude was comforted by word left for him that that his father was eager to meet Claude's wife and son as soon as he returned.

He and Camille moved into a modest hotel off the main boardwalk.

In the weeks that followed Claude threw himself with great passion into his commissions of elegant people on the beach, the sand, the hotels, and the huge, wind-pushed flags of the boardwalk. He painted Camille in a beach chair under an umbrella with Jean digging in the sand at her side. At night they sometimes left Jean with one of the hotel maids and danced under the stars, he somewhat clumsily, laughing. Other evenings they dined with his old friends, among them Boudin and his wife and Claude's friend Marc. A few times they delightedly gambled small amounts at the casino.

He accompanied her to a dressmaker and a hatmaker and, in another pretty shop, bought her pink shoes. He sat waiting in a chair in all the shops, biting his lip, rubbing his head and mustache, almost afraid to leave her. She glittered and laughed, so utterly happy trying on an Indian fringed silk shawl. She turned this way and that before the shop mirrors, and he saw his reflection in the mirror as well, sitting sideways in the back, a moody man who looked a little tired.

She had received a portion of her dowry; he noted wryly to himself that her parents, who lived so well, could only give her that. Still, he was determined that it be spent all on her so that her clothes would be as lovely as they had been when he first found her.

Sometimes, leaving the shop with a hatbox, she touched his cheek and asked brightly, "What's the matter?"

"Nothing! Should there be?"

Silence held between them for a moment. She lowered her eyes and looked away. Her smile faded. He clumsily took her hand and kissed it. They strolled and he bought her a pink parasol. Once when he stopped to purchase tobacco and she went on a little ahead on the boardwalk, he saw her and his son in a new way, as you do sometimes when you see people you love from a distance.

Two months more here will heal us, he thought. Sometime on that hotel bed on a warm afternoon with the curtains drawn and Jean away with other children, we will hold each other and tell each other everything.

He did not know they would not have those months.

WALKING DOWN THE boardwalk on an August day, his easel on his shoulder, he was intensely aware of groups of people gathered here and there at café tables or on the boardwalk; they were poring over newspapers, their faces startled.

He picked up a newspaper that had been left on a bench and read the front page. When he looked up, the very air seemed to have changed. He forgot his easel in his haste to return to their room and had to run back for it, quickening his step as he passed through the lobby of their hotel.

Camille had already dressed and was pacing the room. Her white parasol lay on the bed. "I heard them talking about it from the window!" she exclaimed. She looked at him fixedly, biting the edge of her finger. "I hoped you'd come back. Oh, Claude, what can it mean?"

He put his arm around her, drawing her tightly against him, looking at the bright day beyond the window and then at his son, who was seated on the floor trying to put on his shoes. He said, "The emperor's declared war against Prussia."

"The maid said people will start leaving at once."

"For where? I think they may call it all off." He did not want her to see that he felt shaken. He helped the protesting Jean with his shoe and then sat down by the window to reread the paper. The words did not seem real: "France may be invaded." The sound of the great flapping flags he had painted turned in his mind to what he had read of the cries of war and women sobbing and fleeing before the enemy. He thought of soldiers marching through the mud, the air acrid with gunpowder, fields and vineyards burning. He had heard these things in his days in Algiers. He also knew stories of the Paris government overthrow in 1848, but he had been far away in Le Havre and only a little boy.

In the next few days Trouville turned from a crowded resort filled with prosperous vacationers to a fading, half-empty town. Claude's patrons left. Hotels were closing, and the carousel ceased to turn. The painted wood animals stood silent, waiting for their joyful little riders. Hardly anyone splashed in the waves. *War*, everyone said. In the few occupied tables of restaurants you could hear little else. Still, the bands continued to play each night, and people still gambled with a sort of defiance in the half-empty casino.

What was happening in Paris? He could not see it otherwise than he had left it: a world of artists, cafés, galleries, colorists' shops, a life lived from one canvas to the next with a great deal of hope. It was beyond belief that it could change.

He read the letter that finally came from Auguste while walking on the emptying boardwalk. Camille was beside him, holding her pink frilled parasol to protect her from the sun, and Jean was ahead of them, chasing seagulls.

Claude, I received your letter but we have been so frantic that my mother left it in the kitchen and just this morning remembered to give it to me. You know that I moved home again, having run out of money once more, but I go to Paris every day.

My friend, this is not the city you left six weeks ago. I hardly know the boulevards, for they're full of marching men and flags flying and people standing on boxes making speeches for and against the war. On every corner men bellow for conscripts. Manet and Degas have joined the national guard to protect the city, and Cézanne has fled to the south of France. Pissarro is so distressed he only mumbles into his beard and says he does not know how he can leave his paintings. His house is in the path the bastards will take if they invade us and reach the city.

To the horror of my mother and my sisters, who are so dependent on what I may do one day with my poor paintbrush, I have been conscripted, though I hope I will not have to fire at anyone, as I am incapable of it. And what about you? I know you were bought out, but there are rumors that such things will be disregarded in time of war.

I am aggrieved and bewildered about Bazille! After you left, he broke off his marriage plans completely and began to drink a lot and not paint at all. Now he's enlisted and left to train in the Zoaves in Algiers, though we begged him not to go and his family bought him out years ago. Wasn't that your regiment? He said to tell you that he now has proven he has the courage to stand on his own two feet. What is he talking about? He seemed very angry. Did you fight with him?

By the water, one little girl was intensely digging a deep hole, and as he gazed at her he wondered if she might try to reach the other side of the earth as he had tried to do for hours as a boy. He turned to Camille, who had touched his arm. "What news?" she asked. "Oh, Claude, is it bad?"

He replied roughly, "They're all damn going in one way or another, all enlisting or conscripted. I should go too. How will I manage later if I don't go and my friends are hurt? I had my training."

"You mustn't go! You mustn't!"

She clutched her parasol as if she would hold him as hard as she held it. In a voice so soft he could hardly hear her, she asked, "Is Frédéric going?"

"I don't know," Claude said coldly. He looked at her briefly, and then he looked away.

HE WALKED ABOUT the resort with his hands in his pockets during the next days; sometimes he strolled on the empty sand, kicking it, watching it fly in heaps in the air and settle again. What if the Prussians do invade? he thought. We'll be at war; I likely won't earn any money with my work, and we may be in danger.

When he felt he could walk no more, he stood still for a moment and looked out over the water. Boats were crossing the estuary every day for the port of Le Havre; people had already booked passage on ships abroad.

Claude thought, I'll send her and the little one on alone to England and stay here myself to enlist. What would she do there? We know no one. Where would they go? Still, I must fight. If he's gone, then so must I, for I'm no less a man! Then he flung himself down on the sand and buried his head in his hands. *Putain!* Frédéric! he thought. Why him and not me?

He turned resolutely to the ticket office and then walked slowly back to the nearly empty hotel. Camille was helping Jean make a picture with bits of chalk, and her fingers were dusted with pale green.

She looked up at him, biting her lip. Several strands of hair fell down her neck for she had made her knot hastily that morning as if she must be prepared to leave quickly.

"We need to leave the country," he said. "I thought to send you on alone but I can't. I've got to go with you to look after you and I also don't know if my exemption from the military will remain valid in this emergency. I've booked passage for us to England from Le Havre."

"England!" she cried. "So far? I must telegraph my sister and niece. I shouldn't leave them."

"Suggest they leave the city. Paris may be invaded."

"Do you think so? Oh, that can't be!"

Camille ran downstairs to send the telegram. He looked about, not knowing what to pack first. Kneeling, he opened a small trunk and gazed down into its floral paper lining, feeling only confusion and shame.

As the ship made ready to sail from Le Havre the next day, Victoire jumped from Camille's arms, waddled through the crowd and down the walkway, and disappeared. Jean burst into tears, but the ship was pulling away and all Camille could do was weep. Claude kept his arm about her, yet as he looked out he thought, *Frédéric*. I hit you and you have gone away I don't know where, hating me.

Interlude

GIVERNY

January 1909

As the winter progressed, he worked obsessively on his canvases of the water lily pond. In them time was suspended; he painted the sun and the mist, the movement of the water by the wind or the wavering of the submerged water lily stems, the changing light. The canvases were horizontal, circular, and square. Some had the effects of evening: colors muting and darkening, water still reflecting.

Each day he tried to see the paintings anew.

Some horrified him and sent him into despair. Was this all he could do at this age? One day he slashed several to pieces, amid the protests of his family, and later he stood trembling as if he had destroyed part of himself. I will never exhibit any of these paintings, he thought bitterly, for they all may be bad, even the ones that remain. How do I know what is good or bad? All I have done may have come to nothing and my life may be nothing but a failure.

He stormed into the house and into the kitchen and sat down for a glass of wine. He was still distraught when his chauffeur brought in the day's mail. Among the many letters he saw one he had ceased to expect. Would it be another bitter few sentences? Of all days, he could not bear it! Still, he had to open it, even against his better judgment.

> *Monet,*
>
> *Though I had resolved not to write you again, I will break that resolve but briefly to answer your question of what happened to the letters my sister wrote around the time she first met you. She brought them to my house that snowy night when you and she had to flee your rooms. She forgot them and at one time asked me to destroy them, but I did not. However, I can't find them. Why you would want letters written to another man is something I can't understand. I supposed she bewitched you as she did so many.*
>
> *If I find the letters I will write you again. I cannot give you more.*
>
> *Annette Lebois*

He stuffed the letter in his pocket and made his way heavily back to the studio. One of the gardeners had taken away the pile of slashed canvases stacked outside. He went inside, closed the door, and stood looking at his remaining water lily paintings. More than forty of them had survived his rampage.

He thought, If my work is futile, I might as well let the critics tell me—they have never hesitated to do so. He sat down and wrote hastily to Paris and then looked for his chauffeur to take the letter to be posted.

You may exhibit the paintings in May, his letter had said, with the last words underlined. *But I will not be there.*

Part Five

1870–1871

Cher ami, *the more I live, the more I regret how little I know*.

—CLAUDE MONET, IN A LETTER TO FRÉDÉRIC BAZILLE

ROM DOVER, THEY FOUND THE TRAIN TO LONDON along with another refugee, a young printer who was fleeing conscription. Among them, only Camille knew some English, which she had learned in the convent.

Claude stared out the window at the countryside, which was beautiful but different from that in France. Then he turned morosely away. He had brought several paintings and his paints and a few changes of clothes; he had left the rest in Le Havre and Paris and its environs. Still, to the rhythm of the train wheels he murmured to himself, "Where is my country? Where are my friends?"

The printer told them, "You're likely to find lodgings in the old French immigrant area called Spitalfields. At least we'll be among countrymen there. I'm staying with a cousin. I beg you, madame, be of good cheer! The war won't last long and we'll all be home again."

Claude had never seen such crowds as when they emerged from the train station in London. Someone helped them find a porter and then a cab. They rattled past immense churches and mansions; buses bumped by them with printed advertisements on their sides that he could not read. Two-year-old Jean sucked a piece of shimmering rock candy on a stick, looking around him darkly from under his hair, which partly covered his small face. The boat passage had been rough and overcrowded with fleeing Frenchmen; he had vomited over the rail.

"Spitalfields," said the driver. They dragged themselves out to the street, where Claude shuddered with relief to hear his own language about him once more. The area was old and overcrowded. After a few hours of asking, they found a place behind a restaurant owned by a Marseilles man who had come here years before. The room was small and dark, the one window looking out at a yard filled with barrels and crates and smelling of cat.

Camille put down her bag and leaned against a wall. She had wept so much for her family and for her dog, Victoire, that her handkerchief, which she clutched in her fist, was a crumpled rag.

Claude looked about, hands on his hips. The room was sparsely and badly furnished; the mattress on the one bed was scarcely an inch thick. He sank down on it, and one of the ropes that held it broke. "That's it!" he cried scathingly. "How can I take care of both of you here? I can't even speak the language."

She cried, "If they invade France, my *grandmère* will take *Grandpère*'s hunting gun down from above the fireplace and stand at her door. He's long dead, but she always kept his gun. I'm here, here, and not protecting her. And my sister and her little Nannette and our friends . . ."

He held his breath and let it out. "I didn't tell you about Frédéric. He damn enlisted! What will he do with a rifle? He's never shot anything but a duck."

She stepped toward him, blinking, terror in her face. "Oh, Claude, he's gone to fight? I didn't know that."

He knelt to open a wicker trunk, trying to keep his voice gruff. "Don't worry, the bastard will make a good enough soldier! He enlisted for nothing; we came for nothing. We'll manage here and everyone will be safe. I promise you. You mind Jean. I'll earn money for us."

They hung a few of his pictures that they had brought with them on the wall.

Claude set off early the next morning. The streets off Brick Lane were squalid, lying like narrow black trenches; two hundred years earlier French silk weavers had come here fleeing religious persecution. Now the weaving industry was dead and the community half Jewish. He wondered what he looked like to people. His beard was untrimmed, and his clothes were wrinkled. He asked several Frenchmen if they knew of work and they all said there was none. "I paint," he said, and one asked, "Houses?" He winced and replied, "I could do that." But there was no opening for a housepainter.

He walked far that day and the following ones, asking directions back to the old weavers' houses in Fournier Street. That much English he learned, but the way he pronounced it must have been odd because people looked at him strangely. He finally just asked for "Fournier" and even then was once sent some miles out of his way. A few weeks passed and he had found nothing.

As he walked home one September day he saw Pissarro and his family making their way down the street. Julie clasped her smaller son and looked weary and bewildered. Her older, Lucien, held his ragged stuffed dog and clung to her side. "There you all are!" Claude cried, pushing past a rag collector's wagon to reach them. "I can't say how glad I am to see you! I wondered when you were coming!" He seized up a roped bundle of paintings. "Have you a room?"

Pissarro pointed down the street. "Yes, in that synagogue," he said sadly. "A distant relative here arranged for us to live above it in exchange for cleaning it. An odd event for me, as I have never been a very religious Jew. You've heard the grim news of our forces? The emperor and his troops were captured by the Prussians at Sedan. They were surrounded. We lost seventeen thousand Frenchmen before he ran up the white flag. The emperor!" He spat. "This is what I think of power!"

Claude said, "I heard and hoped it wasn't so. I hardly know how to take that. How can seventeen thousand men be killed? I can't think of so many lives snuffed out."

Pissarro shook his head. "Neither can I, but our friends are safe and so are we, though we have to bear this news in our hearts. One man was from my village. As I was locking our paintings in my stable, his mother was crying, and we are here, living our little lives with the sole justification to paint. Why? Is a painter more than a farmer? Can you work here?"

"No," Claude replied abruptly.

At least our friends are safe, he thought grimly, but for how long?

He hoisted the small trunk to his shoulder and helped the little Pissarro family up the stairs to the rooms above the synagogue. A bookcase held prayer books in Hebrew, and from below came the sound of droned singing.

The weather was warm, and his countrymen lingered in the street when they weren't working or looking for work, talking about home. Many were from Paris, others from around the country. He met a clarinetist who had played in a Trouville restaurant. Some had immigrated here a generation before.

Weeks passed. They gathered every morning after coffee in front of the restaurant; the owner, Louis, would unfold the limp newspapers and translate news of home. Claude stood near Pissarro staring at the cobbles as the news was read, their shoulders tense as the sentences unfolded, none of them good; each sentence broke open his chest and settled inside.

Louis was grimmer than usual one morning. "My friends," he said, shaking his head. "I wish I didn't have to translate this. I'd prefer to burn it. I'd prefer to piss on it. Paris is completely surrounded by the enemy; it is under siege. No one can come out, and no one or nothing can come in. No food can come in, my friends."

A hot, bruised murmur rose among the group until it became a cry. Everyone was talking at once. Many were crying. Claude thought, bewildered, But how can my free city be under siege? That is a medieval thing. What can it mean, "No food can come in"? Very few kitchen gardens were kept in the city; there was little room. Paris was completely dependent on the surrounding farms, which sent food in the earliest hours of the morning to the great market at Les

Halles. Could there really be no piles of vegetables so plentiful that cabbage leaves and carrot greens littered the ground? No baskets of fresh eggs, no pungent cheeses of goat's and cow's and sheep's milk? No lambs hanging from hooks in the butcher shop, no flour in the bins of his favorite baker? It did not seem possible.

Camille clutched his hand. "My sister's there, and my little niece."

Julie clasped her and rocked her slightly; "Come, Camille." she urged. "No matter how bad things sound, you know our country will win in the end. I will make you a nice coffee. It will be all right." Julie led her friend away, coaxing her, with Camille looking back as if somehow more news might come shortly that there really was no siege so far away.

A few weeks later a letter finally arrived from Auguste; he drew sketches of his camp, which was stationed well away from Paris, and said he was becoming a horseman. He added that Paris was sending news by hot-air balloon, which he thought was marvelously innovative, and that he had received word from Frédéric, who was still in training in Algiers.

His friend's name on paper broke something in Claude and the sudden silence between them was too heavy to bear. Not a day had passed when Claude had not thought of the regiment there and his friend.

He penned a letter sitting at a table in the empty restaurant at midday. "Bazille, I hope this reaches you. We are in London and reasonably well. Pissarro's here also. How are you?" It won't reach him, he thought as he posted it to Algiers in the red postbox. But a few weeks later, a wrinkled envelope arrived for him. He walked with it for some time down Commercial Street, past the half-broken houses, until he had courage to open it.

Claude, Auguste told me you were in London, but I was very grateful to hear from you directly and to know you are safe. I am humbled that you were the one to write first and break our silence.

We are training now and soon will ship out to France. I am up at dawn to peel potatoes, which I actually do very well. I had visions of riding a white steed, delivering a message that would save my battalion, but all I deliver is potatoes. I expect you will find this amusing.

There are things I need to tell you. I can't say them in a letter, Claude. I'm sorry if I did anything to hurt you. Don't worry about me. I've too many things to do in this life to get killed. I'll come back. I promise.

As he stood under the spire of Christ Church, Claude said under his breath, "So this is all you say? And will you ever tell me more of what happened between you and her, you bastard?" There had been more; it was over now, but there had been more. Claude sensed it. He tore the letter in two, and then ruefully fitted it together again.

He kept it in a book; he did not share it.

That day he began to paint again.

As CLAUDE HAD in his early days as a struggling art student, he and Camille ate beans and dry bread, and sometimes the remains of a stew from the restaurant. They cleaned the restaurant to pay for their room. Late at night when he came home he would see her mopping the floors and washing the pots, a scarf around her head; he would take the mop from her hands and finish himself.

Tenderly he would kiss her hands and rub cream into them. She pulled them away quickly, and he flushed. She is avoiding me, he thought sadly. She is worried about him. She blames me for many things.

She was always with Julie these days; they shopped together and sewed and sometimes laughed in the private way of women, sitting close and talking of children. In Paris it had been her sister and Lise with her love of dresses and wild theatrical aspirations who had been Camille's closest friends; now it was Julie, the daughter of farmers, with her rough rural accent, her strong hands that could mercilessly wring wet laundry or a chicken's neck, and her blunt, sometimes tactless judgments of the artists, the English, all religious belief, and any garments for children but strong, simple ones that could be readily mended.

Claude heard these opinions frequently, for he and Camille spent most evenings with the Pissarros in their rooms, the sound of men praying in Hebrew rising up from the synagogue. A few of the artist's landscapes hung over a bookshelf of Hebrew books and boxes of candles that had been stored there.

He and Pissarro sat by the window on stools or chairs, smoking their pipes frugally. If they closed the drapes they could pretend they were in the Marais again and one of them might go down shortly to the café to fill their wine jug. It seemed as if they'd hear voices from the stairs and Sisley would come in, throwing off his white scarf, or Édouard Manet would come with top hat and cane. At any moment the English Channel would dwindle to no more than a puddle to step across and all the Prussian soldiers would be blown away to their own land.

Rain fell against the window.

Julie was cooking beans with a bit of meat. Camille set the apple tart she had baked on a sideboard to cool and sat down on a low stool. "My English is getting better," she told them shyly. "I've learned some useful phrases. 'Please, sir, where are the Houses of Parliament?' 'I desire to engage a nursemaid.' 'Yes, sir, I accept your kind invitation to the ball.' "

When she translated they all broke into laughter. They became wild with laughter after a time; they gasped with it until they noticed furious tears running down Julie's face. "Why are we laughing?" she shouted. "Don't you know the news from Paris? The shops are empty; they've *nothing* to eat. It's been weeks now! Someone told me today they're eating rats and horses there. The zoo's been long emptied."

Lucien knelt on his chair and hit the table violently with his spoon. "They haven't eaten the zoo animals!" he cried frantically. "They haven't eaten my lion! They wouldn't eat my lion."

Pissarro drew his son on his lap, rocking him and kissing him. "What can we do but have courage?" he asked. "Every man in the French army is now on French soil. They'll liberate Paris. Let me tell you the story of the first day I arrived in Paris from the West Indies with this mad desire to be an artist . . ."

When he had finished his story, he sang to them traditional songs his dark childhood nurse in the West Indies had taught him; he did not have a musical voice, but it was comforting. They all sat for a long time listening to the softly falling rain outside, with only a few candles they had taken from the synagogue supply lighting the empty soup bowls and glasses. They watched the candles burn low before saying it was late. Lucien had finished his lion picture.

Claude and Camille left to walk to their room, she holding a little bread wrapped in cloth, he carrying the sleeping Jean. The rain had almost stopped. He thought, It's the same rain that falls on Frédéric in his regiment as he makes his way toward Paris to free it. He knew his friend was in France now.

"Soon it will be winter," he said.

CLAUDE WAS GONE every day and often did not come home until dark; he was painting. There was something in the air he had never seen before: the thick, yellowish gray fog that hung over the whole city so that the sunlight was strained as through a dirty brown cloth. You could not part it with your hands. Beneath and through this aberration of light struggled the form of the immense gothic Houses of Parliament behind Westminster Bridge and the tumbling, shuddering water of the Thames, which rolled downstream to the sea. He painted both passionately.

He had brought some canvases and paint from France. He and Pissarro hoarded them, sometimes painting over one. Sometimes he walked around in the parks and saw artists following wealthy people, crying, "Sir, sir, two shillings for a drawing. One shilling . . ." Day after day he became more aware of the poverty of London: the dark, narrow alleys; the rotten food; the naked children; the hands sliding in his empty pockets to find what they could there. He became aware of the hundreds of beggars.

The cold came and the skies were cloudy again. Winter settled in and he and Pissarro ran out of canvases. When they had no more they could sacrifice to paint over, they did not paint but stood on Brick Lane talking about the latest news from Paris. Camille was not in the restaurant; she had likely gone somewhere with Julie. Claude was suddenly very tired. He made his way to his room and lay down, covering himself with the blanket and his coat, and immediately fell asleep.

Someone was knocking at the door, waking him. *"Entrez! La porte est ouverte!"* he called irritably.

On the threshold, wearing a fine cashmere fur-trimmed coat and a top hat and looking about curiously, stood the great painter Daubigny.

Claude rose, stumbling over a shoe. "Monsieur," he stammered. "I didn't know you were in London. Come in. I can't excuse this humble place, but we all do the best we can. If you'll wait, I'll go out for some wine. I'm happy to see you; I can't tell you how happy."

Daubigny glanced discreetly about, and then looked at Claude. "I heard a rumor you were in London but only found you now. I may have an opportunity for you. My art dealer has moved here from Paris as so many of us have. I tried to get him interested in your work a few years ago and now he wants to meet you. You have undoubtedly heard of him: Paul Durand-Ruel. You have been painting London? Good."

HE SELECTED HIS paintings hastily; he could not find a clean shirt. He climbed into a hansom cab after Daubigny and they maneuvered through the heavy traffic, descending at New Bond Street and entering a gallery with the walls full of paintings and racks of drawings. It was so like the Paris gallery where he had tried to show his work and met only refusal from the art dealer's assistant.

On one wall hung a painting by the beloved artist Corot of a forest with trees in blossom. It brought such a longing for rural France to Claude that his eyes filled with tears. He wanted to climb inside the picture. The slightly plump man with prematurely white hair who walked toward him blurred for him. Claude murmured, "*Bonjour;* I am Claude Monet."

"I am Paul Durand-Ruel, monsieur," replied the art dealer, shaking his hand. "How odd we two should meet in this strange city! I see you have brought some of your work. Will you show it to me?"

Claude leaned his canvases against the wall one by one, and the art dealer walked back and forth in front of them, taking in the oil painting of the port of London with all its ships' masts, churning water, and intense clouds above, the Thames at Westminster Bridge with a few distant boats, and a somber, lonely painting of a scarcely populated Hyde Park. At last Durand-Ruel turned to him. He said, "I think I can sell them. I'll take all three at two hundred francs each."

Claude stared at him. He said at last, "When we were in Paris you wouldn't so much as look at my work, no matter how I tried. What has changed your mind, monsieur?"

"Sometimes good things come out of great misfortunes, Monet. I did not expect any good to come out of this, but perhaps it has. I am sorry to have turned you away in Paris. I didn't think I could sell your work there. I do believe I can sell it here. Daubigny guarantees it. I shall pay you in English pounds, of course."

AS THEY RODE away in a cab together, he thanked Daubigny until he had no more words, and when he found himself in Spitalfields again, he stood watching the cab wobble away with the great artist within. Here, in this strange and foreign place, one of the artists he most admired had stood up for him, and he now had more money in his pocket than he'd had since he left Trouville.

He turned to the market, which spilled down the street in front of food shops. He carried his remaining paintings, and now he bought a wicker basket and hurried from shop to shop. From the dairy he bought eggs, cream, butter, and cheese; from the poulterer a freshly killed chicken; and from a sausage maker, two long ropes of sausage. Pissarro would need some too. He bought jars of asparagus and jams so sweet that the seeds seemed to press against the glass. He bought tobacco and English biscuits and hurried with the paintings and parcels down the street and through the restaurant to the kitchen.

Camille had returned. She was washing dishes, her hair under a kerchief, a great apron covering her dress, her sleeves rolled up, and her hands plunged in hot water. "Minou!" he cried. "I've sold three pictures to the greatest art dealer in Paris! I'm sending Pissarro to see him tomorrow and the man will take my friend if he wants anything else from me! He'll sell them all over the world. This is the beginning, here, today!"

She looked at the baskets and parcels and then at him so tenderly. "Oh, Claude," she said.

His desire rose fiercely for having been hidden away these months. He half pulled her into their room, trying to manage her hand and the baskets and the canvases. She laughed first, and then her pretty face grew serious and she drew in her breath sharply, in longing. He stifled her mouth with kisses. He pushed her onto the bed. Her worn, mended stockings were scratchy and left her legs reddened. Her belly was the same beautiful shape, still faintly etched with stretch marks from bearing their son. He was not slow but rough and fast, and she gasped and rose breathless to meet his thrusts. The kerchief came off, and her hair was dirty. Her hands smelled of cheap soap.

They lay close to each other for a moment when they were done, each in their own thoughts. Slowly she moved away and felt for her undergarments. Louis was calling her from the kitchen.

"You're my muse," he whispered. "My woman in the green dress."

"I am a sad muse now, Claude," she replied. "And all my pretty dresses are again pawned or sold. I don't blame you. I only want to be home again. I only want this dreadful war to be over."

He nodded; he wished she would not go. He felt words forming in his throat but they had not time to come.

At Christmas she placed a candle in the window once more to welcome the wandering Virgin and her child. By this time a few things had changed. He knew a little English, mostly curse words. He had sold a few more paintings, and she had stopped working in the restaurant. Through the one small window he saw the snow falling over London, and taking his coat and sketch pad, he went out. He stopped beneath an old market awning no one had taken down, sketching rapidly on a pad he held with the edge balanced on his chest, drawing the world as he wanted it.

THE NEWS THAT France had conceded defeat came in late January as he walked home with his easel over his shoulder. He knew only that the headlines on the papers included the word *Paris*. "We have lost the war," someone said, "but Paris is free." Claude sank to the curb, leaning on the milk cart, stupidly watching the trickle of thin blue milk in the gutter.

Friends gathered in the street, in rooms, in the restaurant that night. "We have lost Alsace-Lorraine to the bastards," someone said. Claude mingled with them and then retreated to his room. Camille followed with their son; she stood with her back to the door as if keeping London away, her face glowing as he had seen it do when he had first taken her to the theater.

He held out his arms and she came into them. "I'll see my sister again," she said. "I'll see my friends." There was a wonder and a determination in her voice; he laughed a little, feeling she would float away just then and go home. All night he heard happy voices outside.

He barely slept. In his mind he was walking with his friends to their independent exhibition at last. He held her and his son, having no words for his joy.

Then he slept so deeply he did not at first hear the knocking on the door. He woke to the first light coming through the one dirty window.

Pissarro stood in the yard, his coat open, his head lowered. "What is it?" Claude asked sleepily. "Are the children all right?"

The artist leaned against the door frame. The white hairs in his beard shone a little by the candle in the tin holder he held in his hand. He said, "Claude, it's bad news. We had a letter late last night from Edmond Maître in Paris."

IT'S NOT TRUE, Claude told himself. It's a mistake. They make these mistakes all the time. He's there in the studio. Why didn't I write him before?

Camille was reading and rereading the letter by the window; he wanted to snatch it from her. "We're returning at once!" he said. "I don't believe it for a moment."

And yet as she packed it seemed that she did not even want him to touch her hand. He stayed across the room, arranging his own things in bags. Jean understood nothing but kept whimpering. "Be still!" she shouted at him in a terrible voice. Claude picked up the child and hushed him. Suddenly it seemed that every unsaid thing between him and Camille was about to come forth. I shall say nothing, he told himself. But he did not say her name under his breath, only that of his friend in the studio in the rue de la Condamine.

The train station was nearly empty but for porters, and they boarded, carrying the sleeping Jean, dragging their suitcases and some paintings. He had asked Pissarro to bring the others to Durand-Ruel. On the boat to Calais he stood for a time leaning by the rail, watching the churning waters until he could no longer see England. Jean was crying with the cold, and Claude took him inside.

The port of Calais was full of Prussian soldiers and French customs officials. One turned over their clothes and a few books. "Traveling is not easy," he said. "The country is occupied, and some tracks have been destroyed."

Camille refilled her water bottle and bought thick soup from a Frenchwoman, who ladled it from a pot over coals. She stumbled a little; she had not slept the whole night on the ferry and little the night before on the train from London. Sometimes she leaned against Claude, and other times she sat apart from him, looking ahead of her.

In the midst of a crowd they boarded the French train, whose doors and windows were icy to the touch. The train rocked through the night, stopping once for an inspection. Prussians came through, opening people's wicker baskets.

Parts of the tracks were gone, and dozens of passengers descended to wait for wagons. For a time they traveled that way, pulled by farm donkeys and then by ferry and wagon again, before rejoining a small, rough train. All the way he heard stories of how the crops had rotted in the field last autumn and the grapes had withered on the vine for lack of men to bring them in.

THEY WERE SILENT as they approached the rue de la Condamine, though they walked quickly. In the end they were running, holding Jean in turn. The concierge was not there and the house door was unlocked. Claude used his iron key and entered the studio, calling, "Frédéric!"

Late-afternoon light fell on all the paintings hung on the wall; dust motes danced in the air. The easels were empty, and the stove was cold. No one had made a fire there in a long time. Claude walked in slowly as if afraid to disturb anything. He sat down in the chair he had sat in that night when he and his friend had quarreled.

Above, someone moved.

A thin soldier came down the stairs, and it was a moment before Claude recognized Auguste. His friend came straight toward them and embraced them. "I saw you across the street from the window," Auguste said. "I'm sorry if I startled you. How did you get back so quickly? I returned yesterday. Well, now I have seen a little of war, but no action. That was left for others. Frédéric and I wrote to each other a bit, you know, saying the whole thing was not as glamorous as we had supposed. Then word came and we telegraphed London."

"It can't be true," Claude said stubbornly.

"We had better sit down," Auguste said. He pulled out a chair at the table for Camille and sat himself. Claude shook his head.

Auguste said, "I came back last night to see how my mother was outside the city—she had no billeting and ate from her garden, bless her—and then I came to the city and went at once to his friend Edmond Maître, who had stayed during the siege. He knows the Bazille family, so I thought he'd have more information, and he did. He had just received a telegram from Frédéric's father confirming the terrible news. So until then I also had some hope."

Claude sat down then. He leaned forward, arms on his knees and hands folded. "Tell me," he said.

"It was the end of November. His battalion was retreating near Orléans. He was tall, of course, so easy to pick out . . . shot in the head, the bastards. Monsieur Bazille traveled to the battlefield under a safe conduct and spent ten days finding him, and then he took his son home in a cart in the snow to bury him in Montpellier. He could get no other transportation. Frédéric's family didn't want him to go. They begged him not to go."

THEY STAYED CLOSE, talking softly for a long time as if afraid to disturb the air. Then Auguste kissed them both and the child, and left them. The sound of his army boots on the stairs faded away and the studio was absolutely still but for the slightly congested breathing of the little boy, who had fallen asleep in Claude's lap.

"He's dead," Claude said at last. "And yet it doesn't seem possible. We fought, you know, about you, and I said stupid things. I said

. . . that he had never had the courage to stand on his own two feet, and he went to war to prove me wrong."

Camille sat with her hands folded in her lap. The lovely hands were not clean, and her dress was dark in the seams from the soot of the journey. "Yes, he's dead," she said. "We've never talked about what happened. Months passed and we didn't talk; not in Le Havre, not in that London room, which seems so far away now."

The child stirred, and Claude stroked the boy's long, dirty hair. "Say what you want," he replied. "I must hear it. I've waited a long time to hear it."

She did not unfold her hands, and she looked at a paint stain on the floor. Her voice was so soft he had to listen intensely. She said, "When we thought you weren't coming back ever again from Le Havre, I turned to him. I was so lonely and frightened. We became lovers. He denied it to you, but it was true. He asked me to marry him and I wouldn't give him an answer because I loved you so. Perhaps if I had agreed to marry him, he wouldn't have enlisted. He wrote me when we were in Trouville and told me about your fight."

"Did he please you more than me?"

He could have bitten his tongue at her horrified face.

Jean woke and began to cry, confused, wondering what this place was with the big windows and the steps to a loft. Claude tried to hold him, but he wailed. "I'm sorry," he managed. "I shouldn't have said that. I left you. I went home to my father and left you and no one knew if I was coming back. I can't blame you. And besides, he was lovely, gentle, kind. He was everything I'm not."

"Yes, you left me. You were in pain and I knew it; I knew it. But it is also true that all you thought of was that you couldn't paint anymore. You couldn't compromise, and you didn't think of how cutting your wrist would make me feel, how it would make your friends feel. Then you came back after three months as if nothing had changed, as if I were one of the cutouts of women from the magazines you told me you pinned on your walls as a boy or the idealized drawing you made of me in a train station. You can close a sketchbook and the drawing doesn't cry out in loneliness, missing you! You can scrub out a painting and it doesn't feel it."

"I wonder if it does," he said with a shudder. "If a painting feels things. *Putain!* So much is wrong with me, Minou. I did think of you. I feel so helpless when I can't paint."

"Oh, Claude!" she cried, turning to him. "There were things he couldn't tell you. Maybe if he had been able to he wouldn't have gone away."

"What things?"

"I can't. I can't!" she cried, bringing the side of her fist repeatedly to her knee.

Claude rose and knelt by Camille's chair, and she turned to gaze at him gravely. "Listen to me!" he said miserably, his hand on her shoulder. "We need to go away. Durand-Ruel thought I should go to Holland sometime to paint. This is a good time. I don't want to be here without him. Come with me!"

She stroked his cheek gently, and he seized her hand and kissed it. "I can't," she said.

"Minou, what do you mean? What am I without you? I need you."

"Don't you understand? I feel so weary. I can't leave this city; I'm afraid it will disappear entirely if I do. I'll work in the bookshop, if anything is left of it. I don't even know where my sister and her child are. You may want to run away, but I need to gather what I can gather. I can't go away again. And with you, sometimes . . . I don't know."

He lowered his head to her hands. "But I know about you. I know how much I love you. Is this for a time or for always?"

"I can't tell you that. I will live above the bookshop and try to sell books."

He slowly rose to his feet. "Very well, then," he said. "I'll take this as a temporary separation only. I'll send money when I can. And one day I'll come back and make a home for you if you want one with me. I promise this." He closed his coat. He saw her still seated with folded hands, looking toward the window with the boy now settling into sleep at her feet and thought, I shall never paint anything this terrible or this lovely.

He opened the door but did not turn again, only said, "It's me you love, Minou; it's me."

1871

The older I become the more I realize that I have to work very hard to reproduce what I search: the instantaneous. The influence of the atmosphere on the things and the light scattered throughout.

—CLAUDE MONET

THERE WERE WINDMILLS, AND THE COLORS WERE ALL different. There is enough to paint here for a lifetime, he thought grimly. At least he knew he could earn money. Durand-Ruel, who was still in London but preparing to return to Paris, wrote that he would buy as many paintings of the Netherlands as Claude could produce. People were interested in that country.

It was winter when he came to the small town of Zaandam and found lodging in a private house. There was a high bed with thick white sheets and huge high pillows, all very clean. For a moment he wanted only to climb into it.

He unpacked his clothes, clean canvases, and new paints and walked out again. The harbor was rich, lined with wood houses behind rising ships' masts. He set up his easel and began to work at once. When he returned to his room at dark, solitude followed him. He did not want to remember the early-morning knock at the London door, the empty Paris studio, Camille's confession and then her refusal to come. He did not even know if she had found her sister. He fell on his bed, burying his head in the great clean pillows. I'll paint and forget, he thought.

In the month or more following he walked or took a cart to the villages and unique windmills outside the city. No one knew his address but Durand-Ruel, to whom he sent pictures. He sent money on to Camille with no note or address. He avoided news of his own country and ate his cabbage-and-buttermilk soup alone in the tavern each night, smoking his pipe.

In the spring he broke his silence and wrote to Auguste. "How are Camille and the boy? You knew about our friend and my wife, I suppose, and never told me." He wrote more and sent it to the Montmartre address Auguste had given him before Claude left the city.

For a few weeks there was no response, and when one came he read it standing by the harbor, staring at the words. He had left a city that he thought would heal, but it had not healed; it had crumbled.

Damn it, Claude, tu es fou!—You're crazy, I did nothing; I was not complicit. You write so accusingly! I only learned about Frédéric's feelings for Camille the night he went away to war. It's almost hard to believe, and then again for many complicated reasons, it's not. Mon Dieu! I also hoped for the old streets and cafés and our meetings again when this bloody war was over, but you fled and she's buried beneath books and there's rioting everywhere. So Paris is as mad as you are, my friend. Consider yourself punched for your words. And . . . I'm sorry, so sorry.

We are falling away from the world of Frédéric's painting of us all in his studio. Even that studio is gone; his father cleared it out and it is a workshop for glassblowing now. How the hell do we keep our dreams of being all together, of going on with our art? Sometimes I think we will never recover, and to be honest, I weep.

If you haven't read the papers, I'll briefly recapitulate the continued sad story of beautiful Paris. The emperor's fled to England and there's a new government formed at Versailles. That government gave many concessions to the bastard Prussians, not to mention part of our country, Alsace-Lorraine. And the Parisians, never slow to react to that which they don't like, have formed a strong guard for the Paris Commune to rise against the new government. Everyone we know has taken a different side, and neighbors report on each other. A dentist was shot by accident and his body left for hours in the street. Half the people have left the city, including you, my old, dear, steadfast friend, fled to the land of windmills. Half the houses on the boulevard Saint-Germain are empty. The artisans and tradesmen are gone, and the students. I am sure papers there carry the news, and I am too sick to write more of it here.

"Steadfast!" Claude thought wistfully. It's kind of him to think of me that way when sometimes I wonder if I'm more than chaff in the wind.

He continued to read closely.

I have not been left peacefully to paint amid all of this. I was working on a picture of the Seine when along came the Commune guards thinking I was a spy! And many others have suffered. Cézanne's in the south of France; Manet had a breakdown from the strain of the siege, as did pretty Mademoiselle Morisot, whose family paintings you so much admire. Pissarro returned to Louveciennes and found that his house had been used by the Prussians and that most of his paintings and yours had been destroyed.

But now, back to beautiful Camille, you poor, jealous man. She and Jean are once more living above the shop with her sister and her sister's child; the sister had left her husband, who turned traitor and had to flee. Camille keeps the shop exquisitely, as if it were peacetime, slipping books in place to keep her world sane while outside people bleed to death on the street. I know she would not come with you but she was wrong. Your son is charming. Do you want to sell him? Seriously, I envy you a son. I am an old bachelor and will never marry. The theaters have closed and Lise is working as a nursemaid, which she hates. She has pretty much

given up on me. I am wise enough, unlike you, to know that a
passion for painting and an erratic income would not keep a wife
content. But if I had a love like yours, I would not throw it over.

Claude hardly knew where he was for a few moments as he tried to see the scenes described in his beloved city.

He wrote her that day, underlining much. "My love, I am enclosing money for tickets. I beg you, close up the shop and join me here. I will come and fetch you. Only say you won't turn me away."

No reply came. But why won't she come? he thought. Does she still love my friend? Did she ever? Will I ever know? With all that he was he wanted to go to her and drag her away, but he could not bear the thought that she would refuse him. He wrote more letters to the shop. Then finally she began to answer. Her letters were maddeningly vague. The bookshop cat wasn't well, and Jean was talking a lot. Nothing about the riots and the deaths and the fires set here and there, as if the bookshop on rue Dante were in another world than the rest of the city. He wrote her desperately: Why won't you come? I have reasons, she said vaguely, and he became depressed. She is impossible, he thought.

Only underneath these things did he think that he had lost many beautiful paintings in the Prussian occupation of the house in Louveciennes.

It was a Parisian man, stopping by the tavern in early June, who told him that the Paris Commune had been overthrown and hundreds of insurgents shot in Père-Lachaise cemetery. The riots in the city had ended.

Auguste wrote sadly:

Some say we have peace again after these horrible few
months. What peace can we have with the Hôtel de Ville and the
Palais des Tuileries burned to the ground? With men I knew
rounded up and shot? And yet in this sadness, what can we do?
We must be able to do something. Now, damn it, will people see

what we have been trying to show them in our paintings for so long—the ordinary daily beauty of our country—which they took for granted and almost lost? Did we have to nearly lose it forever to appreciate it?

Claude packed his things then and thanked his landlady. On a late June day he set out for France by train. We must build our world again, he thought. I will have my love, for love between a man and a woman can also heal what has been destroyed. Neither we nor our art nor our world will ever blow away like chaff in the wind.

1871–1873

Everyone discusses my art and pretends to understand, as if it were necessary to understand, when it is simply necessary to love.

—CLAUDE MONET

IT WAS EARLY JULY WHEN CLAUDE RETURNED TO PARIS by train through the Netherlands and France. Nearing the city, he stared out the window at the burned farms and houses. The destruction hit him as hard as if someone had punched him. He was gasping with rage. Come back, he said. He saw jagged ruins against the sky from places that had been burned by the angry Commune.

He left his luggage and paintings at the Gare Saint-Lazare. There were no taxis to be had and the omnibuses came erratically, so he walked toward the river. Empty barges were moored there, and even the number of homeless had decreased. Notre-Dame rose like a huge, comforting bulk. I am still here, it said. He walked steadily, staring at the cobbles, not wanting to see the water this late afternoon or anything that might touch his heart.

He made his way into the Quartier Latin. The *boulangerie* across the street had opened its doors again and people came and went, buying bread. Shell marks scarred the walls of houses, and one house lacked part of its roof. And there in the middle of it was the bookshop. Not untouched at all, he thought, his heart beating a little faster, for the windows had been partially smashed and were boarded up. Who boarded them up? he wondered. Annette's errant husband? One of my friends? I would have replaced the glass with the air of the man who easily mends things, he thought. But perhaps there was no glass then or it was futile.

He opened the door.

Camille was sitting on a chair inside with the ancient shop cat at her feet, sewing, her head bent, intent on the stitches as if each one marked her future. There was something so peaceful about her, as if indeed fires had occurred over the past months and neighbors had been shot and she had sat in the midst of it unknowing as a nun at her prayers. But when she turned her head, he saw how thin her face was and that she had dark circles around her eyes as if she had been ill. "You foolish . . . ," he wanted to cry, but he did not.

She stood tentatively, and he put the sewing aside and tentatively drew her against him. "Claude," she said. "I knew you'd come. The past few days I've sensed it. Maybe Julie saw it in her tea leaves. Oh, Claude."

"I'm here," he said.

"Yes, you appear again after having been away!"

"I'm not going away from you ever again." He thought, How much space is there between us? I'll never manage it this time, never. But he said confidently, "I'm here; I'm here. I love you. I did write. I wrote and wrote . . . it was you who said little this time. Oh, Minou!"

He drew up a chair and she dropped into her own again, her face a little averted. She looked up at the half-empty shelves. "I know I look dreadful," she murmured. "I can't eat even now that the city's at peace. I keep thinking of things I saw. My supply of books is decimated, and I haven't the strength to try to buy more. I sold them cheaply; I almost gave them away. The price of everything went up again during the Commune as the farmers didn't want to come in. It was horrible, horrible!"

"Where's your sister?"

"Oh, we quarrel if we're together too much! She's found a place of her own and has decided to open a millinery shop. My parents are still in Lyon. Nothing much changed at all for my *grandmère* but for some village boys going to war. She writes that by the priest."

"Why didn't you come to me?"

"You know . . . things between us, what happened. My fault, really, or perhaps not. I keep deciding one thing and then another and then this place seemed a sort of sanctuary. Auguste was almost shot. I haven't been out much, lately not at all. A neighbor shops for me. I missed you terribly."

She looked at him, her large eyes sad. "And there you were! I saw the sketches on the letters; I have the little painting you sent me. Holland seems a paradise, not like here. Why is paradise always someplace else?"

"I could wipe all bad dreams away," he said tenderly. "I could give you a nice life. The one we always planned for. It's so odd that out of such chaos a possibility of something beautiful comes. I thought this wasn't so, but now I believe it. We must make the losses into the beauty, somehow. Will you let me?"

She nodded, and even though she looked down, he could see that she was smiling. "Yes," she said. "All I ever wanted was a life with you. I knew it, but I was safe here. Will you make me safe again, Claude?"

He felt his rising strength, not desire so much as a blinding tenderness. Softly she began to tell him some of the things that had happened while he was away, about her sister's devastation, that Édouard Manet had come by to look in on her, that some friends had remained in the city and come to visit. He felt as she spoke that she was like a little girl walking in careful circles; she danced around any memories of how the window was shattered and what she must have seen when she ran out.

But the memories came anyway and she began to sob terribly, covering her mouth with her hands and pulling away from him when he tried to hold her.

"People died," she stammered. "I ran out when the city was burning. And it all seemed to burn. A boy died before me, shot down. I've not been very good in my life. The nuns raised me to be good, but I've not been. That bullet was perhaps meant for me, not him. I ran back here and waited for it. And it was all ashes from the burning, coming through the window, huge black things that settled everywhere."

She pressed his hand very hard, trying to cry more softly. "I have to ask you. I have to. What do you think it was like for Frédéric to die? Did he have time to be scared or was it all too quick?"

"I . . . don't know," he said. "I thought of it so many times. And other things, what he wanted to tell me. What you wouldn't tell me. I understood a little when I was away, because I was alone so much. I think you'd better tell me. Would you tell me, Minou?"

She waited until she could stop crying before she spoke, looking down at her empty hand open on her skirt. She said, "Yes, we understand many things when we're alone. He had slept with a few women besides the little we had together, but it wasn't only women. For a short time he took a young man as his lover, and his family found out and canceled their support of the art exhibition. It was the summer when you and Auguste painted at La Grenouillère. Frédéric's family behaved wretchedly. I think he wanted to paint like you, to be like you. He loved who you loved and loved you through me. We both cared for you more than each other . . . so even if I had gone away with him, it wouldn't have lasted. Did you know these things, Claude?"

Claude nodded slowly. "I thought it was that. A friend mentioned it once that they thought so and I said no. He never said anything to me. He was tender to me, but we were all pretty tender with each other . . ." He blinked and his throat filled with tears. "Life isn't simple. I want it to be. And then we lose the chance to go back and do things better." He forced his voice into a rougher tone, defensively folding his arms across his chest. "He should have told me."

"He thought you mightn't forgive him; that's why he never told you."

"There's nothing to forgive," Claude blurted. "We were very close. He should have said it."

"He was going to tell you. I think he also went away to leave us together."

"I wish I could have stopped him."

"No one could have stopped him, Claude. His family was so angry about the young man. Frédéric wanted to be a hero in their eyes and then he'd come back and paint here. I think he wouldn't have married Lily. I think he would have grown old here in his studio with all of you around him."

Just then Jean came down the stairs, sleepy from his nap, hair tousled, crying, "Papa!" Claude wondered where this sturdy boy had been when the city burned and the windows shattered. All he knew was he ached for his son and for Camille with every limb of his body and would protect them with his life.

HE WANTED TO rent a house for his family at once. He had sold many of his Dutch paintings to Durand-Ruel and was confident he could afford it.

There was a house he had long admired in Argenteuil, a short train ride from the city, but he had no idea if it was occupied. When the three of them went there a few days later, he saw it was empty; the garden was choked with weeds, and old leaves littered the path. "Yes," a neighbor said when they asked him. "The man who owned it fell in the war and his widow's moved away. It's for rent." Claude thought, Then our love will heal it and we ourselves will heal here.

He and Camille walked hand in hand through the empty house exploring the dining room and the parlor and the kitchen while Jean went upstairs and called back in an excited, echoing voice to tell them what he had found: a great spiderweb, and a view of the river from a window that he saw by standing on his toes. They heard his running footsteps upstairs on the bare floors.

Camille considered it carefully and he could see she liked what she saw. "It's such a short way to the city," she said. "I could go in a lot, but I might not. I think I'd like to make a new life here, a whole new life with you. I'll write my uncle to sell the shop. He's been made an offer for it. Only we must take the cat. I'd miss him, so."

They sat on the floor those next warm days and drew plans for furnishings on large pages torn out of an old sketchbook. Everything he had brought back from Holland, his clothes and paintings, was stacked against the walls. The widow had left only one bed, which the three of them needed to share until they could order another one. They bought cheese and wine and bread in the little shop near the train station and ate sitting on the floor.

They talked as if they could not bear to stop. They sat on the floor holding hands and laughed and spoke of so many things. It was like turning over earth in the garden. And yet there were always a few words he felt he withheld or she did, and sometimes he tried to tickle them from her, crying playfully, "Tell me! Tell me!" and she giggled and fought him; she was surprisingly strong. And by that time they had forgotten that there was anything left unsaid: something sweet or shy or lonely or perhaps something of regret. Something perhaps even more than she had told him about what she had seen in the war.

THAT WAS THE first perfect winter and spring. They found each other again in the light rooms of this house; he had his studio and would make the garden beautiful. For the first time in their life together they had enough money. Claude's pictures were selling regularly, if not for huge sums, and then his father died and left him ten thousand francs. "May it give you the security you so badly need," his brother had said when Claude and Camille had traveled to the funeral. Later Léon added privately, "I must say this now, though. He missed you so all those times you didn't come or write. Sometimes on his birthday he'd sit by the window most of the day looking for you." And Claude had felt the words deep within him and was silent most of the train ride back, holding her hand in his.

He and Camille furnished the house together, traveling into Paris to rent or buy furniture and draperies, plates, sheets, lamps, all the things they had ever pressed their noses against windows wanting and some of the things he knew she had had at her parents' home. He bought and framed Japanese prints, and she chose a bronze mantelpiece clock with a silver bell that struck on the half hour. They hired a maid, a nursemaid, and a cook. Jean played in the garden.

The summer after they had moved in he wrote effusive letters to his friends, lovingly demanding they come. "We accept and will bring easels," they replied. Claude stood in the garden waiting for them that morning amid the roses, lilies, dahlias, carnations. He wore loose trousers, an old shirt, and his comfortable wood sabots. Gently he swung the swing from the tree branch. He heard the train whistle over the birdsong, opened the white gate, and looked down the dirt road in the direction of the station. Édouard Manet and Auguste, easels over their shoulders and arguing over something as always, came toward him past the dry stone wall.

As the three of them sat down to breakfast on the table under the tree, Camille joined them in a white flowing dress with Jean following her. "What news of the theater and of Lise?" she asked, kissing them and taking her place between them. "Now we're here we simply are too lazy to go in to Paris much! I haven't seen a play in months."

"Yes, we read and make love," Claude added comfortably from his chair, looking at her tenderly and biting the edge of his finger.

"Both worthy occupations," Auguste exclaimed. "But neither of which may occupy you today! I'm painting both of you. Look at that sun, just right! Madame will sit under the tree there, please, and the charming little one will lay his dear head in her lap. We'll both paint you! For once I won't paint you reading as I do most of the time." He rose and dusted his hands of crumbs.

"I don't want to lie there; I'm not sleepy," Jean protested, but Auguste squatted down and whispered in his ear, "Do! I'll tell you stories and sing you songs."

"I shall neither sing nor recite," Manet said with his dry humor as he rose to set up his easel. The men prepared their palettes, and Camille settled herself on the ground against a tree. Jean rose and ran about and came back briefly. Claude began to water his flowers. A red chicken escaped from the henhouse and strutted around Camille's dress.

Manet exclaimed, "There the boy goes again! Jean, go to your mother!"

"No, monsieur, I'm bored!" cried the little boy. He ran around in circles.

"Jean!" Camille cried, holding out her arms. "Come here! Something magical will happen," and the little boy came, laughing, careening into her, tumbling. She tickled him and he shrieked and then lay down again, contemplating the leaves above him.

Claude moved among the flower beds. He called, "He always comes for her! Are you going to paint me fat? I'm getting fat."

"We are painting the family and you moved, Monet! Bend over again to water the flowers!"

"Ah, my back hurts. So this is what it's like to model!"

Auguste began to sing an old children's song. The fascinated boy stared at the thin painter and again lay down with his head in his mother's lap. In two minutes, Claude thought, he will leap up to ride his hobbyhorse.

He straightened. "You'll stay at least the week, Auguste?" he asked. The painting was finished and they gathered around the table again for lunch. Lise came down the road carrying her parasol. She kissed all of them and talked of her tedious rehearsals. They sat for a long time drinking coffee under the trees, Lise's stocking feet in Auguste's lap. They had reconciled.

"Both the chicken and the boy moved," Claude said later, looking at the paintings. "I look weary and fat. Madame, if possible, is more beautiful than ever."

Manet left at dusk on the train back to Paris.

Claude thought of that year and the one that followed always as summer, but there was also the winter, when he braved the cold and snow to paint outdoors and then returned to the warm, bright room where Camille was reading or sitting on the floor playing with Jean. She went frequently to Paris to buy hats and gloves and to visit her dressmaker, chattering of lunch with friends, with her sister. She had told him she passionately wished to have another child. He replied with a smile that he would continue to do one of the things he loved best to make that happen.

One soft early autumn day more than two years after they had moved to Argenteuil, a letter came from Pissarro in Louveciennes. "I am overjoyed to tell you, Claude," it said, "that not all the work we left in my stable was destroyed during the occupation. A group of paintings has been discovered in a neighbor's attic. I don't know who hid them. Perhaps since we all have a little more money now, we could think once more of our independent exhibition."

1874

THAT WAS HOW THEIR FIRST EXHIBITION FINALLY HAP-
pened after nine years.

Claude retrieved from Pissarro his painting of the sun rising
over the harbor that he had painted with his old friend Boudin three
years before. They borrowed for the following April a few large
rooms on the boulevard des Capucines that belonged to a photogra-
pher and were wonderfully light. Many colleagues would partici-
pate: Pissarro, Auguste, Degas, and Berthe Morisot; Sisley and
Cézanne. Manet refused; he told Claude that the established art circle would look upon them as vagabonds and turn their backs on
them.

"Oh, we're vagabonds, are we?" Paul Cézanne growled.

Boudin sent a grateful note saying he would join them and sent a
few paintings.

In the cool days of early spring, they hung their work in the
gallery. The gray walls sang with the colors of the gardens of

Pontoise, piles of flowers and portraits of women by Auguste, and the water and island of La Grenouillère. There were ballet dancers and laundresses from Degas, and from Cézanne, the remarkable *House of the Hanged Man*. They had included a few of Frédéric's paintings: a gorgeous vase of flowers with a black woman behind them, a fair nude girl being dressed by two attendants.

Camille arrived on the morning the exhibition was to open, wearing gray silk-wool. Her eyes shone. "You're all ready," she said breathlessly. "You're all here. '*Un pour tous, tous pour un.*'" She walked slowly into the other room. Claude had the oddest feeling then that she would walk into one of the paintings and disappear. His heart began to beat rapidly. He was going to rush forward when she appeared again.

She said quietly, "It is as we dreamt the day after they threw you out into the snow. It's as I thought it would be."

More than two hundred people came that day, some delighted, some critical. In the days that followed they sometimes had only two lone souls wandering shyly amid the rooms. Claude had somehow expected them to push in by the hundreds; that reading the announcements they would trample one another. But compared to the Salon, it was a tiny endeavor.

Two weeks later at ten at night the doors closed for the last time. One by one the painters departed until only Claude, Auguste, and Pissarro remained and, sitting a little apart from them, Durand-Ruel, who had returned to Paris a few years before and reopened his gallery. From the boulevard below, the gas lamps reflected up with the chatter of people.

Auguste took off his new shoes and rubbed his stocking feet. "We sold a few things, at least," he said.

Claude shook his head. "I can't believe that critic called *Impression: Sunrise* 'a preliminary drawing for a wallpaper pattern.' Has he ever seen the sun rise over the sea? Why do people with no gifts have to spend their honest hours making up nonsense about others and tell a man who has lived most of his life by the sea what the damn sea and the damn sun look like?"

Durand-Ruel smiled and, opening a silver case, passed out small, fine cigars. He said, "That critic has done you a favor, Monet. He has given a name to all of you: *Impressionists.*"

ON THE SHORT train ride home, a little drunk, Claude looked out the window at the dark countryside. Camille had not come this last day; she did not feel well and thought she might be pregnant, and he was anxious to get back to her. When he reached his station he jumped out and ran down the path by the stars. Once in the house he went straight to the bedroom, undressed, and dropped his clothes on the floor. He thought Camille was sleeping but instead he heard her low sobs.

He sat on the side of the bed, his hand on her back. "What, dear?" he murmured.

"I wanted to keep you all together, and one went away to die. It was partially my fault. You are all together but for him, and without him none of you could have gone on."

He could not comfort her. Even when he finally slept he could sense her crying in her sleep. He put his hand out to touch her and murmured, "Minou, Minou."

ALL THAT NIGHT he dreamt of the sea and of that night he had run into it with his dead friend and fallen with him in the cold water and shouted with joy at the wonder of the dawn rising through the storm. Camille was still sleeping when he woke the next morning. At the table near the coffeepot was the early post, and amid the news journals and letters from friends and collectors, he found a letter from the Normandy coast. For a moment a shiver moved through him and then he knew the handwriting of his old mentor, Boudin.

Monet, I wanted to express to you my great joy in the exhibition in which you so kindly included me. My pupil had returned any favor I humbly gave him. I thought I was only a lonely artist painting by a windy sea. It seems I am part of a movement of many talented painters: Impressionism. *My dear friend, yes indeed. We are Impressionists.*

Interlude

As the opening of his exhibition approached, he canceled it twice. Then he changed the date. At last he was ashamed to once more inconvenience his bewildered art dealer after announcements had already been made.

He continued to paint thoughtfully, sometimes furiously.

As he painted, the memory returned to him of a lovely morning the previous June when he had taken his easel and canvas and paint box to the pond and had simply sat looking at the water lilies for some time. He heard birds and the slight movement of the flowers and the leaves.

A soft rain began to fall on the pond. He opened his large umbrella and held it more over the easel and the empty canvas than over himself. Light rain splattered on the old wood of the paint box and on the pond and the flowers. He stood fascinated, watching the pink blossoms quiver under the soft, small drops. He heard the rain on the leaves, and then it died away and presently the clouds moved and the water stilled; leaves dripped into the pond and the colors and scent of the flowers washed over him.

Almost without knowing it, he began to paint. He had the feeling that the water lilies came to his canvas more of their volition than his. The flowers and the shadows and the air moved against his brush; they moved from all about him to the canvas. They were outside of him and yet they were inside: they embraced him and drew him inside their world.

He stopped finally, his arm tired.

But I have not made them as beautiful as they are, he thought ruefully when he recalled that ecstasy of painting that had remained with him for several days. Nor did I ever really see how lovely my Minou was when I made love to her, only after when I stepped away and saw her lying on our rumpled bed, her look so tender. No, I must postpone this exhibition.

He did not cancel, though, but wrote again to her sister asking if the letters had been found.

Part Six

1875

This young man will surpass us all.
—CHARLES-FRANÇOIS DAUBIGNY ABOUT CLAUDE MONET

THROUGH THE TWO SUMMERS THAT FOLLOWED THE first independent exhibition, Claude painted Camille many times. He borrowed a huge Japanese robe, so heavy with its thickly embroidered birds and a demon, all gold and bright blues against the thick red silk. It flowed around her, down to the floor. They tacked Japanese rice paper fans to the wall of an empty room and he portrayed her holding a fan, her smile bright and charming. She wore a wig the color of golden wheat.

He painted her reading in the garden under a tree with her luminous white skirts spread about her and then with Jean in a foliage of flowers so thick that she seemed to be rising out of them as something from the earth. She stood by him after, gazing at the work on the easel, leaning her head against his.

"I can't believe I'll be twenty-eight this June!" She sighed.

"I want to give you a birthday party."

Over the past four years their circle of friends had grown and now included not only his fellow artists but the art collector Leclercq, the Durand-Ruel family, and a few physicians and musicians. Her sister, who visited occasionally with her frail, coddled daughter, would also come. He planned the menu himself and gave the cook directions. He hired an extra maid.

The day was overcast, and the trees in the garden above the long tables where they ate rustled now and then as if shivering in the wind. By the time the cheese dish came the branches were swaying, and darkening clouds hung heavily from the sky. Rain fell suddenly, splotching the tablecloths and moistening the cheese. Guests leapt up and began to bring the dishes inside. The maid ran out, and the cook. Everyone was shouting and laughing as they collided with one another trying to get through the door. Crowded in the parlor, the women worried for their hair. Now the rain fell torrentially, beating against the windows.

"No matter! We'll have coffee here," Claude said. He opened the doors to the dining room. "Some can go there," he said. "And some can sit on the stairs." The rooms smelled of coffee, which the maid brought on trays and served, pouring from the silver pot.

"Edmond must play," Pissarro called from his chair by the window. Edmond put down his cigarette and sat down at the piano. "Will you and your sister sing, Madame Monet?" he called. "I recall how you sang that song from *La Périchole* together at your wedding party!"

Edmond played the introduction and the two sisters took hands. Camille's voice began clearly but shortly died away. She shook her head. "I don't think I can," she said. "Oh, I can't." Her face darkened and she looked around. "I don't want to sing that; I don't want to sing anything. I don't want to sing for you." She ran across the room and up past the few people sitting on the stairs. A door closed above.

Claude stood up at once, but Annette put her hand on his arm. "I'll go," she insisted. "Lise and Julie can come too. The women will go," she said, and the three of them hurried up the stairs with a rustle of skirts past Jean and Annette's daughter, Nannette, who were holding hands, biting their lips.

Edmond remained at the piano, touching the keys with delicate fingers. "I shouldn't have asked her," he said. "When she sang that before, our friend was there. Everything brings back memories. People who suffered through the siege and Commune suffer still; some of us will never be the same again. Some losses can't be made up. You think you're over them and they return; it's no longer yesterday but now."

After ten minutes Claude could not bear any more and jumped up, exclaiming, "That's it; I must go up to her!" He was crossing the parlor when the door opened above and the two sisters descended arm in arm, followed by the other women. Camille had been crying. Once downstairs, she went from one friend to another, kissing their cheeks repentantly. Claude felt her remote kiss on his lips; she seated herself in a corner by a lamp, taking out her sewing.

Pissarro and Julie knelt beside her, picking up her thread and touching her sleeve. "There you are, Minou," they said. "Be well, darling Minou." She smiled a little, but tears ran down her cheeks and Claude felt he could not approach her. How strange to feel this, and yet he sensed that something would not let him in.

EARLY IN THE morning he came down to the kitchen, leaving Camille to sleep. He made his own coffee and sat down at the table to drink it. He had slept badly, mulling over not only last evening but also something he had sensed about Camille now and then over the past few years. The changeability of her interests and moods had increased. She had decorated the house, making sure every color was right, and afterward had thrown herself first into writing poetry and then into trying watercolors. She now took piano lessons. She spoke again of the theater and returning to her novel. These things delighted and depressed her both. She told him one evening that if she kept changing her art she would never be anything extraordinary. Does she really want to be that? he asked himself, bewildered. Does she know the cost? Even living with me for so long, she doesn't know it?

Over the past few years they also had been drifting into their old habit of not telling each other their difficulties, and slowly the unspoken words lay within him until sometimes the things he wanted to say got trapped between the things he did not. He did not want to tell her that his inheritance had been spent and that his work was selling more slowly; he would not say that to keep up the house and the servants, the party and her dresses, he was promising everyone to pay them later. Still, Claude knew she was aware of it.

Outside, a blackbird sang.

He heard her footsteps on the stairs but she did not come into the kitchen. He rose with his coffee and walked barefoot through the rooms. There were the gathered chairs in the parlor where he had sat last night talking late with Auguste, there the piano with its closed keyboard. Early sunlight fell on the moss green velvet of the sofa. One coffee cup from the party still rested on the windowsill behind the curtain.

Camille was kneeling on the dining room rug, her loose long hair rippling down the back of her dressing gown, gazing up at his painting of her in the green dress, which hung on the wall. He knelt beside her, slipping his arm around her shoulder.

"Who is that lovely girl?" he asked, kissing her ear.

"Oh, Claude, look at her! She's untouchable! Nothing can hurt her; nothing can change her. I'm growing older and will never be her again. Do you remember the Baudelaire poem I asked you about? 'O you who, like an ephemeral ghost / Trample lightly and with a serene look . . . ' She's like that to me."

"Minou," he said softly, though sternly. "You're still young. What troubled you so last night, eh?"

"I felt suddenly I didn't sing well and would make a fool of myself. Sometimes I feel everyone does everything better than I do. I felt . . . dark inside."

"These past months you sometimes seem to sink into sadness. I worry about you." He added delicately, "Your sister once told me about certain collapses when you were young."

Camille drew her pink dressing gown together. "But that was so long ago!" she said, dismissing it. "They came from the endless difficulties with my mother and my desire to please her and to be free. I remember little except that the doctor was kind. He said my nature was too excitable, that I felt things too deeply. My *grandmère* came and I was better."

She played with her fingers; the nails had long since ceased to be bitten but were neatly trimmed, and she wore both his engagement and wedding rings. "I can't talk to Julie much anymore and sometimes not to Lise. Everyone else seems to go on with their lives but me."

He left the conversation uneasy, still feeling many things had not been said. From that day, though, he became a little more wary of Camille's darker moods, which came without much warning. He sensed that the peace of his house was fragile and threatened as the wind worries the outer walls and will find a way to enter. A window shatters, and the wind and rain blow in and lift the curtains and thrust against the flowers in the vase. The mist blows over everything, even the elegant, delicate dresses behind the closed wardrobe door.

As the winter came on, she not only did not go to her sister or her old friends but also now and then stayed half the day in bed. When he spent the afternoon in Paris negotiating or painting, he never knew what he would find when he came home. Once he discovered nine-year-old Jean sitting forlornly on the steps. "Maman's not been up all day, Papa!" he complained.

Claude ran up to the bedroom and opened the curtains to the last of the light. Leaning over Camille, he asked, "What is it, my love? How can I work with you like this? I need all the courage I can get!" and she said, "I'm so sorry. Has Jean eaten? Oh, poor Jean! I only meant to rest a little while."

But her mood fell steadily after Christmas until it seemed he had no peace. One winter day it snowed and he stomped out to the river-bank and painted. He felt nothing when he worked, not the cold of his feet on the damp, hard earth, not the weariness of his back. He heard his name shouted and saw her hurrying toward him in her walking dress and hat. She cried, "I'm going to Paris for the afternoon. You've hardly noticed me here today."

He exclaimed impatiently, "I'm trying to paint something that will sell. Go to Paris to see your sister. Ask friends in."

"All you do is paint. You don't care that I'm not pregnant and you promised me. Perhaps I won't wait for you. You'll come back from painting and find me gone!"

He knocked over the easel, and the gray paint on his canvas smudged in the snow. With a shout he kicked the easel away so that it landed at the water's edge and lay there. That afternoon, he locked himself in his studio and painted his self-portrait, but he did not finish it because he disliked it so much. Where had the daring, brash young man gone? Who was this exhausted fellow?

He jumped up and hurried to their room, where she lay across their bed, still fully clothed, her hat and its pins on the dresser. "Why do you say those things?" Claude cried. "I love you, I love you."

"I'm so sorry. I love you too. I don't know what's the matter with me! Of course you must paint. It's all I ever wanted for you." She wept in gasps, and he held her to stop the grief.

Winter passed and cold spring came, and with it her moods brightened. She went to a dressmaker with her sister and ordered three more dresses, and he did not tell her he had no idea how he would pay for them, that though he sold paintings it was not enough. He watched her running around the garden with Jean, so girlish and lovely. The dark periods of the winter were entirely gone, though they had left him with a sense of unease that he would confide to no one. Why has this happened now, he asked himself, when some success has truly come? Perhaps it is not enough. She needs another child; I will give her one.

He wanted to surround them with beauty: he bought everything he liked and his friends' paintings and good wine and fine food. He felt strong; he felt he could create everything with his imagination. If he could capture wind and waves and a frozen river, he could make her happy. He wanted in the end to deserve her, to show her parents in Lyon that he had kept his promise to them.

1 8 7 6

Don't proceed according to rules and principles, but paint what you observe and feel. . . . Paint generously and unhesitatingly, for it is best not to lose the first impression.
— Camille Pissarro

THE POSTMAN BROUGHT SEVERAL LETTERS THAT WARM summer morning, walking through the gardens to deliver them. Auguste had written from Paris asking about having a second independent exhibition, and Léon had written with some warmth about a possible visit. There was a letter from Jean's teacher and one from an actress friend of Camille's.

Standing in the garden, Claude turned the envelopes over until he noticed one from Durand-Ruel. Perhaps it was the list of paintings sold and those still in the shop that was sent every half year. He tore open the envelope to find a brief letter on the gallery stationery. Monet, it said, are you at leisure to meet me in Paris tomorrow at one at the Café Anglais? I want to discuss a possible commission with you.

Jean was with his tutor and Camille was practicing scales on the piano when he left for the Argenteuil train station the next morning. "Good-bye, monsieur," the new maid said, curtsying to him as she took his coffee cup away.

An hour later Claude strode into the Café Anglais on the boulevard des Italiens. He had taken Camille here a year ago. Surely the high prices meant something of moment was at stake.

"And madame, how is she?" asked Durand-Ruel, rising slightly from the table. "And your boy?"

"Well, very well. And your sons and daughter?"

They drank excellent wines and ate a soufflé with creamed chicken, lobster in glazed medallions, and then ducklings stuffed with liver. Claude let all the complexities of his life fade away under the delight of the meal. By his third glass of wine, he only wanted to remain here indefinitely with waiters gliding over the carpet and the soft tapping of silverware on fine china.

He reluctantly brought his mind back to work. "So what have we now in our business? How do we proceed, eh?" he asked with the good humor his full stomach had given him.

Durand-Ruel lifted a small bit of cheese on his fork. His blue eyes were warm. "As you might have astutely gathered, Monet, the news is good and profitable; I could not afford to bring you here with bad. One of my collectors stopped by yesterday and bought two of your landscapes. He also has a private commission to discuss with you."

"Who is he? How much money does have?"

"His name is Ernest Hoschedé and he has a family business in textiles and a great deal of money. He owns an enviable apartment on the rue de Lisbonne, plus an old country estate from his wife; she herself comes from a wealthy family. They have four enchanting girls and a lad. He's asked you to go to the Paris apartment tomorrow morning to discuss the particulars of the commission."

GREAT DRAPES COVERED the windows in the apartment on the rue de Lisbonne and art hung everywhere on the walls. Claude noted the silver and bronze statuettes and the enormous Chinese vases. The ceiling was painted with flowers in the decorative style of the last century.

Through the portiere curtains over the door, he heard young girls laughing and someone at a piano lesson. After a few moments, the door opened and two girls around the age of twelve peeped mischievously at him, curtsying. With urgency they whispered to each other, "The artist's come! Does Papa know?"

He smiled as they fled. "The artist," as if a species of being! Claude moved his shoe on the carpet, feeling the depth of it. He felt his old wistful disdain for people who had been born with a great deal of money.

The farthest door was pushed open and a heavyset man in a fine wool suit strode toward him. "Ah, Monet!" he said, firmly shaking Claude's hand. "Sorry to have kept you waiting."

Claude inclined his head slightly. "Monsieur Hoschedé."

"Will you . . . ?"

They sat down together in comfortable chairs and a maid in black brought a tray of coffee.

Hoschedé leaned back, hands clasped together, eyes narrow. "I'd like to engage your services to paint a set of panels for the walls of the gazebo at my wife's château, paintings of the estate. We will of course be delighted to be your hosts for however many months it will take you to complete the work."

The fee was named as an offhand thing, not to be discussed, and Claude allowed no expression of relief to come into his face, though he knew it would support his own household for a year or more if they were prudent. Hoschedé's conclusion broke into his thoughts. "I'm leaving for the country later today; my wife and children go first on our private train. Come with me and take a look!"

THE CARRIAGE LEFT Paris and drove to Montgeron on the River Yerres. Claude looked from the window as they moved down the tree-lined road until the Château de Rottembourg rose above them, pale blush stone with many windows and a park before and behind, running down to the river. "Look around!" Hoschedé said as they descended. "It's a pretty estate. You'll dine with us, of course? And after I'll show you where we'd like the panels to go."

For an hour Claude wandered among the orchards and vineyards,

the flower gardens and fountains, and the stone benches under venerable trees. He walked down to the river and gazed at its flow; he
thought, Perhaps I will have some fortune after all! Who could be
anything but peaceful and content in such a place, attended by so
many gardeners and servants? Monsieur raises a finger and his valet
comes.

His pocket watch indicated it was the dinner hour. He turned
from the river and was nearing the house when he noticed a woman
in a plain blue dress walking from the kitchen garden with a basket of
fennel over her arm. Likely the housekeeper or a governess. "*Bon-
soir*, madame!" he said, now at her side. "I'm Claude Monet, the
artist, come to paint here."

The woman gave him her hand. "So you're Monet!" she exclaimed curiously. "I saw your exhibition two years ago. I'm Alice,
Madame Hoschedé. I'm just going back to see if my girls are dressed
for dinner."

He replied hastily, "I beg your pardon, madame! I didn't know
you. I thought you were perhaps . . . You must pardon me."

She smiled. "Yes, people mistake me for the housekeeper. I don't
mind. I put on an old dress at once when I come here and am so
happy. But we must hurry, for the dinner bell will ring and I need to
change; Ernest likes to dress for dinner."

Taking the basket, he fell in beside her as she walked on rapidly.
They slipped in the back door and she said, "Wait in the library if
you like, monsieur! I hear you'll stay with us. We're happy to have
you, and my children are excited. I hope you won't mind if they
watch you work a little."

"Madame, the pleasure is mine," he said.

The dinner was served at a long table set with delicate china and
crystal wineglasses. Four girls and a boy chattered away, but grew
shyer when he looked at them and bent their heads over their plates.
After the meal, they all walked out to the gazebo, where the maid
would bring brandy and coffee.

Now he saw where his panels would be set, and he placed his hand on the wall. At once he wanted everyone to go away so he could think about them. The feudal aspect of the situation struck him. So were Renaissance painters housed and fed by the great Florentine families while they decorated the rooms and painted the family portraits. He smiled; I have come from the son of a provincial shopkeeper to the life of Raphael. He could not wait to tell Camille.

HE RAN FROM the Argenteuil train station down the path past the stone wall. She was embroidering under an arbor. He bent to kiss her mouth and told her of the commission and she put down her needle. "I knew something magnificent would happen for your beautiful work!" she exclaimed.

"Listen, though, *ma chère!*" he said. "It means I'll be away several days a week, but I'll be home every weekend as fast as the train can carry me, longing for you. It is a great opportunity, but perhaps I should tell them I can't accept it."

She bit her lip and turned away to look at the flower beds. He traced his hand gently down her cheek. He added, "If you don't want me to, I'll tell them no. Something else will come up. The American sales will start again."

Her long, lovely Grecian face was serious when she turned to him. "Do you want to do it?"

"I do, but I hate being away from you."

"Oh, I'll miss you terribly!" she exclaimed, kissing him. "But you'll be painting! We'll write every day. Really, Claude! I'm so content here. The part of me who was so dark and strange this past winter seems like another woman. Lise is coming to stay for a few days, did I tell you? The theater world is just exhausting her, poor thing! And Auguste has no patience for her, she says."

CLAUDE'S ROOM AT the Château de Rottembourg overlooked the lawns and the gazebo, where he would paint. He hung up his clothes in the capacious wardrobe and noted the carved and painted French headboard: this was an old family, having little in common with him and his hardscrabble life. No one would disturb the solitude of this room. He had only to eat fine meals and paint.

Even so, he missed Camille and wrote her nightly, the houseman taking his letters to the small post office every morning and bringing back the ones she sent to him.

Sometimes the Hoschedé daughters stood in the doorway watching him paint. Other times the whole family returned to Paris and left him with the servants and he dined at the long table alone. He went through the rooms then, touching the edges of another life. Once he looked through the open door to the master suite. The walls were papered with a yellow print. He had a great desire to go in and lie upon the large, high, curtained bed. What lives were these, so rich and full, lacking for nothing?

Sometimes he did not see them at all, for on weekends he went home, and that was often when the family came; sometimes he passed them in the train station as their private car arrived. Other times he heard the voices of the children from their schoolroom, and when the door was opened he noticed the map and the globe.

His first three weekends home in Argenteuil were joyful, but on the fourth when he let himself into the parlor, he saw that everything was in disarray and that dishes and pots were piled in the kitchen. He ran up the stairs and opened the bedroom door.

Camille was lying in bed reading. He watched her turning the pages, other books at her side, trying to disguise the sinking feeling in his heart, and bent down to kiss her. "What's the book?" he asked casually.

"Our friend Zola sent us his latest novel about a poor laundress. The cook left four days ago. I didn't want to tell you. We owed her . . ."

"I told her I'd manage it this week!" he said rigidly. "But where's Jean?"

"Oh, he's always at the neighbors' these days after school; their son is his closest friend. He has his meals there; sometimes he doesn't come home until bedtime. Really, he's quite happy!"

Claude bit his lip. His son should be here, but at least the boy had found a refuge until his mother should return to herself again. Were her dark moods returning, during which she despaired about things in the past, things she felt she should be, her worn but steadfast sense of unworthiness? How long would they remain?

He said, "I've missed you both so much! Haven't you been to Paris? No? Is your sister so preoccupied making hats for the wealthy? You didn't go to see Lise in that new comedy? Don't tell Auguste if you go; it makes him too sad. He told me they won't last together. You're too much alone here. Come with me to the château next week."

She shook her head. "It would be strange to be in someone else's house with you working all the time! Only perhaps you can paint more quickly and come home to me. Claude, my time came again. I'm still not with child." She put down her book and held out her arms, and as he came into them he felt how she trembled.

All weekend he watched her face and her moods. Sometimes she was radiantly happy, other times withdrawing. He recalled her birthday, when he had felt so oddly that something would not let him in. He was glad when the hour came for his return to Montgeron. In his heart he had already left for there and walked from the train station, hand in his pocket, bag over his shoulder, watching the sun setting behind the château and all the small windows and the water in the fountain and the yellow jonquils ablaze with the light.

At times the four Hoschedé girls and their brother tiptoed in to watch him create his panel of turkeys. Occasionally Madame Hoschedé came with them, bringing her sewing. Autumn arrived with its cooler air, and sometimes before he slept at night, he took his pipe and went out to the gardens.

One evening as he smoked there, lulled by the rustle of the trees, he heard the door open and saw Madame Hoschedé coming across the terrace.

"What, are you here?" she exclaimed with a smile. "The night's so lovely, I had to come out as well. Are you walking to the river?"

"Yes, I generally walk that way to listen to it in the dark."

"I used to come outside with my sisters at night and exchange secrets. We also hid about the house; it was our special place, full of hidden rooms and stairs. My girls think they know them all, but I discovered them first." She laughed and he looked down at her. She was a little dowdy and plump, her brown hair in a loosely gathered lump at her neck and her walk a bit clumsy.

As they came closer to the river they heard the flowing water. "I feel this place isn't ours, really," she added. "We're keeping it for the children and their children. Many generations will play here. I'll be old and watch them."

When they walked back, he felt the darkness about them and the huge bulk of the château with its many secrets, all preserved somehow in hidden drawers, chests, and corners where children ran and hid and were happy.

AT FIRST HE said to himself, I am not drawn to her. He had to say it, as he had noticed her coming into his thoughts frequently. Sometimes he wondered, What can she think of me? He no longer felt young; he was thirty-six years old, and his age was beginning to show. Auguste said his face had increased in interest. He seldom thought about it, but he did now. How was he seen? Now when she was not there he was sorry. Sometimes he turned around to see if Alice Hoschedé had come in, but it was only his wish. He listened for her voice.

She was so steady. She seemed happy with her husband; she seemed contented. They laughed a little at the table and had their private references. Sometimes she blushed. He felt then bitterly that he had wrong thoughts about someone who was happy, that he stood at the gate looking in, never knowing what he would find in his own home, admiring the security of hers. He knew she was deeply religious, and was rather appalled to realize there was a chapel in the house and that a priest came to say Mass there when the family was at home. He smelled the incense. He remained defensively atheistic. He suspected his mother's faith had kept her unhappily with his father. He was polite enough to say nothing and yet he wondered if some of Alice Hoschedé's stability came from the deep order of things her religion gave. There was an answer to everything and some celibate priest to explain it. He doubted it and yet envied its comfort.

"You seem so happy," he said to her one day as she sat with her sewing in the gazebo as he painted.

She carefully took another stitch with the blue silk thread on the pattern that would decorate the sleeve edge of a child's dress. "I am! I don't know if there is such a thing as perfect happiness, though; not on this earth. We have to keep it within ourselves, a little steady flame. Perhaps your painting does that for you."

"I am merely a craftsman," he said gruffly.

"A little more than that. You show me the beauty of this place. I hope one day you'll paint my children. Do you paint people?"

"Yes, I have painted my wife a great deal."

"What is she like, your wife?"

He hesitated, the white paint on his brush not yet descending to the turkey feathers. "She's lovely and radiant and at times incredibly courageous."

"I see you bring letters down each morning as I send mine to Paris. I saw the portrait of her in the green dress years ago when it was first exhibited. Monsieur Durand-Ruel has said she acts and sings; he saw her in Paris a few weeks ago and she told him she was planning to go on the stage."

"Ah, did she?"

Alice Hoschedé leaned forward, blinking a little shyly. "My only gift is for sewing, which I can't claim to do very well. Claude . . . I may call you Claude? I am fortunate to have been born to such a good family because really, I have no gifts. If I were a man, I think I would like to do what you do, to paint such wonderful things."

He shook his head and smiled. He found himself breathing more quietly than he could ever recall. He was tired and yet alert. He watched her hands, the freckles on the back of them, and the meticulous way she stitched.

THEIR RELATIONSHIP WAS delicate; even when she called him Claude there was a formality in it, as if she was aware of the intimacy. He felt so odd calling her by her Christian name that he generally mumbled and called her nothing.

She never gave him the weekly money herself; the house steward left it each Friday morning in an envelope on his breakfast tray, which held brioche, warm milk, hot coffee, jams, and butter. Yet even in the lovely breakfast china he felt her presence, as if someone watched over him. He had not felt that way in a long time. On weekends going home he was more thoughtful.

Slowly he began to form the conceit that she somehow needed him, though he realized this was probably nothing but pride. Why should she need him or anyone? She came from wealth, and her husband adored her. Claude was a painter struggling on the edge of security and growing weary: he was not the young man he had been. His shoulders were a little bent. And yet as he rode the train back to the château on Sunday nights, his thoughts went not only to his work, which compelled him, but to the suspicion that Alice Hoschedé needed him.

When he arrived on a cool late autumn day with the wind blowing up from the river, the housekeeper told him, "Madame and the children left for Paris. Your meals will be served at the same hour in the dining room or on a tray brought to you, as you wish. She asked me to convey that she sends all good wishes for your work this week." And he felt as he mounted the stairs to his room that Alice had perhaps gone for many reasons and one was to avoid him.

IT WAS LONELY suddenly without her there; he felt her in every tree and in the fountain filled with leaves. He received a long letter from Camille saying she had been twice to see Lise in her comedy and truly hoped to gather the courage to audition once more. Her parents were not very well, and her *grandmère* begged them to visit. For a moment his eyes filled with tears, and he felt his distance from her, a distance far greater than a short train ride. He was relieved to read the funny and badly spelled letter from his son, full of puzzles and riddles about snails and old men. Claude saved both and reread them a few times.

Still, as he painted, thoughts of Madame Hoschedé would not leave him. By Wednesday he could not see his work anymore and took the train to Paris to visit Durand-Ruel in his art gallery on the rue Lafitte. He had promised to visit and he had some questions forming in his mind.

As always, he first surveyed the walls of paintings to see what was new and what had not yet sold. A few new paintings by Pissarro had just arrived and he helped uncrate them. "How is my old friend?" he asked. "We only meet when we exhibit these days."

"He's looking for fortune still, as we all are. Renoir does better with his beautiful rosy-cheeked girls and dancers and lovers; he has several commissions to paint children. People would rather have that than Pissarro's country market women and abbeys. How are your panels coming?"

"Slower than I expected," Claude said.

They walked out down the street to a modest restaurant and ordered fish and chicken and the house wine in a carafe. A few young men played chess in a corner. There were new possibilities of American sales, the art dealer told him.

At the end of the meal, Claude said casually, "I'm curious about my patrons. They are ever kind and generous, but she intrigues me. She seems too fine for him, and yet she loves him."

Durand-Ruel sank back in his chair and lit a cigar. "Yes, it's a love match, or it was one. Years change things, I think, though she still adores him. She married him at seventeen against the wishes of her family, but then she has old money and he was merely a very bright entrepreneur. He was rising fast and building his fortune, and she joined hers to his. Recently—this stays between us, Monet— there have been distressing rumors."

"What rumors?" Claude asked, lighting a cigarette.

Durand-Ruel kept his voice low. "He's in financial difficulties. How much we can't say, but we hear it's not good. He's handled his affairs rashly, ineptly; he's spent much more than he's earning. This has been going on for some years, apparently, and he covered it all up. His partners, one of whom is a client of mine, have discovered some crisis in his mismanagement and want him out of the business. Her family will have nothing to do with her now, as she married against their wishes, so she's dependent on him. I have always liked her better than him. She's very loyal and will stand by him if he goes down. I find it sad indeed."

"Is there any danger they will go down?"

"No one knows. Are you being paid?"

"Yes, actually."

"Good."

Claude took the train back to the château, feeling a great heaviness of heart as he walked the long road and saw the house rise before him between the trees. That this beautiful place that seemed to promise the most envied stability might be endangered! He was being paid; how were they managing it? Did even these people pay some bills and not others? How much of what he had heard was true and how much rumor? How much did Hoschedé know, and how much did he conceal from his family? And how could it be? He could not imagine Madame Hoschedé apart from this world she loved.

The rest of the week he sometimes stopped painting and then, too distracted by his thoughts to work, sat in the château salon reading, listening to the ticking clock. He could feel this place considering leaving, as if the very stones and carved headboards could shake themselves loose and walk away.

When he returned the following Monday she was still not there, and he set to work. At midday his concentration was broken by the sound of the carriage and voices. The girls hurried into the gazebo to greet him, commenting on his work, taking his hand. He heard Alice's voice, and the hair on the back of his neck quivered. He hardly saw her as she came toward him and he felt bad that he had asked Durand-Ruel about her.

"Are you well?" she asked him. "Don't let the girls bother you!"

"They're not bothering me. And you, are you well?"

"Quite well," she said, and he breathed, much relieved. My art dealer saw things as worse than they are, he told himself. Everything here would remain as it had always been for generations to come.

SHE STAYED AT the château but her husband did not come. Letters from husband to wife arrived daily, and Claude saw Alice Hoschedé pacing in the long salon reading them with a frown and once again felt something was wrong indeed. Still, the space between him and her was great. She was his patron also in a way, and thus he was her servant. She read, her hand to her lips, as he passed the room, but she took no notice of him.

She has no one, he thought; no one but the children.

He remained reading in the library every evening, hoping she would come in. The hundreds of old books surrounded him as he sat in the fraying chair with his feet on an embroidered footstool, eating cakes and drinking wine from the tray a servant had left for him.

On the third evening she came across the carpet with her slightly clumsy walk. She wore a dark shawl, as if she could not be warm enough; she held it close the way women do who feel alone. He put down his book and stood slowly.

"I've disturbed you," she said, looking at him anxiously.

"Not in the least."

She motioned for him to sit again and took the chair near him. She sank back, pulling the brown shawl tighter, and gazed up at all the books.

"It's odd," she said. "I'm a little afraid tonight, a little lonely. This beautiful château! I'm afraid it will somehow disappear if I leave it. I didn't see you at dinner. I hoped you'd come in. The children hoped you would."

He replied, "I forget the time when I paint." He did not want to say he had avoided her.

She took out her one of the girls' plaid pinafores and began to mend the pocket seam. She sewed as practically as a nursemaid in some upper room might by candle. He said, "I'm also a little lonely tonight. I sometimes don't remember people exist when I paint, and when I stop I look up and wonder why they've deserted me! I've always been like that."

She nodded. "You've heard rumors, I'm sure," she said softly. "My husband's finances, which I trusted, are in disarray. There may be some losses. We sit here in my family's beautiful house, which has been ours forever, and I don't know what will happen. He's too ashamed and uncertain to do anything but cut himself off from me."

Hᴇ ʟᴏᴏᴋᴇᴅ ʙᴀᴄᴋ on the next few days as something out of time. He felt her in the air, when he woke, when he breathed. He could neither paint nor read. He positioned himself in the house or the garden in respect to where she was. Then two days passed and he did not see her. Where could she be? She was in the house. Neither did he hear the children. He realized at last that they had gone away, but where and when he did not know; he knew only that she remained. He sensed it.

At dinner alone at the great table, he asked the servant, "Madame does not come to dinner?" and the man replied, "Madame is a little tired tonight and dines alone." Then his heart leapt. In his mind he swept away the servants, maids, cooks, and gardeners. He was here alone with her in the château by the river. He finished eating and went to the library to wait. She will come to me, he thought.

But hours passed and she did not come.

He mounted the stairs to the bedrooms with a candle. The master bedroom was to the left down the corridor and his was to the right. He stood in the hall with the wind outside the château walls, not knowing which way to go. He walked to the left, past the old green flocked wallpaper and the stiff portraits of her ancestors from centuries before, until he came to her door.

He put his hand on the handle and turned it. The door creaked, and he was caught momentarily against the portiere curtain. At once he heard her listening. "It's Claude," he said then.

Her voice from behind the bed hangings sounded far away. "I thought I was alone in the house but for the servants."

"You knew I was here, surely!"

He approached the dark blue bed hangings, seeing the shape of the carved testers by his candle and the portraits on the wall and his own shape with the candle reflected back from the oval dresser mirror. "Forgive me," he whispered. "I shouldn't be here, but I can't help myself. I've waited days for you, sensing where you must be. I stayed in the library for hours not reading, waiting for you. I feel so tenderly for you, Alice! Tell me to go away, and I'll go at once."

She said nothing. He bent over the bed and touched her open hand and then bent forward to kiss her forehead. She reached up and drew him closer. How rich and deep and still she was, and would be that way today and tomorrow and always! I can ask no more than this, he thought.

He doused the candle and lay down near this rather plain chatelaine. They moved together and reached for each other, arms at first caught oddly beneath her cotton nightgown and his trousers. They made love then, at first cautiously, then their breath came faster as they pushed away all reticence. She was passionate; she cried out at the end, and he placed his hand over her mouth gently.

They lay looking at each other in the near darkness. "It was lovely," she whispered. "We joined together; we melded. I thought of where you could be in the house and willed you to come here. It was the loveliest thing in the world, but it's wrong."

"Religion!" he said, still dazed by her touch. "Why doesn't it stay on church walls where it belongs? What is it, to say that the coupling of two lonely people who see good and truth in each other is wrong?"

Her answer was patient. "Because we not only are promised elsewhere but we still love elsewhere. And those other people think we're true. Forgive me; I needed you so! I called for you and you came. My husband's been too unhappy to touch me for quite some time, but it's more than that. You are somehow in my heart and have been since I first saw you. For some moments I knew what it was to paint, to be Claude Monet . . ."

"Don't wish that," he whispered. "I've no certainty, and my youth has left me. I started out determined to make no mistakes and now I have made so many I can't escape them."

Gently she pushed him away, sat up, and felt for her dressing gown. "We mustn't do this again, Claude," she said. "I love my husband, though he has turned from me, and you love your Camille. I'd better go now. Please don't follow me!"

But he cried, "Wait!" hurrying after her as she went swiftly down the dark hall. He could have overtaken her, but he kept back a little. He was barefoot and only in his shirt. The house was full of servants. Though the clock showed three in the morning, one would come from a door or down a step, perhaps holding a lamp.

He caught her arm. "Where are you going?"

"I don't know . . . to the chapel. How you move me! But why should we expect to be happy in this world?"

He stumbled back to his room and lay heavily down on his bed, his arms wrapped around himself, staring into the darkness. He saw Camille again waiting for him and beat the pillow with his fist time and again as if he struck himself.

He slept late and heard Ernest Hoschedé's voice rising from the garden before he rose. From the bags in the hall, Claude knew the man had just returned, and when he came into the breakfast room, bright with sunlight, he saw that Alice was already at the table, hair neatly combed, wearing her loose morning gown.

"Ah, Monet!" Hoschedé cried. "How are the paintings coming? Have you seen them, Alice?"

Alice looked up from pouring the coffee. "I am quite pleased," she said.

HE PAINTED BRUTALLY that day, unhappy with everything. Later he asked the servant for supper in his room and went there at twilight to find a letter from Camille on the table. It lay in its blue envelope, accusing him. She must know somehow, she must sense . . . what had he done? The best thing would be to finish the panels, take what money he could, thank monsieur and madame, and hurry away, not hearing the sound of rumbling and tears as this place was surrendered as once his paintings had been surrendered for debt. For he understood clearly from words that rang out down the hall how dire Alice Hoschedé's situation would become.

He found in his shirt pocket a blue cloth button from her nightdress; he had no memory it had torn away. He stuffed it into the side pocket of his carpetbag, where it jammed under the lining folds.

The writing of the letter from his wife blurred for him; he looked away from it, walked back and forth, poured a little wine, and tried again to make sense of the words. Surely they said, "I accuse you," but they did not. They said, "Dearest Claude, I long for you and I have lovely news to share."

Yes, he thought, what madness! What madness it was to take someone else in my arms when she's waiting for me. Now it is I who have a secret that can never be told.

He took the train home the next day. Camille ran out to meet him. He picked her up and swung her about, smelling her hair, feeling her warmth against him. Jean ran out as well, all thin and boyish, crying, "Papa! I have new friends . . ."

The new cook had prepared fish and they all three ate together, the boy chatting about his schoolmates. Gradually Claude quieted his terrible sense of shame. What had been between him and Madame Hoschedé anyway? Nothing, a shadow. Both pairs of lovers, both married couples, had been reunited. His essence left in the folds of her body would be buried under much else: duty, prayers, he could not say what. His face burned. And if the Hoschedés lost much, what was it to him? They could not begin to know of loss.

He walked upstairs with Camille, his arm about her waist.

She pulled on her nightgown and sat at the dressing table, brushing her hair. "Let me do that," he exclaimed, rising. Her face in the mirror smiled back at him.

He demanded, "Tell me your news. Come! I'll make love to you until you do, showing no mercy. Now at once, madame!"

She stood up and ran her fingers down his mustache. He bit her fingers gently. "I won't tell you then for days because I'm longing to make love with you!" she said. "But I also can't wait to say my news. I'm with child. My breasts are tender. Don't squeeze so! Ouch! Are you happy?"

"Yes," he said, and his voice broke. He cried firmly then, "Yes, so happy."

Later he lay sleepless thinking with her beside him. He was glad the panels would take no more than a few more weeks to complete, and he suspected Madame Hoschedé would take the children and go to Paris during that time, absenting herself. The château would be his alone with the servants until he packed his clothes and paints for the last time and returned home to Argenteuil.

Interlude

As the exhibition drew closer he found he ate little; he walked back and forth in front of his selected forty-eight canvases, once more apart from them. The paintings had been framed, and people from the gallery were to take them away tomorrow to hang them.

When he returned to the house to put some distance between himself and his work, he found a small, thin parcel addressed to him on his dining table. He knew the handwriting. He carried it upstairs to his bedroom at once, closing the door before opening it.

There were no more than twenty letters tied together with a blue ribbon, some written on the bookshop stationery, some on pages from a school notebook, some on paper that he guessed had been scented but now just smelled rather musty. Some were dated, some not. Because of the handwriting and style he guessed they all had been written between her sixteenth and eighteenth years, before and at the time she first met him. They were passionate letters, full of girlish longing. "I am thinking of you today. The spring is sweet, and you're not here. How tired I am waiting for you! I think I will give up courage and turn to someone else." Likely they were meant for her fiancé, that ridiculous old man. Or perhaps for schoolboys or a dead actor.

He fell asleep with the letters. That night he was certain he heard someone calling him from the water garden. He rose from bed in his nightshirt and made his way with his cane across to the pond. The moon was on the lily pads, which had not yet blossomed. He splashed into the water. It was not very deep, up to his waist.

He returned to the house, hoping no one would see him, ashamed of his actions. It was madness, he thought. I'm merely anxious about the exhibition.

He stripped off his wet nightshirt and slept.

Camille came to him in his dreams and pressed her soft body against his, and her long loose hair tickled him as she whispered into his ear. *I'm not in the pond, darling Claude! I'm in the paintings.* He woke suddenly, hours past his usual time. Then the paintings are mine alone and too private to show, he thought. He threw on his clothes and hurried downstairs.

He was too late. They had been taken away by car half an hour before to Paris.

Part Seven

1877

I remember that, although I was full of fervor, I didn't have the slightest inkling, even at forty, of the deeper side to the movement we were pursuing by instinct.

—CAMILLE PISSARRO

IT HAD BEEN NEARLY THREE YEARS SINCE THE FIRST independent exhibition in the photography studio on the boulevard des Capucines had closed. The emotion that arose before and after Claude's friends had risked their money and reputations on what a few frames could hold still stirred among them. They were bound together by the name *Impressionists,* and yet in spite of the many times they had painted the same snowy lane or bunch of flowers together, their styles and temperaments were very different.

And what was this thing called the school of Impressionism composed of? It was always changing; if anyone expected it to stand still, they were wrong. There were the visible brushstrokes of pure color, the emphasis on changing light, the beautiful world of modern daily life throughout the country. There was also their now famous recognition for painting *en plein air.*

A month before the latest exhibition, Claude had walked into the Gare Saint-Lazare and addressed the stationmaster. "I am the artist Claude Monet, my good man!" he had said. "And I wish to paint here. It is convenient for me to do so tomorrow morning at ten? Would you be so kind as to stop the trains at that time briefly so I can paint them?" His friends were amazed that the stationmaster complied. Claude had worked there many times over a few months. To capture the energy and shadow of the great glass roof and the smoke, he had created rich browns and grays from many colors. Even the shadows were shot with color. He was always exploring, always experimenting.

At the opening day of the exhibition, with two of his finished train station pictures on the walls, he thought, Yes, for good or for worse we're yoked together: Sisley, Cézanne, Auguste, Pissarro, and the others. He saw in their faces the weariness once more of brushing their best suits and smiling at strangers in the crowded rooms. Auguste complained of stiffness in his legs, though he was scarcely past his middle thirties. Pissarro's beard was whiter and he had more children. Sisley's beloved wife was ill.

Later Claude walked through the streets alone to board the late train back to Argenteuil, sitting back on his plush seat as he sped through the night, already thinking of Camille. She had not been pregnant after all, or had miscarried early, and she struggled against her sadness, for she wanted a large family.

She was waiting for him in the kitchen in her pink dressing gown, drinking a tisane and eating a cake. A cup had been left out for him. "How was the exhibition?" she asked, rising to kiss him. "I heard the train whistle and knew you'd be here. I'm sorry I didn't feel well enough to come."

"You were missed! Some people reserved paintings to buy, never as many as we would like, of course, but the paintings will hang for a time and we're sure to have more sales."

"There's hot water. It's lovely tea: chamomile blossoms with bits of dried apple and cinnamon. Sit down."

They drank the tisane and he took some sausage and cheese from the cupboard because he was suddenly hungry; the clock struck the hour and then again an hour later as they talked and laughed together. He teased her a little about spoiling Jean.

He left the thing he hesitated to tell her until last. "I've had some good fortune," he said, looking at the wet blossoms in the bottom of his cup. "My friend Caillebotte, who exhibited some of his work with us tonight, offered to give me a studio on the rue d'Isly. I'd like to paint there sometime; I want to finish more of my train station pictures."

She rose and settled herself on his lap. "I'm glad about that. You need time away from everyone. From all your friends, and from perhaps me."

"Oh, not from you, my love! I'll be home every evening. I've also been thinking. You remain too alone here. As soon as I can afford it, let's move back to Paris."

"I'd love that! I miss my friends, and I never can see my little niece enough. I don't want to live away from there anymore. I didn't want to tell you."

"But you can always tell me things," he said. The clock was striking two in the morning when he rose, setting her on her feet, and led her upstairs.

THAT WEEK HE took possession of the Paris studio. He shut the door behind him, bolted it, and sat down on a stool in the middle of the room, looking around with his hands on his knees. Some paintings he was working on stood against the wall. He could hear the sound of his own breath and his heartbeat and, underneath, the murmurs of all the paintings he wished to make.

We are alone, you and I, he said to his paintings. No one can come here.

Claude went home almost every night, but when work kept him late, he sometimes slept on a narrow cot in the studio. Once on waking he thought he was twenty-four again and in his first studio, on the rue de Furstenberg, and that Frédéric was calling him.

Coffee's ready. Don't worry about me. I've too many things to do in this life to get killed. I'll come back. I promise.

On the cot, Claude stared at the early-morning sunlight through the curtains and the floorboards. He whispered, "You broke your promise, and I never had a chance to thank you for everything you did for me. Have you forgotten me, wherever you are? She and I stumble a little and you're not here to steady us, for you always did in a way, you complicated fellow. I miss you, *cher ami*, and so does she."

1877–1878

It's on the strength of observation and reflection that one finds a way.

—CLAUDE MONET

ON A WARM SUMMER EVENING IN THE HOUSE IN ARGENteuil, Claude made his wife pregnant again. They did not know until she began throwing up in the mornings. Turning her head toward him, she began laughing. He laughed too and took her in his arms.

"A girl!" she swore.

"No, a boy," he said, his hand over her belly. "I feel him!"

But she was more ill from the start this time than she had been with Jean, and again Claude resolved she should not be in Argenteuil alone with the boy for another winter. There was something about her that made him uneasy. She seemed to search for her strength. All the dreams she had had for many things turned into the making of this child.

"We're moving back to Paris after Christmas," he told her.

He found elegant rooms on the rue Moncey in Paris and led her through them one by one, showing her the wood paneling, tall windows, and immense doors. Now in her sixth month, she followed him with her hand on the small of her back under her loose blue dress to ease the weight of her stomach. Jean ran ahead. "I'll come as long as my friends from Argenteuil can visit me!" he exclaimed. "Did we ever live in Paris? I don't remember."

With Camille, Claude rented furniture and arranged what things they had; she ordered calling cards engraved *Madame Claude Monet.* "Now you can call on your old friends," he said a little wryly when she showed them to him. "Those women we met once at the opera when we were in the balcony and they were seated in the parterre boxes!"

"Yes, I will sit there this season. I like engraved cards; my mother had them."

"I remember," he said gravely.

They gave their first soirée on a February evening; from the street below they heard carriages slowing in the snow in front of the house and the muted sound of horses' hooves as they moved away again. Edmond Maître arrived with his new wife; Pissarro brought a painting, Sisley carried hothouse roses, and Auguste and Lise wore the indignant look of a couple whose fractious quarrel had barely ceased. A few other men who collected Claude's work came: Dr. de Bellio and Comte Beguin Billecocq, who had met Claude many years before.

Camille sat on the sofa in a loose silk-wool dress, charmingly swollen with child, and the others gathered around her, some sitting on chairs and leaning on the sofa back, one or two on the floor. After a time, she rose to the piano and sat down. She sang one song in English that she had learned in their days in London, leaning forward, fingers cautiously moving from one key to another as she accompanied herself.

That night when Claude was sleeping soundly, he heard her cry out from another room. He leapt up, stumbling against a chair, stubbing his toe—he hardly knew what direction to take. His heart was beating fast. He ran into the parlor and saw her dark shape, her nightdress showing her swollen belly, standing on a chair with his painting of her in the green dress down from the wall, barely resting on the chair's edge and leaning against her. She could not move for its weight.

He cried, "What are you doing?" He ran forward and lifted down the heavy picture first and then her from the chair. "You could have asked me to take it down," he said. "I would have. It's the middle of the night! You could have hurt yourself and the child."

"I suddenly didn't want it there. I'm fat now and she's a reproach to me. When I'm old you won't love me anymore."

"I'll love you more!" he said tenderly, trying to control his voice. "And besides, you must be fat to have a baby. Even your blessed Virgin grew fat. We'll put up another painting instead."

HER LABOR WAS longer than the first one; the baby did not want to come. Claude thought as he had the first time, I will never touch her again. He caught glimpses of her fierce, anguished face until Lise came running in at three in the morning and walked him gently back and forth across the parlor. Annette had arrived at once with a midwife she trusted. Jean wandered in and out in his nightdress, thin and barefoot. It was not until the next evening that Claude's new son was born. When he heard the cry he went in to Camille and held her.

HE HAD MANAGED to put away most thoughts of the Hoschedé family since Camille's pregnancy and since the move to Paris. He did not see them, and oddly, he did not hear of them. It was a few months after Michel's birth, reading the morning paper early in May with his coffee, that news of Alice and her husband and children came to him through a small article.

Camille and the baby still slept and Jean had tied his books with a strap and left for school. Claude dressed rapidly and walked through the streets past shopkeepers washing their sidewalks to Durand-Ruel's apartment. Waiting for his art dealer in his salon, he studied one of the many floral panels he had created on and above doors.

Durand-Ruel came toward him pulling on his coat. "Claude," he said, surprised. "I was on my way to the gallery. May I offer you a coffee? Is all well?"

"I saw something in the paper this morning about my old patrons the Hoschedés. Can it be true?"

Durand-Ruel's round face grew somber and he nodded his head. "It's true," he said. "They've lost everything—the art collection with your pictures, the château. You know she had another child some eight months ago. She delivered the boy on a train, fleeing from her estate and the bailiffs. The conductor stopped the train and some-one took the other children into another car. And Hoschedé is now serving a month in prison for financial fraud."

"*Merde!* I had hoped it wouldn't happen!" Claude replied.

"The poor woman must find herself in a strange world. She hasn't a franc and she and the six children are living with her sister. I have asked her to my soirée in a few days and hope she'll come."

That night in his own comfortable rooms in the middle of after-dinner coffee with guests, he rose and looked into the leaping fire in the fireplace. His glass of brandy was warm in his hand. His old pro-tective affection for Alice Hoschedé came flooding back to him. What shall I do? he thought. I must see her again, at least to offer some kind words and find if I can help her in any way. And perhaps her child is mine, from the one time I took her in my arms. Perhaps he is mine.

When he turned from the fire, the rest of the room blurred.

CLAUDE HAD INTENDED to arrive early at the soirée, but then he walked about anxiously for a while, hesitant to go. By the time he mounted the steps, the salon with his painted panels was already crowded with artists and patrons and friends. He moved through the crowd, greeting people he knew, shaking hands or kissing cheeks, all the time looking for Alice Hoschedé.

She was standing by herself in a small room off the salon near a harp, her fingers absently touching the strings. Her dark brown hair—hair that had tumbled over his shoulders amid the linen sheets that one night that now seemed a lifetime ago—was gathered at the back of her head. The sight of her brought a rush of confused feelings to him, among them the old peace he had felt with her at times, peace as simple as a child feels when he knows all the world about him is orderly and well.

As he walked forward, she raised her face. Behind her rose shelves of books on the great artists of the past: Leonardo da Vinci, Michelangelo Buonarroti, Fra Angelico. He realized then he would rather read the titles than look at her. If only he could have looked at her without her looking at him! Claude thrust his hands in his pockets.

"Alice," he said.

"I hoped you'd come," she said simply. "I'm glad to see you, Claude." He saw them both in an oval mirror, her back protected by her evening shawl, his shoulders hunched in his evening suit and gray silk tie, his face wary under his beard. He stood a few feet from her; he would not venture closer.

He kept one hand in his pocket, reaching the other out to grasp the back of the harpist's gilt chair. "I'm glad to see you too. Durand-Ruel told me some of the news. I can't say how sorry I am. It's beyond what could be conceived."

"Yes, my children won't have the château now. I meant to keep it safe for them."

"He tells me you and the children are living with your sister."

"We are, but even before Ernest went to prison, she wouldn't have let him stay, she's so angry with him. I need to leave there when he comes out to be with him, but we don't know where. It's so odd we have no place to go. So many people who often dined with us won't speak to us. Very few people here this evening have come to greet me."

Staring at the blue flowers in the Oriental rug, he said suddenly, "True friends don't leave. What can I do for you? Alice, my hands are so empty. I have little money myself now. We men are wretches, aren't we? We make promises and break them. We say, 'I'll manage!' and then fall on our faces."

She was looking at him with her old sweet look. "You have another child, I hear."

"Yes, and you as well."

"I do." He could not ask her now; he could not. Once again he was drawn to her quiet steadiness and wanted to pull her against him, but he could not do it here, and besides, he dared not. She spoke her husband's name with love and sorrow. Still he felt, oh the pity of it! Oh, the pity of living, and yet she will at least have her husband again and I am loved more than I deserve to be.

Someone called him and he excused himself. When he returned, the small room was empty and one of the maids said that Madame Hoschedé had left suddenly and alone.

CLAUDE WALKED A long time through the city. He passed many a beautiful house, many churches, and the locked gates of parks. Ernest Hoschedé's fall had both hurt and warned Claude. He himself owed everyone here more than he ever had in his life; it was only a matter of time until it all closed in on him with bailiffs and an even more dreadful scene occurred to his wife and children than had occurred before. His Parisian life, which seemed always to call for another seat at the Opéra Garnier, another expensive dinner, was choking him. He had to leave here; he had to move again. Once more his painting had slowed. He wanted to escape to the country, far from all this, with only Camille and the children. They would live on next to nothing. They would read together. They would grow their own vegetables and drink fresh milk. He would paint the countryside every day.

A lamp burned in the nursery when he came home, shining on Camille nursing her little child. "You're so late!" she scolded. "You look tired. Give me a few minutes and I'll make you a tisane. The maid's long gone to sleep."

"Let me talk with you, Minou."

He pulled up a chair so that their knees touched, and he gazed at the lovely shape of her breast and the infant who did not bother to acknowledge him but remained absorbed in sucking, one little fist clenched. He heard the sound of the country inside of him so intensely that it seemed as if any moment she too would hear the crickets.

She said, "Talk to me, Claude."

He said clumsily, "The truth is, I've failed again. I can't keep us here. I finally was able to give you what you always deserved: calling cards, dresses, afternoon concerts. I see you're happy, and yet for me . . . I'm not. I want to be away in the country to paint, in a deeper part of the country than our little town in Argenteuil. I feel like the mists of the river call me. I want to dig in a garden and walk out before dawn the way my old mentor and I used to do. It would be a nice life! You'd miss your operas and ballets, but I'd build a small riverboat and take you with me when I painted. And when I have money we can come back. I promise you. I swear it."

She hesitated a long time; he watched her breath rise and fall even as the child suckled, and her elegant profile turned to the window, outside of which lay the Paris street. She said, "I always know what you feel before you do. Some men came to the door today about what we owe. They'll be back, I'm afraid."

He cried, "I'm so sorry, Minou!"

She grasped his hand. "We'll go," she said. "You'll sell more work and we'll be back again. I love you."

"How can you love me when I fail?"

"But you don't fail, Claude," she said. She rose to put the baby in his cradle and he watched her shape as she bent, the roundness of her bottom under her nightdress. "So it's settled. We'll go. Do you have a place in mind? Ah, I thought you did! If you're inspired to paint we'll soon pay these wretched people. Now, who did you see this evening? Tell me."

He stood, hands in his pockets, for a moment too moved to speak. "Many people," he said casually. "I saw my old patron, Madame Hoschedé. They've lost all their money and property, and they were so wealthy! I used to draw the girls funny pictures in their château.

They're sweet: the eldest is perhaps fifteen and the littlest not yet six. There's a boy a little younger than Jean and an infant too."

"Oh, how dreadful for her!" Camille cried. "All's lost? What will she do?"

"I don't know."

"She must feel as I do. Men have to work all the time, and most women can't make their own way. I wish I could pay for things. I wanted to be a great actress or a novelist like George Sand or George Eliot; I know now those are only dreams. Sometimes I feel quite use-less."

"Never!" he insisted. "You give me all the strength I have. We'll rent a house this time, but someday we'll buy our own and live in it forever." In the lamplight she seemed pale, and she touched chairs and walls as she went as if she was very tired. She had seemed more tired since this last birth.

The pain passes, but the beauty remains.
—AUGUSTE RENOIR

THOUGH TWENTY MILES FROM THE CITY, THE VILLAGE of Vétheuil was remote. First there was the train to Mantes, which curved around the River Seine, and then a cart and horse or a regular local coach that took you on. Sitting on the cart's hard bench beside the driver, Claude gazed out as they jerked up the slope of Saint-Martin-la-Garenne. There was little here but the water, fields, and woods. He descended the cart and walked to the old village with houses built around the church. Wherever he looked, he saw landscapes he wanted to paint.

Even the smell of the air filled him with great joy. He would have liked to have begun painting at once, but he had to rent a house and bring his family here.

He moved Camille and the children within days, leaving promises everywhere in Paris to pay what he owed when he could. He did not doubt he could. He felt in his body the paintings he would do. Also, the house held an enchantment for him the way new houses and rooms always did: new spaces, new ways to look at and paint the world.

They went through the dark rooms with a lantern, Jean running ahead and shouting back. Claude felt for drafts and made a note to mend places in the walls. They had not brought the maid or the cook, but he had engaged one of the farm girls to cook and clean and her slow-witted brother to help about the house. Still, the house was so big it seemed to echo back to them.

In the morning he ran down the steep stone steps that led from house to garden. "Do you mind if I go out to paint?" he called back to Camille, and her voice echoed from the kitchen. "No, do go. I'll unpack." He went then, striding through the village to the fields, his easel on his shoulder. Autumn was coming, and the haystacks were slowly forming. The trees were heavy with apples. He breathed in everything and set up his easel at last, painting as if starved. Some farm boys came to watch him. He heard the call of the men stacking the dry hay and the boys on top tamping it down; he heard the hay falling softly.

He stayed away all day, then strode back, stomping up the steps from the garden. From inside came the smell of dinner and the clink of china. The hired girl had made a soup, and he and Camille and Jean sat down at the table in the unpainted kitchen to eat. The baby slept.

He ate hungrily and asked, "And, both of you, how was your day?" He ruffled Jean's hair and the boy shrugged away a little, offended. "I miss my friends in Paris already," he said darkly. "And now I won't see Pierre from Argenteuil anymore. How do I know if I'll like the boys here? I don't understand why we keep moving."

Claude put down his spoon. "I'm sorry," he said.

"But it can't be helped," Camille said tenderly to her son. "And magical things will happen here too, as they always do. You know they always do."

She ate carefully, stopping now and then to look out the window at the darkening trees. She crumbled a bit of bread and said, "Claude, I keep thinking of Madame Hoschedé and her poor husband. You said he had been released from prison. I keep thinking she has no place to go, poor woman, and that perhaps they could come to us for a while."

He swallowed some wine. "You'd have them here? I don't think that's best, Minou."

"But it is!" she exclaimed, both hands on the table edge and her eyes very bright. "Imagine if it happened to you when you owed money, if you were sent to prison! And besides, it would be company for me. I'd love to meet her girls. One day perhaps I'll have a daughter. I know you, how you paint and forget the world. I'd also like to ask my *grandmère* to come. Claude, let's ask them all. This house is large enough for fifteen people. Shall I write?"

"No," he said. "If you think it best, I will." He could eat no more.

While she washed the dishes with Jean and the girl, he sat at the cleared table drinking his coffee and writing the letter. This is madness, he thought, the back of his neck warm. He walked to the village in the morning and reluctantly posted it to Durand-Ruel, asking him to forward it if he had an address for the Hoschedés.

Three days later a reply came from Hoschedé himself, delivered by the local post boy. Claude drank his coffee and shook the letter open. The heavy script pierced the paper in a few places. "I have been through hell," it said, "and you are most kind. *C'est très gentil à vous,* Monet! I insist on paying half the rent and expenses. Life delivers what you do not expect. We will come Saturday."

Camille looked back from arranging their dishes on a kitchen shelf; she wore a bright blue cloth over her hair and a blue apron. "Will they come?" she asked.

He bit his lip, folding the letter. What would Alice, the former lady of a château, make of this old place that smelled of mildew? And for what deeper reasons had he agreed to this madness? He did not like Ernest Hoschedé—he never had—but that was the least of it. They should not come, he thought roughly: I shall write them not to come. Perhaps Hoschedé himself had changed his mind. He walked down the steps to pick flowers from the garden and put them in a glass.

As CLAUDE NEVER wrote the letter, the Hoschedés did come: two carts arrived in a few days, laden with trunks, Alice riding with the driver in her plain dark dress, her one-year-old son in her arms and the somber four young girls and their brother walking. Hoschedé strode among them as if shepherding them, carrying his fine ash walking stick with the lion's-head handle. Claude watched them approach; he stood at the bottom of the stone steps, which were now lined with flowerpots.

The two men shook hands.

Hoschedé said, "Well, now we'll be quite surrounded by your paintings, Monet! No need to commission them, eh? But I'm sorry to tell you our visit will be short. Yes, within a week or a little more, we'll have a place in Paris again!"

But what have they brought? Claude thought uneasily as he helped Hoschedé and the driver carry the trunks up the steps. Alice came after, clasping her baby, her daughters and older son following closely. Now Claude could see that she had been crying.

Camille stood at the top of the steps in her blue apron, her own baby in her arms. She kissed each girl in turn as they slowly entered the kitchen, and she held Alice's hand. "I welcome you, madame," she said gravely. "You have had a terrible loss, and I'll do my best to make you feel at home."

Alice raised her head and said softly, "You are so very kind to have us, Madame Monet." The clasp of hands and then the grave kiss between the two women took only a few moments, but Claude hardly breathed. He stared at the floor, hands in his pockets, and then gradually raised his eyes to the eager little boy who was struggling to be set down in the kitchen. The boy crawled happily toward Claude's legs and pulled himself up on Claude's trousers. He looked very much like Ernest Hoschedé. Claude sighed. At least he did not have to contend with that.

"We all welcome you," Claude said, picking up the boy.

Hoschedé clapped Claude's shoulder. "Poor mites!" he muttered. "I've put them through a lot. My wife's a saint. I'm going back tonight. I have prospects. I'll send on five hundred francs in the morning. This plain country living will be healthy for all of them, and they're fond of you, Monet! My second daughter, Blanche, likes to draw a little, you know."

"I know; she showed me some of her sketches. A few days, then, and we'll see you," Claude replied. He stood on the steps as an old man from the village arrived with his cart and donkey to take Ernest Hoschedé back to the city.

THE LARGE HOUSE was no longer empty: girlish voices called softly, timidly, uncertain of this new world. The oldest girl, Marthe, was fifteen and the youngest, called Germaine, was five; all followed their mother so closely they almost trod on her skirt. They kept to their rooms unless coaxed down, and then hardly said a word. By the end of the long afternoon Jean had decided the older Hoschedé son, Jacques, who was a couple of years younger than he was, might be worth knowing, and took him off to the riverbank to consider building a tree house.

The rest of that day and in the evening as they made up beds and found towels, Claude made a great show of chasing away mice with a broom so that the girls would laugh. He often came near to Alice, brushing her arm in the hall or finding himself going through a door before her. "Will you excuse me, monsieur?" she murmured, her face flushing, and under his breath he muttered, "What is this 'monsieur'? Alice! It's not your fault."

Near tears, she murmured, "It's difficult to accept such kindness from your wife. She's so lovely." Then the girls hurried up the stairs and he turned and smiled at their pale, timid faces.

"More mice?" he cried. "Show them to me! Mice and spiders cringe when I come near them. I chase them away with a paintbrush; they fear me!" Marthe smiled a little, staying close to her mother, and then he led her, followed by the other girls, in a spider hunt.

Afterward he trotted down the steps to the garden because he had promised to help with the tree house. Seated on a branch, securing the small wood platform to the trunk with the two boys looking up at him, he felt warm all over and strong. Just then two of the girls laughed brightly from inside the house.

Sunday he woke early as always and had just made coffee when he saw Alice and her family in their best clothes, the older children carrying prayer books. They were going to church, of course. After that they had a Sunday dinner with both women cooking. They moved together as if they had always known each other.

But days later, coming in with a pail of milk and a basket of eggs from a nearby farm followed by two of the girls, who had gone with him, he heard Camille weeping from their room. He ran up the stairs and then paused before the closed door. Within he could hear both women murmuring, and Camille's choked phrases. This is it, then, he thought darkly, and opened the door.

Both women were sitting on the bed, holding hands. "Oh, Claude!" Camille cried. "I just heard from my *grandmère*'s priest that she's broken her hip and can't come to see us!"

"Well," he murmured. From the kitchen he heard the girls discussing where to put the eggs and the sounds of the boys from the incomplete tree house. "I'm so sorry, Minou. She'll come when she's better. We can have omelets for supper if you like."

DURING THE NEXT several days Alice began to take over the management of the house, the days the laundress should come, the purchases of cloth, thread, coffee, and milk. First she planned the meals together with Camille and then more and more sat at the kitchen table with her Blanche and wrote out the menus. The small pile of what money he could give her sat on the table. Sometimes when he sat down to dinner he felt the lovely girls looking at him as if to say, "But monsieur *le peintre*! You used to make Maman laugh. Won't you again?"

Camille was teaching the girls to embroider.

Blanche and Suzanne liked to paint; he began them in watercolors, and they often worked together by a window, whispering back and forth. Marthe was the best housekeeper, the most serious. Little Germaine often sucked her thumb and clung to her mother's skirts. They sometimes laughed brightly and then seemed ashamed of it; he remembered them racing over the gardens of their château and his heart ached with a love for them he barely understood.

No one went to school; they talked of hiring a tutor. Alice tried to arrange some regular lessons and gave up. They would be leaving any day now so it could be postponed.

Every night when they all went to bed, carrying lamps up the creaking stairs, kissing in the hall, the girls separated with difficulty from their mother, and Alice's son Jacques and Claude's Jean slipped off in relief to the room they shared to whisper of pirates. "Good night! Sleep well! *Bonne nuit! Couchez-vous bien!*" they called.

He lay awake, hearing once more in his mind the soft closing of Alice's door and sensing her in her white soft nightdress alone in her bed with the tree branches moving outside and the moon shining softly through the almost closed curtains of her window.

COLD CAME SUDDENLY and swiftly from the river, from the earth, from inside the trunks of trees. Leaves turned and fell. December had arrived, and Claude walked out every day to paint, coming back to the white house thoroughly chilled, walking up the garden steps with his easel on his shoulder, preparing to make his sometimes clumsy transition from color to words.

All the children but the babies were gathered about the kitchen table. Camille kissed him and Blanche jumped up as well. "Hello, Monet! Papa wrote all of us and you. Your hands are cold, monsieur! I'm going to knit you some mittens." She took his hands shyly and rubbed them.

After supper he sat down at his desk in a small room off the kitchen. He did not make a fire, not wanting to use the extra wood. Lighting the lamp, he read the letter from Hoschedé, which was no different than the previous ones. "Monet, I know it has been several weeks since my family has lived in your care but now I am absolutely assured that we will have our Paris apartment within a week, at which time I will also reimburse you for any expenses. Meanwhile I send profound apologies that I have been unable to send my share of the rent and food as promised. Circumstances . . ."

Claude clasped his hands behind his head. His thick hair was graying and curly, the front a little receded.

He waited until he heard everyone going to bed, each tapping on the door and calling gently, "Goodnight, monsieur!" or "Goodnight, Papa!" He heard them climb the stairs.

For a time he was too tired to move, and then he too climbed the stairs in the dark. He stood listening to whispers from the rooms and to late acorns falling on the roof. The wind seemed to speak. He closed his own bedroom door behind him.

Camille was sitting in bed with her knees drawn up and her long hair in braids to her waist, a shawl around her shoulders. He pulled on his nightshirt and stretched out beside her on his back, looking up at her. "Is it soon?" she asked anxiously. "Is it soon he's taking them away? Oh, I hope it's not soon. I love having them here. It will be too quiet without them."

"I don't think they'll be going too soon."

"I thought Alice would be plain. She's not beautiful, but she has a great deal of character. She endures everything without a murmur."

After she fell asleep with her head on his shoulder, he stared into darkness, listening to the sounds of the people in this house. Debts were beginning to pile up here too. He had been building the tree house and helping the girls with their drawing, but now he had to get back to work. There were eight children and two women here and he had to provide for all of them. He would provide for them.

HE HAD HOPED to leave for Paris before anyone was awake, but when he went downstairs he found Alice up already and grinding coffee. He felt he blushed a little when alone with her, and he tried not to look at her directly, though he sensed her now as he had those days in her château. She knocked the coffee grounds carefully into the pot to avoid spilling any.

He said buoyantly, "I'm off to the city to see about selling my work. There's a regular coach to the train now that I can catch."

"Do you have time for coffee and bread first? Marthe will bake more bread today. May I walk with you, Claude? I need to buy needles in the village."

"You may walk with me, of course," he said with a slight frown. Nothing could cure her of addressing him with a slight formality, aware of her debt to him. He would have preferred to walk alone, but he could not refuse her.

He fetched his paintings, protected by canvas and tied together with a rope, and they walked side by side down the dirt path to the village, where the coach would stop before the church at seven. But the shop is likely not open yet to buy needles, he thought. She just wanted to walk with me.

They stood together before the twelfth-century church with its rising tower and surrounding graveyard, looking out for the coach. For a time they were silent and then he said, "I'm going to ferry across the Seine when it snows and paint the church again."

"I remember what a beautiful picture you made of it in autumn! Is that one of the paintings you're carrying to sell?"

"Among other things. I want to paint the same scene in different seasons. If you look at that tree, it is different than when passengers stood here yesterday. I see it more, not less. One day I thought I'd see it less, but the more I feel inside of me, the more it turns to color." His voice dropped and he looked down at his new mittens, which Blanche had finished. "The subtleties of people elude me utterly, the subtleties of myself. I can't explain it. I explain it when I paint. What good it does others I don't know."

A priest in a long dark cassock and cloak emerged from the church, nodding to both of them. Alice bent her head and turned back to Claude. She said hesitantly, "I wanted to have this chance to say how kind you are to keep us all. What I have lost is nothing; what my children have lost is everything. My husband means well. But he tries. He can't face me."

Claude shook his head. "I know that, Alice; I know how he feels. I said this once before. We are such fallible creatures, we men, and you women put your lives into our weak hands. But you are strong, strong. He'll come for all of you soon, and I'll miss you very much."

"I'll miss you and your wife; she is like a bright little candle. I'm happy to do what I can when I'm here. I love your children too. Will you all come to see us in Paris sometime? Be our dinner guests?"

He replied, "Yes, of course, and I'll manage the lot of you lovely ones until then."

"Of course we will have a terrible time leaving you! My Suzanne was learning embroidery from Camille yesterday; the girls love her. And our sons are inseparable! Do you know they were playing pirates by the river yesterday and fell in? They climbed back to the house soaking! And the clean laundry had not come back. I put them in blankets. Oh, the mischief they get into every day while you're off painting!"

"It was the same with me and my friends when we were young, but still, I will speak to them sternly."

Alice laughed. A wind came, stirring the bare trees, and she hugged her chest. She said very softly then, "Claude, I want you to know that I haven't forgotten our time together. No one will ever know, but perhaps the memory of it will somehow come into your canvases? In all seasons as the years come, you will be here painting the church and village. I will be in Paris, and you'll be here. You'll have daughters of your own. As you paint you will, as you do, forget everything. And your dear feet will be so cold, so cold from standing at your easel, and your dear fingers so cold too."

The coach came around the bend, the horse's hooves stirring the dirt. She kissed his cheek and he looked after her as the coach bore him away and she walked back to the house in her long skirts and dark coat.

THAT WINTER, THE neighbors said, was one of the worst they could remember. Snow and cold blanketed everything, but it could not keep him inside. He had to paint; he was utterly possessed by the beauty of this place. That February morning he had set up his easel in Lavacourt, where he had an excellent view across the Seine of his village of Vétheuil with the church tower rising against the sky. He painted the cold and the church, using cool blues, grays, and violets. When he saw the light was leaving this short day he reluctantly packed his things and ran swiftly down the wet wood dock to wave for the ferryman.

"Last trip tonight, likely," the man said as Claude climbed on carefully. "River may freeze. Ice floes all down the river and still you're out painting, monsieur." Claude watched the oars cut the gray water, pushing aside the ice. It was only four o'clock, but darkness was falling early. Now, returning to Vétheuil, he slowly felt the passion of his work leaving him, replaced by thoughts of what he would find at home.

Hoschedé had found work with a Paris newspaper, though he still lived only in a rented room, and delayed bringing his family until he could assure them an apartment. Now it seemed only a matter of time until he would do that, likely by early spring. Claude would miss them all; sometimes he felt it impossible they would not be there to greet him each night.

He walked up to his house, which rose white and dusky above

him, a few lamps burning in windows. As he opened his garden gate, Alice hurried down the steps, wearing only a shawl over her dress. "Go back inside; it's cold," he scolded. "How is everyone? I painted until the last minute and almost couldn't cross the river to come back!"

"The woodman was just here," she said. "We waited too late to ask him to come. We're only lighting the stove now. Camille's sick and hasn't been downstairs since the morning. Everyone's been with her. I could bring her some broth once the stove is going."

"What's the matter with her?"

"I don't know."

Claude bit his lip. Camille had had no dark moods since her pregnancy with Michel. Could she be pregnant again? She hoped for a daughter, but he knew she still had not regained her old strength. And now they had no wood most of the day. In the name of all that was reasonable, why did they not? He thought, I left them all day without heat in this cold.

The girls were kneeling by the stove to light it, and he knelt between them to help. When the broth had been heated, Blanche poured some into a blue-patterned cup with little handles and set it on a plate with a bit of fresh bread. He carried it up the stairs and pushed open his bedroom door with his shoulder.

A lamp showed that the children had been here: the sketchbook and one of the boys' books on pirates were on the table. Camille sat halfway up in bed with her coat over her shoulders and the warm sleeping baby beside her. She was looking out the window. "There's such ice in the river," she said, turning to him. "And you were away on the other side of the Seine all day! Jean was worried you'd be stranded there. Oh, Claude, I'm so cold! I can't stop shivering."

He put the broth down on the table. "*Ma chère,* if you come down to the kitchen you'll be warm. I'll make a fire here, but it'll take time to warm the corners."

"The stairs seem so long today."

In the dim light she turned to touch the baby, her hand descending to pull up the covers. The hand moved so slowly. Suddenly his heart began to pound. He sat down next to her on the bed. "Are you really sick?" he asked. "Is it . . . do you think . . ."

"I don't know. I don't think I'm pregnant. I'm bloated here in my belly, but it feels different."

"But Minou," he said, taking her hand, "you've been so weary; you must be pregnant. Would you mind if our friend Georges de Bellio came to see you? He's been threatening to visit me in this remote place, and this will give him an excuse. Come downstairs now! It's lovely in the kitchen. I'll show you my painting. I hurried home as fast as I could when it was done."

THE SNOW WAS even thicker on the ground when Georges de Bellio descended from the cart a few days later. The girls had swept the steps. Their father had brought them a guitar on his last visit, and they were inexpertly studying music from a book in the kitchen and quarreling over whose turn it was. On the floor by the stove Jean and the young Hoschedé boy were struggling over a game of chess, using small stones in place of a missing knight and queen. Blanche was sitting at the table drawing the stove, her mother by her side.

The middle-aged, balding physician stamped his feet and greeted everyone. "I saw Monsieur Hoschedé yesterday," he exclaimed buoyantly, "and he tells me he'd be here with all of you if it were less arduous to go back and forth. What a ride from the train! I missed the daily coach and was bumped and shaken in that cart. I tell you frankly, Monet, if you hadn't wanted me to look in on your wife, I would have deferred coming until spring. Another difficult pregnancy for Madame? I'm so sorry! I remember how she suffered last time."

De Bellio kissed the children and said to Alice, "Your husband sends his love. I would much appreciate a coffee! But first let me see our lovely Camille."

Claude watched him mount the stairs and sat down in the kitchen.

The boys spoke softly over the chess game. He was about to give Blanche a few quick words about shadowing when he saw she sat with pencil raised, looking quietly at him. Alice had taken up her sewing. It was as if sound had withdrawn from the room.

"Will someone start coffee?" he said suddenly, clumsily.

The bedroom door had closed upstairs.

He rose and walked outside and into the garden. Snow had been swept from the swing, and boot marks showed that a few of the children had been out here today. He sat on the swing and looked up at his bedroom window, whose glass winked back a little with the dull sun. His feet were cold now and his chest, for he wasn't wearing his coat. What was taking so long?

He heard the doctor's voice in the kitchen and ran up the steps.

De Bellio said, "Come, my friend," putting his arm around Claude and drawing him into the room where Claude kept his desk and his accounting books.

The doctor turned to him with a grave face. "It's bad news," he said. "It's not pregnancy. Poor darling, she's very sick. She has a uterine tumor, and it's fairly large."

Claude stared at him. "A cancer?" he repeated. "Camille has a cancer? But you must be mistaken. No, really." He walked back and forth, gazing for a moment at one of his son's school notebooks used for dictation. (Had Jean done his lessons? They ought to have a tutor here.) This was not possible.

He kicked the edge of the thin rug. "I thought it was . . . she's moody sometimes and thinks she's ill but then she recovers. You don't think . . ." He threw his bent arm over his mouth for a moment, trying to look back on the last weeks, the last months.

De Bellio sat down heavily and half pulled Claude into another chair. "Brandy in the coffee, I think," he said.

"Can it be operated upon? Yes, that's what we'll do. Get your coffee. I must go up to her."

He ran through the kitchen, feeling them all looking after him. Had they somehow known? Not the specific thing, but had they feared something as they were here with her day after day and he was away somewhere lost in the ecstasy of his work? He climbed the stairs, holding on to the banister, and flung open the bedroom door.

Camille lay in bed, her head turned to the window. He hurried across to her and she looked at him, puzzled. "He told me," she said, her eyes darkened in her lovely oval face.

He exclaimed heartily, "You mustn't worry at all. He'll arrange everything. We must schedule surgery."

She pushed him away, her breathy voice rising. "No, I won't allow anyone to cut me!" she cried. "I know how it can be made better. I must be happy and get more exercise. I'll go to church with Alice. She's always asking me. I'll burn candles. It's nothing, really. If we need another doctor, we'll send for one. It's the cold. Truly, I'm quite all right, but tired. Hold me until I sleep. I'm a little shocked, but I'm not scared, for it's not true. You can't be scared of things that aren't true."

Claude held her tightly until she slept. De Bellio knocked on the door, but Claude whispered that he would be down shortly. By the time he had covered her tenderly and put more wood on the fire, he heard his friend's footsteps on the path toward the coach stop by the church.

He knew everyone was waiting for him, and still on each step of the stairs he hesitated. Through the kitchen door he saw them at the table, chairs crowded together. Empty coffee cups, half a loaf of bread, and a pot of jam sat in front of them. The two smallest boys were sitting on the floor on a blanket with their blocks and bits of bread, looking as messy as young children can.

Claude pressed Jean's thin shoulder. He tried to smile at everyone, but he sat down suddenly, covering his face with his hands. "He told you, I suppose," he said. "She's really sick, and when I look at her I see all the things I couldn't do for her." He began to cry wrenchingly and felt the girls gather about him, their arms around his shoulders, their hair falling down his shirtsleeves.

"Oh, please don't cry, monsieur!" Blanche said. "She'll get well. We'll burn candles, won't we, Maman?"

He raised his face and saw Jean's terrified look as he sat with his napkin crumpled in his hand. "She'll be fine," he said to the boy. "Don't worry, my love."

"God will watch over her," Alice said.

SPRING CAME, THOUGH for the first time in his life, Claude felt indifferent toward the season. He cared nothing for the wild fields of daffodils and poppies or the flowering apple trees. Letters went unanswered; he submitted paintings to the new independent exhibition and forgot he had done it. He would not go to Paris.

There was only one thing he wanted, and that was Camille's health.

He read eagerly the encouraging stories sent to him by friends of women with the same symptoms who had recovered perfectly. Julie sent a bottle of holy water. Hoschedé came and went, saying they must have heart and he had no faith in doctors. Every moment of the day centered on how Camille felt, how she looked, whether she was happy or sad or frightened.

Lise wrote weekly and came once, distracted from the long journey, worrying about her rehearsals. "But you must get better quickly and come stay with me in Paris!" she exclaimed. She held Camille's fingers tenderly. "Don't you miss the theater? Yes, come soon! Next season I have one very wonderful role."

Camille was well enough to sit in a chair by the bedroom fire; she preferred it because she was always cold, and often at least two of the girls came to sit with her. When he carried up some food on a tray on an April day as he did every evening at dinnertime, he saw her at her embroidery frame, stitching with concentration, as he had once painted her under an arbor. Suzanne Hoschedé stood by her shoulder, watching her, and Blanche sat at her feet, reading a novel aloud.

Was she better or worse? He asked himself that so many times a day, but today he had turned over an idea he felt he must share with her. "I think we should write to your parents," he said.

She shook her head. "No," she said. "There's no need to alarm them. You know they'd come from Lyon with great fuss, and my father has those heart pains. And they'd write my sister in Rome at once, and you know her new marriage is in difficulties."

Claude picked up a spool of blue thread from the carpet and said casually, "De Bellio feels you should be seen by a few doctors."

"But why? I feel better! I was just telling the girls I plan to come down to sit in the garden tomorrow. Claude, you look at loose ends! When you're like that, I'm afraid you're not painting!"

"You know I can't paint when I'm worried about you!" he answered.

"Promise me you will."

"There, I promise," he said, kissing her forehead. As he tramped down the stairs, he swore he would. He needed the money, anyway; they were borrowing from everyone, including all of his friends but Pissarro, who had nothing. He had sent off every small thing of value to Paris to be pawned.

Still, we'll manage, he thought. I'll sell many things at the private exhibition. Then we'll move away from here; she loves Paris. When she's better I'll move her back in time for the theater season. I'll encourage her to take her audition. She can write another novel on a desk by a window overlooking a boulevard. Her sister's coming back from Rome in the autumn and they'll shop together.

She did come down to the garden the following morning, holding on to him. After that she came down every day. It's all right, he told himself. He studied her carefully; she was thin but he could feed her.

He walked back from painting on an early July morning and hurried to the bedroom, calling, "Come, we'll have late breakfast outside! The girls have baked. Minou!"

From under the covers she whispered, "Oh, Claude, the pain's bad and I feel dreadful." She began to cry in gasps. "I started to feel it again a few weeks ago and thought it would go away."

She turned on the pillow to look at him.

Her lips were dry, her face and neck very thin, and her hand on the pillow almost translucent. In that moment he knew. He cried, "That's it. Get up, get dressed. You're going to have the consultation for surgery. I'm taking you to Paris!"

She clung to the iron bed, shaking her head; her thinning hair flew about her. When had her hair thinned like that? Why hadn't he noticed? He tried to pry her hands from the bed and she would not let go. "It's your fault!" he shouted. "Now you listen to me." The coach would take her to the train, and somehow within the next few hours she would be at the hospital, drugged with laudanum; a skilled surgeon would remove the tumor from her, and within weeks color would come into her cheeks again. She would run up and down the steps laughing.

He got her hand away from the headboard and lifted her in her nightgown. She weighed nothing: her breasts and thighs were so thin. She managed to cover her face with one hand. "I won't; I'm scared," she cried. "God's going to take me."

The door opened and Alice came toward them, throwing down the clean sheets she held. "Put her down, Claude!" she shouted, seizing his arm. He had never heard her shout before. Looking directly at him she mouthed, "It's too late."

Camille had collapsed onto the bed, half falling over, and he knelt before her and touched her knees and whispered, "Minou, Minou! The worst thing is for you to overly excite yourself, Minou!"

HE WATCHED HER body melt away all summer, until it seemed she could not get any thinner and the pains increased, and she would start with wide eyes and a gasp and press her hand against her abdomen.

He dreaded those gasps, after which he went to her and held her, and Alice held her too.

Georges de Bellio came once more from Paris, thoughtful in his long coat, hands behind his back. "There, my dear," he said, sitting by Camille's bed and patting her hand. "Years before I met you, Madame Monet, I saw the picture of you in the green dress and fell a little in love. You mustn't tell your husband; he would be jealous. He was a mere painter and you were divine. I am even now a little in love with you, Madame Monet."

"Are you, doctor?" she said, smiling.

De Bellio came downstairs more heavily, with Claude at his side. "A few weeks more at most, I think," he said. "Give her laudanum for the pain if she can keep it down. She keeps nothing down now, does she, poor beauty? You must resign yourself, my friend."

Claude ran from the house and sat on the steps between the large pots of sunflowers that lined them. When he looked up Jean was sitting beside him. "What is it, lad?" Claude asked. "You're not playing with Jacques Hoschedé anymore. What about your tree house? Go make up with him."

The twelve-year-old boy shook his head fiercely. "I don't want to make up with him! It's all his fault."

"How can it be his fault, eh?"

"It is," Jean shouted, his voice breaking. "It's all the fault of them coming here." He ran down into the garden, setting the swing crashing back and forth.

ON THOSE WARM, lovely days with breezes from the river and haystacks being made on the farms, everyone waited. The laundress came; the farm girl cleaned the stove. Bread was baked; coffee was ground and brewed. His easel was empty. He walked a few minutes away and came back terrified, racing up the steps. She dozed a lot now, the curtains drawn in her room, Alice or one of the girls sewing by the bedside or reading to her.

He did not sit with her all the time; he stayed away downstairs, but at a creak he ran up, listening to her breathing. He forgot there had been any other life with her. Then the pain worsened. Even with the laudanum and the brandy, it overwhelmed her and she would start up, her back curved, crying and sobbing. He was there in seconds then, but he could not hold her tightly enough to make the pain go away.

She finally slept at midnight.

He walked down the stairs, not knowing where to go.

Alice was mending one of his shirts in the kitchen. He sank into a chair, took her hand, and kissed it. She flushed. "I've something to tell you, Claude," she whispered. "It's important, and you mustn't scoff. Camille told me today she's afraid she won't be allowed in heaven because she never married you properly in church."

"Can she believe such a thing?"

"She does, and she would like to have a priest come for the sacrament as soon as possible if you consent."

Tears filled his eyes. Alice put down his shirt, took his hand, and led him to her bedroom. He was aware of her lumpy bed in the corner more than anything in the world. He watched her, motionless, as she made to unfasten her top dress button. She whispered, "Would it make you feel better?"

"Yes, very much," he whispered. "But afterward I'd feel like jumping from that window, and you'd be wretched. Dear Alice, you're healthy and strong as she was; you're like what she was. I want to bury myself in you, but I can't. I can't."

HE DRESSED IN his best suit two mornings later, standing in his son's room. The girls and Alice had suggested he leave his bedroom to let them dress the bride. The bride, he thought. His collar stud broke. He swore. The suit hung on him; he had not been able to eat. He walked down to the garden and picked some flowers.

Toward ten he saw the tall priest walking solemnly from the village. Claude shook his hand. The bedroom window opened and Blanche called down that the bride was ready.

The room was full of flowers that the girls had gathered, and he gave his small bunch to Camille. Her hair had been arranged under a pretty lace-edged cap, and she wore her wedding and engagement rings on a ribbon around her neck as they long ago had slipped off her fingers. She had on a pretty bed jacket he had bought for her when they first moved to Argenteuil. Claude wished for the splendor of a church and boys singing and an organ for her sake, but there was only the bedroom, quite crowded with the Hoschedé girls, two holding the babies; the boys; Alice; and the priest.

The priest kissed and donned a stole. "Monsieur," he said formally, "are you ready to marry this woman before God?"

"Yes," Claude said.

"Take her hand, then."

Camille made her vows seriously as he held her hand.

Jean stood by his mother gently rubbing her shoulder, staring out the window. He looked as if he was waiting for her to rise and dress and go for a walk with him, as if he believed all this sickness and the priest would leave them and she would be the beautifully dressed woman on a hilltop in his father's painting with him sprawling impetuously in the grass, flowers rising about them.

Jacques threw his arm around Jean's shoulder.

The girls served cake and wine around the bed, though Camille could take no solids and gagged on a sip of wine. Claude wanted only to escape to his attic studio and sit there with his arms clasped about him.

Toward two in the morning he woke to her cries of pain and he jumped up and ran to the river at the end of his garden, crashing through the high summer grass. I can't bear it, he thought. I can't. The cries echoed through the night. If only I could paint, he thought. As far as he ran he could hear her cry: "Make it stop, Claude!" and he cried out by the river, "I can't do anything for you! I can't do anything for you!"

FOR TWO DAYS she shouted and cried, and threw up what medicine they gave her. On the third day, when he was downstairs writing her mother, Alice called him to fetch the children and come. Camille lay on the pillow, blinking a little to concentrate on the faces bending above her. She looked at Claude as if she did not know him and then tried to focus. Her lips moved as if she wanted to say something.

"No," he whispered.

The priest came again and anointed her with oil, burning a candle and praying. Everyone knelt. Then Marthe led Jean away, the baby Michel in her arms. Gradually the other children slipped away. Only Alice remained.

They listened to Camille's shallow breaths. By that time he was too weary to hope, and yet he did. It was a time after the breaths ceased before he understood. Camille's chest was still but her hand was warm. Alice held her rosary on her lap, her fingers on the last bead she had prayed. Her face was wet with tears. She held him close to her, whispering, "My dear, I'm so very sorry!"

He broke gently from her and left the room, returning with his easel and canvas and paints from the attic and setting them up by the bedside. He said, "Will you be so kind as to leave us for a little? And say nothing to anyone yet?"

"I will. You'll call me when you need me?"

"Yes."

She touched his arm as she went, closing the door behind her.

Camille was absolutely still. "I am going to paint you, dearest," Claude murmured.

He had never painted anything like that in his life.

She lay there very pure and pale and still but he saw colors rise and swirl about her. He painted her face as almost a spirit, with a violence of color about her, slashed and feathered with his brush. He painted against time. You are light, he murmured, and if something of you remains here yet, it is leaving me. He gritted his teeth as he painted, murmuring, "Stay, stay. I don't want life without you. Is this all that life is, then, Minou, in the end, suffering? Do we ever know another person truly? It is better to go than to feel this."

He heard only the sound of his brush. As long as I paint, she's not yet gone, he thought. And then the painting was done and still she lay there.

Later that night he beat the wall with his fists. Young Blanche clung to him and cried, "I will always stay with you, Monet."

FOR DAYS AFTER the funeral Claude lay in bed unable to sleep, then sleeping a little and afterward saying, "Why? I am awake, but why should I rise?" He saw Camille's dresses in the half-open wardrobe, her brushes and powders on the table as if waiting for her. If he looked in the mirror, he could see her reflection; he could see himself come behind her, his arms about her.

Hoschedé visited for a while and did his best to be comforting. He left, and Alice and her daughters kept the house. Sometimes Claude came to dinner, but he could eat little. Many letters of condolence came for him, but he could not even read them. Then he jumped up and looked for everyone he loved. They were there when he needed them; they stayed away when he had to be alone. From one of the trees Jean whispered to Jacques in their half-built tree house.

Claude sought Alice; he only touched her arm or sometimes held her.

"Listen to me," she said gently. "Go work in the garden. A garden is healing." He nodded and went outside in his oldest clothes with his old black brimmed hat jammed on his head. He heard the voices of the children from another part of the garden. The tree house above the swing was empty. He knelt in the dirt and began to cry. He sat on his knees helplessly gasping with sobs.

After a time he raised his face. Camille's sister, Annette, was standing near him in a black mourning dress. He rose clumsily, wiping his cheeks, and stammered, "How did you find me here! Oh my dear, I'm so very sorry!"

"Are you, Monet?" she replied.

He blinked. He would have kissed her, but her tone was so cold that he drew back, studying her as best he could. Her dark skirt was spattered here and there as if she had knelt on the ground. He supposed she had been to the graveyard. He said, "It took a while for you to come from Rome, I know. I also wrote to your parents. They couldn't come because of your father's heart condition. I don't even know if your mother has told him. I wrote your *grandmère*'s priest."

He indicated a chair by the white wicker table and brushed away some leaves from the cushion. "Come, sit down," he said compassionately.

Annette seated herself carefully and looked around her. "So this was my sister's final home," she said. "A rather remote one for a girl who lived for the world of Paris."

"We were going back eventually. There were circumstances . . ."

She held her gloved hands tightly together on her lap, her lip raised slightly. "Ah, but with you there have always been circumstances," she said abruptly. "I have merely come to see my sister's grave. You also wrote I could have one of your paintings of her. Then I'll go away again."

"Come and choose, then," he said, holding out his hand. She shook her head and indicated that he should go before her. So unforgiving and so easy to judge, he thought as he walked wearily into the house and up the stairs to the attic. Her first husband had felt it and her second marriage also did not go well. Camille had worried about it.

Opening the door of his studio, he motioned her inside. "Take any one you want," he said. "She made me take them all down from our walls. If it's too large, we can send it." He leaned against the wall, unable to raise his eyes for the beauty of his wife, whom he had painted so often.

He heard Annette's footsteps on the floor and when she stopped. "There she is with that little dog. She looks so serious." She walked on, her voice floating back to him, a little softer now. "And the one in the green dress, of course. I won't take that."

The footsteps ceased and he heard her gasp. "What is this thing . . ."

He had forgotten his deathbed painting on the easel. He rushed forward to throw a cloth over it, but it was too late. Annette stood before it, sobbing in rage; her voice rose. She cried, "What is this thing? What is it? Is it . . ." and he said, "Yes."

She shoved him hard. "What kind of monster are you that everything, my sister's life and now her death, must be consumed by your work? If she had stayed with your friend, she would have been alive and happy."

He cried, "She loved me."

"Loved you, the foolish girl! I know all about you, as does half of Paris. I saw de Bellio in Paris before I came here and he told me you asked him to redeem Minou's locket from a Paris pawnshop so that you could bury her in it. She died as she lived, impoverished by your ridiculous dreams. And then that woman and her children live with you and her husband never comes. Minou knew you loved that woman; she knew you would leave her for her."

"What!" he cried. "I would never have done that."

Annette shouted, "She wrote me privately when I was in Rome. She told me she'd known she was sick for a while before you chose to notice it, before you wrote de Bellio to come. She wrote, 'I don't much care what happens to me because he no longer loves me.' "

"Come, choose your picture! For God's sake, take one and stop wounding me when I can't bear it."

"I don't want any of them!" Annette ran out to the stairs and almost fell. He put out his hand to stop her, but she struck him away and sat down on a middle step, weeping. She cried, "Did you sleep with Madame Hoschedé while my sister was alive? Did you? Did you?"

"Annette, I wish I were a better man than I am; I could wish it a thousand times," he replied. "All I know is that Minou loved me and I loved her. You wanted a certain life for her, but she had to choose her own. She chose me and my work. I'm not separate from my work. She was very clear in what she chose, and she didn't choose to die. I'll never believe that. And if I ever betrayed her, I'm sorry a thousand times. Did you see all the pictures? Do you know how many more I made and painted over, or those I made that I kept only in my heart? And that never will I do anything worthy of her, ever."

She looked at him. "And the last painting? How could you?"

"To keep her . . . the last one. To keep her."

CLAUDE WOULD HAVE walked Annette to the coach that stopped before the church, but she refused him. She did, however, accept a chalk portrait of Camille, which he wrapped in paper as best he could. After she left, he stood by the swing and saw that the table had been cleared of coffee cups and plates. The children and Alice were still in the other part of the garden and likely had heard the shouting.

He walked past the garden down to the river, where he gazed at all the wildflowers he had painted with such joy. That joy seemed remote to him now. Never had he felt so empty. He was not even air— he was less than air.

He sat down on the riverbank with his head in his hands.

"You loved her," Alice had said earlier that morning. "You loved each other, but so much was against you. We try to love each other and we never do perfectly, but what we cannot do doesn't erase what we have done."

If only, Claude thought as he looked at the flowing river, in the end the good I have done in this life outweighs the bad, if I have succeeded more than I have failed, not only in my work but in my life. My love for you is deep, deep inside myself like something below the water. Only with my brush when I can paint again will I express it. Whatever I do in the rest of my life, my love for you is part of it, and in everything I paint I will remember you and say with my work what you were to me.

His mind, exhausted by his emotions, turned to the practical. He was, after all, his father's son, and he sat a little straighter on the riverbank. I have to shelter those I promised to, he thought. I will keep my promises.

His body ached. He leaned on his stick as he mounted to the road and walked toward his house, where his son Jean and young Blanche were calling for him. He replied as loudly as he could, "I'm coming," and continued along the path home.

Epilogue

This endless measure of his dream and of the dream of life, he formulated, reprised, and formulated anew and without end in the mad dream of his art before the luminous abyss of the Water Lilies *pool.*

—GUSTAVE GEFFROY

AT THE LAST MOMENT THE OLD ARTIST DECIDED TO attend the opening of his water lily exhibition; he dressed in his best suit with his lace cuffs and climbed into his car for his chauffeur to drive him into Paris. During the ride he felt anxious, often on the verge of telling the driver to take him home again.

When he walked into the gallery with his cane, he saw that the rooms were already quite full. What he had created from his own dream was now on the walls for everyone to see. In every painting he felt Camille's presence. Of all his portraits of her, these paintings of the water lilies were the truest ones, for within them he had captured her beauty, her variability, and her light.

Some people had tears in their eyes; some pressed his hand. Did they see her as well? Perhaps and perhaps not, he thought. They would see their own dreams and losses and hopes and the terrible brevity of life and imperfection of love.

During those hours in the gallery he also felt the ghosts of all the young painters. One ghost moved among the crowd, taller than anyone else there. Claude wondered if his friend also saw Minou in the paintings in all her infinite variety.

THREE DAYS LATER amid many words of praise and offers for purchase and positive critical reviews, a letter he could not have expected arrived for him. He had stayed long at the opening, hoping she would come. When she did not, he did not expect to hear from her again. Sitting at his table with his wine, hearing the sounds of the gardeners outside the window, he opened the letter slowly.

> *Monet,*
>
> *I write you because of something I have learned that came as a great surprise to me. I don't know how to take it. My daughter, who admires your work, insisted we go to your exhibition, of which everyone in Paris is speaking. Your art dealer, Durand-Ruel, was there and knew me. He told me that when I returned to Paris almost penniless ten years ago, the anonymous benefactor who gave me the means to begin my business was you.*
>
> *Since you have showed me such an unexpected kindness, I will tell the story behind the letters I sent on to you last month, which Camille confided to me the night she came to me in the snow. They were not written to her actor or her fiancé or any Sorbonne student. Before she had met you, she wrote them to the great love she hoped to have one day, to a young man she sensed*

would come into her life. Then you walked into the bookshop. So these letters are for you, and belong to you alone.

I will say more. She never wrote me when she was ill that she wanted to die because she had lost your love; she never thought that. I lied to you.

One day perhaps we will meet again. I miss her too, every day of my life.

Through most of the next few months he was very busy with responses to the exhibition, the many articles sent him, and the news of sales. When all that settled down he reread Camille's youthful letters, with their eroticism and tenderness. He read them until he memorized them, and then he fit them in the lacquered box.

One day if he became ill and his eyesight deteriorated further, he would cease to paint and be unable to see the letters and the other things in the box. Perhaps he would die before Alice. She might find them and be hurt by them; she had been mostly a calm and loving wife these many years, understanding his moods, raising their children, and he did not wish to hurt her. He never told her he thought often of Camille.

Autumn was coming in. He could sense it at every moment; the flowers sensed it. It would soon be time for the last water lily blossom, and then the gardeners would take the tubs in which they were planted from the water to keep the roots from freezing over the winter. The leaves would fall from the trees and the pond would freeze on cold mornings. For months most of the garden would be still.

One late afternoon he placed the letters in the Japanese box and wrapped the box well in oilcloth. Everyone was in the parlor after dinner when he slipped from the house down the stairs and along the path, walking down to the water lily garden.

He looked about, choosing carefully until he decided on the foot of one of the willow trees. He knelt and began to dig a hole with his small shovel. He had to try a few places, for he struck roots. He touched the oilcloth over the box and lowered it into the earth, covering it quickly. He sat on his knees for a while afterward, his hand on the place where he had buried it.

He rose stiffly. Ah, he thought, old age. Still, perhaps I will ride into Paris this winter to see her sister. We can talk further then of things we do not want to forget or things we never understood. I do not need the things in the box; I have memorized them.

He stood on the bridge. I am not done painting my lilies, he thought. There is always, as there is with love, more to say, but now I am tired and pleased. Yes, I am pleased.

He left his shovel leaning against the tree and walked back through the upper flower garden toward his supper and his waiting family.

THE IDEA FOR THIS NOVEL came to me while attending an exhibition at the Metropolitan Museum in 1995 called "The Origins of Impressionism." In it, the curators had gathered many paintings from the young artists who would eventually be famous. The artists were mostly poor then; they slept on one another's floors or painted the same vase of flowers side by side and stood "shoulder to shoulder" against the world, as Renoir would later say. Of all the paintings in that exhibition, two haunted me more than the others. One was Claude Monet's *The Point of the Hève at Low Tide* and the other the fast, rough painting by Frédéric Bazille of his friends in his studio. A small painting, it is a microcosm of a whole world. I was startled to read on a placard that Frédéric had died in the war just before he turned twenty-nine. Why had a young artist gone to war?

The novel is based on history; some events have been slightly altered or fictionalized for dramatic strength and continuity.

All the world knows Monet as an old man in his gardens at Giverny, but the genesis of that revered painter was a very determined and handsome young man: proud, sometimes haughty, and sometimes humble, in need of love and understanding and someone to buy his work. If he had not stood his ground through all his hardships with the help of those who loved him, there would be no water lily paintings today. I wanted readers to know him as he was to better understand what he became: where the determination came to paint his gardens year after year, still seeking deeper expressions of their beauty. I wanted to write about his great love for the girl whom he painted in a green promenade dress.

At the time I began to write the novel, I could find very little about Camille Doncieux. Late in my writing, I discovered parts of a recently discovered diary kept by a nineteenth-century art collector that revealed a little more about her charm, her amateur theatricals, and the good family from whom she ran away to throw her lot in with Claude Monet. As with many models for the great artists, little of her personal information remains. No single letter to or from her has been found. Claude adored her; he painted her more than he ever painted anyone else. She died young before he could give her the things he promised her. What complexity or trouble in their relationship caused him perhaps to turn to Alice Hoschedé? The ménage of the two women and eight children in his house toward the end of Camille's short life caused considerable gossip in Paris at the time. Claude was wild with grief when Camille died. And he did marry Alice in the end.

Of the three major characters, Monet's best friend, Frédéric Bazille, was perhaps the most complex. A few of his paintings suggest a possible sexuality that he himself did not understand. He was immensely fond of Camille, choosing to buy the picture of her as four women in a garden above all other paintings, but the conjecture of his intimate relationship with her and any other person grew from my imagination alone. The last twenty years have brought a retrospect of the work of this young painter and good friend.

The gardens of Giverny have a wonderful true history.

Four years after the death of Camille, Monet and Alice Hoschedé rented the Giverny house and moved there with their children. When Alice's husband died, Monet married her. It was some time before he had enough money to actually buy the property and begin his gardens. These expanded over the years to include the great water gardens and famous water lilies. Alice's daughter Blanche eventually married Monet's son Jean.

At the age of sixty-nine, Monet gave his first exhibition of his water lily paintings. Still he continued to paint them. In his eighties, just before his death, he completed the great paintings of his gardens for the Paris Orangerie at the urging of the prime minister of France.

The grown children of both families had scattered but Blanche, now a widow and an accomplished painter herself, lived on in Giverny as the keeper of her stepfather's memory. When Michel Monet also died in 1966, it was found that his father's personal collection of his own work and that of his friends had been kept in the son's country house, stuffed under beds, piled in the cellar, and in cupboards. The property at Giverny was in terrible condition. Rats overran the gardens. The greenhouse panes and the windows in the house were reduced to shards after the bombings of World War II. Floors and ceiling beams had rotted away; a staircase had collapsed. Three trees were even growing in the big studio.

The paintings went to the Musée Marmottan in Paris. It took almost ten years to restore the gardens at Giverny to their former magnificence. Fortunately, Michel had made the Académie des Beaux-Arts heir to the property, and in 1977 Gérald van der Kemp was appointed curator. The gardener André Devillers helped him reconstruct the gardens as Monet had created them.

The new custodians expected only a modest number of visitors, but to their surprise, the numbers grew steadily until they now exceed a half million each year. They come seeking the peace of the place that inspired the art—peace hard-won by the artist, who left the gardens as his last gift to the world. One of the Giverny guides writes a poetic journal in French of the daily world there; she has now also added selections in English. It can be found at http://givernews.com.

Frédéric is buried in Montpellier. Camille's grave can be found in Vétheuil in the église Notre-Dame. Claude Monet is buried on the grounds of the église Sainte-Radegonde a little way down the path from his house in Giverny.

SOME PAINTINGS MENTIONED IN OR OF INTEREST TO THIS NOVEL

Monet, Claude Oscar

The Seashore at Sainte-Adresse. 1864. The Minneapolis Institute of Arts, Minneapolis.

The Point of the Hève at Low Tide. 1865. The Kimbell Art Museum, Forth Worth, Texas.

Luncheon on the Grass.1865–1866. Smaller version. The Pushkin Museum of Fine Arts, Moscow. Two surviving panels of full version: Musée d'Orsay, Paris.

Camille, or The Woman in a Green Dress. 1866. Kunsthalle Bremen, Bremen, Germany.

Women in the Garden. 1866–67. Musée d'Orsay, Paris.

The Magpie. 1868–1869. Musée d'Orsay, Paris.

Jean Monet on His Hobby Horse. 1872. Metropolitan Museum of Art, New York.

Garden at Argenteuil. 1873. Private Collection.

Impression: Sunrise. 1873. Musée Marmottan, Paris.

The Gare St-Lazare. 1877. National Gallery, London.

Church at Vétheuil with Snow. 1879. Musée d'Orsay, Paris.

Camille on Her Deathbed. 1879. Musée d'Orsay, Paris.

In the Woods at Giverny: Blanche Hoschedé at Her Easel with Suzanne Hoschedé Reading. 1887. Los Angeles County Museum of Art, Los Angeles.

Paintings of the Giverny gardens and water lily pond can be found in most major museums in the world.

BAZILLE, JEAN-FRÉDÉRIC

Studio in the Rue de Furstenberg. 1865. Musée Fabre, Montpellier, France.

The Improvised Field Hospital (Monet with an injured leg). 1865. Musée d'Orsay, Paris.

Portrait of Renoir. 1867. Musée d'Orsay, Paris.

Family Gathering. 1867–1868. Musée d'Orsay, Paris.

View of the Village. 1868. Musée Fabre, Montpellier, France.

Portrait of Edmond Maître. 1869. National Gallery of Art, Washington, D.C.

La Toilette. 1870. Musée Fabre, Montpellier, France.

Studio in the Rue de la Condamine. 1870. The Louvre, Paris.

RENOIR, PIERRE-AUGUSTE

All of Renoir's approximately twenty café wall paintings have disappeared.

Lise Sewing. 1866. Dallas Museum of Art, Dallas, Texas.

Frédéric Bazille at His Easel. 1867. Musée d'Orsay, Paris.

*Lise and Sisley (*sometimes called *Alfred Sisley and His Wife).* 1868. Wallraf-Richartz-Museum, Cologne, Germany.

Camille Monet Reading. 1872. Sterling and Francine Clark Art Institute, Williamstown, Massachusetts.

Portrait of Claude Monet. 1872. National Gallery of Art, Washington, D.C.

PISSARRO, CAMILLE

Entrance to the Village of Voisins. 1872. Musée d'Orsay, Paris.

CAROLUS-DURAN, CHARLES AUGUSTE ÉMILE

Portrait of Claude Monet. 1867. Musée Marmottan, Paris.

Portrait of Madame Alice Hoschedé. 1878. Benno and Nancy Schmidt Collection, Wildenstein Galleries, New York.

MANET, ÉDOUARD

The Monet Family in Their Garden at Argenteuil. 1874. The Metropolitan Museum of Art, New York.

ACKNOWLEDGMENTS

I read far too many books about Monet and his circle during the writing of this novel to list them all. I would particularly like to name *Monet and Bazille: A Collaboration* (Champa, Pittman, and Brenneman); *The Impressionists at First Hand* (Denvir); *The Unknown Monet: Pastels and Drawings* (Ganz and Kendall); *Claude Monet: Life and Art* (Tucker); *Monet und Camille* (Hansen and Herzogenrath); *Hidden in the Shadow of the Master: The Model-Wives of Cézanne, Monet, and Rodin* (Butler); *Frédéric Bazille: Prophet of Impressionism* (Musée Fabre Montpellier/Brooklyn Museum); *Frédéric Bazille and Early Impressionism* (Marandel and Daulte); *Monet* (Gordon and Forge); *Monet, Narcissus, and Self-Reflection: The Modernist Myth of the Self* (Levine); and all the work of Daniel Wildenstein. Any divergence from their excellent research was in the service of fiction.

Many kind friends read early drafts of this novel, sometimes more than once. I am grateful to Judith Ackerman, Robert Blumenfeld, Russell Clay, Ann Darby, Michael DiSchiavi, Susanne Dunlap, Laura Friedman, Philancy Holder, Katherine Kirkpatrick, Barbara Quick, Amy Rosenberg, Alice Tufel, Bina Valenzano of Brooklyn's Bookmark Shop, and Bob Weber, as well as my late father, the painter James Mathieu, and my stepmother, Viraja. Special thanks for the amazing support of novelist Susan Dormady Eisenberg and actress/writer Christine Emmert, who not only read many drafts but sent me daily encouraging e-mails.

Much gratitude to my family for their constant support: my son Jesse Cowell and his friend Erica Langworthy; my son James Nordstrom, his wife, Jessica, and daughters, Emma and Hanna. Love to my two sisters, Jennie and Gabrielle, and their spouses and to my nephew and my late mother, the artist Dora. Also to my husband's large, supportive family: his mother, Genia, his brothers and sister, Glenda, sons, spouses, grandchildren, and our cousin Lynnda.

Rachel Benzaquen and Monique-Marie Bray helped with my struggling French. My lifelong friend Renée Cafiero visited Giverny with me and was patient when I cried over paintings at the Musée Marmottan. Thanks to Robert Blumenfeld for French and his book *Tools and Techniques for Character Interpretation*.

I cannot possibly list all the friends who cheered me on, but I thank all of you. I also must mention the clergy and parishioners of St. Ignatius of Antioch, St. Thomas Fifth Avenue, and the congenial Sisters of the Community of the Holy Spirit, all of whom sustain me spiritually, as well as my friends and colleagues at MDRC.

I am deeply grateful to my agent, Emma Sweeney, who advised me patiently through several drafts of the novel; and to Eva Talmadge and Justine Wenger of her staff; to my gifted editor, Suzanne O'Neill, Heather Proulx, Emily Timberlake, Tina Constable, Patty Berg, Annsley Rosner, Emily Lavelle, and to all the staff of Crown.

And, as always, thanks to my husband, Russell, who listened to all my hopes and fears and cooked for me. The characters in my novel lived with both of us so closely that he always expected to find Monet painting away in our living room and would, of course, have asked him to dinner.

READING GROUP GUIDE FOR
Claude & Camille

READING GROUPS: If your group is reading *Claude & Camille* and would like to be considered for a visit from Stephanie Cowell, either in person, by phone, or by Skype, please e-mail contact information and a description of your group to claudeandcamille@gmail.com.

QUESTIONS FOR DISCUSSION

1. Do you think Claude should have found some sort of work to support his family? Was he right in his insistence on following art only? Was he not capable of compromise? Do geniuses live by special rules? Would you have seen the situation differently from his father's point of view, not knowing the end?

2. Camille was a very complex girl: loyal, secretive, and duplicitous. What do you think drove her secrets and lies? Could she help herself? Back in 1865, people did not know much about the workings of the mind. Discuss the complex reasons for her behavior.

3. Do you think Camille would have been happier if she had left Claude for Frédéric?

4. Do you think Claude compromised his career and artistic focus by breaking away from his friends to pursue his relationship with Camille?

5. Do you think Claude's artistic achievement would have turned out differently had he not suffered so much hardship and loss? Would he have been able to create such complex masterpieces as the Water Lily series? Why or why not?

6. Annette holds Claude responsible for the death of her sister. Is there any justification for that? Do you feel, perhaps, in any way that she was envious of her sister's ability to live a free life?

7. Could Claude have prevented Frédéric from going to war? How could he have behaved to prevent his friend's tragedy?

8. There are many different turning points in the novel—Claude leaving for Paris, the first time he meets Camille, Bazille enlisting in the army. Which do you think had the most profound effect on his life and career? Which do you think resulted in the most growth?

9. Monet's paintings of his water lily pond and gardens are arguably the most beloved paintings in the world. How and where did you first find them? Everyone sees them in his or her own way. What do they mean to you?

10. Have you visited Monet's house at Giverny or would you like to? Now that you know some of the hardships Monet endured before he was able to make his garden and paint it, will you see it in a different way?

ABOUT THE AUTHOR

STEPHANIE COWELL is the critically acclaimed author of *Marrying Mozart*, *Nicholas Cooke*, *The Players: A Novel of the Young Shakespeare*, and *The Physician of London* (winner of a 1996 American Book Award).